# Acclaim for AUSTIN CLARKE

"Clarke makes West Indian speech into a form of
music and poetry... tremendously versatile in what it
expresses and exhilarating to read."
*The Globe and Mail*

"Austin Clarke [is] one of the most talented novelists at work in
the English language today.... His fiction is unique, surprising,
comfortable until the moment when it becomes uncomfortable.
Then you realize you have learned something new that you didn't
want to know — and it's essential knowledge. And so on you go,
alternately congratulating and cursing Austin Clarke."
Norman Mailer

"Uncommonly talented, Clarke sees deeply,
and transmits his visions and perceptions so skilfully
that reading him is an adventure."
*Publishers Weekly*

"[Clarke's] characters are so real you can reach out and touch them."
*Saturday Night*

"Clarke is magnificent in transferring to print the music, the
poetry, the complete aptness of West Indian dialogue. It is comic,
it is tragic, it is all shades in between. And as prose it is
as near poetry as prose can become."
*Charlotte Observer*

"Clarke is a major Western wi
*Greensboro Daily News*

D1616126

"Brilliant is the word for Austin Clarke's depiction
of his highly ebullient characters."
*Canadian Forum*

# Books by AUSTIN CLARKE

*Fiction*
The Origin of Waves
There are No Elders
In This City
Proud Empires
Nine Men Who Laughed
When Women Rule
The Prime Minister
The Bigger Light
Storm of Fortune
When He Was Free and Young
and He Used to Wear Silks
The Meeting Point
Amongst Thistles and Thorns
The Survivors of the Crossing

*Non-fiction*
Pigtails n' Breadfruit
A Passage Back Home
Public Enemies
Growing Up Stupid Under the Union Jack

*Selected Writings*
The Austin Clarke Reader

**Austin Clarke** was born in Barbados and came to Canada in 1955 to study at Trinity College in the University of Toronto. He has enjoyed a varied and distinguished career as a broadcaster, civil rights leader, professor, and diplomat, representing Barbados as its Cultural Attaché in Washington DC. His many honours include Lifetime Achievement Awards for Writing from both the Toronto Arts Council and Chawkers–Frontier College, an Honorary Doctorate of Literature from Brock University, the 1998 Pride of Barbados Distinguished Service Award and, most recently, the Order of Canada. He is, formerly, writer-in-residence at the University of Guelph, and the 1998 inaugural winner of The Rogers Communications Writer's Trust Fiction Prize. Author of eight novels and five collections of short fiction, Austin Clarke is widely studied in Canadian universities. He lives in Toronto.

# The Meeting Point

# AUSTIN CLARKE

VINTAGE CANADA
A Division of Random House of Canada

FIRST VINTAGE CANADA EDITION, 1998

Copyright © 1967, 1972 by Austin C. Clarke

**Canadian Cataloguing in Publication Data**

Clarke, Austin, 1934–
The meeting point

First book in the Toronto trilogy.
ISBN 0-676-97160-1

I. Title.  II. Title: Toronto trilogy

PS8505.L38M4 1998    C813'.54    C98-931310-7
PR9199.3.C526S75 1998

Cover Design: C.S. Richardson
Printed and bound in the United States of America

10 9 8 7 6 5 4 3 2 1

To
Melva Da Silva
with love;
and to
Robert Weaver

# 1

# THE EXPERIENCE OF ARRIVAL

When Bernice Leach got the job, thirty-two months ago, as a domestic for the Burrmann family, she was expected to cook three meals a day. Nothing else. As things turned out, she had to cook only one meal, supper. It was a meal which required a lot of work to prepare. There were lots of snacks for the children, especially on weekends: grilled cheese sandwiches; cheese blintzes which Bernice had to learn how to make. The family drank many bottles of Coca-Cola and other soft drinks, which Mrs. Burrmann called collectively, "pop." Mr. Burrmann hadn't the time or the disposition for more than a cup of coffee at breakfast; and this he drank "clear," that is to say, without cream, milk, or sugar. He would sometimes drink it while standing up; and even when he did sit down at breakfast with his wife, Bernice noticed that his head was always buried in the business section of *The Globe and Mail,* or in some other newspaper of his thoughts. She nagged him for not having a heavy breakfast before going to his law office; and he argued that he was all right, that a heavy breakfast was only for peasants. Bernice would watch him, standing, drinking, and with a tipped cigarette in his left hand; and he would glance at his pocket watch, and she would shake her head and say, Boy, you sure running your damn blood to water! Mrs. Burrmann would continue to grumble and continue to eat her porridge, her bacon, her eggs and her Ryvita biscuits; and for the rest of the day (between drinks) she would slouch in her favourite couch, reading paperback novels. When the days were long, like Sundays in winter, she drank more and read less. She was at present reading *Herzog*.

There were two children in the household: Serene and Ruthie, healthy and red, the only persons who had three square meals a day. Bernice made herself four: tea, breakfast, lunch and dinner.

But time passed, and Mrs. Burrmann got used to Bernice, and to her singing in the kitchen. And Mrs. Burrmann overcame her earlier reservations about having Bernice's black hands touch her white bed linen and her silver cutlery. She grew accustomed to Bernice; and permitted her to graduate from merely preparing meals to serving them at table. But Bernice very often wondered why Mrs. Burrmann wanted a servant: she was such a diligent housewife — and this in spite of the novels and the whiskey. The way she could plan the household expenses for a month; sometimes cook a four-course meal and attend to the children, and still find time to have a nap in the afternoon, convinced Bernice that Mrs. Burrmann was a better domestic than she. Bernice did find out, later, why she was ever engaged: it was during a husband-and-wife bout of secrecy and whispering, when the word "treatment" was dropped. Apparently, Mrs. Burrmann was taking "treatment" for something; and Bernice began to notice her leaving the house, every Wednesday afternoon at a quarter to two, punctually as a bill collector.

She began to handle Mrs. Burrmann's Royal Doulton chinaware, with its golden wheat sheaf stamped in the middle, as if it belonged to her. With her own two black hands, she would tuck the lily-white linen bibs under the chins of Serene and Ruthie, who were seven and five respectively. She began to move like a conqueror round the table, and about the house.

There were many parties: sherry parties; wine and cheese parties; cocktail parties, masquerade parties, and dinner parties. Bernice liked the parties which were usually attended by a jolly, prosperous man named Silverstein who revelled in hilarious, dirty jokes, and jokes about the Jews. But at these parties to which Mrs. Burrmann insisted on inviting many artistic-looking men and women, and some radio producers of the Canadian Broadcasting Corporation, Mr. Burrmann behaved as if he were one of the invited guests. His wife would be domineering and distant; sophisticated and arrogant, giving the guests the impression that she was the artistic one in the family; the cultured one. It was so obvious that Bernice could not help noticing it; and soon, the guests themselves started talking about it. Mrs. Burrmann was the boss in the household. She had come from a very rich and respectable Jewish home, "one of north America's best *diasporas*," as she liked to say at parties. Mr. Burrmann was the poor Jew, who had brains, but no social acceptability. Mrs. Burrmann had supported him for the three years he spent in the University of Toronto Law School. At this time they were already married and he was undoubtedly in love with her, yet he resented this dependency.

Mrs. Burrmann's behaviour at some of these parties, and in the home generally, greatly distressed Bernice; and in time she too began to resent her mistress. She could not understand what kind of a wife would hold a party when her husband was absent: perhaps on a business trip in Hamilton; or in his office or his study, studying and pretending to be sick from the recurrent headaches which Bernice felt were the frustrations of his marriage. For Bernice, failure in marriage meant failure in bed. Early in her employment in this wealthy household, she began to feel the tension, and see the first signs of a division; and so, on more than one occasion, she had to shake her head, while standing amidst the rising evening fog of steam from the boiling pots, and say with some sympathy in her heart, "Mrs. Burrmann, God, you giving that man a dog's life!"

But Mrs. Burrmann continued to drink; and to read. She was subject to bouts of great affection; and would come into the kitchen and talk about herself, and about the children. And she would say how Sam was so disappointed he didn't have a son; and how close and fond he was of Mrs. Gasstein's little five-year-old boy. She would talk more about the children than about herself or her husband. She said once, perhaps overcome by Bernice's warmth, that sometimes she felt her husband resented her, almost hated her, because, after four pregnancies and two miscarriages, she had not given him a boy child. But it remained a superficial kind of friendliness: a probing, with short laughs and sniggers; and on Bernice's part, broad smiles like the sunrise. After more than two years of these outings with affection, Bernice never felt close enough to Mrs. Burrmann to tell her that she herself had left an illegitimate child back in Barbados. And in spite of this affection, she always saw herself as a servant; a sort of twentieth-century slave. It was mainly the amount of hard work which reminded her of her status. And also, the small wages.

Relations improved, nonetheless, between the two women. Bernice's wages did not. Mrs. Burrmann began to feel so much at ease with "this, this-this — *woman*" (that's how she first described Bernice to her friend, Mrs. Gasstein) that in addition to having Bernice bath and dress the children, she gave her permission to take them into the nearby city park on Eglinton Avenue, and for walks along Marina Boulevard, where they lived. The children were very intelligent, but not too well-mannered; not sufficiently whipped and scolded to satisfy Bernice's own principles about bringing up children. The fact that they knew they were wealthy; and conscious of their position in this cadillac-and-fleece-lined, suede-coat-and-fur-and-sable-reinforced section of Forest Hill Village, added to their being precocious in the most embarrassing situations. Bernice was nonetheless very impressed by the wealth of the Burrmanns. Sometimes, you thought it was *her* wealth as she reminded her Barbadian friend, Dots, that Forest Hill was superior to Rosedale. "Good God, Dots!" Bernice said, one day. "There's money on everybody' face and clothes, up here in Forest Hill!" Dots, also a domestic, said the same thing about Rosedale, where she worked.

But Bernice knew her place. Sometimes, it was pointed out to her that on this street she was to remember she wasn't a housewife. A head would lean out of a passing car; or would draw back a window blind, to wonder and to consider the possibility that the two healthy-looking children belonged by blood to the woman into whose hands they had entrusted their hands. One snow-filled afternoon, a woman driving a blue Cadillac stopped and waited until Bernice and the children got alongside; and when she thought they could hear and were in smelling-shot of her Estee Lauder Youth Dew perfume, she pulled her spectacles down her long Semitic nose and said, "Well!" in that short aggressive manner, as if she really meant to say "shit." That was the day Bernice wished everybody in Forest Hill, man, woman and child, dead; the day when a tear came to her eyes, and shimmered her entire view of the road and the world.

But it was Bernice's facility for work, long hard work, which knitted her into a glove of affection on to her mistress's hand. Mrs. Burrmann would brag to all her friends on the street, and at the pottery and watercolour classes which she took at the YWHA on Spadina Avenue. She would tell Bernice, "Leach, you're a wonderful worker. Really!" Bernice would smile sweetly and openly in her presence; but within, she would say, You don't have to tell me that, woman. I know I works hard as hell in this house, and for peanuts. The smile would brighten on Bernice's face a second time, and Mrs. Burrmann would contract this disease of happiness, and would smile; and the entire household would brighten for the remainder of that day. But Mrs. Burrmann never knew and couldn't imagine how deep Bernice's hostility was. One day, Mrs. Irene Gasstein had trouble with her German immigrant maid, Brigitte. Brigitte had remained in her quarters in Mrs. Gasstein's house, taking a rest from a touch of influenza and a bout of overwork. Mrs. Burrmann came to her rescue. "Forget about calling an agency for extra help, darling. That costs money. I will send Bernice over. She can do the work of a mule, two mules, ha-ha! and look, you don't even have to bother paying her anything. Bernice will come, darling."

"Oh I couldn't do *that*!" But she had already mentally accepted the offer of Bernice's sweat.

"Forget it. Don't spend your money foolishly."

"But . . . ah, would Bernice come? You know how these West Indian women feel. . . ."

"Will Bernice come! Irene, are you forgetting Bernice is my maid? That's what I pay her to do."

When Bernice raised no objection, this silence was mistaken for surrender, for acceptance. Silently, she grew to hate Mrs. Burrmann even more than she hated winter and the snow. To her, Mrs. Burrmann not only symbolized the snow; she symbolized also, the uneasiness and inconvenience of the snow. Her loneliness grew, too; and so did her hatred of Mrs. Burrmann: deeper and deeper, the same way as December, January and February piled snow on the ground. Added to this, Mrs. Burrmann refused to raise her wage from the ninety dollars a month, with which she had started, almost three years ago in 1960.

The burden and demands of her new life in this country were becoming too much for her, when one day ("Bam! bam! bam!" she actually clapped her hands in joy, three times and shouted, "there's still a God up there!") chance and God placed Mrs. Burrmann in her hands. What she saw the mistress do that night almost terrified the maid. The discovery upset Bernice, and she had to struggle hard to keep it a secret, because an idle word *would make Mr. Burrmann tear loose in this woman's backside, if he is a man in truth. Lord, a idle word on my behalf could do a lot o' harm in this household! and look how I have the balance o' power in my hand!* Her power cascaded into laughter. The laughter carried her into the kitchen, the kingdom of her service that was now a dominion; and she put her hands over her mouth to control her laughter. When she withdrew them, she was a different woman. "I'm going to blackmail her arse!" She laughed, and added, "I will whitemail her backside, clean clean clean!" She thought about it; and she conceded, "That isn't a christian-mind thing to do, though."

For many nights, Bernice dreamed about what to do. In all her dreams neither the colour nor the enormity of the incident was altered. It had happened on a Thursday night. The house was smelling of incense; rose in the sitting-room; sandalwood in the pantry, because "guests're coming here tonight, Bernice darling, so we have to cut down the awful smell of your cooking"; jasmine in the downstairs toilet, because Ruthie did not have time in the split seconds of need to get upstairs and relieve herself of her stomach flu, cabbage, minced steak and Boston beans. ("Christ! child, why you always having the belly? Your guts always running. I think something basic is wrong with you.") All the normal house-smells had to be counteracted. Mrs. Burrmann had had some bunches of roses, red roses and white roses, delivered earlier in the day. She had draped a red satin cloth on to a round table, and on this, she had placed her "priceless, absolutely priceless" candelabra with its five candlesticks ("Those thieving bastards down there in Yorkville Village, selling a lot o' junk for art!" But she had bought it for seventy-five dollars; and insisted in company that it was a bargain), four red candles; and a black one. When Bernice went into the sitting-room and saw it, she was speechless. She wondered if the black candle was her presence. She was thinking: *Mrs. Burrmann, do you have ghosts in here? You have as much candle and incense in here to bury a dead man and raise him up again from the dead. All these blasted candles! Mrs. Burrmann, I swear you is a fortune teller, or some damn thing.* The room was charming; and Bernice loved it. To her, it looked like the inside of Beth Tzedec, like a very sacred place; and this worried her, because she knew Mrs. Burrmann never went to the synagogue. And then the guests began to arrive; and Mrs. Burrmann, dressed to look like a sheath in a dress with two slits at either side, showing her blue-veined calves, greeted each guest man or woman with, "Darling! how sweet of you to come." For the men, she had a kiss on the cheek. For the women, she had a kiss on the cheek. Bernice could not understand what was happening. As the evening wore on, the guests relaxing with drink, their desires rising, it suddenly occurred to Bernice, that Mr. Burrmann was still absent. She saw Mrs. Burrmann put down her glass of port; pass her hands over her cheeks as if she was removing a stain, or pain; look purposely frustrated, and alien amongst the happiness, and go to the telephone in the hall. The stereophonic record player was giving out the soft, cool jazz of the MJQ. Nobody was listening. Mrs. Burrmann rested her left hand on the table top, to steady herself; and she dialled a number. Mr. Burrmann had left the office, his secretary said. Was he coming home? Or was he going to see a client? "He said he was coming..." and instinctively, the secretary paused, considered her salary, unemployment stamps and old-age pension, and then added in a new voice, in a surer lie, "Mr. Burrmann said he was coming home *after* seeing a client who he had to see earlier today, but who couldn't see today, earlier, because..." The expression on Mrs. Burrmann's face changed. She replaced the receiver before the secretary had finished; she struggled briefly and arrogantly to steady the drink in her legs and said, "Bastard!" It was a whisper; but Bernice heard it. And then a tall man, well dressed, slightly older than Mr. Burrmann, came to her. He carried two glasses of whiskey. He leaned over. He rested his lips on her lips and forced her, gradually, gently, against the telephone table, until the table sagged a little and the receiver slipped off. Mrs. Burrmann took a glass from the man's hands; put it on the table; wrapped her arms round the man's waist, and seemed to surrender herself to him. The glass fell and the whiskey was spilt. Nobody came from the sitting-room to find out why.

"Not coming, eh?" the man said, as if he was glad; as if he had pre-arranged Mr. Burrmann's absence. "Can't make a buck and a party, too! Hey! that's a great one...I should be in show business!"

"Sam'll soon be here," Mrs. Burrmann said, reassuring herself, and trying to give the man the impression that she was not completely neglected by her husband. "He's coming," she added, struggling not to appear cheapened by her loss of control in kissing him.

And as the hours and the guests lingered; and the hours became smaller, so too did the party become choral and rebellious. Stockings came off feet; men loosened ties and inhibitions; and soon everybody was singing *We Shall Overcome*, and other Negro spirituals. Bernice had heard some of these songs on the radio and television. Hearing them now, she could not at first recognize them as the same beautiful melodies. The guests did not know them. But this did not deter the man (the man who had kissed Mrs. Burrmann), from singing at the top of his voice, off key. Bernice heard it, and saw some of it, and got sick; and pronounced Sodom and Gomorrah on this household. *Lord in heaven look down! To look at this house from the outside you never will dream o' the things that takes place behind these expensive curtains and drapes. I glad as hell I is a poor, black, simple woman!* She used to remain downstairs, out of curiosity, until these parties wilted and ended; but after she was accustomed to them, as soon as they became sing-songs, she would leave in disgust and listen to the radio in her quarters on the third floor.

Midnight was coming. The wife of a talkative wine-faced man (at least the woman this man had arrived with; Bernice couldn't tell who were husband and wife after eleven o'clock at these parties) was sitting on a footstool, beside the player, listening to the folk music. She was the only one who could not sing the spirituals and freedom songs; and she said so, by listening to them. She had sat on the stool the moment she arrived and at eleven o'clock was still there, in spite of the crashing of glasses and the martial alcoholic friendships and the noise and the dirty jokes which the large prosperous man, who everybody called, "Jerr, baby," was telling about the Jews. Everybody (except this lonely, bored, vigilant woman) liked his jokes and said so by trying to laugh the loudest. Bernice was puzzled, even after having witnessed so many times how these people could laugh at jokes about Jews, when they were all Jews themselves. She moved through them, this group of wealthy people trying to be happy, falling off chairs, their eyes drooping from sleep and drink and their cigarette and cigar butts dropping ash on the expensive rugs. She pitied the woman, sitting and silent, listening and exhausted (or asleep) and she wondered what she was going to say to her choleric husband when she got him home in bed.

It was almost time to go up to her room. Bernice washed a new supply of glasses and swept up the broken ones. She said goodnight to Mrs. Burrmann; and the man who had been hovering over Mrs. Burrmann's honey the whole evening, buzzed "Nighty-nighty, Bernice!" and stung her with a pinch, on her jello under the white tight-fitting service dress she was wearing; then he winked at her.

"Darling, you shouldn't." Mrs. Burrmann felt compromised.

"Oh, what the hell! I believe in intergration."

Turning to Bernice, with a trace of embarrassment on her face, Mrs. Burrmann said, "Goodnight, Leach. And thanks for helping." Before Bernice turned to go, she saw that the man was now pinching Mrs. Burrmann on her behind.

Bernice left her door ajar, to hear the noise and the laughter and the occasional smashing of glasses that kept her company. All night long, she waited for Mr. Burrmann to come home; and when he did, finally, about four in the morning (five minutes after the last man left) Bernice at last fell off to sleep. She felt safe now. Suddenly, she was awakened by a noise and thought she heard a fight downstairs. Her sense of justice almost made her go and tell Mr. Burrmann what had happened in his house, in his absence: how the man kissed his wife, how he pinched her. But she could not. She knew she had to keep all this evidence within; and there, she decided to keep it.

Mrs. Burrmann must have realized how vulnerable she was now that Bernice had such evidence. And after some time, she fell off to sleep again. However, Bernice knew that a time would come when she would have to blackmail Mrs. Burrmann.

The time came a few weeks later, when Mrs. Burrmann refused to give her time off to go to the airport to meet her sister, Estelle, who was coming up from Barbados on a short holiday. There was a cocktail party set for eight that night, so Bernice would have to do her work first. When Dots heard of Mrs. Burrmann's attitude, she told Bernice plainly, "Gal! I would have blackmailed her long time!" Mrs. Burrmann knew that Bernice's sister was arriving; but she did not know the exact date. Bernice hated to pester her about it, because she had planned (unknown to Mrs. Burrmann) to have her sister stay with her. She was sure Mrs. Burrmann would resent it; might even dismiss her. She had mentioned Estelle yesterday, and Mrs. Burrmann waved her aside. Now, Estelle was arriving at ten this very evening. And nothing was being said about it. Bernice had to go to the airport to meet her. And today, of all days, *on my blasted day off, that whore in there, telling me what?* The emergency of this party and her general disposition had developed into a crisis. Bernice was nervous. Nothing was going right: she couldn't get the pickles out of the jar; the bread was sliced the wrong way; and every two seconds she had to wipe perspiration off her forehead with the tail of her apron, although the kitchen wasn't humid. *Be-Christ! stand up for your rights, Bernice. Don't let her walk all over you, man. No, it ain't true.* Bernice remained in the kitchen, keeping her distance from Mrs. Burrmann, who was watching television. She heard her laugh shortly. Then she heard the rattle of ice cubes in a glass. The television voice grew louder, and Mrs. Burrmann laughed again. And then, the room was quiet. "Look at her, though!" Bernice said, putting down the knife she was using. She took it up again, looked at it, and thought of murder. She wiped her face again with the tail of her apron. She pushed the knife far from her, on the kitchen counter: she had seen clearly, frighteningly clearly, the repercussions of that thought. She went into the sitting-room, without the knife, to speak her mind. Mrs. Burrmann was engrossed in the programme. Her back was turned towards Bernice, who stood a full thirty seconds watching the programme, before she had the nerve to interrupt her. "Mrs. Burrmann." The programme ended before Mrs. Burrmann replied. The news came on next.

"Oh, Leach!" she exclaimed. "I thought you were a spook!

You frightened me." Without turning round, she added, "Get me some ice, will you?" As Bernice served the ice, the announcer was saying that the Reverend Dr. Martin Luther King had led 2,500 Negroes in the shadow of the State Capitol here today.... "Praise God, it doesn't happen here," Mrs. Burrmann said, a noticeable relief in her voice. "We're even better than Britain."

"Mrs. Burrmann, I want to ask you a question."

"Sure, Leach." She seemed glad to have a reason for turning off the news. And this she did; and when she turned round and faced Bernice, Bernice thought she saw a certain blush on her face.

"It is about Estelle, ma'am."

"And who is Estelle?"

"Estelle? Estelle is my sister, ma'am. And as I have told you," Bernice said, being careful with her speech and grammar in front of her mistress, "I told you Estelle is coming in today, and..."

"Oh, yes, of course, that's right, too. Now, how is your sister, Leach?"

"Estelle better than me. But she coming in tonight, ma'am, on the ten o'clock plane."

"And how're you going?"

"I haven't arrange' transportation yet, but..."

"I mean in the kitchen, Leach."

"Well, I don't really know if I going or coming, 'cause as you see I still have a hundred and one things to fix for the party, and..."

"Don't forget I'm having eight guests."

"I know that." Bernice was becoming aggressive. "I know. And that is why I hurrying like the devil to finish up in time, and run up to Malton Airport." Mrs. Burrmann remained arrogantly aloof. She pretended there was a speck of something in her whiskey. "It's about Estelle and her coming-in that I want to talk to you about, ma'am...."

"Please don't forget there'll be eight guests."

"No, ma'am."

"And that means eight place-settings."

"You don't need to tell me that, ma'am."

"I'm not *telling* you anything." Her voice was rising; and her cheeks changing colour. You damn West Indians, she said to herself. "No need to have a chip on your shoulder. I'm merely reminding you...."

"But Mrs. Burrmann, listen to me! Are you forgetting that when I came to you as your servant, I came with the best papers and references. Look, I been setting table and laying knife-and-fork since I could reach the table with my head."

"Now, what about the sandwiches? And the other things?" Mrs. Burrmann's tone now suggested that she didn't expect an answer, rather that she wanted to remind Bernice who was maid and who mistress. This was her favourite technique when dealing with Bernice; and Bernice had always kept silent. She stood there and abused Mrs. Burrmann in her mind. Behind the smiling face, Bernice was telling her: *But, oh Christ, woman! I am not a child this time o' day. 'Course I know that eight guest mean eight place-settings, so you don't have to remind me, or tell me that!* And Mrs. Burrmann, who didn't have the power (or the desire) to listen to Bernice's thoughts, was saying, "...all I want to know, Leach, is that you have set the table for eight persons, and that you haven't forgotten that I told you, twice so far, this morning, that eight persons're coming. It is almost three o'clock now, and you still have lots to do ... the children, the groceries, and you have still to go to the drug store for me...." *Be-Christ, look woman, I didn't even have time to look at the blasted table, you had me so damn busy the whole day. You in here from daybreak to dusk, sitting down on your fat behind drinking drinks, whilst I out there, in that hot kitchen working off my fat, for peanut-money. From the time I come into this country, I been working. Working, working, working hard as hell, too. I really don't know what get in me to make me do a damn-fool thing like emigrating to Canada, saying I working as servant and maid for somebody like you...* "Leach!" Mrs. Burrmann was screaming. "Have you gone deaf?" It was a long time before Bernice heard her voice. Mrs. Burrmann was now on her feet, her hands at her temples, as if she was feeling great pain. "Leach, haven't you heard me asking you for my pills?"

"No, ma'am."

"Well?"

And that was all it took to defeat Bernice, once more. It was always like this. Whenever there was a serious matter to discuss with Bernice, Mrs. Burrmann always felt sick, suddenly. It had happened last week, when Bernice first mentioned that her sister was coming. Then, Mrs. Burrmann had developed a migraine headache, and asked for her tranquillizer pills. She'd taken twice the amount prescribed by her doctor; and for the rest of that afternoon had escaped to her bedroom to sleep it off. When she appeared the following day, smiling and charming ("Oh, Bernice, what a lovely winter day! You know, I think you're putting on too much weight." And she even patted Bernice on her behind, where her weight was heaviest), Bernice's defeat was so complete that her previous aggressiveness turned to sympathy.

"You taking it with water, ma'am?" she asked now, insinuating that Mrs. Burrmann might take it with whiskey. "I hope the head feel good soon, ma'am." *But she was hoping the blasted pill stick in your damn craw, and choke you dead, dead as hell! 'cause you think you buy me; but you didn't purchase me, you hear? You can't, nor won't ever buy Bernice, oh no, darling. You have your riches and your mansion and your broadlooms thick thick as grass, but you don't think for one moment that could make my heart flutter.* Mrs. Burrmann took the pill, and then reached out a hand and turned on the player which was part of a streamlined, expensive walnut cabinet that also contained the television. Without getting up from her couch, she chose a record; and then turned up the volume. She did not intend to continue the discussion with Bernice. Bernice waited to see whether the volume was turned up so high by mistake; but realizing that it was done deliberately, she flounced out of the room. Hate piled up within Bernice's heart as the eaves of the house piled with snow into shapeless mounds near the side door. The record was Beethoven's Sixth Symphony. Bernice had heard it before: Mrs. Burrmann played it every day, at least once, from beginning to end. And so, Bernice found herself liking the record, although she never knew why.

The music echoed through the entire house, like a storm, Bernice began to notice that this music, and the volume at which it was played, coincided with their quarrels. So many things went through her mind this afternoon, like children's fingers running at random through sand on a beach: thinking of Mrs. Burrmann, *unfair as hell, because today my day off, today is one Thursday I wanted to be free. Thursday's is my day to be off, as the regulations say. I didn't say so, and I certainly didn't make them regulations. You don't think she is a damn advantage-taker? Estelle coming in at Malton, and that princess in there, God blind her. . . .* But the music was upon her, coming back to her, like the memory of a kiss. It had reached the part she liked best; the part she always listened to, and which made her think of home, because she could see the lines of corn in the small plot of land her father tilled behind their house; and see women wearing hats of old rags on their heads as shields from the violence of the sun; women bending down, bending over like hairpins, pulling the weeds from choking the corn. Sometimes, if she listened attentively, she could see the blackbirds and wood-doves calling one another. . . . And then the telephone rang.

"Phone, Leach!" (Bernice called out in her mind, You can't hear it ringing yourself?) "Leach? The phone. Come and answer it."

"Mrs. Burrmann's residence?" she asked the phone; and when she recognized the voice, she exclaimed, "Oh Christ, Dots! That is you?"

"Guess."

"What?"

"Gal, guess."

"Boysie get the job in the civil service. . . . "

"I told you to guess, not *dream*." She filled Bernice's ears with her throaty, sensuous laugh. "Gal, that man been job-hunting since he come to this country eight months ago, and you think he could get a job? But I ask you to guess. Guess!"

"I can't guess, man," Bernice whispered. "Working for this bitch here has took away all o' my guessing powers. I here fighting with her to let me go up to the airport to rescue Estelle outta the hands o' them immigration people up there. And up till now, that woman hasn't even picked her teeth to me, to say yes, or no."

"But I ask you to *guess*."

"What happen now, eh?"

"Lottie dead." There was a pause, a long pause, before Bernice could speak.

"*No!*" she gasped.

"Lottie dead," Dots repeated, without too much emotion; as if she was reporting the death of a dog in the street.

"Yuh lie!"

"*Dead.* I just hear the man on the radio called out Lottie' name."

"How?"

"Crosswalk."

"When? When it happen?"

"Appears Lottie was going up Bloor Street, and she put out her hand to cross through one o' them blasted crosswalk-things, and..."

"If I had my way, Dots, if I was Mayor Givens, look! if I was a woman o' power, I would wipe out every last one o' them things. I calls them death-traps, not crosswalks."

"...and even though Lottie put out her hand to point, that man driving the mottorcar came right on, and *bruggadung-dung!...*"

"Poor Lottie...."

"Jesus Christ, Dots!" And for a long time, neither said anything. Dots began to talk again. "And to think, just think, that Lottie and me was sitting down here in my room, talking 'bout the nice things she bought down in Eaton's for the wedding. That girl spent so much money for the wedding...."

"Perhaps...perhaps, it is a good thing that Lottie dead, though."

"But gal, how the hell it could be a good thing when somebody dead?"

"Well, she was marrying the wrong man...."

"You vexed with the gal becausing she had a white man in mind? So what the hell so precious with black woman marrieding white man, gal? Look, I tired telling you that if you go on waiting for a black man, or even a Westindian man, to come and put wedding ring 'pon your finger, be-Christ, you will have your wedding day 'pon your death bed! Heh-hee! or you will surely die with yuh maiden intact, gal!" Dots laughed again, more maliciously, more sensuously. Bernice didn't see it as a joke. "Look, gal, times changing. And a man is a man."

"But still, Lottie…" and she realized she had better change the conversation.

"She dead. And I say it is a blasted shame that she died the way she had to dead. Still, it ain't a damn thing neither you nor me could do, save follow Lottie to the grave, at the funeral."

"I still sorry, though. 'Cause she is one o' we." Just then, Mrs. Burrmann called her. "I have to go now. You hear this one breathing down my neck?"

"I am not deaf, gal."

"Well, don't forget tonight. Estelle coming in, and when you come round here, we going have to talk some more," and with that, she put down the receiver. "Lottie, dead," she said to herself. "Dead?" The tragedy came in upon her with power. She felt lonely all of a sudden; and she felt cruel with the world. Immediately, she hated Mrs. Burrmann a little more, and blamed her for Lottie's death. But she talked herself out of this heavy judgement; and soon felt strong enough to face Mrs. Burrmann, once more, to talk about Estelle.

Beethoven's music was mournful now, as if it had reached that section purposely, on Lottie's behalf. Bernice waited until the hearses and the black of the funeral were out of the melody, and the feeling was new and rising and lighthearted as sugar cane trash tossed in a strong wind, before she moved off towards the sitting-room. She stopped. She stood. She thought. She came back and stood beside the kitchen counter, looking into the backyard of the neighbouring house, watching the snow fall, and counting the snowflakes dropping like marshmallows. The music was still loud; but it was distant now. It was something that could not be reached out to, and touched; something that melted, like the snow, the moment it came in contact with you... *Lord, a young woman! coming all this distance up here in this cold place, and You mean that You let her died? Lottie dead? just like that? What the hell that mother o' Lottie is going to say when she find out? And the same Lottie who was thinking o' sending for her brother to put him in a technical school to learn how to be a welder. All the money that poor girl saved up, all these five years working off her arse, and saving ninety-nine cents out of a dollar, turning her eyes 'gainst the luxuries o' this world, and setting them on necessary things, and now, out of the blue, bram! A blasted motor-car...*

"Miss Bernice! Aunt Bernice! Auntie Bernice!" It was the children. They had just come from school, one day early in winter with Mrs. Gasstein's two. Bernice held down and picked up Serene, and kissed her on her forehead. Serene kissed her on her lips; and Bernice stealthily but firmly passed her hands over her mouth, wiping away the kiss because it had chewing gum on it. The two of them were shut off, through their kisses, from the others. It was their little exile of happiness together. In the midst of this, one of the children, Mrs. Gasstein's son, commented, "She's *black*." (Bernice had not then liked the word "black" used to describe her colour. It was before she began reading the Black Muslim newspaper, *Muhammad*

*Speaks.*) Bernice flinched. She could feel the tension grip Serene's tender body, as she held her darling. The little boy was a fierce, little pink pumpkin of a boy. "She's *really* black." This made Bernice stiffen; but she pretended not to hear. "Look, Deirdre! Look! She is really black," the litle boy told his sister.

"So what?" Serene demanded. "Wise guy!" Serene had learned her lesson a long time ago: once, she came downstairs and called Bernice Miss Nigger, and her mother heard and slapped her on her mouth. "Never again do you let me *hear* you say that!" As viciously as she could, Serene said again, "Wise guy!"

"She's black. But our maid, Brigitte, is white," he said, savouring his last word.

"Mummy says Brigitte is a kraut," Deirdre said. Bernice felt it was such a heavy, ponderous and final pronouncement for a small child to make. But then, she felt she understood, seeing that she had always regarded these Jewish children (those on her street) as little spoilt brats. "Anyways, Mummy says we must never call a Negro person black or brown. They're persons. Mummy says we should call them coloured."

"And Mummy called the woman on the pancake box, Aunt Jerimima, Bernice's sister, because she is a nigger. Mummy says she is the same as Bernice. She looks like Bernice." After all this talk, the little wise guy was more serious, more inquiring than vicious and malicious. It was as if he had been working out these difficulties in his mind, to himself and for himself, to see whether he could find any logic in them. But by this time, Bernice was fierce. She was stiff with tension, with shame and with hate. Her right hand was quivering.

"Anyways, she's our maid," little Ruthie said, talking up for the first time. "And she is a *person*." Had it been on another occasion, in different circumstances, Bernice would have smiled and patted Ruthie on her head. But now, she saw just a child, one of four white children; *and children or no children, adults, old people, be-Christ, this whole damn world is the same all over.* And her hate thus became a corporate hate.

"Miss Bernice," Serene said, hugging Bernice, "don't listen to him."

"But what is wrong with you-all tribes, eh?" she asked, certain that at least one of them would not be offended by her harsh words. "You-all come running in *my* kitchen, walking-over this clean floor I just sprained my back cleaning. You-all looking for cookies, I bet yuh." She said it fast, gathering as much feeling as she could in this outburst of mock resentment. "Is cookies you-all want, ain't it?"

"Gimme a cookie." It was the fierce, little, wise boy, demanding.

"Don't give him any, Auntie Bernice. He hasn't any manners."

"She *has* to," Wise Guy said. He was now red with indignation. Bernice looked down on him, hardly three feet above the floor, and she wondered *why this little white bastard don't have no manners? Wonder what would happen if I bashed in his little arse with this cookie tin.* "She has to give me, I don't have to be nice to *her.* She is only a maid!" A quiet, like the quiet of the interval between new, unintroduced, faltering conversation, settled on the kitchen. *Boy, if I wasn't in this house, I would tar your little red arse now!* Serene tried to push the little wise guy of a boy out of the kitchen, before he said more embarrassing things; but he was too strong for her. *It is the same thing all over this world, big and small; and this bastard is bad bad, and strong to boot!* Serene eventually gave up trying to throw him out. And Wise Guy was quiet, and nice again. Bernice went to the top of the refrigerator for the large toffee tin in which she kept her home-baked cookies.

"Miss Bernice," Deirdre said, eating a cookie, "see my new bracelet. I just got it. I got it for my birthday." She held up her hand; and Bernice inspected it. Deirdre gave her brother a dirty look. It was impossible for her to relax in his presence. And just as Bernice was about to touch the bracelet, and run her fingers over its embossed patterns, Deirdre withdrew her hand. "It cost fifty dollars. Mummy bought it. But Daddy paid for it. And Daddy says I should have got a much better one. A better one cost *seventy*-five dollars. This is not a better one. This is a cheap one." It grieves my heart to see how your mothers spoil you children, she thought; but aloud she said, "You have a nice Mummy, dear, to spend fifty dollars on you, for that."

"You're *black*!" Little Red Wise Guy had not forgotten Bernice.

"She's six," Serene said. "She had a party, though. Not a very good party. I invited only twenty of my friends...persons. My Daddy says when I am thirteen, I am going to Europe for my birthday present. And..."

"How old you is now, please?" Bernice asked.

"Six."

"Looka, you-all come and take these cookies, please." Bernice was disgusted by the waste of wealth on these children. "I have work to do."

The children grabbed more cookies; and pushed their hands into her tin. Bernice smiled. Within her heart, she felt that these children were just like those she knew back in Barbados. Wise Guy came right up to her; rested his sticky red hand, softly, on her hand; and said, quizzically, "You're *black*." He touched her gently; perhaps even with love in the gesture. But how was she to know? After what he had been calling her? Swiftly, like electric current, Bernice's hand, her right hand, moved. And just as swiftly, something told her, *No! don't do that, you fool.* She looked at Serene and Ruthie, and realized that they did not know what to do with the little boy, their friend. The situation was too large for them. "My Mummy says you people are nasty," he said, eating a few cookies, and allowing some to crumble down his mouth. "And my Mummy says you shouldn't live among us. You're different from us."

"You're not even white, wise guy," Ruthie said. "You're just a lousy little Jew, like all of us."

"Oh God, man! you shouldn't call your friend by them hard words." And Bernice shook her head in sorrow.

"I'm not a Jew. I am white. And, and-and-and...she's black then, anyhow." The situation was now out of hand. Completely. Bernice remained clenched with anger, beside the counter, biting her lips, trying to evade the stares of Serene and Ruthie, her two dear sweet children, whom she knew would never say bad things like this; and she cried in her heart, because she could not strike the little boy dead. "Un-eeny-meeny-miney, moe! catch a..." he continued. And then he smiled, as soon as he reached that part in the nursery rhyme; he stopped; he looked up at Bernice, and smiled again. Instead, he merely added, "...catch a *dolphin* by his toe!" (Bernice exhaled all her hate.) Still staring at her, he went on, "...and if she hollers, let her go, eeny-meeny-miney, moe!" Bernice had closed her eyes by now, against the catastrophe that almost happened. She would have slapped all life out of him, had he uttered that word. When she opened her eyes, the little boy was standing at the kitchen door, with the door and the door-post squeezed against his head, showing only the eyes and that part of his head which had no ears. His mouth was turned up in a sneer; his tongue was hanging out in derisive contempt. "And eeny-meeny-miney, moe! and catch a black nigger by her toe..." But he did not have the chance to finish it. Bernice's shoe struck the aluminium screen door with a bang; and he fled with the remainder of the insult, terrified within him. His sister flounced. She placed the partially eaten cookie, scalloped by her tooth-prints, on the counter; juggled her fifty-dollar bracelet on her wrist; and left. She did not even bother to close the door behind her. Serene looked at Bernice, and then at Ruthie. And then she said, as if a great fatigue had come over her, "Come, Ruthie. Let us go upstairs." She seemed much older after she said it. They left Bernice alone; with the tears falling down her face, like icicles melting from the branches of the tree on the front lawn.

Many times during the thirty-two months she had worked for the Burrmanns, Bernice made up her mind to leave, to run out on Mrs. Burrmann, without notice, and with the kitchen sink full of dinner dishes. Always, her mind was changed for her by the terror of facing a Canadian winter without a job; and also by the comfort and near luxury of her three-room (living-room, bedroom — which were really one room — and washroom) apartment on the third floor, which was part of her wages for working as a domestic. It was her self-contained shelter, against herself and other racial fall-out. It became, in time, her home away from home. This apartment contained more facilities than she had ever known back in Barbados. It was clean; she kept it clean. It was large, for her; she was accustomed to sharing a bed with her sister, Estelle, all her life in Barbados. But it was lonely.

One day, in a pit of depression, Bernice went down to Eaton's department store and brought back two hundred dollars in dresses plus a ninety-dollar swim suit. She put on the dresses; but she did not wear them out of the apartment. There was nowhere to go. And so she called her friend, Dots, and the two of them alternately dressed themselves in the dresses, and modelled the swim suit which left a mark on the swivelly, jowled and jelly avoirdupois of their behinds. The next day, Bernice telephoned Eaton's to pick up the clothes. Eaton's gave her charge account a two-hundred and ninety-dollar credit. Dots had liked the swim suit; and wanted to keep it. But she remembered in time ("Where I would wear this thing, eh, gal? In the backyard in the summer? 'Cause I have never seen *one* Negro person in any o' these swimming pools they have all over this city!"), she took a final appraisal of her figure; took the swim suit off, and wrapped it in the soft, noisy paper into the box. Bernice cackled as if she was really happy, and said, "You could model it round the house, for Boysie, though."

"Look, gal, Boysie only married to me, you hear? And that don't give him the rights to see my body. And let me tell you something," she added, laughing, "we does do *that* in the dark." She laughed so loudly, that she had to put her hand over her mouth. Bernice laughed too. It was like therapy; and it made her feel better. Some of her depression left her.

But this depression would always come back. And once when it did, she withdrew from the congregation of the Toronto Negro Baptist Church, and transferred her soul and its care to the Unitarian Congregation, on St. Clair Avenue, West. This was a much better church, she felt. (Mrs. Burrmann used to go there; but she stopped shortly after Bernice came to work for her.) It was a cleaner wealthier church than her old Negro Baptist Church; and the congregation was all white — or mostly white; and they did not come to church to moan and groan, and exchange experiences about white people and about racial discrimination. Bernice felt purged, in a way. She chopped an inch off the hemline of her dresses, stopped wearing nylon stockings with seams and began stepping out into the pearly white, white virginity of winter and broadminded liberal Christianity, clickitty-clacketty, in a pair of Italian three-quarter heels. She had bought them the day before with her Eaton's charge-o-matic plate. One immediate result of this change in her place of worship, was that she stopped thinking Mrs. Burrmann was the devil; and consequently, stopped thinking of leaving the job. Life became a little less unbearable. She could stomach Mrs. Burrmann, who at this time, was going to the University of Toronto, doing a part-time course in Social Anthropology. Mrs. Burrmann had less time to herself; less time for the whiskey; and she spent most of the day studying. Bernice spent all her time caring for her personal appearance; and the appearance of her mind. She herself, following her mistress's influence, took out a subscription to *Life* and *Time* magazines, because she thought she was not quite equipped to engage on formal studies. But reading these two magazines, diligently, caused her to think a great deal about her life in this new, vast country; and about the world; and of course, about Mrs. Burrmann. Reading them even prompted her to put her thoughts on paper, in a letter to Mammy, confessing that *I following the lead of my mistress, and trying to improve my mind. She gone back to school, taking lessons. She is this big, rich Jew woman. So, I figure there must be something very special in doing that. That is why I subscribe to two nice magazines which I reads every night after work. I am convince there is something in learning, Mammy. Some damn thing. This lady, Mrs. Burrmann, have learning already, and money too. I don't know yet which road to follow. But I intend to follow both; and get some of both. If she can go back to school, at her age, and she already have a lot of certificates on the wall, and other papers testifying to the fact that...* and here her thoughts forsook her.

... and all these things come back to her, working eternally it seems, in this kitchen; listening to Mrs. Burrmann play Beethoven's Sixth Symphony as often as there is snow in winter; listening to the complaints, the small defeats and successes of the two children; and at times, giving some asked-for advice to Mrs. Burrmann about a dress — advice which was never taken. Listening now to the music, as the music possesses the room like human harvesters of women possessing a field, and leaving the field without corn, the music makes her think of home in Barbados; and it makes her say these thoughts out aloud, to herself, as she is accustomed to doing, while working in the kitchen. Sometimes, she argues aloud, to herself. And sometimes, her voice frightens her, as she hears it answering her; and she fears she is hearing the knell of a beginning insanity; and *remember, Bernice, do you remember Gertrude? and what happen to her? Never a soul with who she could exchange a word with, and comment on the colour of snow, even. Days and days pass, and not one o' we women from the West Indies ever went up to Orillia and see how Gertrude making out; and Orillia isn't as far as New York, and they always rushing down there, as if they have gold down there. Nobody won't go up and see how Gertrude making out in life, living amongst all them white people. Lord,*

*and when all of us was thinking that things up there was rosy, that*
*Gertrude was making money like water, Gertrude, oh dear loss!*
*flat on her back in a mental hospital. Gertrude let the loneliness*
*and the hard work go to her head, and it send her straight inside*
*the insane hospital. Up there in the wilderness, all by herself, ain't*
*have a chick to visit her, not a thing to do with her time, save go*
*and sit down in a church, four times every Sunday. Gertrude, like*
*the rest o' we, marching her behind inside somebody church....*
(One Sunday morning, when spring first peeped into Gertrude's boredom, she went to church, and was asked to testify.
A week before, she had "taken Jesus as her personal saviour."
The church was packed. Word had walked through this resort
town that a Negro woman from Africa (Gertrude was born
and bred in Grenada) was giving a speech. When the day came
and the church was hushed just like that time, in biblical
times, when spirits of foreign languages were falling on disci-
ples like tongues, Gertrude rose, red as a rose in a dress, and
said aloud, as if her whole body was a resort in which the Spirit
was rejuvenating, "I thanks the Lord for saving me and keeping me, from the rising of the sun till the going-down thereof.
I am saved, amen! and I have been washed in the precious
blood of the Lamb, and be-Christ, all of you brothers and sisters in here now can see that I been washed whiter than snow,
amen!" Gertrude was so black, that sometimes even Bernice
used to make jokes about her colour. Dots never liked her, and
called her Coal Dust. Nobody in that Orillia, tongue-tied congregation, could understand the meaning of her words and
nobody said amen!)....

The party (which Mrs. Burrmann had called a cocktail party,
but which was now being renamed a dinner and cocktail

party) was now a few hours off. Bernice was still working hard, making sandwiches and other tid-bits. Mrs. Burrmann shouted above the music, asking for ice. Bernice ignored her. She refused to tell herself she had heard; but she set about preparing the ice, nevertheless. "Estelle coming in, in exactly four or five hours and I haven't heard a word yet from that princess in there, now asking me for ice, blind her!" When she took the ice, she found Mrs. Burrmann sitting on her favourite chair, a reclining creation of teak from Yugoslavia. She held up her glass to receive the ice. Her eyes were almost closed, as if she could not hear the music with them open. Bernice was hearing the music perfectly, and she had to serve ice. *But why this woman close her eyes just to listen to this music? Man, this is music to make you want to dance and jump up and throw your dress over your head...* "That is a very nice tune you playing, ma'am." This caused Mrs. Burrmann to open her eyes. She sat up too.

"Beethovun," she pronounced, as if it was unquestionably beyond Bernice's comprehension to know what the music meant. "*Classical* music."

"So, that is what it is!" The triumph in her voice was the triumph of new knowledge. "I like it, though. It sound real good."

"Beau-ti-ful!" Mrs. Burrmann tried to impress upon Bernice the genius of this creation. "I'm never tired of hearing the power and the conflict of this very great mind...."

"Pardon me, ma'am," Bernice interrupted her, "but you want to know something? I don't see nothing like power or conflicts in this music, as you telling me you could hear. It reminds me o' women back home reaping corn, and putting that corn on their heads, and singing all the time they putting..."

"I am sure, Leach, that you don't really understand this symphony, dear."

" . . . and, a moment ago, just before I bring you this water and ice, I could swear that the music was telling me 'bout winds blowing, and a storm gathering up in the clouds and the skies. . . . " By this time, Bernice was talking to herself, because Mrs. Burrmann had left the room. She lingered for a while, looking at the dust jacket of the record. She decided she must own this record, to play it to herself, in her apartment when it got lonely and cold at night. Going back to the kitchen, she could hear Mrs. Burrmann moving about upstairs. Once or twice, Bernice stopped her work to ponder how and why this woman could be so offensive. *Satan does always find work for idle hands; and that is what she is: idle hands.* She was finding it difficult to concentrate on her work: her mind was on her sister arriving; and then it settled on the letter she had received from Lonnie back home, the day before. *Pay-day don't well come before I ain't getting all kind o' love-letter from that bastard. He think I up here to support a man? Well, he lie in hell! Man made for supporting woman, and not the other way round, Mister Lonnie. No, darling.* But she took the letter out, and sat in the chair beside the refrigerator to read. Part of her mind was on the high-heeled movements upstairs. She did not want Mrs. Burrmann to catch her sitting down in the middle of the afternoon. Lonnie's letter was written on crisp, expensive onion-skin paper; and she wondered where he had stolen it, since he never had money. *Darling, sweetheart Bernice* (this salutation, which she had read four times, put a sharp pang of desire in her body. She had read it, last night, just before going to bed — just the salutation; but she didn't read more, because she knew the rest of the letter would be asking for money, and

telling her how he missed her "in that certain way." Bernice
was not strong enough to read this kind of letter, while she was
alone, and uncomfortable in bed, thirsty for the warmth of a
man's body next to her skin. "Lonnie, when are you going to
learn how to write me a love-letter like any other man would,
without asking for money in the same sentence? Heh-heh,
Lonnie, you is a real case, in truth," she said, as if she was talking to him, across all those hundreds of miles) . . . *this is Lonnie.
I writing you because Christmas soon here, and things down here
in Barbados still rough as hell with me. The sugar cane crop-
season was a real bitch this year, Bernice. And the estates start the
season laying off mens, right and left, like flies. I only had a five
weeks job this crop-season. Furthermore, a piece of sickness had me
flat flat on my back the whole of last month, and I had was to give
up a little picking a fellow by the name of Boulee, who uses to be
a garbage collector in a donkey cart in Christ Church parish, told
me about. You remember Boulee? The job he told me about was a
night watchman job at a new club open by a Canadian fellow
whose name I can't call to mind right this minute, because only
heavy things like money resting on my mind these days* . . . The
letter made her think of her son, Terence. Terence was left
with Mammy, with strict instructions not to let Terence see his
father, Lonnie. The moment the plane took off from Seawell
Airport, Bernice put Barbados and Lonnie out of her future
plans. But she was going to send for Terence, when he was big
enough, and put him through university, if she had to beat the
brains into his head. That was her plan for her son. "Hope it
won't be too long, Lord, I hope it won't be too long before
Terence grow up." She looked at Lonnie's letter, put it down
because she had to wipe the recollections of tears out of her eyes
with the tail of her apron; and just as she was about to read it

again, Mrs. Burrmann crept into the kitchen (she had already seen Bernice sitting down, in the middle of the afternoon!) as silent as Putzi, her cat, who followed her now, and who followed her everywhere she went. Bernice jumped up, and in her haste forgot the letter lying open on the kitchen counter.

"I just this minute sit down here, ma'am, to rest my poor foots," she said.

Mrs. Burrmann ignored her. "I was dreaming," she said. She seemed as if she was still in the dream. Bernice saw the lines from the pillow case, and from her fingers, etched into her face. These marks looked like wounds that did not cut deeply enough into the flesh to draw blood. "I was dreaming about a little boy." She returned to the dream which was not too clear in its imagery. "Now, let's see... this little boy, now that I think of it... I can't for anything remember who he looked like... but this little boy, with a big head... I remember that... and big eyes... you know that little boy across the street... Mrs. Gasstein's... what's his name...? anyways, that little bastard wanted to make love to *me*...! ha-hah..." (Bernice went back in her mind, to this afternoon, when Wise Guy was in her kitchen: eeny-meeny-miney, moe! catch a dolphin... heh-heh-hehhh!... Well, what a terrible experience that would have been for that little boy...) Mrs. Burrmann then stretched her arms horizontal; and made her body look like a crucifix. The cat curled itself round her ankles. A sadness came over her face. "What a strange thing! I can't remember the dream."

"Leach."

"Yes, ma'am."

"Do you believe in dreams, Leach?"

"Me, Mrs. Burrmann? Believe in dreams?"

"Do you, really?"

"Well, to tell the truth, ma'am, my whole life is one big never-ending dream."

Mrs. Burrmann either did not understand the meaning of Bernice's words; or she was not concerned about them. She took up the cat, Putzi, and held it to her face. Putzi, black and sleek and sneaky, cuddled up like a naughty child in the spoiling hands of a doting parent; closed its eyes, because it was secure; and listened to Beethoven. Bernice saw the cat open its eyes and put its long pink tongue out, and plant a kiss with its tongue like a pink snake, right on Mrs. Burrmann's mouth. *Jesus Christ! this blasted woman and that cat! That cat will surely give her the tizzick, as good as a cent! I am sure that this woman believe in black magic and witchcraft.* But the cat re-coiled itself into a black ball, in Mrs. Burrmann's hands. Mrs. Burrmann told it, "Putziputziputzi, darling, mother's gonna feed thee, eh, Putziputzi, eh? you're a sweet person . . . *(God blind her and that black cat in my kitchen! She must be sleeping with that blasted black cat, or something just as bad!)* . . . eh, Putziputzi?" She was talking to Putzi, as if she had forgotten that he was a cat. She then put Putzi down; and the cat, transformed from a person into a cat again, transformed itself into a horse-shoe token of goodluck, and curled itself against Bernice's fat ankles. "Putzi loves you, too, Bernice," Mrs. Burrmann said. *("Blind you, cat! if she wasn't here, I would throw you right in a tub o' hot water! Now, get to hell from offa me, cat! I don't like cats.)* Bernice smiled with the cat; and waited until Mrs. Burrmann had looked off, before she jabbed it with her toe.

"Putziputzi," she said, imitating Mrs. Burrmann.

"I'm going out now."

"But wait, missis. And what about the party?"

"Forget the party, I'm going out."

"Forget the party? But you mean to tell me, Mrs. Burrmann, that you had me stretched-out in this kitchen from the
time I wake up this morning, till now, past five o'clock, and
just like that, you telling me forget the party?"

"Forget the party," she said, and she took Putzi from the
kitchen counter where he was eating some of the sandwiches,
and put him on the floor, and called him after her, "Come
Putziputziputzi, darling, come come, Putziputziputzi...." The
cat went to her like a black worm; it looked up into her eyes;
aimed with its eyes and tensed its body, and then sprang
into Mrs. Burrmann's arms. "Honey!" She was still speaking to
the cat.

"That *animal!*" Bernice spat into the kitchen sink, as she
said it; and then she ran hot water over the substance. She
sat down as soon as Mrs. Burrmann went upstairs. The letter
from Lonnie was still on her mind, and she wanted to remember what home was like... *remember, at this present moment,
because things resting heavy on my mind. Things real tough as
I said, down here in this island, although we got the deep water
harbour that Grantley Adams promised to the people since Adam
was a boy in short pants. Christmas soon come, and I want to
go to church five o'clock Christmas morning, at the Cathedral,
because the news is that the new bishop of the island coming to
preach there, and everybody say he is a good preacher who does
preach long long sermons. I want you to try to get me in Canada
one of these days, Bernice, because you will remember that the
night before you left, we was talking about that. You remember?
And the nice time we had behind Mammy's paling, when I really
thought you was my woman, and would help me out in the
time of need? Well, that time come now. Cuthbert the tailor fellar,
since he went up in the States and in Canada and all over the*

*outside world, he now come back down here in Barbados, charg-*
*ing everybody something he named luxury tax, and if you don't*
*put that luxury tax inside Cuthbert hand, he not touching your*
*suit at all....* "Not one blasted word that man ain't say 'bout
Terence! I don't know if Terence sick, if Terence playing tru-
ant from school, if Terence walking 'bout with his backside
at the door, if his pants wants mending, nothing at all he
ain't write...."

"I run all the way up here, Bernice, gal," Dots was saying. She
was still panting and sweating. She bent her head forward, and
wiped the back of her neck, and her forehead, with the hem of
her dress. "It so blasted cold, and I sweating like a mule, hah-
hah!" Dots had waited very patiently, and somewhat peeved,
to see the attention Bernice had given her winter coat: pulling
out the sleeves and putting it on a hanger in her clothes
cupboard. It didn't make sense to Dots, to waste time on the
coat, which had been given her by Mrs. Hunter, her employer.
"Well, what gone wrong with you, this time, gal?"

"Estelle."

"She's not coming anymore?"

"The quicker I leave Mrs. Burrmann," Bernice said, already worked up, "the sooner I leave, the more better for me,
and the better for her."

"Yes, gal. I understand. But I ask you 'bout Estelle."

"I think I hate that woman so much, that..." she paused,
and then said, "that I could have *kill* her this afternoon." This
was what she wanted to say at first, but she didn't think Dots
would have appreciated it. She needed Dots: in times like this,
when there was no other person on whom to lean for support.

"But I don't see it as a matter of hate, or hating, gal. Nor like, nor liking. I see it as a attitude. Gal, attitudes is things that don't stand up for excuses like hate or love."

"I don't know what to do," Bernice said. "I was much better off in Barbados, and ... (Dots was thinking: like hell you was! you, like the rest o' we, if you didn't come up here, and if Canada didn't rescue you, you would still be as poor as a bird's arse) ... though we didn't have these modern conveniences, things wasn't as bad."

"Give every man his due, gal. Give every bastard his due, and the world would be a better place and everybody would be happy."

Bernice went to the window, to look out, perhaps to see if the answer was written on the house where Brigitte worked. She didn't see an answer there. After all, Dots was right: she was as poor as a bird's arse, back in Barbados; and still, she couldn't afford to let a stranger know that. (Dots was thinking; anybody would think this retired whore was really something back home. The way she carries on! "The work too hard," "the missy too bad," "she don't have any money," "the pay too small," good Jesus Christ, Bernice, you was not the Queen o' Barbados.) Bernice said, "Child, it is at this window, looking out almost every night, that I think I could see the meaning of the whole world." Dots went to the window, not to look out, but to be near Bernice. She peered through the mists of warm breath blown against the window pane, out into the snow-banks, and she saw snow, and not the world, as Bernice boasted.

"Snow, gal," Dots said. "Snow, and more snow. Snow climbing up outta the sidewalk, and up on the houses like a thief climbing through a window."

This made Bernice mad. She thought Dots was regarding her as a mad woman. "It mean more to me. Dots, it mean and connote more to me than mere icicles and snow. In it, I can see that princess down there, and the way she tries to ride me and ill-treat me." Dots disregarded her. She was thinking of her husband, Boysie: what that damn man up to now, I wonder. I wonder if Boysie really down there at Henry's place, playing dominoes as he say he left home to play? Or if he is after some white woman, now?

The two women were quiet now; silent, through the agreement of close friendship: Bernice, standing beside the window and Dots, sitting on a chair, looking into her lap to see if she could see there, the image of the white woman her husband was in bed with. Dots would look up; or pass gas, and then say, "Excuse, gal"; and Bernice would make another biting observation about her life in Canada. "Estelle coming in tonight, and up till now, *she* down there, hasn't pick her teeth to me, saying Bernice, or Leach as she like to call me, go and meet Estelle."

"Nothing at all?"

"Not one word."

"That is life!" She paused to allow the snow to fall, in silence. Then she added, "Estelle coming. But where she going live? With you?"

"She not staying at the Royal York Hotel! I lives here! So my sister going to stay here, and get some o' them benefits!"

"Now you talking like a lady, with sense, gal." Dots burst out laughing. "Don't forget you have something on Mrs. Burrmann that you could use as blackmail. You have her, coming and going." Bernice started laughing too, but the suggestion of blackmail made her serious. "What's wrong with you, gal? You are *Lady* Bernice, now! You could milk her, with a stiff piece o' blackmail, till she really turn *white*."

"Not blackmail, though." Bernice was cautious, and very moral about this. "Oh God no, Dots. Mrs. Burrmann *is* bad, but she isn't so bad. And blackmail ain't a Christian-minded thing, neither."

"You too damn stupid."

Here, conversation stopped. Music was playing. Bernice smiled, and leaned her head to listen. Bernice looked at the letter from Mammy, reading it to herself, all the time making facial expressions in comment, as the letter pleased, or displeased her. Bernice wondered why Mammy's letter, dated a week earlier than Lonnie's, had reached Toronto a day later. ("Lord!" said Dots, making a comment on her boredom, her misery in Bernice's company and her general mental state.) The letter told Bernice, *Dear Bernice, love, I have received the money which you posted to me in March last...* it was now March again.... *And I have been reposing myself at the front window, at which you used to sit, in the evening, waiting for the postman to knock. I remember that you used to sit down there, and sing those beautiful songs which you learned at the Fontabelle Christian Mission Church in Christ. And everytime I see Berry, the postman, pass across on his bicycle, my heart gives a shudder, and tears sometimes come to my eyes, because I know then that you have not sent me anything....* "A year pass already?" she asked the letter.

"What you say, gal?" asked Dots, coming awake.

"I talking to myself, child." Dots apparently went back to her dreaming; and Bernice to the letter. She threatened to let Mammy sit down at that window till the undertaker removed her, before she would send another penny to her. *You have not remembered me. You have forsaken your own mother. Don't you know that you left a child behind you? I mean Terence. And Terence has been sick every day for the past month....* It saddened

Bernice very much to think of home, and of Terence. She must withdraw some money tomorrow from her bank, and send it for Terence. But she couldn't help remember that poor as Mammy was, she still raised two daughters, Estelle and herself; and that she sent them to school, and to church, plus Sunday school every Sunday. Mammy did her best to make them the two "most decent girl children in this village"; and she went further and sent Estelle to high school, which at that time was very expensive. Bernice had already decided that school didn't like her: but it was really the other way round — she hadn't the brains to pass the entrance examination; and she started to work at the Marine Hotel, as a housekeeper. She remembered the small, one-room leaking house; and the flattened skillets that once contained butter from Australia (which butter neither she nor Mammy could afford to eat) which Mammy nailed on the roof as shingles to keep out the sun and the rain and the wind; this house — like many others of the fifty in the village, lodged on loose coral stones — was their mansion, their castle which hid the penury from the eyes of the other poor villagers. The worst thing she remembered about Barbados, and home and the village, was the closet which always had cockroaches infesting and infecting it; with its oval hole in the middle of the seat like the hole in a coffin; and the ten-gallon galvanized bucket underneath ("What that bucket used to have in it, Bernice?") catching everything that dropped: filth, excrement, the blood, the rags-and-the-blood; and once upon a time, something that came from Bernice's womb, or belly or stomach (and Mammy never called it by its name) which had to be got rid of, because Mammy said so, because Bernice was too young for that... *and although Terence has been sick, that no-good man you found yourself with, I mean Lonnie; Lonnie does not even come round and say, Take this, to Terence, meaning a six-cent piece.* At this point, Dots came alive, to ask what time it was.

"The missy home?" she asked.

"You mean that music, eh?" Bernice asked, smiling.

"That damn rock-'n'-roll waking me up," Dots grumbled. "She don't know that is heathen-music?"

"My missy don't play *that* music, darling! It is the children you hearing." Bernice assumed great pride in defending Mrs. Burrmann's tastes.

Dots was apparently impressed. "Oh!" she said, with great relief; and straightway, like an animal awakened from its hibernation by a small disturbance of no consequence, she retreated into her reverie. It was part reverie, and part silent appraisal of Bernice's apartment, which she envied because it was always kept so clean; and also because it was a room larger than hers. She reached out, and touched the animals from the north of Canada, all dead, all seeming to be prancing, or grazing on grass that was the colour of green clay: animals roaming in glazed and plastic enthusiasm. They were on the centre table. Dots ran her fingers over them again; and then she touched the jungles of false trees: maples, spruce, pine; trees coniferous and deciduous. A miniature waterfall bubbled and gurgled when she held it in her hand. She turned it upside down; and was shocked by its origin: MADE IN JAPAN. "Christ!" she exclaimed, "Niagara Falls, gal!", although it was not the first time she had seen the Falls, in artificial reproduction.

"You ever went there?" Bernice asked, noticing her interest; and coming awake from her own thoughts.

"Niagara Falls," Dots repeated, noting the likeness.

The room was quiet again, as if a door on a noisy city

street was shut against the din of traffic. Bernice, wishing that Dots wouldn't talk so much, returned to the letter which her wandering thoughts had interrupted. *All Lonnie comes round for, is to ask me if Bernice send the thing? I don't know why you don't put an end to Lonnie. Lonnie is no good for you. Lonnie, since the day you left for Canada, has been running after ever thing wearing a skirt. Lonnie does not even take Terence to Gravesend Beach on a first Sunday, for a sea bath. He passed round here once, which was a month after you left, and he took Terence to the Garrison Race Pasture. Terence came back in here at eleven o'clock at night. Terence tells me that he lost Lonnie who went drinking rum with his friends, and if it wasn't for a police, Terence would still be lost. By luck, the police found Terence, and somebody happened to know that Terence belonged to you, meaning that you is Terence's mother, and that you far from here, up in Canada. I had to bathe Terence in licks for doing that trick to me, because I think he is too big to say he getting himself lost.* Bernice had to laugh at Mammy: she ain't change a bit, that Mammy. And looking up, she saw Dots inspecting her dressing table, which was the largest piece of furniture in the room, and Bernice's priceless possession. There was a looking glass attached to it. On this dressing table, Bernice had placed every bottle which contained manufactured tricks to improve a woman's facial beauty and personality. Some bottles contained a fluid thick as molasses, but white; one boasted, and backed up its boast with a guarantee, that it had the ability to transform Bernice's personality and complexion in such a way that men would trip over her. And this was the bottle Dots was examining. Others contained complexion-lighteners. These Bernice had discovered in Harlem where she had recently spent two weeks, visiting a cousin. Except for her complexion-lighteners, the entire collection of miracles were manufactured by Avon. Mrs. Burrmann had called her downstairs, and had given her this collection.

Bernice broke into Dots's thoughts, grumbling, "Lady Burrmann expecting friends, and I expecting a sister. I have to forsake my own flesh-and-blood so that the princess down there could drink her whiskey till her damn face is as red as a cherry, and she and her guests start singing Negro spirituals and folk songs, and carrying-on . . . holding up their clothes in front o' the men, and swapping mottor car keys, and . . . "

"No! *They* don't do them things, gal!"

"Them?"

The room was so quiet, that the snow seemed to be making noises as it fell. Dots sighed again. "I wish I could lay my hands on Boysie!" And a lifetime of disappointment and frustration seemed to rise from her sight. "Every night, each night, Boysie comes in at three, four, five, and one morning that bastard creep in Dr. Hunter's house, at *seven*. Christ, gal! and I was so shame in case the doctor see my husband coming in at that hour. Boysie crawls home late, like a dog, tired as hell, and saying all the time, the car break down, something wrong with the car, and be-Christ, when I call-on 'pon Boysie to give me little loving, Boysie licked-out like a wet rag. Bernice, gal, sometimes I envies you, 'cause you don't have no man-worries to worry you. . . . "

"You have a lot on your mind, too."

"Boysie running after white woman, gal. My husband in love with white woman. But I swear to you, in the presence o' God up there, be-Jesus Christ! let me just catch Boysie with one o' them!"

"Lord have mercy."

"And I telling you now, Bernice, that I don't intend to stay in that damn place by myself, night in and night out. I am going to get myself a nice, young strapping white man and put a horning in Boysie's backside that will learn him sense. Let Boysie take that! 'Cause he don't know how to appreciate a nice black woman."

"But what you saying at all?" Bernice was nonplussed.

"Many's the night. Bernice, you know not, because a woman can't tell everything concerning her life, not even to her closest bosom friend . . . many things goes on between my husband and me that I can't break to you. Them is things I have to keep buried inside here." She patted her breast heavily; and Bernice nodded her head, in sympathy. "Many's the night, gal, I sitting down at the edge o' that bed, and I watching that hour-hand as it move round from eleven, twelve, one, through two, and three and four o'clock, and my husband isn't in my bed beside me. Where the hell he could be? In somebody bed? Tell me."

Bernice could understand this way of feeling things, and this way of expressing them. But she was still stunned by the compromise in Dots's words. "For a decent person like you, to say that," she said, "is nothing but a damn surrender to the past and the past histories that used to be the way o' life for my great-great grandmother. Mammy tell me all that happen in them days. And I telling you now, so you won't mention no more past-tense thoughts and commit no more fornications and suicides, with those thoughts. Mammy tell me that in them black days, any excuse for a man, as long as he was white, could hold on 'pon her grandmother by the hand, or grab her grandmother by the neck, or by her behind and drag her in the nearest canefield or behind the pig pen, and

lay down flat on top o' she, and work off himself and his
unwanted substance and seed in her belly. And on the back o'
that, leave her to the four winds. Jesus, Dots, you mean to tell
me that you want them days to come back? Is that why you
want to go with a white man?" (Dots was twisting and turning
uncomfortably.) "Look, child, I reading some serious knowledge these days, since I went down in Harlem. I think you
should go there."

"It does happen every day, gal!" Dots did not give the
impression that she had been joking all along. "It happens
every damn day, black woman and white man. I ain't the first
and I won't be the last, and there ain't nothing you could do to
stop this modern trend." Bernice remained unimpressed. Dots
had to go further; and with mock exasperation, she added,
"But have you never pass through Yorkville, Yorkville Village?
Near by Bloor and Avenue Road. Or the Little Trinidad Club?
Toronto integrated now, gal. It is a technicolour city, now."

"Technicolour, or no technicolour, I still say what you just
tell me has a damn lot to do with histories."

"Histories, my arse! — if you would pardon my vernacu-
lar, please."

After this, Dots flounced into silence and sulking. Bernice,
somewhat humiliated by what had been said about finding
a white man, went back to her letter. She got up from the
chesterfield, and sat beside the window, counting the snowflakes passing her window. Dots was looking at the chesterfield, which was a couch by day, and a bed by night; and
she felt very sorry for Bernice, because she knew the chesterfield had never been occupied, at night, with Bernice locked
in the thighs of a man's satisfaction. Perhaps, had there been
a man, Dots thought, Bernice might not have reacted so

violently to what she had said a moment ago. Although I tell the old bitch I was joking, Dots thought, throwing a glance in Bernice's direction.

Just then, the telephone rang, and frightened them. Dots's expression said it was the airport calling about Estelle; perhaps the flight was delayed. But Bernice knew it was the princess downstairs. And that was who it was.

"What she want, now, gal?"

"I have to fix dinner for *he*. *She* going out to the YWHA, she say. Mr. Burrmann eating by himself again tonight. Four times this week, already!"

"These people ain't have no damn respect for their husbands. Suppose you hear the way Mrs. Hunter talks to the Doctor? Christ, gal, if that was Boysie, Boysie would have lickin my arse with the broomstick already... and Boysie isn't even what you would call a real husband to me, neither!"

"Dots, he is a good man to her, Mr. Burrmann is, a damn good man," Bernice said, shaking her head from side to side, to let Dots know how good a man was Mr. Burrmann. "Good man. She ain't lacking in clothes, pocket money, mottor car, fur coats, nothing. The broadlooms in this house is enough to hide a man in...."

"Like a dog..."

"He kisses the dirt that bitch walks on."

"But you can't buy love, gal. You could maybe buy anything saving *that*!" Dots yawned. She stretched, and while stretching, she tickled herself under her left arm; and smiled. Bernice smiled too. "Well, gal, what about tonight, and Estelle?"

"Child, everything fix up already," Bernice said. "Observe how I plan to operate on that princess down there! I have already pinch three bottles o' Haig-and-Haig scots whiskey, and I put it under my bed, three months ago, when I first knew Estelle was coming up. I have a big piece o' ham left back from last Christmas. That hide away too. A half dozen bottles of her nice Jewish wine that helps to make her face red as a beet, well, that Jewish wine will have to help give me some thrills tonight! Even though I can't turn red as a beet when I drink it, heh-heh-heee!... and some eatables and deli-cacies, deli-deli-delicacies, that I been hoarding up on her arse, on the sly." Dots convulsed into laughter. "Look, you have to use your head with these people, man. I telling you, you have to sit down a long time, and think how to outsmart these bitches and bastards living in this world with you." Bernice noticed that Dots was suddenly very quiet; and when she looked back, Dots was getting her coat from the cupboard. "You going, child?"

"I am going, gal, I going."

"What about tonight? I having something for Estelle."

"I don't know if I coming," Dots said irritably. "I ain't coming. And I going tell yuh why. Gal, I am tired sitting down and looking at a bunch o' damn frustrated women who don't have no man, and can't find no man. Usually, I am the only one who bring a man. And he is my husband, Boysie. Every woman in the place always have her eyes on him, and I tired as hell always having to watch my husband." After this, Bernice was silent. There wasn't anything she could say to change Dots's mind. You could hear the snow falling, it was so silent in the room. Dots gathered up her things; said, "I going, gal," once more, and then walked towards the door. When she turned the doorknob half in its circle, she held it there for a moment. She looked back at Bernice; said something very awful about Bernice in her thoughts; and left. Not yet arrested and handcuffed by this desertion, Bernice watched the door-knob as it moved back throughout its circle.

Bernice didn't know how long it was since Dots had left. She could hear the music climbing the stairs; but not Mrs. Burrmann's music. And this made her feel even more displaced. The music was what Dots liked to call, "White people' music, gal!"

A little blue light, twinkling like a star, said the snow was going to fall and fall, as if winter had decided to compress itself into one day, and drown the land. Bernice experienced a sensation similar to strangulation: things were moving, but moving slowly and only with the permission of the snow, which held life itself in a cold neck-tie. The blue star of light, of night (although it was not yet eight o'clock), brought a melody to her mind. She sang it until her memory snowed the words from her tongue; and she had to begin again at the beginning, and come to that same snow bank which she could not climb in the first instance; and then the melody was buried. The light of blue, the night star, was the star of light on the snow plough which passed under the window of her memory; and it passed once more; and just then, the melody returned to her:

"*Twinkle, twinkle, little star,*
*How I wonder what you are . . .*
*Up above the . . . so high . . .*" and when the melody died finally, and the snow plough left Marina Boulevard, unreality returned. She began to talk in conversation with herself. She began where the reality of her earlier conversation with Dots had ended: *You have to learn how to use your head, Dots; and how to sit down at a window and think, and focus your attention and thoughts on things above; and learn how to out-smart them*

*bitches and bastards, and use them the same way they uses you; and you have to learn how to use the same weapons they use on you; and you have to understand what them weapons is. Lemme tell you: them weapons is brainpower and brainwashing; and I know, 'cause I come across it in a magazine I got in Harlem, when I was visiting there. Brainpower and brainwashing...* "Come here, Dots," she said aloud, in her make-believe conversation, "come and let me show you something." *...you see them things running 'bout in the trees, looking as if they is big big mice? there, on Mrs. Burmann's lawn and all over the sidewalk? What you think their name is, Dots?...* "Squirrels, gal." *...you're blasted right, they is squirrels. And I wish that you, Mister Squirrel, you dark-brown one down there, had the sense to read my mind when I throw you a piece o' stale bread; and I wish too, Mister Squirrel, that I could, some day, come down there and talk with you, 'cause you have open up my eyes to many mysteries of this place...* "Gal, are you telling me there is something important with a simple thing as a damn squirrel? Christ, a big woman like me, and wasting time talking 'bout squirrel? I must be going mad as hell!"*... you ain't going mad, child; and if you going mad, you going mad only to learn sense. Don't forget every mad person is a sensible person in some way. I come across that in a book, in Harlem, too; a lot o' things and mysteries I come across in Harlem ... but Lord, at this moment, that isn't a damn use to me, because there ain't one man I could call on to ask for a favour from. Not one blasted person, white, black or blue, or pink! the only person I could think of, is Brigitte; I inviting Brigitte tonight, that German girl from 'cross the street; never mind she is a, a-a-a, what Mrs. Gasstein boy called Brigitte?...* and the steam in the breath of her conversation melted, and the glass in the window returned to the window; and she looked down and saw it. And she called Dots to watch. Since the steam in her conversation had polished the glass in the window, and she could see, and she knew she was seeing, there was no need to pretend that Dots was still in the room with her. She had to see the act for herself: there were two men, standing beside a tree, while their two dogs (Bernice didn't know the pedigree of the dogs) were bent stiff as icicles, in their shivering act of easing their bowels. A brown, dotted line of spaghetti, dit-dotted and dot-ditted out, into the cloud bank of snow. The men stood near-by, like landlords. They were pretending: they were pretending their presence was based on the pretences of the past, and all the time, the endless sausage was coming out of the two dogs; and they pretended they knew it was going to end. They were jerking their heads, up and down the street, at second floors and bottom floors, to see if anyone was going to raise a window, and screel down at them, *Take your goddam dogs, and scoot, or!* But the dogs, both white, continued to shiver and to strain from the exercise and the exertion of their deliverance. A smile came to the faces of the men, as they saw the faeces of the dogs, still bent like two skeletons of a dinosaur, curved backs, still in the position of the act, although the act itself was now only wind, and air, and gas. "Now, watch," Bernice told the presence of Dots, which she felt in the room. "You watching, Dots? Watch something now." The dogs were finished now. One of the men, the tall one, with wisps of grey hair at his temples, raised the left side of his winter coat, and pulled out a piece of tissue paper, the colour of snow and blood mixed, the colour of pink. And he was about to bend down to the snow and to the dog that was his dog, when Bernice turned away her eyes. (She made Dots's presence turn away her eyes, too.) And she said to Dots's presence, "Jesus Christ, no! No, no, no! he don't

intend to do what I think he intends to do! No, he couldn't be
such a . . . " But the man did what she thought he was not
intending to do. He reached down. Down to the dog and the
snow. And he wiped the dog's behind. Twice. Clean. With the
tissue paper that was pink as dirty snow, mixed with blood.
He looked up sharply, like a man caught stealing. He tried
to wipe the other dog. But that dog wouldn't have any of it.
He pranced off, as if ants were stinging his balls. He pranced
and shook and scratched many invisible, stinging ants out of
his balls and his ears. (Bernice thought of Putzi kissing Mrs.
Burrmann with his pink tongue; and of the times, when eating alone, she would put Putzi on the table, to lick, wash, rinse
and dry her plate.) When the man was satisfied that his dog
was a clean dog, he looked anxiously up, to see whether anybody else knew his dog was a clean dog; and then he lifted
the left side of his black winter coat with the black fur-
trimmed collar, and he pushed the pink tissue paper back into
his pocket. "Jesus Christ!" The shock was so great, that Bernice
really thought Dots had seen the act. *Now, you have seen*
(Bernice was not only talking to Dots, now; she was addressing the world and the room, which was the world), *now you
have witness with your own two eyes the manner in which this
world does spin round, from this window. I have seen them two
niggermen pass here, and I have wonder if, because o' the things I
see, they aren't two she-she men. What you think? Nobody can't
convince me that when two young, clean, strapping gentlemens
walk 'bout the place, holding hand in hand, something ain't
wrong! As soon as darkness fall, they holding hands, as if one
frighten for the darkness, and the other, for the Lord. And they
think nobody don't know? Christ, I been seeing them in this inci-
dence days on end . . .* "Jesus God!" . . . *and it resting heavy on my*

*mind, Dots; heavy, heavy, heavy. When I tell you that one day I see those two sammy-geese pass 'cross here with their two dogs, and the two o' them four-legged dogs dressed off in clothes. They were dressed off, and their two dogs were dressed-off, too, to suit. Man matching dog and dog matching master. Man, master and dog matched-up. On another occasion. One afternoon. Catching my breath before going back down in that steaming kitchen. When, I ups and see them two missy-missy men, standing up and waiting till their dogs did their number one, and number two, next to Mrs. Burrmann maple tree. Number one and number too, I tell yuh! Then. They bend down, both o' them men. They bend down and wiped them two dogs . . . "This is an advanced place, gal!" . . . They wiped those two dogs as how you or me or the next human being would cleanse ourselves after going to the bathroom, and . . . "They say this place is a civilized place, gal!" . . . but a man, any man at all who does a thing like that to a dog, who is only a animal, that man isn't really and truly a human being anymore. No, Dots; that man cease to be a man and become a dog, too. And if I had never seen a dog back home in Barbados, and if I had never witness how people back there treats their dogs, which after all is only animals, now that I'm in this country, this civilize place as you refer to it, I couldn't discern a dog from a human person, at all! heh-heh-hai, looka Dots, I licked my mouth long enough, so let me crawl back downstairs and see what Princess Burrmann calling my name for.*

The night Estelle arrived in Canada it was cold. As cold as a dead man, dead a long time ago. Estelle filed past the Chinese stewardess, while jets of white fire came from the mouths of the other passengers, and from her mouth, as if she was a dragon. She looked at the shining macadam of ice, and at the words of the aeroplane attendant, spoken in cold vapours; and she wished she had never left Barbados.

"Have a nice holiday, ma'am," the Chinese woman said, "and goodnight." She smiled, and took Estelle's parcel from one hand, and placed it under Estelle's armpit. She was now able to negotiate the shaking cold iron steps better. Half-way down, she looked back up at the Chinese stewardess for moral support, and the smile on the latter's face carried her safely down the steps. But still, Estelle was not in a good mood. In her mind she carried the face of a small boy, who had looked at her during the flight, and had then looked at his mother and shouted, "Aunt Jemima." It could have been that the woman was not his mother; that she was his aunt, Jemima. But Estelle assumed immediately that he was calling *her* Aunt Jemima. After the incident, the Chinese lady (Estelle felt she was the only lady on the plane) had given her some chewing gum, and a copy of *Maclean's* to read. The Chinese lady had winked at her, when the other stewardesses were not looking, and had nudged her and said, "Never mind."

She was walking in the dead-man night, in the long line of passengers, filing like crabs, shuffling and scratching; silent as monks and nuns going to vespers. The line was going towards a door at which a man in white coveralls was standing. He held a torchlight in his hand. The bulb was red. He was the same man who had brought the plane to a stop, with the same red-bulbed torchlight. Now, he held the light, the bulb off, pretending that it was nothing at all for him to bring a big jet aeroplane safely from air to ground. He didn't even smile himself a pat on the back! "This way, please, this way, please," he was saying. When Estelle drew alongside him, he stared at her; and a puzzled look came to his face. Estelle

became tense. Looks are so deceiving, Estelle, so deceiving...
the man was staring at her because the temperature was *ten
degrees below zero*; and he, a born Canadian, wrapped in two
pairs of longjohns, three sweaters plus his insulated coveralls
— and she, from the tropics ("Hey! look at that goddamn lady,
from the south! Well, goddamn!"), was wearing a silk dress,
with no coat; walking as gaily as a nightenbird, goddamn and
I'm clapping my hands on my shoulders one crossed over the
other, like a goddamn penguin, hey! Bill, look at that goddamn broad! And Bill, who had already seen her, and had
looked and had disbelieved, was himself like a penguin, flap-
ping and breathing from his mouth like a humidifier, whispering, this is a bitch! — meaning the cold. The crabs before
her were walking too slowly. The two men remained outside,
like ice sculptures, clapping with vigour and vapour, pounding
themselves and the cold which sneaked into their bodies, while
they watched Estelle. But Estelle was boiling inside.

At last, she reached the gate marked INCOMING PASSEN-
GERS; and she scratched along with the others through a shin-
ingly bright passageway, through a glass door which swung in
her face because the man in front was not a gentleman. The
door struck her gently in the face. Finally, she was in a large
room, on fire with electricity. Looking around, searching for
a face to smile with, her eyes caught sight of a black woman
sitting on a large bench. At the other end of the bench — it
seemed miles away — was a white woman. Although they
were both on the same bench, Estelle felt they were sitting on
two different continents. Her eyes roamed again. In another
corner was a black family: man, woman, two children and a
box marked CAPTAIN MORGAN RUM, all huddled in a family
portrait of warmth from the cold of stares, and fears of the

winter. They looked so strange in their winter garments that Estelle found herself laughing at them. This family possessed and ruled a bench all by their dictatorial-selves.

Then the passengers went up to a man with CANADA CUSTOMS printed in gold on his shoulders (Estelle noticed there were four others dressed similarly, waiting for the passengers), showed him their passports; said something to him, in that close, secretive manner she had come to notice so well on the plane; and then passed on, without too much fuss, into another room, where some other CUSTOMS men stood guard. Trunks were tumbling onto a revolving conveyer platform; and some red caps, vague and suspicious about the best-goddamn-tipping-arrivals, were studying the passengers, as if they were studying the markings on a spinning wheel in a gambling casino. The family group of man, woman, children and Captain Morgan, was watching Estelle. They had been watching her very closely: (once, out of boredom, Estelle passed her hand over her behind, and just caught herself in time, before giving it a satisfying scratch; and frightened to be caught scratching she glanced round, and there! staring at her, with rivets in their eyes, were Mr. and Mrs. Captain Morgan, the children and the rum case).

Her satin dress shone like coconut oil on a road at midday; her compressed cardboard valise was in her left hand; another valise of cardboard which was used to ship Country Life cigarettes before Estelle made it into a valise (and which contained five dozen flying fish fried in lard oil; a Christmas great cake, although it was not even near Christmas; a bottle of pure Caribbean sea-water for purging Bernice's bowels) was in her right hand. The parcel which the Chinese stewardess had placed under her armpit, was really a box which once contained Lifebuoy, and which now had a large cooked meal of increased-peas and flying-fish, steamed in case Estelle felt peckish in mid-air. But Estelle had felt too embarrassed to be seen eating so much food in mid-air. To her, it was definitely sinful.

The family group was smiling now. But still they looked like a portrait snapped while they were dead; a portrait snapped and snatched with a smile on their dead faces. The smile bothered Estelle. Theirs was similar to the look she thought she noticed on everybody's face, on the plane. She smiled at them, with them; and straightaway, they looked in another direction. This upset her. In Barbados, everybody spoke to almost everybody. Her eyes wandered again to the black woman sitting on her half of the hemisphere of the bench with the white woman. She smiled at the woman. The woman held down her head, and covered her face under the broad brim of her straw hat which said NASSAU. And Estelle's smiles were soon buried in the footprints on the cement floor, among the pools of melting snow which outlined the season of the year. When she looked up again, she was standing before a man in a black uniform. CANADIAN IMMIGRATION was written on his shoulders.

"Where were you born, ma'am?"

"In Barbados, in the West Indies, please."

"Passport, please." Before she could move, he was saying, "What's the purpose of your visit to Canada? How long do you intend staying?"

"Just a minute, please, just a minute." She was fumbling with the parcel under her arm. She put one valise on the floor. The passport was in the valise. The valise was tied with a heavy kind of shaggy hemp rope which Mammy had wrapped round and round it; and this gave the valise a battered appearance, as if the bodies of many snakes were curled around. The rope was knotted in many places, for safety. Estelle realized she would have to untie all these knots, before she could...but when she looked up, the immigration officer had *that look* on his face. Turning to the man behind her, she said, "If I could only get this parcel opened, if I could get some person to help me get this parcel, hold on to this parcel for me, please." She turned to the gentleman for help. "Would you, please?" He took the parcel. The same time, the immigration officer held up his hand to prevent the man (who was a minister of the church) from taking the parcel.

"Lady," he said, in a tone that was both pleading and authoritative, one which had always brought obedience. "*Please.*" The six or seven passengers behind reacted with impatience, shuffling their thawing feet on the snow-polished floor. Somebody further back said, in a soft voice which carried more than he had expected, or intended it to, "...hope Canada don't get like Britain!" No one commented. Estelle was still digging deep down into her valise for the passport. "Lady, *please!*" This time, the immigration officer's voice was tired. "Would you mind stepping aside till you find it, so's I could attend to these ladies and gen..." But the man of God had raised his hand, signifying a different kind of authority; and the hand caught Estelle in the act of leaving the line. "Continue, my dear," he said to Estelle; and to the immigration officer and the others, "I don't mind waiting my turn, sir." He was a middle-aged man, with grey spreading round his temples. Underneath his white scarf, worn neatly under his coat, was the parson's collar, barely visible. The immigration officer hadn't seen it. "*Please,* lady!" This time, there was more of a threat than a plea in his tone. "There're others in the line." He gave the others (all except the man of religion) *that* look. They returned the look. The nervousness of trying to locate the passport, rushed from Estelle's hands and erupted through her lips. She swung round and faced the immigration officer; and when the words, *But who the hell you think you is?* spewed out of her mouth, she realized with terror, that she was not in Barbados. And she said, in a more respectful manner, "But don't you see me looking for the passport, please. I won't be too long." She then lifted her valise and placed it on the counter, in front of the officer. And when she did this, when he realized that it was blocking his vision of her, he shouted, "*Lady!*" He was coming round in front now, off his stool; but Estelle remained undaunted, outwardly: inwardly, she was terrified.

"My dear man, please attend to her," the man of God said. He too was becoming anxious.

"But sir!" the immigration officer pleaded, both to the minister and the other passengers. The man of God was firm. He said it did not matter; there were others in the line, he admitted; but right was right; and it was the lady's turn to be served . . . and Estelle, finding it impossible to locate the exact corner in which the passport might have been placed by Mammy, not knowing in which corner she had last seen it, whether in the Seawell Airport in Barbados, or in the Main Guard police station where she had got it, where where where the hell did Mammy put the thing, now? when Mammy puts down something, she really puts it down for good! Lord, the last time I saw the thing was . . . I wonder if Mammy put it in the left hand corner that was my left, or if it was Mammy's left! But where the hell is my passport, could it be that the plane shifted the thing in the valise, while the plane was moving about over Boston. . . .

"You will have to stand aside, lady."

...you, listen to me, Mister White Man...everybody in the room was listening and watching; and the black woman, and the black family were looking, with *that look*; and they were more embarrassed than the others, because it was one of them causing all this disturbance. It made them very uncomfortable in front of all these white people. The other immigration officers stood idle for a while, to watch and listen; and a few of them smiled. The minister of God was enjoying himself...Christ! you think that because I am a stranger in this damn country, you could treat me like dirt! Let me tell you, I am a Bajan, a Barbadian by birth, and we don't treat foreigners so! I looking for the passport, so wait a minute, please, Mister Man...and just as the minister laughed, and as the scene was becoming tense, Estelle found the passport. It was in her bosom. She held it up, in the air, triumphantly. But before she gave it to the officer, she took her time closing the valise (some of her underclothes were visible)...All these blasted white men's eyes looking at my panties!...and re-tied the knots.

"This is my passport, please."

The immigration officer opened it, flicked the pages without actually reading anything on them; and then gave it back to her. Estelle thought: I could have done without the damn passport, if that is the way you read, my man!

"Name?"

She deliberately refused to answer at first; but she thought better of it, and said, almost shouting at him, "Estelle!"

"Last name, or the first?"

"Shepherd!"

"Is Shepherd the first, or the last?" He too was deliberately obstinate.

"Estelle Shepherd!" and to herself, she wondered, You can't read? But he must have heard, or read her thoughts. He ordered the immigration officer nearest him to attend to the minister and the other passengers (his line had been served by this time); and in a rage, his face full of blood and cherries of anger, fumbling with his ball-point pen, taking three attempts to get it clipped into his breast pocket, he himself snatched up her valises and the parcel, and said, "Come with me, lady!" He went in the direction of the cubicles, glassed-round and penned-off, and on fire with an even stronger bulb of electricity. When he moved off, he did not even look back. He was confident that she would obey and follow. The black family held down its head in shame and embarrassment; the black woman sitting on the other side of the ocean from the white woman, averted her eyes; the man of God was now busy talking to the other immigration officer, and Estelle suddenly felt cold and lonely. Once more, she saw the pink face of the small boy on the aeroplane; and it was close to hers, peering into her eyes; and she could do nothing now, for the face was suspended in mid-air, and it had no neck and no body. She felt she was in the plane again, and the Chinese lady was not there. And the plane was spinning. A moment before she entered the glass cell, she looked back; but the black woman and the black family had already anticipated her gesture for sympathy, and they had already started to count the lakes of the melting overshoes, in the floor patterns. Estelle then looked up, and noticed the round electric clock on the wall, which said it was nine o'clock. She wondered what time it was back in Barbados.

All the way to the airport, Bernice was grumbling about Mrs. Burrmann, to Dots and her husband, Boysie. Boysie was making the 1942 Chevrolet compete with Cadillacs and Corvairs on the highway. Before Bernice could leave the house, she had to settle the children in bed; she had to bathe them; she had to cook their dinner of boiled potatoes, boiled carrots, boiled lamb, and warm milk. She'd turned her back to run upstairs and make up their beds, and when she returned, their plates were clean, except for swishes and curves of gravy where the forks had passed swiftly over, as the boiled potatoes, boiled carrots, boiled lamb had skidded into the garbage pail. *But God blind you, kids! You-all don't know they is thousands o' children all over this world tonight starving like hell? and you two, you-you-you...* Bernice was in a rage. "Mrs. Burrmann!" she shouted. But when Mrs. Burrmann came into the kitchen (where the children regularly ate their dinner), Bernice decided not to inform on them. "I was, I was wondering if you need more firewood in the fireplace, or something, ma'am." Mrs. Burrmann looked puzzled; stared at Bernice for a while, and went back to the sitting-room where she was lighting small cones of incense. (The party was on again: but it was being called a sherry party now.) The children sniggered. They were not hungry, they said; they wanted wiener-sausages and potato chips, which Bernice gave them. They ate it, bathing it in tomato ketchup, and washed it down with Coca-Cola. And they were happy as angels. And after they had fought and screamed in their battles of pillows, and had lost and won, they settled down.

One evening last year, when the summer was beautiful and Bernice had put the two girls to bed, she went down to help Mrs. Burrmann with a party she was having. Mr. Burrmann was away on a business trip. But the guests were happy. Mrs. Burrmann, trying to take the whiskey out of her hoarse voice, and out of her balance, was trying to piece together in coherency, the Negro spiritual, *Steal Away to Jesus.* And when Bernice heard her, it made her sick to her stomach: *but why the hell they always trying to sing spirituals whenever they have one-two drinks in their arse!* One of the guests was going up to each woman, tilting his champagne glass precariously and deliberately near the half-exposed brassieres of the women guests, and then laughing uproariously. The women waited, expectantly, for the cold drink to put some life into them; and when it did, they laughed a very high-pitched nervous laugh, like pure steel. And then again, Bernice saw Mrs. Burrmann sit in a man's lap; and feed him some of her whiskey. She got up, and the man placed his hand gently on her behind; left it there, as if both hand and behind belonged to him, as if his hand had changed into plaster of paris, and then folded his hand gradually over into a fist; he pinched her, and then slapped her, *plax!* on the right half of her velvet sheath dress. The dress was red in colour. She turned to him, and said, "Now, Jack; now now *now!*" scolding him playfully with her finger.

"*Great!*" another man observed; saying it in such a way that Bernice (she was standing just behind the door post) could not decide whether he was commenting on Mrs. Burrmann's sensuous body; or on his own exuberance; or on his faith in the never-ending flow of Canadian Club whiskey. "This is great!" he said, pushing one of Bernice's sandwiches into his shining fat Old Spiced jowls. He was also fat in the middle. He held out a hand and stuffed three more sandwiches into his mouth. Bernice smiled: her handiwork was excellent. "Great!" he said, as some piece fell on his jacket sleeve. He pinched them up, between thumb and index finger, held his mouth back, whispered, "Great!" and closed his mouth on the pieces, like a trap door. He wobbled away, and lifted a very fragile, over-dressed, over-done-up young lady, up to the ceiling. Her underclothes were showing. And this was when Bernice, like a tablet of ten commandments, flounced away in great disgust: *these people doomed doomed doomed,* she told God.

And now this evening, a year later, before she went upstairs to dress to go to the airport, *this same lawlessness, Lord! lawlessness to the height! I too glad I is a poor black woman!* Mrs. Burrmann came to her, "Oh, Bernice," she said; and handed her two envelopes. "These came earlier. And thanks." Suspicious always, Bernice took them, and did not open them until she was half-way up the stairs. One envelope had the Burrmann family crest stamped into it, and Mrs. Burrmann's bold handwriting saying, *Have a good time, Leach, with your sister, Estelle. Love, Rachel Gladys Heinne.* After the word, "sister," in brackets, was a large question mark which was drawn over and over more than three times, so that it looked shaggily written. Inside the envelope were five crisp ten-dollar bills. All Bernice could do, was roll her eyes and laugh; but her heart was touched, and a tear escaped from her. *Lord, the more I cuss that woman, the more kinder she is to me! She may be bad, Lord, but she ain't so bad, though. Have mercy on her, for me, please.* Mounting the stairs, and shaking her head all the time, she passed the children's room where Serene was telling her younger sister, Ruthie, that Jesus was not born on a farm. And Ruthie was laughing. Bernice examined the other envelope. It was from Lonnie. When she got into her room, she put Lonnie's letter in a drawer and forgot it instantly. "That bitch think I made outta money!"

The old Chevrolet was clapping, and its muffler pipe was shrieking. Bernice waited until some of the noise subsided,

before she continued her story to Dots, about Mrs. Burrmann.
"...and the whole damn afternoon that princess breathing-
down my neck. 'Bernice, give me a first-class job, tonight,
dear. Important people coming.' As fast as I make a sandwich,
she got it in her damn mouth! talking up in my face, and all I
could smell is the whiskey on her breath. Well, I not shamed
to confess to you, Dots, that more than one time I imagine
myself cutting off Mrs. Burrmann hand with that carving
knife...and the onliest way I could get her from offa my tail
was to tell her that before I stooped so low as to bring myself
to come in this country servanting for her, I was working
for the Governor o' Barbados, otherwise call' His Excellency,
yes! I tell her that, and be-Christ, she believe me, too! White
people believe any-damn-thing you tell them, they stupid so!
And in case, I says, in case you don't rightly *comprend*, Mrs.
Burrmann, what that means, it stands for the biggest and the
best..." and Bernice lost herself in the psychiatry of the lie,
and went on talking to Dots, as if Dots was Mrs. Burrmann:
*and I don't want to sound as if you is not a proper lady, whiching
I know is the case, otherwise; but I have experienced the experience o' setting table, laying knife and fork for Her Highness,
Princess Margret, whiching as you know, is sister to the Queen,
and for a hell of a lot o' other high and mighty people. Yes, man!
they have sit down at that dinner party I fix for eighty people, not
eight like you getting so excited over, but eighty! — eight, nought!
and they eat, not with knife and fork as you would expect royal
people to employ in their eating, no! they put down them eating
tools outta their hands, and when they saw the Barbadian cuisines
I laid on 'pon that table in the form o' dried-peas and rice, with
a piece o' corned beef boiled-down in that pot, and some good thick
dolphin steaks, it is bare hands they eating with, as if they was*

*borned and bred in the Island o' Barbados, like anybody else...*
Dots was finding it difficult to concentrate both on Bernice's
story and on the highway. She did not trust Boysie behind a
steering wheel. A narrow escape had just prevented them from
crashing into another car. When she had chastised Boysie with
a nasty look, she turned to Bernice and said, "A little lie don't
hurt to put these people in their right and proper perspective."

"But a German fellar tell me once," Boysie said, talking
out of the corner of his mouth, so as not to take his eyes off
the highway, "a German friend o' mine tell me that the Europeans is bigger liars than anybody else when they come over
here. He says everyone o' them does say they was counts or
kings back in Europe. Nobody don't be no plain, simple immigrant, no more."

Bernice was going to make a comment, but Dots cut in,
changing the subject, and therefore ignoring her husband.
"Food tastes a hundred times more better and sweet when
you could take up a handful o' rice, holding that handful 'twixt
your thumb and these four other fingers, so, look! look at my
hand, Bernice, right so! and when hand and mouth meet, and
mouth tastes what hand deliver, Christ, gal! well you would
have to be something more than a royal kind o' man or
woman, to want to divert back to knife and fork."

"Just like them Indian people," Boysie commented.

"And what the hell so special 'bout them?"

"They eats with their bare hands, Dots," Bernice said.
"Everybody knows that. You don't know that?"

"I know they eat with their hand, but..." She tried to
hide her ignorance; but only Boysie knew she didn't know anything about the Indians. She hated to see Boysie with a new,
intelligent idea.

"And you know why they uses *that* particular hand that they uses in eating with?" Boysie asked Bernice, who didn't know. "Because. Because..."

"What?" Dots snapped, confident that he didn't know.

"Because they uses the other hand to wipe their arse clean with!"

The car was death still, for three minutes of mourning for Boysie's uncouthness. Then Dots said, "Have more respect for Bernice, you hear? If you have none for me, have some for her!" Again, three minutes of death fell in silence; and after a respectful lapse of time, Bernice asked, "This thing have a roof light, Dots?" She looked at Boysie and asked again, "This old dump that you carrying us to our graves in, this limousine, have in a roof light?" Boysie pointed to the light switch, and at the same time the car swerved. Dots shrieked. "Christ, Boysie! you want to kill me?" Boysie ignored her; but in his heart, he said, *Yes*, gorblummuh! Then the light was on; Bernice took out her letter from Mammy, and turning to Dots, said, "Listen." Bernice read: "...*everytime I see Berry, the postman, pass across on his bicycle, my heart gives a shudder, and tears sometimes comes to my eyes, because I know that you have not sent me anything*..." Bernice put the letter back into her handbag, while Dots moaned and shook her head, in sympathetic sorrow.

"The way those people down there expect to get money every week!"

"But you don't think that is ungratefulness to the height?" Bernice asked.

"We is millionaires," Boysie said, this time without taking his eyes from the road. "The moment they see we emigrate, they think we elevate, heh-heh-hee!"

"Nobody would think, after hearing that letter, that you,

Bernice, sends that mother o' yours at least twenty-five Canadian dollars a month, every month, for the past three years. They won't think so, gal." Dots did not know whether this was the truth; but she said it, nevertheless. "If I didn't know you as a decent daughter to Mammy, I would swear that you is the ungrateful brute that that letter making you out to be, gal. . . . "

"Some mother real ungrateful, though!"

"Shut your damn mouth, Boysie," Dots snapped. "This ain't your business . . . and besides, that is the woman who gave birth to Bernice. A mother is a mother, and you could only have one."

"*You have not remembered me. You have forsaken your own mother.*" Bernice was reading from the letter again. "But to think . . . " and then she sighed.

"Christ!" Boysie said in sympathy. He was sorry for Bernice; because she had always been kind to him. Many times (unknown to Dots) Bernice had lent him money for beer and other "accidentals for this blasted old Boer-war Chevvy"; and she had never asked him to repay any of it. And once, out of gratitude, Boysie got away from Dots, and sneaked out with Bernice, and took her down to the Little Trinidad Club, where the two of them danced calypsoes until Bernice was tired and cramped. But when Boysie tried to kiss her, she turned away her face in shame. However, she never forgot his kindness. "Dots, you just said a mother is a mother? But I know some mothers who don't get on like no blasted mothers at all. I mean, just because they happen to make a blasted mistake and born a child, it don't . . . "

"Was you borned, though, Boysie?"

"Are you infirming that a stork bring me into this world, then, woman? Looka, God blind . . . "

"I inform *and* infirm that! yes. Because, for the way you treats me, and the way you..." Boysie looked back.

"Oh, God, look out!" Bernice screamed.

"Lookout! look out, man!"

The brakes screeled. The old Chevrolet swerved and rattled. Their bodies bounced against the torn upholstery and against each other. When Boysie had the courage to turn on the ignition, after the rush of blood to his head, the engine held its silence. He pressed the starter, and the more he pressed, the less happened. "Gorblummuh!" he swore at the engine and at the women (but they felt he was cursing the car, only). And then the engine turned over. He pressed the gas, the wheels whined; and the more he pressed, the more the wheels whined. He had put the car to bed, deep in a snow bank.

"You don't intend to get out? Looka, get out and start up this blasted car, do! You don't see we are late as it is already?" Dots was furious. "We late, so get out and do something, man." Bernice knew it was her place to remain quiet. Even after Boysie got out (still cursing), and did certain things with the front bumper and did the same things with the rear bumper; and after many jerkings and heavings and curses and drops of sweat, and the car was back on the highway, still Bernice remained silent. She had been saying her prayers.

After many miles, Boysie said, "But look at that snow, though! Look at it, man." He was looking at the snow out of the corners of his eyes. "That damn snow real pretty, like if somebody forget and throw a big big pail o' white paint all over the whole land. Boy! say what the hell you like 'bout living in a warm place, like back in them Islands, *any morning*, give me a cold place that have snow. Any morning. 'Cause the snow is the prettiest thing I have ever see in my whole kiss-me-arse life." Boysie had been living in Canada for eight months only. "Looka that blasted snow, eh!" He saw Dots out of the corner of his left eye, as she sat like a large snow-woman, inanimate, and with a vexed expression on her face. "Have you ever see snow back in Barbados?" But Dots pretended he wasn't speaking to her. "You ever seen snow back home in Barbados, Bernice?" And immediately, Dots was exasperated. She snapped, "Look man, how the arse could she have seen snow in Barbados, a hot place?"

"I ask *if.* I ask if she ever . . . "

"And I say, how the bloody-hell, *if,* or no *if,* could you expect to find snow in . . . "

"What Boysie mean to say, Dots, is that *if you ever had the* . . . "

"Tell her for me, Bernice," he said, welcoming support and explanation, although he didn't know what Bernice would say. "Tell this kiss-me-arse woman I married to, because as far as she is concern, I ignorant as a ram goat."

" . . . the, the-the-the . . . *if you ever had* the occasion, or the experience, or the pleasure of the fact of that experience, of having seen snow. *If* . . . "

"*If,* man, *if!*" Boysie said, echoing her.

" . . . if ever at any one particular time, back in Barbados. It don't matter if Barbados is a hot place, or a warm place, or a cold place. What I think Boysie mean, is that because of the absence of snow from *that* land, *this* land, meaning Canada, is a more prettier and appealing place, as far as Boysie is concern." She waited a while to see whether Dots was following her logic; and whether she had anything to add. But Dots was still fuming: exasperated at both their stupidity. She was finding consolation in the telephone poles slipping past like stakes in a fence round a field. "That is what Boysie mean," Bernice concluded. Immediately after, she was sorry she had intervened.

"Bernice, you just take the exact words outta my mouth," Boysie said. Dots was still counting the telephone poles.

"But the snow makes me want to puke, though," Bernice added. And then, for a long time, during many furlongs of telephone poles, nobody said anything. Conversation and life in the car were dead. They were passing fewer cars now. The whirring of the worried engine, and the frequent rasping noises made by Dots's teeth, was all the company they had. The monotonous telephone poles sped past them, like never-ending comb-teeth. "You don't know, that travelling is a damn funny thing." It was Dots who spoke. "Travelling, I say, is a funny funny thing." They could see the lights at the airport. And the engines of jets came to them, even in the noisy car. "Travel, and travelling, is a funny thing. I remember back home, reading in a book that somebody lent me, something about people travelling and seeing telephone posts going in one direction, whilst the person who is travelling, was going in a different direction, altogether. Now, isn't that a funny thing? That is what I mean. And all I try to think, I still couldn't understand the ins and outs of what that book was trying to tell me. Until now. I just happen to look through this car window as I tossed out that piece o' chewing gum paper." She paused to see who was listening. Boysie caught a glimpse of the retreating poles, out the corner of his eyes; and Bernice, alone now (since the mishap in the snow bank) on the rear seat, was studying them, too. "Them telephone posts going fast in *one* direction. And we going just as fast in the *next* direction."

"True," Boysie said, as if it was his idea, in the first place; and a brilliant one at that. "Travel and travelling is a bitch of a thing, man. And I think it is the lack o' such that causing Bernice' mother to think we is millionaires in this country."

"But Dots," Bernice said suddenly, "do you think that the postman, Berry, could have thieved any money that I send down to Mammy?" Bernice knew this was a possibility; but she also knew she hadn't sent any money to Mammy for a long time. Yet she flirted with the argument of the theft, in her imagination.

"Possible *and* probable." Again, Boysie claimed the observation as his. "It could happen, and it does happen. There was fellar back home, a postman-fellar, too!...what the hell his name was, now?...you know the man, man. The fellar who thieved all the money from the boys in Curaçao and the boys working on the farms in Florida picking oranges for the Yankees...."

"Air Mail!" Dots exclaimed. "You mean Air Mail."

"...he thieved every blasted money-order that come into Barbados from Away, for three years!"

"That is Air Mail!" Dot shrieked, in delight.

"...and he was so damn rich from thieving money-order and postal-order, that..."

"Isn't he the one who went to the dentist?" Bernice wondered.

"The very same beast! Gal, he went to the dentist-man and ordered the dentist to pull out every one of the teeth in his head, clean clean..."

"Clean as a whistle!" Bernice said. She was remembering the scandal now. "Air Mail demanded of that dentist to extract every individual tooth, and..."

"He put in gold teeth, in their place."

"That was back in the war days, and Christ! when Air Mail smiled, Jesus God!"

"'Twas like the stars in the heavens was fallen inside Air Mail's mouth!" Boysie said, laughing, but still holding on tight, to the steering wheel.

"Air Mail!" Dots said, shaking her head.

"Air Mail," Bernice agreed.

"But I wonder what happen to Air Mail?" Boysie wondered.

"Oh, Jesus-heh-heh-heh-Christ!"

"Air Mail, man!"

"Air Mail was a . . ."

"A plane!" Bernice shouted. She wound the window down, and looked through, and up, towards the skies.

"It coming in," Boysie said, somewhat unnecessarily; and with not too much joy in his voice. "That is the plane Estelle on," he added, as if he was sorry her journey would end their journey to the airport; and their joy of expectation.

"What is the time, Dots?" Bernice asked. "Estelle landing at ten. If that is really Estelle' plane, she landing at ten."

"Is quarter-past, gal."

"Past what?" Bernice asked. She was very anxious.

"Nine, gal. We still early."

Going across the road off the main highway to the airport, the car was quiet again. The road was under repair. The imminent arrival, which they had all experienced before, was beginning to tell on them. They felt something was going to happen to Estelle: not a plane crash; not air-sickness; but something after arrival; something to do with immigration. Bernice was tense; and her mind was jumping the hurdles of immigration and difficulties, even before she could see them. And then she mentioned the telephone poles, which everybody had forgotten about. "Look at them telephone posts running down this dirt road to meet we. Telephone post after telephone post, one after the other, one following 'pon two, and two preceding behind three and four and five...all the time, never stopping never ending, more telephone posts than the snow." Boysie kept his eyes on the gutter; and Dots kept hers in the air, tracking down the aeroplane. They remained quiet, as if to give Bernice this liberty of expressing her fears, so as to help her relax herself. They felt she must have this freedom of thought and imagination, this fantasy running away from her, and she from it; just as the poles were running. But then, the camouflage of her real thoughts blew off, and she said, "You think Estelle got the passport in order? I wonder." No one answered. They knew, though. But they did not answer. They knew that to come into this country, even with a passport and papers in order, was a difficult matter: if you were a black person. Dots tried hard to think of something else to take Bernice's mind off passports and papers.

"Hey, Bernice! Boysie says he contact Henry, and Henry say he coming and bringing some more men, for tonight. We have three men now, counting in Boysie, here. And with you, and me, Brigitte the German girl from 'cross the street, Estelle..."

"Suppose the passport that Estelle have, isn't made out properly, though," Bernice asked herself; and them. "What you think they could do to her?"

"Everything all right, gal. Everything in God's hand now, and it couldn't be in a more better place, at this moment. Anyhow, it damn late to start worrying 'bout passport and papers. And we arrive."

"We here!" Boysie said, unnecessarily; and driving into the parking area.

"What you think them immigration people going to do?" But Bernice started to weep before Dots could think of an answer. Boysie became very confused. There wasn't much space to turn the car around; and he could think of nothing to cheer Bernice with; and the lack of space and the women getting on like women . . . and then Boysie saying "Gorblummuh!" over and over again. And the tension was reduced.

"Bernice, Henry say he coming to the party, and he bringing another man," Dots said. But she knew it didn't matter at this moment. It was all she could think of saying; she, being not a very imaginative woman. "Henry says he coming, and bringing another man."

They were standing, the three of them, with their faces pressed flat against the glass partition of the waiting room, at Malton International Airport. They were standing near the door through which all incoming passengers from overseas had to pass to enter the Dominion of Canada. It was now thirty minutes past ten. And Estelle was nowhere in sight. A black family of a man, woman, two children and a large box marked CAPTAIN MORGAN RUM was leaving just as they arrived. A black woman was waiting very patiently, while a customs officer searched her bags. Estelle was invisible. Each time a gust of people came through, they would press their faces even flatter against the glass. Boysie had just returned from the departure lounges; but no one had seen a woman called Estelle. She was not in the airport bar (Boysie had a quick double rum, to cheer himself up while inquiring); not in the restaurant; and just as he stumbled at the *Ladies-Femmes-Senoras* door, by mistake, a black red cap waved him aside, saying, "This is a hustling night, baby! *Move!*" Boysie was furious; and all the way back up the escalator, he called the red cap a "blasted nigger, a blasted black Negro!"

Boysie became suspicious of Bernice's arrangements for her sister. "The men in the immigration place back in Barbados could have made the mistake, yuh know. And the immigration people here, could make the same mistake. I mean, they could make a man who went to Oxford look like a damn fool. So, I asking you, Bernice, to remember if you tell Estelle all the things she had to do...Did Estelle have a passport, though?" Both Bernice and Dots ignored him.

"Don't mind him! Estelle coming, gal. She 'bliged and bound to pass through this door."

"The worst things that could happen to Estelle, according to that black fellar, the red cap fellar..."

"Look, Boysie, nobody ain't asking you for no opinion, man!" And to show him how disgusted she was with his attitude, Dots moved to the other side of Bernice, far from him. She rested her hand on Bernice's shoulder. "Christ! man, you is nothing but a black cat in my path, bringing me bad luck on top o' bad luck."

"Sometimes, gorblummuh woman, you makes me feel you too decent for a man like me, you don't know? You sorry you married me?"

"We are not asking you for no advice, Boysie!"

Boysie fell silent. Bernice fell silent. And after this, Dots herself was silent. For some time, they remained standing in front of the new crowd which had gathered; waiting, waiting for Estelle to appear from inside. Bernice had already made up her mind that the "worst thing" had happened. Dots thought the worst *had* happened. Boysie was sure it had already happened. Still, none of them said what he really thought. Then, a voice belonging to one of them, shouted something. It took some time for them to realize whose voice.

"Look, look!"

Boysie was pointing at something inside the glass partition. "Look!" he exclaimed. And they looked. But they saw nothing. Dots was about to swear at him again. "Look at that valise, man! the valise there, tied-up with a piece o' string, a piece o' string that could only come from one place, namely, Barbados. That is *we* string, man!"

"Oh Christ, yes!" Bernice was jumping up and shouting. "And look! the valise has Estelle's name on it. And it address to, to ... *care of Miss Bernice Leach, Forest Hill* ..."

"Oh God, she come!" Dots said.

"She here, man, she here!"

"She come, she come, Estelle come!" Bernice said. "And didn't I tell you all the time she ... "

"Estelle in the land, and I did know all the time, that you two stupid womens was only moaning ... "

"Looka, Boysie, shut your damn face, do! You were guessing. How the hell could you alone, outta the three o' we, have known a thing like that?"

They waited a little while longer before they saw Estelle come out. She was mad. Carrying a parcel in one hand, her passport in the other, she was looking round for a face she knew. The black woman sitting on her side of the fence was still there; and Estelle looked at her, and said within her heart, I beat you, you bitch! but still it saddened her to see the black woman sitting so long on the bench; and without much hope. And then saw Bernice; and she wanted to scream for joy, for relief; but she realized that many people were watching; and she restrained herself. And she wished she was back in Barbados, because back in Barbados, she wouldn't give a damn, she would shout as loud as she liked because she was home and

free to shout, *Bernice, good Jesus Christ, girl, I land, at last!* She
glanced round and saw the black woman, exiled on her bench,
smiling. She too, would know the feeling of exhilaration, had
*she* been back home. "Little, little Estelle, who I used to hold
in my hand, when she was a little baby..." Bernice began; but
tears were in her eyes now. She took out a lace handkerchief
which Mrs. Burrmann had given her for her birthday, and she
moved it in front of her face; and when it reached her mouth,
she rested it there for a while, while the water continued to
come out of her eyes. And when they passed the fatness of her
jaws, they stained the glass because she was still leaning against
it. "Little, little Estelle..."

"She come," Dots said, "because we can see her standing
up there, like a lord, like-like-like a queen. She sure come."
Tears came also to Dots's eyes, as she spoke. They slid down
the white powder on her face, leaving a black mark across the
whiteness of the powder. They flowed over the plains of her
face, and she did nothing to regulate them, or restrain them.
Uncontrolled, they rambled over the powder on her face, that
was like snow. Out of the corner of her eyes, she saw Bernice;
and Bernice saw her. And she gave the lace handkerchief to
Dots, and Dots took it. But she did not wipe away the tears.
She let them run. "You know why I shedding tears, gal? I crying because I happy. Estelle come through, and she beat them.
Be-Christ, they can't keep we out o' this country, no matter
how they contrive it! We is good, hard-working people, and
they need us, God blind them — pardon my language, gal,
but I happy, happy as hell now!" They were her tears of victory; and Bernice's tears of victory. It was their victory over the
experience of arrival. Boysie saw them crying; and he played
brave, and sucked disgustedly on his teeth. But he could not

regulate the convulsions of his body. And when they moved, the two women, arms round each other, to the door to kiss Estelle, and to throw their arms and their kisses on her, Boysie lingered behind so he might wipe away the sorrow from the joy, with the back of his hand.

"It was the first time I ever was in a plane. I remember flying over America, God! that America is a place of places! In a way, I wish it was to America, I was going; not that I'm grumbling that it is to Canada that I come; but I couldn't help saying to myself, that America is really God's country on earth." Boysie cleared his throat to object to what Estelle was saying about America; but before he could say anything, his wife interrupted.

"You in Canada, now, gal!" she said.

"I know," Estelle said, "and this is a good place too, 'cause a white lady in the plane asked me where I come from, and where I was going. And when I say, Canada, she said, My goodness! And she went on to say that jobs easy to get here, and there isn't any problem finding somewhere to live. But I told her I was coming on a holiday, to stay with my sister in Forest Hill, and she didn't say another word."

"Take your time, Estelle," Bernice cautioned.

"...when I say I was living in Forest Hill, that white lady didn't say another word. I wonder why." Boysie started sniggering. Estelle went on. "Though this is the first time I ever flew, I wasn't nervous. I was sitting down beside a white gentleman, for more than five hours, and he and I talked about everything under the sun. And when the plane reached the ground, guess what? Christ! when you see that plane putt-putt and landed, I never set eyes on that man again. "'Twas as if he was going to a different world altogether."

"He would see you a thousand more times, on Yonge Street or Bloor Street, and he won't even fart on you," Boysie said.

"I don't see how that could be true, though, because he gave me his telephone number to call him, if I need anything. . . . "

"He *what?*" Dots shrieked. She saw she had lost control of her emotions, and added instead, "What you say he do?" Estelle showed them the card with the man's company, his name, and his telephone number at his office. Bernice took the card out of her hand, and threw it through the window. Boysie expected a row to follow; and he was surprised when Estelle said nothing. After the tension left the car, Estelle began to talk some more about her flight.

"Well, anyhow, in that plane, I fell in love with a Chinese lady, who was one of the four stewardesses on the plane. And do you know what struck me as being funny on that plane? She was kept chipping, on her toes, the whole flight, whilst them other three brutes was in the front o' plane licking their mouths and laughing with the other first-class passengers."

"They have Chinese stewardesses, these days?" Dots wondered.

"Progress," Boysie commented. "That is one reason why I like this country, and hate Amer'ca so blasted much. Things tough, here. That is true, 'cause I been trying to track-down a job for eight months now. Still, you could see a star o' progress, here. And that Chinee on that plane is one."

Estelle was very excited. She talked and she talked; and she told them about the small boy in the plane who called her Aunt Jemima. "What really made the devil get up in me, was that I was waiting for that child's mother to scold him."

"You still waiting!"

"Boysie, this is one time you utter a mouthful, boy,"

Dots said. "White woman apologize to you? Well, gal, you just come and you got a lot to learn *and* unlearn. One thing I going tell you, in case this sister o' yours forget to tell you. And it is this. You weren't born here. You were not born in Canada. And furthermore, the people who born here, they ain't black, eh, gal!"

"Be-Christ, Dots! if I wasn't behind this steering wheel, I would kiss you 'pon your mouth."

"Look, niggerman, mind your manners, eh?"

"Dots is right, Estelle. We were not born here. We in captivity here."

"All the time," Estelle said, continuing her story, "all the time, I could see my five fingers printed plain plain in that boy's behind. That is the way we treat children where I come from — if they don't have manners."

"Huh!" Boysie sniggered, "you try it here!"

"Rudeness is rudeness," Estelle said. And she said it as a final pronouncement on children, and upon the whole world.

"The childrens in this outside-world is a different breed o' beasts altogether, from the ones I uses to know back in Barbados," Boysie said. All the time he was talking, he never once left the road with his eyes. "They watches too much damn television. Everytime you pass near somebody living room, be-Christ! all you hears is *bang-bang-bang!*"

"Violence, gal!"

"But that is children, though, Dots."

"Children, my arse — excuse me, Estelle — you mean this brand o' children." Boysie was really mad. His words affected everybody in the car; and for some time, there was a general re-shuffling of positions and comfort. Estelle took out a package of Barbadian cigarettes, and made a big stage-show in lighting one. Bernice made a mental note that she wasn't going to smoke in her apartment, oh no!

"I would never forget how, one day, Mrs. Burrmann' second girl-child nearly caused me to go to the gallows," Bernice said. She paused there, while a little more attentiveness crept imperceptibly into the car. You could hear everybody breathing, as they settled back to listen. Bernice herself had to think hard to remember what she was going to say, because the fact of Estelle's smoking worried her greatly: she never thought Estelle was a woman who smoked. It was too much. She couldn't stomach Mrs. Burrman's drinking and smoking; and Estelle's smoking, too. She recalled her story, and said, "'Twas during the first days I was working for that princess, Mrs. Burrmann. One day...I think it is the first time, too...she ask me to bathe them two brutes o' hers. Well, I got the firstborn, Serene, in the bath tub, and she licking all the damn cold water...those two children love cold water! they are like eskimoes, heh-heh-heh!...Serene throwing all the blasted cold water up in my face, all in the bathroom, and making the water into waves as if a storm brewing up in the tub. The soap burning my eyes. I feel I losing my sight, but I still laughing with the child all the time, *hee-hee-hee-water-water-water cool, cool water!* me and she playing we are two children playing. But I vex as bloody hell, and any moment now, I feel I going strangulate or drown the blasted unmannerly child..."

"Ho-ho!" Boysie brayed; he was enjoying this.

"Listen, man. The next bastard, Ruthie, the second-born, she come round behind me. Well, I paying attention now to the next one in the tub, seeing that she don't drown by mistake, and have all o' Forest Hills and Mrs. Burrmann out looking to lynch me, *blind them*!... although, to tell the truth, that was exactly what went through my head. But, murder is murder. Then, as I telling you now, I feel this thing running down my leg, right from up under the middle o' my behind... pardon me, Boysie, child... in the soft part o' my behind. Christ! a fright take a hold o' me. Wait! am I wetting myself already? A young woman like me, starting to wet my trousers so early in life? And then, as I telling you, something told me look round, look round, Bernice, a mind tell me, and inspect thyself when nobody ain't noticing, and *see*. Could the water you feel crawling down your leg be your own water, or water from the bath tub? And Jesus God, Dots! when I turn round, that little white bastard was *up under my uniform*...."

"But wait!" Estelle exclaimed, because she could think of nothing else to say.

"... and her hand was 'vestigating what she didn't put down."

"Gorr-blummuh!" Boysie said; threatening the whole world. He spoke the threat again, equally viciously, in two distant murderous syllables. "Gorr-blummuh!"

"But look Satan, gal!" Dots tried not to laugh. "Jesus Christ, what was she searching for, Bernice?" But her laughter was too much for her, and she collapsed, loud, and sensuous and throaty. "Look the devil!" Her heavy breasts were jerking up and down like two pneumatic drills.

Estelle was vexed; and she asked Bernice, as if challenging her, "And what did you do?"

"I turned round, and I say, but Miss Ruthie..."

"Miss Ruthie, my fat arse!" Dots screamed. She was almost hysterical. "Miss Ruthie, hell! You should have slapped her arse till it is still black-and-blue. Miss Ruthie? Miss Ruthie?"

"Do what, Dots?" Bernice asked, obviously embarrassed and humiliated. "You ask me to touch that woman's child? And lose my head? And lose my job?"

"But what *did* you do?"

"Look, Estelle, don't you come playing you could talk to me like..." But Dots cut her short.

"Look, it is high time you forget all this shit 'bout Miss Ruthie and Miss Serene outta your head, hear? Miss Ruthie, my backside! Call the little monster by her real name, gal!"

"I say to her," Bernice continued, her voice shaking and wet with a few tears in it, "but Miss Ruthie, why are you spying up in my behind like that? Has you lost Mummy or Daddy up in there?"

"And what did she do, then?" Estelle asked.

"She laughed, she just laughed."

"And what did she say?"

"She tell me that a little girl...Mrs. Gasstein' girl..." Bernice said, breaking down now in shame and tears, "she tell me, that this little girl's father tell her that black women..."

"Be-Jesus Christ, I don't buy that at all!" Boysie said. "Look, we gotta be fair. Perhaps the child father say so, and perhaps he didn't tell the child so. I have to buy that the blasted child make up that story. Some children is lying bitches!"

"I believe the child's father tell her so," Dots shouted.

And Bernice could not finish her story, because the shame was too much for her; and the censure in Dots's voice and in Estelle's eyes was too bitter. Boysie's silence after what he said, was perhaps the greatest weapon. Dots started to shake her head, characteristically, from side to side, in sorrow; in sympathy. Bernice tried hard to forget what happened on another evening:... *I think it was a Sunday, though it could be a Saturday,*

*'cause Mrs. Burrmann had take the kids for a drive afterwards,*
*yes! it was a Sunday, and Mr. Burrmann was somewhere in the*
*house . . .*

"How old is this little girl?" Estelle asked.

"Four," Dots told her.

"And you mean to tell me . . . "

"Gal, white people teaches their children some o' the
worst things 'bout black people, you hear me, gal? . . ." *. . . and*
*he had called Bernice to bring him a hot drink; and when she*
*opened his study door he was lying on the floor, with his head*
*touching the large speaker, and the music . . . jazz, I think he called*
*it, was as loud as Mrs. Burrmann's Beethoven; and the lights in*
*the study was out, and I was so frighten . . .* "you will soon find
that out for yourself."

"You know something? You really want to know something?" He slammed his foot on the brakes, and the car jerked.
It was too sudden for Dots to start cursing him. "Listen! It
does really pain my arse to hear how you, both you and Bernice,
does say such good things 'bout Mrs. Burrmann and Mrs.
Hunter *one minute,* and gorblummuh! the next moment, both
o' you saying Mrs. Burrmann is cheap as hell, Mrs. Hunter
is a bitch; Mrs. Burrmann nice, Mrs. Burrmann bad; Mrs.
Hunter is a lady, Mrs. Hunter is a whore! What I want to know
is when you-all going stop talking with both sides o' your
mouths! Make up yuh minds, because, gorblummuh, Mrs.
Burrmann and Mrs. Hunter couldn't be queens today, and
whores tomorrow! That is what I have to say." He allowed his
last words to sink in for a while, and then he started the car,
and drove on. They were still and scolded, like children. In her
heart, Dots was pleased that she had a man who talked up like
a man. But she kept this satisfaction to herself. Bernice was too

shocked to say anything; and Estelle, the newcomer, pretended she was looking at the scenery passing her, and she passing the scenery, like photographs taken out of focus. It was a long time, before Dots had the courage to say another word. And when she said, she was humble. Boysie noted her humility, and smiled in his heart. Gorblummuh, I gotta put my foot down more often!

"But still, after all, Boysie, you will have to remember that it is Mrs. Hunter who gave me the down-payment for this car you driving."

"It ain't a gift, Dots. Woman, it isn' no blasted gift she give me. It is a repayment. And be-Christ, if you let them buy you out, they can't and isn't going to buy out Boysie. Not me!"

"Is Girlie still living in the old house behind Mammy?" Bernice asked her sister, after she felt it proper to change the topic.

"And what happen to Lord Nelson?" Boysie asked, thereby implying he wanted the topic changed. "Lord Nelson' statue still standing in the middle o' town, directing traffics? Nobody ain't blow-down that blasted statute yet?"

"He still there, too!" Estelle said.

"And how Mammy?" Dots asked.

"I get a letter from Mammy this morning."

"Mammy still there, living, in the name of the Lord, as she likes to say."

"I hear the Deep Water Harbour build," Boysie said; although he knew it had been built, completed, even before he left the island.

"It's built, Boysie, it built. It was built a long time now, man. You're behind the times. The Deep Water Harbour finished, because the people *made* Grantley Adams get up off his sit-down, and build it. And if Adams didn't harken, we intended to get a better man, like Dipper Barrow to build it for us. The people down there in that island, are tired with the lack o' progress. The tourists taking over the whole damn island. And if Adams was still in politics, I think the people would have killed Adams, because Adams was the same as a tourist. Nobody never see him!"

"Adams is a hell of a man, though!" Boysie said.

"Adams likes the people; but he *loved* the white people," Estelle said.

"Be-Christ, that is why I always tell this woman I married to, that I voting strictly Conservative in the next Canadian elections. I votes Liberal as a rule, at least the last time I voted Liberals. But I find out through Henry, that whilst the Liberals was running this country, it was hell for a black man to get inna this country, as a immigrant; 'specially when a man named Picklesgill was Prime Minister. Well, I telling you now, I voting strictly Conservative next federal elections. And I intends to remain so."

"The island making progress, but it is a public progress, not really an individual one. Big public buildings, government buildings, and government offices. But it isn't making progress in the way of putting food in the mouths of poor people, like me and..."

"That is exactly what I mean, Estelle," Boysie intervened. "That is what I mean 'bout voting Conservative. Now, in a lazy-faire system, whiching as you know, is the system under the Conservative type o' political system..."

"Mark your last words, Boysie, boy," Bernice cut in. "Estelle, look on your right hand. You see something?"

"The building? You mean the building...ohh!... Palmolive!"

"Yes! P-A-L-M-O . . . "

And Estelle, excited as a child, completed the spelling, "L-I-V-E! *Palmolive!*"

"We uses to use that same soap, back home."

"Yes, man. Palmolive! with them five little beautiful white girls on the soap. . . . "

"I wonder whatever happen to them five girls?" Bernice asked. "A long time I haven't hear nothing 'bout them."

"They grow up, Bernice," Boysie said. "You think they is still children? They grow up. They was the Dions!"

"Christ, yes! Gal, they must be big women now."

"I wish somebody could give me *five* children right now, this very minute," Estelle said. "I would get a hell of a lot of money. Christ! it won't be no trouble at all for me to have five every year, neither."

"But what are you saying, gal?"

"She only joking, Dots."

"That's a damn funny joke to joke with."

"Boysie, a joke is a joke, man," Estelle said. "That's all. You and Dots and Bernice are so tense. From the time I stepped off that plane, all I can feel and see, is a tenseness. You-all so tense, that nobody didn't ask me how I enjoyed my trip."

"How you enjoy the trip?" Boysie asked.

"The trip was good, man. First class."

"You had a good plane trip?" Dots asked.

"And what about the immigration people?" Bernice asked. "We was waiting for you a long time."

"Well, that is where I had a little trouble. That is what spoiled the whole trip for me." It was going to be a long answer, they felt; so they sat back to listen. "The first trouble really was with the passport."

"Mark your last words, Estelle," Bernice cut in. Estelle was a little annoyed at the interruption. "You see the name on that sign?"

"Cadbury!"

"Remember how we uses to eat them?"

"Chocolate, Cadbury Chocolate. Well, bless my eyesight! To think that I live to see the day, and the place..."

"Continue," Bernice said.

"The man took me in this little room with a bright light, and started asking me questions. Child, you would have thought that I come here to rob the Bank of Canada, and not merely to get a little rest! What is my name? Have I got relatives here? What am I coming for? And am I coming in as a domestic? How could I say that my sister is Bernice Leach, when my own name is Estelle Shepherd? Well, that man had me so blasted vexed, I don't know..."

"That immigration man was outta his place, if you ask me," Boysie said.

"Be-Christ, look!" Dots said. "Look, it is not a matter of being outta his place, or not being outta his place. No, it ain't that. For there is a lot o' German whores and Hungarian whores and Polish whores, not to mention the droves o' Eyetalians who comes to this country every month, and the government pays their transportation. And I bet you that not one o' them immigration men *dare*...you hear me?...*dare* ask one o' them Europeans what their name is. They do not dare."

"Tell me how they could dare, when they can't even speak the language, Dots?"

"Boysie, I could kiss you. You just spoken a mouthful!"

"And when he insisted on bringing his freshness to me, I stared him in his face, and I said to him: Now, listen to me,

Mister White Man...I have to call you Mister White Man, because I do not know your name, and on account o' the way you treated me, I can't address you in a better fashion...you haven't no right being worried about the dissimilarities in my name, and in my sister's name. I am a Shepherd. And she is a Leach. And I am Shepherd because I am divorced lady...."

And when they stopped laughing and shaking their bodies on one another, they were entering the district of Forest Hill Village. Estelle became quiet now. Bernice was preoccupied with the difficulties of adjusting to Estelle, and her ways and her smoking, in the small apartment. But most of all, she was worn out by her sister's experiences of arrival. Everyone was worn out. But everyone was happy. All Bernice had strength for now, was to point and show Estelle the banks and churches and other stores they were passing.

"One...two...three...six, *seven!* Seven banks in one district?" she exclaimed. "Barbados only have *five*, I think."

They were passing the meat stores; in their windows were sausages pouring down from hooks, and looking like red cylinders; and a few late shoppers were buying groceries and other goods with their eyes through windows; and Estelle wondered why steam was coming out of their noses and mouths, whenever words came out. As Boysie drove sight-seeingly slow, she asked the question she had long been thinking about. "Where are the coloured people who live here?" Nobody answered for some time. She asked the question again. "Where are the coloured people who live in Canada, Bernice?" Boysie guffawed. Dots had to poke him to keep him quiet, and respectful. Bernice turned her head away, pretending to take a sudden interest in the surroundings where she had lived for thirty-two months; and which she had deliberately ignored for the length of that time. They reached the cinema at the corner of Bathurst and Eglinton, where Boysie said, a lot of Jews went to the movies, "because the film stars is Jewish, that's all!"

"Samson and Delilah," Bernice said, aloud; naming the current film.

"Where the hell are all the black people you've been writing me about, Bernice, child? Bernice? . . . Dots? . . . Boysie? . . . well, somebody, Christ, say something, eh?"

"Estelle," Bernice began, in a tired, hoarse voice, "we four in this car, is the only black people you are going to see in this neighbour, at this moment. The four o' we. But don't worry, darling, you going have to get accustomed to it, too. We all have to learn how to survive 'mongst these white people. It really do not matter, though, Estelle, if you see a black person today, tomorrow, or the next year. . . ."

"Gal, the less you see of *them*, the better off you are, I tell you."

". . . but you will have to get accustom to seeing all white people round you, for the rest o' your stay in this country."

"I wonder then," Estelle said, as if talking to herself, "I wonder, if that is why that little bastard in that plane said I reminded him of Aunt Jemima . . . perhaps, he never saw a real coloured person, before, in his life! . . . well, yes. It could be that, yuh know, it could be that."

"You really think so?" It was Boysie, getting in the last word.

The record had just come to an end, when Boysie and Henry exchanged dancing partners. Their partners were Brigitte, the German maid from across the street, and who was Bernice's friend; and Agatha, a young Canadian woman, of about twenty-nine, who was studying Zoology, at the University of Toronto. Bernice and Estelle and Dots were sitting together, on the chesterfield, like the pink roses printed on the chesterfield, like Lilies-of-the-night, since eleven-thirty when they returned from the airport. The time was now one-thirty. They were sitting, not because they could not dance, not because they did not wish to dance; but because neither of the two men available cared to dance with them. There were two other black women present. One was a registered nurse at the Toronto General Hospital. Priscilla. A fierce, black woman, whose face was lined with the lines of some kind of emotional frustration; a woman thwarted out of all her expectations, it seemed; except for her extraordinarily good taste in clothes. Tonight, Priscilla the Condemned, was wearing a woollen suit, bought at Holt Renfrew. (She had already told everybody that she bought it at Holt Renfrew when *there was not a sale on.*) Priscilla's suit, like a suit of mail to suit her present disposition, was red. The other young woman was a student. Large like Bernice, but much younger; she, Miss Carmeeta Anne Bushell ("I'm in third year, Hons, polly-sigh-and-ec," meaning Honours Political Science and Economics), was also at the University of Toronto, a student like Agatha, but until tonight, unknown to, and by, Agatha. These two ladies had heard of the party, and had decided to come. They had had nothing on for the night anyhow; and though it was rather late to go to a party (Mrs. Burrmann had let them in through the front door, when they arrived; she excused herself from her own party to lead them upstairs, into Bernice's apartment, to wait for Bernice and the others) they had come. Miss Carmeeta Anne Bushell wore a shiny material which looked like scales on her body every time she wriggled in her uncomfortable seat. Two minutes after

Priscilla and Miss Carmeeta Anne Bushell arrived, their excitement sank to the level of the broadloom in the room. They were sitting now like dying flowers on the trunk of a tree. They were tense and sad and angry: both at Bernice for not explaining what kind of party it was; and at the men for not noticing them. It had happened so many times before to Priscilla especially (Miss Bushell had learned her lesson about these parties a long time ago; and she usually remained in residence, studying and learning her lessons) at parties given by West Indian students: the worst one Priscilla experienced was given by a tall Grenadian law student at his place on Huron Street, where she first met Miss Carmeeta Anne Bushell; "Well, listen, Meeta, I put myself out so much just to come to this fête. Azan the hairdresser had so many girls waiting, to get their hair done, it seem that every Sam-cow-and-the-duppy had a man taking her out this weekend. I had to beg Azan to give me a' appointment. I spent most of Friday night and Saturday morning shortening this dress, 'cause I know that West Indian men like to see their women looking sharp. And now I come here, what? What make me come here? I could be home in the little room I rent, or I could have told the head-nurse I was coming to work tonight. All these black men after the white girls, child. You can't see that?"; and when she told this to Miss Carmeeta Anne Bushell, she was in turn, made aware that Miss Carmeeta had experienced some of this, at the Little Trinidad, a calypso club on Yonge Street.

"It seems that our lot in this country," Miss Carmeeta Sweet Bushell said, with a heavy sigh in her voice, that night at the Little Trinidad, "is to watch our men dance with white women, take out white women, and spend their money on white women." She had just pushed a cheese stick into her mouth, when a white girl, a classmate and room-mate she had brought along sat down beside her. "What a lovely bunch of guys," the friend commented. "I've never had such a lovely time in my life! not even at a fraternity party. You must bring me more often, Carmeets." Priscilla javelined a side glance at Miss Bushell, and she got up and went into the washroom. That was three months ago. Now, at this party, they were sitting (along with Bernice and Dots and Estelle), watching Henry and Boysie teach the two white women the intricacies of the calypso dance. Some time ago Henry took Bernice to the West Indies Federation Club, called the WIF, on Brunswick Avenue. He took her there about three times on a Thursday night. Thursday nights were free admission night. But Bernice had enjoyed herself, and had even got a chance to exchange a bit of gossip with a Trinidadian girl who had come up on the domestic scheme with her. But Henry didn't like Bernice too much. He found her most aggressive and unattractive; and he told Boysie afterward, "Goddamn, never again mention that woman's name to me, you hear? Goddamn, in this bright day and age, that goddamn woman wearing white ankle socks with a pair of stockings with a seam in them, and winter boots, goddamn as if she is a blasted teenager at this stage o' middle age. And the more I tell that bitch 'bout a certain Guianese fellar I know, who is a good dentist, and I hoping Bernice going to take the hint, she only saying, *Henry, I is a lonely woman, you know! I don't like Canada, Henry. It is too lonely here. And people don't speak to you on the street car. I don't like this place, it too cold.* Goddamn, Boysie, they don't speak to me, neither! And the Jewish fellar who lives in the room next to mine, he tell me they don't speak to him, neither. The more I hint, the more she moaning and groaning 'bout how she don't like Canada. Bad breath! old man! Goddamn, it is enough to make me kill a woman dead, even if I am on top o' she at that particular moment. Bad breath! goddamn."

But unknown to Henry, and for a different reason, Bernice did get around to going to the dentist; not the one Henry had recommended, but a Jewish dentist Mrs. Burrmann recommended. And she had stopped wearing those "teenage" clothes.

Tonight, however, Henry had arrived alone. But when he saw the women in the room, ("Goddamn, these skins ain't sharp enough, Boysie!") he asked Bernice to let him use her Princess; and Bernice, expecting he was inviting more men (he had said something vaguely about "let me see what I can do to liven up this fête, girl"), whispered the word around that Henry was "bringing more people"; and then she winked. All the women understood the wink. And they relaxed for a while. Miss Carmeeta Anne Bushell reached out her long, well-shaped arms, with the long, polished, clipped fingernails, and took up a sandwich which had its edges trimmed. She put it into her mouth and looked round to see who saw. The table was full of food when she came in; but no one offered any to the guests. And then they heard footsteps coming up. Bernice stiffened, prepared herself for men, and went to answer the door. When she opened it, she gave out a short gasp of surprise. Two more white women were at the door. Miss Carmeeta Anne Bushell swallowed the sandwich paste in her mouth, and Priscilla glanced at Estelle, felt sorry for her and then felt glad: Estelle was seeing in one night what they had seen many times before. Henry rushed to introduce his friend, Agatha, to Bernice; and Agatha introduced Debbie who "is staying with me for the weekend, and I hope you don't mind; but after

Henry called and said that you needed more..." Agatha lived nearby, on Roselawn Avenue. She was wearing a bulky fur coat, the only fur coat in the sweltering room of hostility. Debbie was part Japanese, a very sweet, a very small, a very gentle woman, who seemed to carry centuries of mysteries of her race and her love in her partly closed eyes. Boysie liked her on sight. He saw sensuousness in those eyes. He made a note to dance a calypso with her; dance close close to that body, man, and feel that body 'pon mine, and feel the passion which he saw in her eyes and body. Dots and Bernice immediately smiled at the two women and immediately hated them intensely. Estelle looked up from her lap, where she was look-ing into the future of her unhappiness at this party; looked at the two men, Boysie and Henry, and wondered what was going on. Miss Bushell and Priscilla did not even say good evening. The German maid, Brigitte, standing close to Boysie across the room, took an ingrained dislike to Agatha. Agatha, who was Jewish, bore herself with supreme dignity, like a princess.

"Come come, man," Bernice said, trying to salvage her party, "you-all come to this party, to sit down and eat? Come, Boysie put on some Sparrow, some hot calypso, and let we dance, man! This is a party to welcome my sister, Estelle, into Canada."

And Boysie, Dots's unbeloved but legal untender husband, ignoring his wife all night, was now sweating and entranced by his little German maid. He had been teaching her to swing her classical hips three times fast to the swinging rhythms of the calypso. Sparrow was asking his audience, in the song, whether they (meaning the men, more than the women), had ever tasted a "*white beef yet?*" Three times fast, Boysie told Brigitte to swing her hips. He was saying while they danced away from Dots's eagle eyes, "You does dance like a real West Indian, though! You does do this dance good good for truth!" And Brigitte, liquored-up and lacquered-down to her toenails, transformed from her maid's uniform into this strange cinderella fashion, dropped her head on Boysie's shoulder, telling the rest of the room and the world, that she was happy; and she grunted, from time to time, from the pit of her ecstasy, "Yahh! yahh!"

Boysie turned the record over, and a rousing tune capsized the room, embracing Boysie and Henry, who was now holding on tight to Agatha, in a certain sexual assurance that *not a woman ever complain yet, with me; I ain't boasting, but I know I got durability...* Dots could see only a graveyard with leaves falling on a grave, and Boysie in that grave... *if a woman ever tell you that I, ever left her dis-satisfy, she lie! she lie! she lie!...* Bernice swallowed, and she thought she could feel pebbles in her saliva; she glanced to her right to Estelle, looking prim and proper in a dress she had borrowed from Bernice; and looking sad. Oh dear, tonight is Estelle's night, this party is for Estelle, in honour of her arriving in this new country! And she looked again at Dots, and saw the grief oozing from her mind onto her face; and at Estelle again, sitting stiff, in that West Indian attitude of utter boredom and distant respectability, her hands folded into her woollen lap: the fingers like a piece of dead ebony, scratched in thirteen places where the sculptor had tried, in vain, to create life out of matter. Oh dear, this is Estelle's welcoming party! Bernice's mind wanders over to Brigitte, clutched to Boysie like a snake; Brigitte whom Bernice herself has invited; Brigitte who now claims fifty-per-cent of the male population in the room. She sees Brigitte hold Boysie, and

Boysie take Brigitte into his arms, and she sees the look in
Brigitte's eyes; and she glances quickly at Dots, to see whether
Dots is too drugged by hate to see the beginning of the taste
of the apple.

The room is warm; no man, it damn hot. Bodies are
beginning to perspire. The ten different body perfumes and
body odours, are finding it hard to circulate, because it is
winter, and the windows are closed; and the room is already
overheated. There is the fire of the music, and the fire in the
brimstone white-rum which Estelle has brought up from
Barbados; and the fire in the liquor which Bernice stole from
Mr. Burrmann's liquor cabinet. There is also the black, white
and red pepper in the rice and peas, laid royally on the table
that has a white Irish linen tablecloth borrowed from Mrs.
Burrmann's pantry, food which Agatha, Carmeets, the young
Japanese woman and Boysie and Henry, have tasted. I waiting
to see if neither one o' the two o' them bastards isn't going
to ask my sister for a dance! Her eyes follow Brigitte, always
Brigitte; Brigitte the maid, Brigitte the same maid as she;
Brigitte the man-stealer, the husband-stealer, Brigitte the
Second Cinderella. Look at that damn woman, though; and
look how tight her corsets fitting her! and look at the lipstick she wearing: lipstick that look so damn natural that it
look as if she ain't wearing no lipstick at all. I should wear
some o' that natural-looking lipstick, myself, and see if man
will notice me. But what the hell I would be wearing *her*
lipstick for?... perhaps, I should start wearing corsets on
this tumbling-tumbling-botsy-rumbling-heh-heh-heh-behind
o' mine and make it stop jumping 'bout the white man road!
And that time, remember, Bernice? when I was fixing the
table, and turned round, and my-Christ! there behind me, not

two inches away, was that scamp, Mr. Burrmann, examining my behind. But what the hell he was after, though? . . . look how close Boysie have Brigitte riding up on him, look how close! as if they is two siamese twins; and look at that whore's face, she isn't even 'shamed, she don't care how she crawling up on Dots's husband, she don't even know they is people in here noticing him and her, and *in front o' the man's wife, to boot!* But look at these white women, eh? they would come in a man' bedroom and take him from on top o' his lawful wedded; not one ounce of shame! But Boysie feeling his oats, now, boy! he feeling himself and smelling his piss; and look how Boysie making Fredastaire and Arthur Murray, wrapped up in one, look stupid as anything. Boysie so damn pretty on them two foots o' his, and that footwork, a wonder to behold and a joy to follow! And look, look at Dots. Stupid stupid Dots, sitting down here on her backside and watching her husband, her man, winding-up his fronts all over Brigitte. Christ, I could run out there and pull rotten Brigitte from offa Dots's husband; give that Henry one cuff, and teach the two o' them monkeys some sense, 'cause there is four ladies, not counting myself, for I old now and retired from man, four ladies sitting down here, the whole night, waiting for somebody to notice them, and ask them for a fox-trot. *Praise Christ, Boysie isn't my husband! 'cause it would be bloodshed by now.* And look how Boysie squeezing Brigitte on her hips every time their backs facing Dots; look how Boysie have his fronts pressed close to Brigitte's fronts, and the look in that nigger-man's eyes, the look in her eyes. And Bernice remembered: you remember, Bernice, the morning Mr. Burrmann came into the kitchen in a rush, looking for his clear cuppa coffee, with the cigarette in his hand; and you was bending down, dusting out the coffee grounds outta the coffee-thing, before putting on more water? And plugging it in? And you happen to turn your eye in the direction o' satan, and that sinner, Mr. Burrmann, dressed in clothing like a wolf had *that look* on his blasted face, the same look that is now on Boysie's face...? I wonder what the hell Mr. Burrmann was looking at, or for...? She inviting Boysie to come across the street and to bed with her, the brute! And look now, look quick! yuh see Dots? getting blue as anything with jealousness? Every once in a while, she takes her eyes offa the girl sitting down beside her, Miss Carmeeta Anne Bushell and she fix them on Boysie, 'cause she want to make sure she have his warm body beside her tonight, if yuh please! But Boysie not noticing wife, tonight, boy; not Boysie. Boysie noticing woman tonight. Tonight is white woman night. Tonight isn't even Estelle's welcoming-party night; no. It is Boysie's woman night...but Dots, you don't hear the lady, Miss Bushell just asked you, are you a student, too? Not you, Dots, you is a student all right; but you studying *man*, 'cause man studying woman...and twirl your backside on her proper, Boysie; give her a good twirl; and I hope you put a proper black man breeding on her, too! Boysie, twirl-up, man, like you is in Queen's Park Shed in Barbados, dancing at a bram-party. Yuh see, God, you see how that jezebel begging Boysie to hold her close? And look at Mr. Boysie, pretty for so! pretty as hell, footworks, *hah-daiii*! Gyrations, letting-go, breaking-away, and letting-go and coming-to-she again...the wind in that gal's tail now, Boysie boy, in her skirts, and she ready. Look at them, the two o' them both, like two tired-out fishing boats coming back into Bridgetown harbour, fagged-out, danced-out, oh Christ, happy happy happy as anything; and I, Bernice, the one who invited

them into my place this blessed, *blasted* Thursday night...
"*I ain't boasting, but I know I got durability*"...Christ, I wonder what is really going on through Estelle's mind, and Dots's
mind, and Priscilla's mind, and Miss Bushell..."*if a woman
ever tell you that I, ever left her dis-satisfy, she lie! she lie! I say she
lie!*"...The record is finished.

Bernice jumped up before either Boysie or Henry could
touch the player, before anybody in the room could move or
think. "Come come come," she said, "come, and eat some o'
this. You-all must be damn hungry. Dancing the whole night
on a empty belly!" She went to the table which was close to the
bathroom door, and began placing food on paper plates which
she had stored away under the chesterfield, from a carton of
Christmas paper plates Mrs. Burrmann had used last Christmas. The paper napkins also had a Christmas motif of red and
green jolly holly on them. Dots edged up to her, and turning
her head towards the rest of the guests, whispered out of the
corner of her mouth, "Gal, what the hell occurring in your
place tonight?"

"Well, how you mean?"

"You ain't seen how the two o' them taking over?"

"Child, what I am going to do, eh? They are my guests
too."

"Like hell, they is!" Before she could say more, Agatha was
upon her, smiling, happy and a bit exhausted. "Would you like
some o' this, Miss Agatha?" And as she said, "*Miss,*" Bernice
gave her a sharp reproving, but playful, stare.

"This is dee-licious!" Agatha was beaming. "Dee-*licious,*
indeed! Henry's always bragging how nice you women can cook
your native dishes. You are *born* cooks." The other women,
Miss Carmeeta Anne Bushell, Priscilla and even the young

Japanese woman, heard and saw something distasteful in the comment. Henry came from talking to Boysie, and patted Dots on her shoulder, affectionately.

"Hey, sweetness! How you tonight, Dots? I going to have to dance a little thing with you after all this food, girl." And Dots rested her right hand on her left shoulder, covering Henry's hand, and grabbed it, and removed it, forcibly; and looked him straight in the eyes, and said, "*Haul!*" Henry understood what she meant.

"Pardon me, please," she said to Agatha, smiling; but Agatha too, understood. And Dots, seeing there was no point in hiding her real feelings, added, "You hasn't seen me in here the whole night? Christ! *Iffing* I was so badly off as to be sitting down on that chesterfield, waiting 'pon you to come and ask me for a dance, well, Henry..." She checked herself, and added aloud, because she had just glanced Boysie retreating into a corner of friendliness with Brigitte, "You don't see that I have my *legal wedded* husband here, with me tonight?" (Everybody stared at Boysie and caught Brigitte removing her hand from his hand.) "You don't see Mr. Boysie Cumberbatch there? He is still *mine*, man!" And she laughed out aloud, in her sensuous and infectious laugh; and soon everybody in the room (except Boysie), was laughing.

"Hey, sweetness!" This time Henry was addressing Bernice. But Bernice, glad at the notice, smiled sweetly at him, and inclined her head to hear what he wanted. "Sugarcake, you got any filter cigarettes?"

"Henry, I don't smoke, man."

"I going out and get some, then."

"I have some," Agatha said. "You don't have to go all the way..."

"Not my brand," he said; and on the way out, he whispered in Boysie's ears, "We better dance with some o' these black women, old man. I'm going to call some of the boys."

"My old lady vex as arse."

"That ain't the word!" And he went out. He closed the door too hard and Bernice called after him, "Look, you, this ain't my house, yuh! Don't wake up that princess down there, and cause her to march up here, and..." and knowing he could no longer hear her, and that he really didn't want to hear, she turned her attention to the young Japanese woman and invited her to eat some food. "You would like this, miss. I know your kind likes rice, and this is some o' the best."

Henry went down the stairs, taking one step and not taking a second until he had heard all the goblins and ghosts behind corners (once he had slept in a women's hall of residence on St. George Street, and he had had to creep out, like this, down the fire-escape ladder, or were they stairs? He couldn't tell, he was so drunk with fear and the cheap sherry his woman-for-a-night had served him in her room which was opposite the don's; and each terrifying crunch in his descent of winter and sinful extra-curricular, extra-marital love, he prayed that he would never again fall prey to his desire for a woman), going out, slowly, carefully. And as his hand touched the door-knob, he heard a voice from downstairs.

"Hey!"

His body stiffened. The first reaction his only reaction in times like this was to run.

"Hey, mate! Enjoying yourself?"

"Please," a woman's voice said. "Behave."

"Having a ball, mate?" And before the man could disclose more of his happiness, the woman rested her hand over his mouth and inclined her head to Henry, signalling him to leave. The man was going to talk so long as there was someone around. Just before Henry went out he heard laughing and talking; someone opened a door and he heard music. They were having a party downstairs. This cheered him up and he decided that on his return, he would drink, laugh and be happy. He took a rather full pack of cigarettes from his coat, lit one and puffed on it as if he had just purchased the house he had left. He was going to call some more boys to help out with the party; perhaps, even to divert Dots, so that Boysie could "do a little thing with that nice German beast." He found a public telephone box, just before he reached the corner of Marina Boulevard. There was one man who would never let him down. Freeness! Freeness lived almost at the end of the east end of Toronto, but this did not prevent him from coming to a party at the west end of the city. Freeness even went, once, to a party in Hamilton, when he got the call from Henry, one morning, at three. Freeness borrowed a car, and drove the forty-odd miles to Hamilton, in time to have the last drink from a bottle of South African port, which nobody wanted to be caught drinking, because at that time, there was much talk about anti-Apartheid boycotting.

"Man, what happening?" Freeness's tired voice, miles away, said he was tired, and in bed. But when Henry outlined the situation on Marina Boulevard, Freeness brightened. The yawns went out of his voice.

"Oh-Jees-and-ages!"

"Some domestics, man. A lot o' food and drinks, man."

"Jees-and-ages!"

"Women like peas! And only two men. Me and Boysie."

"Oh-Jees-and-ages!"

"A Japanee thing here, man, would make yuh mouth run water for a mile, and . . ."

"Oh-Jees-and-ages!"

"Take down the address. Come in through the side entrance. And don't mind it is late, the landlady, or the missy, or who the hell she is, having a big worthless party downstairs, man . . . and Freeness, listen, man. When I was coming out just to phone you, guess what?"

"What happen?"

"I bounced up 'pon two people screwing . . ."

"Oh-Jees-and-ages! I'll be there!"

And Henry, with the mission accomplished, walked back easily across Marina Boulevard, holding his cigarette cockily at a corner of his mouth, with one eye shut to prevent too much smoke from getting into his eyes.

There was a car, blended into the darkness of the side of the road and the shadows from the trees. Henry noticed the car, thinking that a man was doing something to a woman inside. A fellar get a lot o' licks, once, for just looking through a window of a parked car. And as he was getting near, he slowed down, and a thought came to him. Christ, Henry, that is a damn risky thing, man; and besides, it is maliciousness; but he slowed down and lingered beside the car, peering through the window, and there was no one in it, this is damn funny! 'cause I swear I saw a man in this blasted car . . . and just as the thought struck him he was unnerved by a form which dashed from hiding on the other side of the car. The form grabbed him, by the arms, pushed him up against the car and frisked his pockets as they do in crime movies when searching criminals.

"What're you doing up here, Mack?"

"How you mean what I..."

"Come on, don't give me no goddamn cheek, nigger!" The form was becoming serious now. "Come on! Come on! What're you doing up here?"

"You really want to know, Mister Officer?"

"Come on, Mack!"

"Well, I came up here to rape three white women!" Henry could feel the man's hands loosening their grip on his clothes. "But shit, man, you're preventing me..."

"You smart black son-of-a-bitch!" and just as the form's hands left Henry's clothes, Henry backed away and threw a straight right. It caught the man unawares; and he slumped over the hood of the car. Henry put him back into his car, and there, he noticed the radio system, and the spotlight and the clip-board with a lot of scratchy writing on it. He had struck the Law. Panic did the rest. He slammed the door, ran back to the house and before he went in, cross-examined himself in his mind; convinced himself that it was too dark to be identified; shrugged the man's handprints and suspicions out of his clothes, and shrugged off his concern going back up the stairs, as if he had really gone out for a packet of filter-tipped cigarettes. He did not see the man or the woman who had seen him go out. But he had heard and recognized Beethoven's Sixth Symphony. "That is a goddamn funny piece o' music to play at a party!"

The guests were eating now. But when Henry looked round for the young Japanese woman, he didn't see her. He didn't see Miss Carmeeta Anne Bushell. He didn't see Priscilla. "They gone," Bernice said, unable to hide her triumph. "They gone!" Estelle was sitting, with a drink in her hand. Henry went and stood in front of her. She looked up at him and smiled. Encouraged, he sat beside her. And she moved to give him more space; and again she smiled.

"Well, how?" he asked her.

"I here, boy." She was not smiling now.

"And how the trip?"

And without answering, she got up, gave him a look, which if it had contained razor blades would have sliced him to pieces. With the weight of his humiliation on him, he attempted to smile, but as his lips formed themselves, he happened to see Agatha looking at him and that made him even more confused. Goddamn! And he got up to talk to Boysie. Boysie led him far away from the women. Dots, Bernice, Agatha and Brigitte were eating. Estelle remained sulky and morose. Agatha looked up from her plate, and smiled at whoever caught her smile; and then held her head back down to her plate. Then something happened. A bone lodged itself sideways in her throat. She closed her eyes, filled with water and swallowed hard. The bone was dislodged. "Emmmmmmmm!" she said, clearing her wind-pipe. But Dots mistook it for her pleasure and satisfaction with the food; she got up and said, "Get up, child; and help yuhself." Agatha did just that.

"And what do you do?"

"You mean me?" Dots asked, behaving rather obstinately and deliberately, to regain her pound of disappointment for having lost her husband the whole night, talking in her Barbadian dialect. "What you mean what I does do?" She glanced over to Bernice to see whether Bernice approved. And of course, Bernice liked it.

"I meant, oh ahh, are you a student, too."

"A big old-time bitch like me, you asking if I is a student?" And then she laughed out loud in her cackling way.

"Goddamn," Henry said to Boysie, away in the corner. They knew what was happening.

"My kiss-me-arse wife!" Boysie said. "Trust her to fuck up my life!"

"Are you a nurse, then?" Agatha tried again, uncertainly; but not really uncertainly, not after having heard Dots speak, and having compared her with Miss Bushell and Priscilla. She felt she had to ask these questions, so as not to appear prejudiced.

"Yes!" said Dots, in a curt, punctuated tone. "Yes! I is a nurse. A nurse-maid. Chief-cook. Bottle-washer — *everything!*" And she laughed again. And Agatha could think of nothing else to do, but laugh herself.

"She's a domestic," Bernice said, simply.

"*I'm* sorry!" Agatha said, and wiped some crumbs from her mouth; just the two corners, with her Christmas-paper napkin. As she wiped, she raised her eyebrows, although she was only wiping her mouth, not her eyes.

"Why you sorry?"

"Oh, what I meant was that, that, that-that..."

"Ha-haaaaa-ooooo-Lord!" Dots screeled out, bending over, and pressing her right hand into her soft, undulating, jello-shivering belly.

"God knows, as a Jew..." Agatha began; but before she could say more, Henry came to her rescue.

"Come, man, some Sparrow, man," he said, with forced gaiety. He selected a Sparrow record, and put it on. "Come, Estelle, let we do this thing, girl." And he went to Estelle, bent down, outstretched his hand, and prepared himself in his mind, to rest them under the plump softness of her breasts. Estelle got up; Henry, full with anticipation, held out his arms for her, and she moved away from him, like a ballet dancer, and went into the washroom. "I too tired, man," she told him; and as she was about to close the bathroom door, she held her head out, and added, "And even so, Henry, I don't dance with black men. You too black!" Henry's body jerked to make a violent comment. He was mad. He was mad with Estelle. He was mad with Agatha for behaving like a fool in front of all these West Indian women. He was mad with Dots for being deliberately uncouth. He was mad with Brigitte because she was white; and because she said nothing. He was mad with Bernice for being...goddamn, I could kick this little poor-great bitch!... and since he could not have kicked each and every one of the women; and since he could not really kick *any* of them; he merely walked over to the table, and poured himself a large whiskey. He remembered, as he raised the glass to his face, that he had just beaten up a policeman in the street outside.

"Hee-hee-oh-Christ!" Dots bawled out. She clapped her hands together, and made them sound like two strips of thick, wet leather; and all the time, she was shaking her body like a bowl of Jello. Boysie looked at her, and wished an awful thing would happen to her; and he wondered whether he was really married to her. "Oh Lord, oh Lord! the thing turn round now! the thing turn round now, as good as a cent!"

"Shut your fucking mout,' woman!" Boysie screamed. There was madness in his manner, as there was in Henry's. The venom in his command took Dots in such chilling surprise, that rather than shut her mouth, she had to keep it wide open, because of the shock. Brigitte forgot what she was laughing about; and she stood at attention. "Come, Henry, man," Boysie said, gripping Henry by the hand, and spilling some drink in the movement. "Let we get to arse outta this place." He pulled Henry to the door with him. He turned round as he was going out, and said, to no one in particular, but really to Dots, "When you ready, I outside." And he slammed the door after him.

Estelle emerged from the washroom, looking less tense and more relieved, and said, "What happened just now?" Nobody answered her.

"Gorblummuh!...gorblummuh!" Boysie said over and over, going down the stairs. The lower he went, the louder and more venomously he uttered this exhortation. It seemed he did not want its earnestness to be diminished by his descent and exit. "Gorblummuh!"

"Women make my arse laugh!" Henry, said, and spat noisily on the street.

"I should make that woman o' mine walk home, you don't know?" He sniggered, and then turned on the car engine. He turned it off. He turned it on again; and finally turned it off. It was dark; for some time, they sat there, silent, looking up at the forms moving about in Bernice's window.

"Brigitte nice, man!" Henry said, after putting a cigarette in his mouth. "That German beast, real nice, man. I hear that German women really like black boys, though."

"Agaffa nice, too."

"You telling *me*?"

"Jesus Christ, I wish I weren't married!"

"That is your luck, boy."

"You think I could do something with Brigitte, though?" There were no secrets between Boysie and Henry. "You think she would give me piece?"

"You didn't hear what I just say? German woman *nice!*"

They were both sitting in a relaxed position in the car; Boysie, his feet on the steering wheel; Henry, with his hands under his head, and his legs spread under the dashboard. Henry was talking in a kind of audible thought-recollection. Boysie was scheming little spider webs of snares in which to trap Brigitte: and between the anticipated effectiveness and the ineffectiveness of these snares, he would hear Henry's voice droaning:... "I have travel this territory from the Atlantic to the Pacific, *free*, as a railroad porter when I was still a railroad porter, and that is a advantage..." (...Boysie had just got Brigitte out of the party, and in his mind he was going through the alleyway where they were parked now; up through the side entrance, to her room on the top floor, and...) "I have seen prime ministers, cabinet ministers, ministers with, and without portfolios and goddamn plain ordinary ministers, gold-miners, students, university professors, Indians, male, female and juvenile and be-Christ, I say to you, tonight, Boysie Cumberbatch, I say to you..." (Boysie was wrestling with Brigitte's rustling skirts, in the imagination of her room.)

"What?" he asked Henry.

"They *pukes*! That is what I say to you, you are looking at a man that *know*, a man that know. This goddamn country adopted me, nineteen, twenty years ago, and I don't have one arse-hole beef 'gainst this country, except that I am a black man. And I know that a day is coming when they won't have no more goddamn use for me, and all the rest like me, Smitty, Willy, Harewood all o' them from Nova Scotia, hanging round The Paramount; and there won't be no more goddamn train to run, no more shoe to shine, no more boot to lick, clean and polish, be-Jesus Christ, Boysie Cumberbatch, no bags to lift. And you will understand there won't be no more tips to bring home, and no more tips mean no more draught beer at the Paramount Tavern, heh-heh! could you see me, a big motherfucker like me, without my draught beer and southern-fried chicken wings from Mr. Ting Ling, the Chinee man at the Paramount, heh-heh? don't laugh, Boysie Cumberbatch..." (Boysie had left Brigitte by this time, because Brigitte had shut up her lap tight tight tight, like Hiddy-Biddy; and he had turned back to Estelle: Estelle lonely as hell, she come up here to live with Bernice, and all Bernice know is church and church-music, and and and you know, I had two good looks at Bernice tonight, and she don't look too bad neither; but I wonder if Mr. Burrmann does get a taste from Bernice, 'cause she always praising him, and praising him...) "And Boysie Cumberbatch, you know something? I already plan for that day. And who you think caused me to think of that emergency? Well, I going tell you. That goddamn white woman sitting down up there with them black bitches, Bernice and Estelle...excepting Dots your wife...them bitches who was cursing the woman because she is a Jew and she dance with me, Godblindthem!" He rolled down the window, and spat the butt of the cigarette outside. He clapped his breast pocket, and laughed, in a superior manner. "And, Boysie Cumberbatch, I have a nice piece o' land up in Rosedale. You ever heard of Rosedale? Well, this black son-of-a-bitch sitting down humbly beside you, owns land up there with the bigwigs. And look at my trial balance, Boysie, man." He struck a match and showed Boysie the bank book.

"Jesus God!"

"That is my old age pension, Boysie Cumberbatch. Pension, beer money, whore money, sick money and hospital money." It took Boysie some time to recover from the shock of seeing *fourteen thousand dollars* in Henry's bank book. He never expected a black man to have that kind of money. "A white woman put that kind o' sense in my head, and nobody like Bernice nor Estelle, nor even your wife, Dots, could make me ignore Agatha. Boysie Cumberbatch, I is not only a one-woman man, but goddamn, I have found out that that woman have to be white!"

"You want to know something?" Boysie asked, emerging from his dreams and schemes. "You talk a lot o' sense, and powerful sense, too, concerning life. But all you been talking to me is 'bout pension and death-money. You didn't say nothing 'bout *living-money*. I want to hear 'bout the present time."

"Make yuh point, Boysie Cumberbatch."

"Look, man, I had a job in a paint factory, once. In the east end o' the city, at a place name Flow Glaze. And gorblummuh, before I even draw my first week's wage, some damn man came asking me for pension-money, income-tax money, and various kinds o' benefits like group-insurance. Christ, I wasn't even suffering from a head cold! Now, I ask you, as a man who have seen many things in many shapes and forms, how the hell could, or should, a thirty-seven-year-old bitch like me be thinking 'bout pension-money?"

"You looking at this proposition wrong. If ever the boss man say to you, You fired! God-blow-me, Boysie Cumberbatch, where are you getting tomorrow's cup o' green tea from?"

"But why should a thirty-seven-year-old man like me, worry 'bout deading for?" When Henry could think of no good reason, Boysie went on to say, "You want to know something?

I come into this country, as you might say, through the back door, meaning I come in only in the behalfs of swearing out an oath that I was going to marry that stupid woman, Dots, in a specified time. Not that I had no fucking choice in the matter. I had as much choice as a rat in a burning canefield. I either married Dots, gorblummuh in that specified time, or *out goes me!*" Henry had heard this story before. "And in a sense, you could say that I is a man *on loan* to Dots, 'cause if Dots wasn't so damn lonely down there in Rosedale, Henry, I is not such a blasted fool that I don't know it is loneliness and *not* love, that signed my passport and turned me into a landed immigrant. That is how I come to be here, tonight. Otherwise, I would still be in some kiss-me-arse canefield, or chasing whores in Nelson Street, or on a ship bound for Brit'n, like the rest o' arse-hole West Indians. But it pains my arse to think o' myself, as a man sponsored, and sponsored, gorblummuh, by a woman at that! You stand all right, Henry, because you standing up 'pon dollars and cents. I also know where I stand. You know 'bout pensions and old age, but let me, Boysie Cumberbatch tell you something 'bout marriage and young-age!"

"Make yuh point."

"Well, my point is this. I wake up one morning and find myself in bed with a woman, married and be-Christ, I don't like what I married, 'cause I wasn't no blasted free agent in the choice o' that woman. I know I wasn't no free agent, 'cause when I see skins like Brigitte, or Agaffa, or even Estelle, I know that being married to Dots as I *had* to be, wasn't no choice...."

"You is a man, Boysie Cumberbatch, in neutral gear, so to speak."

"Prefuckingzactly!" The rum had worked a kind of mad

poetic articulateness throughout his system; and in the poetry
of his words, he could hear his voice moving on. "Now, I do
not know, or care, what immigrating or living in this damn
place does do, or has done, to women like Bernice and Estelle
and the other two farts who was up there at the party. I only
know what it do to Dots, 'cause she is the woman I had to say
*I do and I will,* to. I see a big change come over Dots, through
immigrating. You didn't see the mad insane way she was
getting on, up there? There is two Dotses now. The Barbadian
Dots who uses to sell comforts and lollipops and parched peanuts in the Bus Stand in Bridgetown, *and* the Canadian Dots,
who spends every blasted night putting her hair up in curlers
and filling up the bathroom with nylon stockings and black
panties that she do not even wear no blasted place. Because I
do not take Dots no place. I don't think a man should take out
his wife, too often. And gorblummuh, I do not take out Dots
*at all.* But something wrong, Henry, something like a vast
transformation come over my wife. Something wrong with
the woman' head, too. Every morning, she singing the same
tune: *Boysie, you sleeping? it is time we put down something for
our old age. Boysie, is time we get children. We should have a
child, or two. I getting to be a old woman.* Dots is a young
woman, thirty-five years, and she telling me she getting old?
Why every-blasted-body in this place, Canada, always thinking 'bout death? When it isn't children, or a house be-Christ,
it is pension! *Boysie, let we move outta this place, and get a roof
over we head. A roof with our name and initials in it. Let we
move outta Dr. Hunter place. Don't mind it is rent-free, and Mrs.
Hunter is a lady, sometimes. She is my friend today, but tomorrow
she might give me a frown instead of a smile.* Jesus Christ, Henry,
the place we lives in now, is the best place I ever lived in in all

my stumbling through this damn Chinee world. And it is the best house Dots ever lived in, too. And she talking 'bout moving outta *that*? Man, tell me what gone wrong? 'cause something gone wrong. House! child! old age pensions! gor-blummuh, and I been in this country for months and months now, and I only had one part-time job. I got fired from that, for going to work late, *three times.* Three times in two months! not thirteen, three! and I been looking for a permanent job for the past six months." Henry, who was unemployed, had nothing to say to this. "But when it was me who suggest to Dots that she should have left the job when the missy, Mrs. Hunter, gave her her cheque one Friday, half-hour after the bank closed, Dots turned round 'pon me like a centipede, call-ing me ungrateful-this, and ungrateful-that, and ask me if I remember who put the down-payment 'pon the car, meaning this car we sitting in now. That is the kind o' woman I married to. Ninety-five dollars and ninety-five cents a month. Five years now, Mrs. Hunter giving my wife that salary, and Dots insist Mrs. Hunter is a lady."

"That is life, boy."

"Whilst I was dancing with Brigitte, I happen to ask her, just outta curiosity, how much she does get, and Brigitte tell me she does get *two hundred* and eighty-five dollars a month. Brigitte is the same kiss-me-arse domestic as my wife!" Boysie sucked on his teeth, with exasperation. Henry coughed, and said nothing.

Agatha had meanwhile organized the women in a parlour game. She had missed Henry; she would have left but knew he would come back to take her home. ("I hope he's not up to any of his tricks, like the day I dressed and waited for him for three hours, with Mother screaming her head off, and he turned up late, *as usual,* without an excuse." He had never left her like this before; and she was a bit nervous.) The game they were playing, was Botticelli, a game of guessing. Dots liked it, although she did not really understand it; and she was screaming her head off. Estelle remained sedate, tired, bored, but slightly happier now. Bernice, once or twice, opened the door, and listened to what was going on downstairs at Mrs. Burrmann's party, and when she caught snatches of the civil rights song, *We Shall Overcome,* she smiled, and went back to the game. Neither she nor Dots had guessed anything correctly; (Estelle just watched, and exchanged an occasional smile with Brigitte, who was listening to the radio) and Agatha purposely *mis*-guessed, so as to allow the other women to win. But they did not. Agatha, nevertheless, persisted in making the chances of their winning very great; and only once did she actually *wonder,* "if their IQ is really correlated to their cultural deprivation...."

Boysie drove to the end of Marina Boulevard; and then reversed. He did not turn on the car lights. The engine was still running when he stopped. He reversed again and came back to the original parking spot. Henry said nothing about this odd behaviour. Perhaps he didn't find it odd. And of course, Boysie did not think he had to explain this small diversion. Back to where they had set out from, twice, Boysie eventually turned off the engine; and he reclined in his seat, as before, and began talking. "I wonder, what the hell them women doing up there?"

"Forget the women, man. We is men."

"They must be giving that poor woman, Agatha, a damn hard time!"

"Or they could be treating her like a blasted queen, too."

And this stopped further comment. Henry closed his eyes, and found that his eyes and his entire head were revolving; and his body began to revolve, and the car too. And when he opened them, the revolving stopped. He knew he was drunk. He closed one eye, his left eye, and the revolving did not begin. He closed his right eye, and it didn't begin, either. He was drunk in a strange way. Boysie was talking: "... you want to know something, man? I goes home at night, late late sometimes, gorblummuh! Sometimes I don't reach home till the morning following the night that I left; and I does lay-down beside Dots, in the same bed, but the two o', we does be in two different worlds, altogether, entirely. And once, on a night like this night, I get suddenly frighten, frighten as arse. And I jumped up outta the bed, and all the time, Dots rubbing my back and the back o' my neck with limacol, thinking I was having a nightmare. But the blasted nightmare I was having, *was Dots*! I wasn't having no other nightmare. And I run outside the bedroom, and into the indoor-shit-house, and Henry, you want to know something? I puked and puked and puked, till I thought that all I had inside o' me, was puke and not guts."

"You was drunk."

"No, man. I wasn't drunk no drunk."

"You was having a nightmare, then."

"No! I wasn't drunk and I wasn't having no damn nightmare. What cause me to spring-up like a blasted tiger cat outta the bed, was that sudden so, before my eyes, just as I come outta a deep sleep, *I saw my wife, Dots, in old age*, as a old woman, be-Christ, and she had false teeth and rimless glasses, and she was peeing herself left and right, and was too feeble to perform the ordinary duties o' life, like going and coming from the bathroom. And you want to know something? Gor-blummuh! it was me, me a young man, who had to clean and wipe Dots. Look man, Henry, I was never scared so much in all my life! I was shaking like two leaves, when I crawled back in that bed, that night. And from that night, I *never* make love never, never had a piece o' love with Dots."

"Jesus God!"

"I have kept this to myself for almost seven months now, seeing as how I know you in all that time, and I never picked my teeth to you with a indication of it... look man, from that night, seven months, running into almost eight months..."

"You mean to tell me that in seven months, you haven't lay-down on top o' your wife, and did a little thing, old man?"

"Seven fucking months!"

"Be-Jesus Christ!"

"Seven months! November the 'leventh gone, is seven months. I cannot tell you neither, what is the colour, nor the embroidery, o' the bloomers and panties Dots, my wife, does wear. Seven months."

"Seven months is a long time, man."

"Don't misunderstand me. Don't mistake anything in my words. I not saying that once in a while, when I come home drunk as arse, or when my outside-woman playing the arse, that I don't lay-down on Dots' belly. I am not saying that, at all! But what I am saying to you, is that each and every time I do that, my mind does be wandering, and I have to imagine it is Brigitte or somebody else I laying-down on top of..."

"Wait! you mean to tell me that you hit that German stuff *already?*"

"No no no! you misunderstanding me, man." The poetry in the rum in his head, was wearing off. He noticed he was finding it difficult to get his words out. "Instead," he said, "instead o' thinking and telling myself that I am laying-down underneath Dots, whilst in the act..."

"Laying-down *underneath*?" Henry exclaimed. "Man, you should be on top! You is the man. A man should be on top!"

"I say laying-down *on top*, man."

"No, you say, underneath! Jesus, I am not deaf, man. I hear you say, one second ago, Boysie Cumberbatch, *that I am laying-down underneath Dots...*"

"Anyhow, that ain't the point, so forget that." Boysie was becoming a little mad. "What I trying to say is, that the once or the twice when I laying down *on top of Dots*, I have to tell myself that I am laying down on top of somebody else, *entirely* different. And I don't even have to know that person. Understand? That person do not have to exist. That person could exist, but I don't have to know that the particular person is really an existing person. I just mention Brigitte by name, because she looks like the kind o' person it could be. But it could be Mrs. Burrmann, or Estelle, or the Japanee girl, or anybody else. Instead o' me laying-down on Dots, it is Brigitte in this instance, that I laying-down on top of. Understand?"

Henry was very uncomfortable with all this involved talking. His head was registering circles of argument and logic; and when he closed his eyes to think harder, it was worse. Eventually, he gave up; and luckily for him, when he looked towards the house, to take his mind off Boysie's problems, he saw Bernice leading Agatha, Brigitte and Dots to the car.

Brigitte said goodnight, and clip-clopped groggily between two houses, and out of sight. Henry pinched Boysie on his leg. Then Bernice came round to where he was sitting, and said,

"Estelle say 'night." And to Agatha, she said, "I glad to meet you. You's really a lot of fun." And Agatha shook her hand, and waited until Dots invited her into the car. The two women got into the back, and Dots said, "Boysie, let we go home and jump in that bed, boy. Tired as a ox!" She laughed a short sensuous laugh; but Boysie, fearing she might say something more personal about their married life, switched on the radio; and when he found a rock-'n'-roll station, turned up the music so loud, that nobody could talk. Just as they were about to turn off Marina Boulevard, they saw somebody walking fast towards them. Dots recognized him first. "But where *he* going this time o' night? And in this district, at that?" Boysie slowed down; and instantly, Henry recognized Freeness, walking briskly, with shoulders hunched, probably in determination and in anticipation of drinks, eats and women. Boysie and Henry burst out laughing. Although Agatha did not really know what was going on, she laughed too.

"Oh-Jees-and-ages!" Henry sniggered, imitating Freeness; and in that mood, they turned off Marina and travelled towards Agatha's home, which was to be the first stop.

"But where he could be going, this time o' morning, or night?" Dots wondered, aloud. She was very worried about Freeness; and her worry must have become contagious, because instead of moving off with the green light, Boysie turned round in the middle of the road and headed back for Marina Boulevard. "Boysie, are you drunk? Where the hell you taking we? . . . excuse my language, Miss Agaffa, dear." But Boysie said nothing until he spotted Freeness, slowing down in front of the Burrmanns' house. Then she knew. She breathed easily, and then laughed. She put Freeness in the back seat with her and Agatha.

"Man, that's a funny funny thing, pardners," Freeness said, excited, without having first told them what he was talking about. "A funny funny thing! oh-Jees-and-ages! boy, when I got off that street car, a police rushed me, and start asking me a lot o' questions! Good thing a white woman get off with me, and could tell the police I just got off, too. Jees-and-ages, wait! this place becoming as bad as New York, pardners!" Henry remained silent, and allowed Freeness to talk.

Bernice lingered for a while by the gate, after the car left. She looked across the street, up to the third floor of the house that faced her. She saw a light in Brigitte's room. She wondered if Boysie was up there with Brigitte, then remembered that it was Boysie who had driven Dots and the others home a moment ago. And Henry had left in the same car.

A car was parked across the street, a little distance from where she was standing. Looking round further, she noticed the long line of garbage pails standing at the front gates, like stubby fortresses. She looked at her own gate. No pail: she had forgotten to bring out her garbage. But she wasn't thinking of garbage tonight. Go to hell, garbage, she said. And then she was sorry, for she was a clean woman. She stood in the cool air, thinking; the wind was tugging at her hair; and she felt the wind kiss her cheeks. Her mind now went to Estelle: Estelle got in safe, praise God; but I have to see whether me and she could set horses together. And she thought of Mrs. Burrmann; she thought she had heard them quarrelling as she passed them on the way out with her guests. That poor, lonely, unhappy woman! Lord help her, for she shouldn't be always having to quarrel...Bernice and Mrs. Burrmann, two sad women, two lonely women, sad and lonely for two different reasons. Bernice wondered whether she knew the reasons for Mrs. Burrmann's sadness. She wondered...

It was time to sleep: time to get outta this blasted freezing wind, gal. Tomorrow morning does come too damn quick in this country. I have a hell of a lot o' things to do in that kitchen in the morning, and Estelle living with me, now; and I can't say yet how living under the same roof as her, will turn out, 'cause I hardly know her. And then she went back inside. She was going up to her room when she stopped and heard: "*Sam, I think I've been a good wife to you, I think I've tried to keep your home as a home, I've always kept myself tidy, because I remember when Serene was born and things were a bit tough, you remember? when you were doing extra studies in Law, you used to comment on the shabby way I used to look around the house... but then, things were hard then, remember? things were hard, then...*" and as she moved off, she loved Mrs. Burrmann very much; a woman with a heavy responsibility of being a woman and a wife and a mother and an employer; and she forgot the amount of time Mrs. Burrmann spent drinking. She told herself that she had to drink, in order not to let life, and those hard things in life, get the better of her. Mr. Burrmann, when I come to think of it, is a real brute to treat you as he treats you, she said. That woman spends all her time in this house, looking after her children. Christ! it took her nearly twelve months before she would let me touch them two girl-children, even to bathe them... all the time she does spend knitting things for that Mr. Burrmann, and for the two kiddies, and she have enough money that she could buy everything brand-new and at the most expensive o' prices and still, she treats him as husband and man. Lord, these bitches you put in this world as men and husbands! Help me not to get myself trapped with one o' them, do, Lord, heh-heh-heh!

She passed the squabbling which came from Mrs. Burrmann's bedroom and walked along the silent corridor to the children's room. She opened the door, and walked in, in the vague night light. She tip-toed up to the larger bundle of striped bedclothes and she unknotted the sheets from Serene's young body. She spread the sheets properly, then kissed the peaceful face on the left cheek. She moved over to the other single bed and tried to take the coloured doll out of Ruthie's grip; but Ruthie, conscious in her sleep, of this intended rape, clutched all the firmer. Bernice rested the small india-rubber hand on the child's breast. She kissed Ruthie too... "You too damn young to suffer because your two parents in there don't have any decencies...!" she climbed the stairs and she could feel tears coming down her face. But she did nothing to stop them. Mrs. Burrmann, poor soul, poor you, Mrs. Burrmann.

When she reached her apartment, she called for Estelle; but Estelle was already asleep on the chesterfield with her clothes still on. Bernice was mad. It was an insult: Christ! this girl didn't even ask me *where* she going to sleep, but she bound off and sleep!

She pulled the blanket up over her sister. She sat by the window. (Estelle had not pulled out the chesterfield to make it into a bed.) Bernice was too tired to wake her and so remained by the window. She turned off the lights and closed the plastic curtains so she might see outside, without being seen. She was studying Brigitte's window. A car came along worm-slowly; blew its horn very softly and immediately, a light went on in Brigitte's room. The car honked again, softly. The light went off and came on, twice, like a blinker sending a message.

Bernice listened carefully. Then a man came out of the car, closed the door without a noise; and walked beside the house, Brigitte's house. Soon, Bernice was seeing images behind the curtains in Brigitte's room, which had not been closed properly. It must have been a long time that Bernice sat there, in the freezing, lonely night, because just before she got up to go to the bathroom, a milkman dropped a white bowling pin of a bottle on the front steps of the house opposite.

# 2

# THE TASTE OF THE APPLE

Bernice had grown accustomed to her triangle of life, in thirty-two months of working with Mrs. Burrmann. It was a life that centred round her kitchen, her radio and her princess telephone. It was a life, which, although restricted by virtue of her being a domestic in Forest Hill Village, nevertheless, was an interesting perspective into the world around her, the world of riches in Forest Hill itself. Because of which, she never considered changing this world. Nobody could get her to change her daily pattern of existence. "I happy as hell in Canada," she once told Dots; and Dots had to wonder whether it was the same person who had said last week, "Canada, Mississippi, Alabama, South Africa, God, they is the same thing!" And when Dots asked how, Bernice added, "As far as a black person is concerned." This made Dots very unhappy and confused. But it was this ambivalence which Bernice entertained even with the Burrmanns: on Monday morning, she hated Mrs. Burrmann for what she had done to her over the weekend, and by Friday, she was in Mrs. Burrmann's corner, blaming Mr. Burrmann for his wife's drinking. And she would say he was giving his wife a dog's life. And sometimes too, she would say,

"Child, it is Canada that liberate me, you hear?" One Thursday afternoon, when Dots was visiting her, Bernice pulled from under her chesterfield, a handful of wrinkled and dog-eared *Muhammad Speaks* (the newspaper of the Muslims in America) and some *Jet* magazines. She had been introduced to these by her cousin in Harlem. "Look at the facts o' your life," she said, holding them in Dots's face. "Here! read the truth 'bout yourself." And she tossed them into Dots's lap. Deep inside her, Bernice really felt she could be happier living somewhere else; maybe even in Harlem. (She had never considered going to Africa.) She thought of returning home; but she knew the chances of living happily there, depended upon the amount of money she could save here; and after hearing Estelle talk about the number of people unemployed back home, and after talking with some domestics who had gone back on holidays, Bernice decided that going back to Barbados to live, was not such a good idea after all. She was, in a sense, as happy on Marina Boulevard, as she could be (as a black woman) anywhere else in North America.

Before Estelle's arrival, Bernice could not conceive of anyone living in her apartment with her. She resented the intrusion upon her cleanliness, tidiness and order. Yet, the closer her sister's arrival drew, the happier she became. She was going to have someone to talk to; someone with whom to share her loneliness. But the moment Estelle arrived, Bernice saw the mistake. It might have been better to have brought up Lonnie: at least Lonnie is a man... Lonnie that damn woman-hound, always wanting something, always writing asking for something as if he think I am up here working off my backside in his behalfs...! And she thought of what Estelle's presence would do to her on Thursdays, her days off; her day for putting her wages in the bank; her relaxation and visits downtown; and sometimes, her little laughing and drinking ("Just a Coca-Cola for me, Mr. Geary, please. You don't know I is a Christian?") at the WIF Club. On those Thursdays which coincided with her wage-days, Bernice would take a bus from Marina Boulevard to entrust her wages to the Personal Chequing Account she had opened with the Royal Bank of Canada, near the corner of Eglinton and Yonge Streets. Something about the name, and the impressively printed *lion*, yeah, the British lion! and her name — her own name! — on her own cheques (a prestige she could never have hoped to attain in Barbados, in her class) drew her, like a magnet, to put her money into the safe-keeping of this bank. The very name — *Royal Bank!* — impressed upon her, the worthiness and durability of the bank: a bank where her money would never be in danger. But it was only recently that she had come to regard banks as being safe for her money. She could not forget that night in Barbados, when the flames vied with the moonlight for the possession of the Penny Bank; and they fought the moon's fluorescence for all the life-savings of the poor villagers. That night, Lord, it was in the dry season, I think, and the dollar bills and the shingles off the house burn and turn into leaves o' black brittle wafers, or like crusts of soot; and they blow all over the village, like if they was interests o' grief. Lord, and I would never forget how, even before the last speck o' black burned-up shingle-money had disappeared from the skies, like black-birds flying home, that man, Mr. Toppin the owner, manager, president and inventor o' the Penny Bank, was already halfway on his way to Harlem, New York City, America. Five years! and fifty dollars and forty-five cents I had saved-up, all the money to my name, to pay down on a house with. Five, ought, forty-five and five!

But it was different in this country, with banks. They were built so beautifully, with large glass windows which exposed to her, the tellers and the people doing business in them; and the managers (these Canadian managers were not hiding like Mr. Toppin, in a room with the door under lock and key: they were there, in the open, to attract money and banking-people and borrowers, like fly-paper to attract flies) all visible; and the women who worked there, dressed so clean in their anonymous personality of the bank clerk, so plain and pallid and trained to smile and to be courteous, and to look poor and honest... and I like to see the way they smile every time I come through that swinging door marked PUSH; which I *pulled* one time, and continue walking in, and I walked right into the blasted glass door, and cut myself and my dress was ripped up in pieces, and I felt so 'shamed and embarrassed! as if my petticoat was showing, which it was. Yes, the Royal Bank of Canada was a special thing in Bernice's life. No one can imagine the satisfaction she had, when she received her first cheque book. The word, *Royal,* gave it that special flavour and prestige. (That same afternoon, she called Dots on her princess telephone, and yelled, "Dots, child, I got it! I get the thing, man. You must come and see it!" It was only a cheque book: not a loan.) It told her that never never, in this world or in the next to come, would this bank ever go bankrupt on her, and burn down, while she was sleeping. It was safe and sound. Safe as the continuation of kings and queens who were royal; whose births and deaths were linked like the beginning is linked to the end, in a line of water flowing through a circular pipe. "Lord, don't matter how I cuss this place, Canada," she said once on the bus going home, after a pang of conscience, "no matter how I say Canada is this, and Canada is that, be-Christ, look!

three thousand dollars, *three-ought-ought-and-ought*! thousands not hundreds; on my own personal chequing account cheque book. My name, Bernice Leach, *Miss* Bernice Leach write down in it, *if yuh please*, and my address and telephone number printed in it, too. That is what Canada have done for me. This is my testimony to this place, called Canada. And Lord, I am glad as hell that I come here, that I is a Canadian." But this did not prevent both Bernice and Dots from lambasting Canada that very week, when they saw a story in the newspapers that a certain West Indian nurse couldn't get an apartment on Bathurst Street, to rent, because she wasn't white. Subsequently, they both agreed, volubly, that "Canada ain't worth shit!"

"This is a place, too?" Dots said, the very next day. "This is no place for a person to live in, and feel like a human being, gal. And when you are a woman, and not married, well..."

"I feel the same way as you," Bernice said; but she hastened to point out a condition which she felt would extenuate this denouncement: "But I still have to think of when Thursdays come, pay day. For that, and that alone, I think Canada ain't such a bad place."

"You know something, gal?" Dots was now laughing in her sensuous way. "You want to hear a piece o' the hard truth, today? Well, listen. No matter how we two bitches sit down here in this white woman' place, and say the worst things 'bout Canada *and* the white woman, 'cause she is as Canadian as Canada is, God-love-a-duck! had it not been for that woman *and* Canada, where the hell would we, both me and you, be, right now, at this very minute..."

These were things that Bernice felt she could discuss only with Dots: similarities of experiences in this country. They could not tell them to Brigitte, because they did not want her to know. They could not tell them to Estelle, because she was a newcomer. And even if Estelle had showed any interest in knowing the hard facts — she told Bernice the morning after she arrived, she wanted to remain in Canada to work — there was a little incident which had already soured Bernice's mind against her sister.

One remark, made in the car coming back from the airport, had bothered Bernice like a bad toothache. It was about the man who sat beside Estelle throughout her flight; and *he and me talked about everything.* Bernice remembered Estelle's exact words. She wondered what else they talked about; she wondered *what* they talked. And she was glad that when the plane landed, the man disappeared, without giving her his name... but no! Estelle has the man's telephone number! But she remembered she had tossed the card through the car window. She felt safer. I know he had *one* thing on his mind, one thing. She was so preoccupied with this fear of her sister falling into danger, that the first thing Friday morning when Estelle woke up, with Bernice cold and cramped from having spent so much time in the chair at the window, that before even saying, "Good morning, Estelle, how you like Canada, your first morning in Canada?", Bernice demanded, "What you intend to do, with that man?"

"What man?"

"The man you meet coming up on the plane. That is the man I talking 'bout."

"But Bernice..."

"Now, look here. Let me tell you something. You are in Canada now. Not in Barbados. I can't tell you what to do, 'cause you are a big woman, twenty-nine years old. But I just want to say that you had better not get yourself mixed up with any man — particular *that* kind o' man. In my time here, I see many things, many women having to go back home with their lives mashed-up. So, I just warning you, in case you have intentions of calling that man, whoever the hell he is."

"But Bernice, I told you the man didn't even as say How-d', the moment he touched ground."

"And that is the way I want it to stay. As I say, I not getting into your business, but I been here too long." Bernice wanted more than that; much more, but she was too timid to say exactly what was on her mind. She wanted to tell Estelle, "Have nothing to do with that white man," because of the way they had treated her herself, in the past (she was thinking of the subway; and one old, vague, decrepit man who spat green-and-yellow just as she was a foot from him). She tried again, saying, "Estelle, look. We who have been in this country, a long time before you, have seen the ways of this world..." (To hell with the ways of this world, Estelle thought.) "... and I can only tell you, as a mother would, and as Mammy would, if Mammy was here, that it do not look good to see a black woman walking with that kind of a man. That is all I have to tell you."

"But Bernice, in Barbados, I have seen many girls I went to school with, walking with..."

"This is Canada."

And instinctively, Estelle knew this was the end of the discussion. Bernice's outspoken words raised many questions in her mind. Although she did not give much thought, or desire, to going out with *that kind of a man*, she could not help being tempted by Bernice's extremism on the subject. In a way, it fascinated her.

Bernice did not like her victory: it was more of a moral capitulation on Estelle's part. And to give her position more justification, she deliberately amplified her grievance: "I would never forget what Brigitte told me, one day. She told me, right here, that she is a German, and she proud o' being a German; and when I mention to her, all the evil and sufferation and tribulation that her German tribe poured on this Christ's earth, all Brigitte could tell me, right here, holding one o' my Chinese teacups in her hand, was, Listen, Bernice, darlink, a frog was in a pond, one day; and a scorpion ask that frog for a ride on his back across the water to the other side. No, says the frog, you think I is a damn fool? Carry you on my back, and let you sting the living daylights outta me? Please, please, Mister Frog, says the scorpion, I am not going to sting you, 'cause I begging you for a ride, and I know that the onliest way I could get 'cross that water, is on your back, Sir Frog. Well, the frog say Okay, and the scorpion get on the frog's back, and they even exchanged a joke or two, in transit, 'cross that water. And just as they reached the other side, just as the scorpion could touch land, Jesus Christ, *pinnnng!* he put such a sting in that frog's behind, that all Poor Froggy could say is, But man, I thought you say you wasn't going to sting me, man? And guess what that wicked scorpion say? *I is a scorpion! I can't help that, Froggy boy!* And as you may guess, the frog died. Well, think 'bout that, because *them* is the scorpion, and we, the blasted frog."

Estelle was trembling. Bernice knew that her victory was now worth something; and straightway, she left to go downstairs to do her work. "Heh-heh! I got the bitch with that story, now, though!" But before Bernice got to the bottom of the first landing, Estelle shouted behind her, "But Bernice. I don't see why you're so worried." And because she herself could not see *why*, she went back into the apartment, and broke down in tears. She remained alone in the room; and in the world: and she promised herself right then, to get out from under Bernice as soon as she could.

Bernice could think of no better way to introduce Estelle to her new environment, than to take her to church. It was her first Sunday in Canada. Church to Bernice, was one of the great diversions which was able to seep into her life, and disrupt the iron-gloved triangle of her existence. No matter how sweetly the voices from over the Andes Mountains cooed; no matter how many sins and evil thoughts she confessed to the invisible, washed-in-the-lamb preacher over there in the Mountains; no matter how her imagination placed her in the *front* pew of that other gospel-singing radio church in Alabama, or in Mississippi, still something was lacking. She had to go down to Shaw Street to worship with her other West Indian co-Christians, men and women. Going down there, in that immigrant street, dressed as if she was going to a cocktail party in Forest Hill; and sitting on the seats that drove pins and needles up through her body, she felt, she *knew* she had a little cornerstone of involvement in this community of people. It was a community of immigrants: immigrants who were not Anglo-saxon. Like her, these immigrants had suddenly realized they were lost in a foreign land. And like her, and her West Indian friends, they came together like seaweed on pieces of drifting wood, in a sea with a current that went no way. Bernice knew there was something closer than social ties, and acceptance based on the largeness of your car: it was colour. And it was blood. Dots had said, once, about this street, "This is the only street in this place, this Shaw Street, where people talk and walk in a million and one different nationalities and languages, and nobody doesn't stop talking the moment I walk by, or you walk by. And one thing on this street I notice: nobody don't look at you with wonder and scorn." Bernice had to confess too, that, "Yuh know, Dots, I don't feel that I am either a black person or a white person. Not on this street. This is like home in Barbados."

After church, Bernice took Estelle into the basement. There were many other West Indian women there. Most of them had not seen home in many years. Most of them had not read a West Indian newspaper for as many years. But they were expressing opinions about the West Indies, as if they had just come up. Estelle noticed this; and wondered what else they could talk about. They talked about Barbados and Trinidad and Jamaica, and sometimes about the smaller islands. Even the women from these smaller islands, like St. Vincent and St. Kitts, kept silent or talked about Jamaica and Trinidad. Bernice asked somebody, "Who come up lately?" and without waiting for a reply, she asked, "You hear who getting married?" And a young woman from St. Lucia, with the heavy burden of her life reflected in her face said, "But tell me, *oui*. Which one of us have a chance of finding a decent man in a place like this, *oui*?" And all the women (including Estelle) laughed; and the laugh was cut in half by someone saying, "Doris from Trinidad five months pregnant. She come by my place yesterday, moaning and groaning, saying how she don't want no baby, she don't want no Canadian baby; and that she going try and get a nabortion because her line isn't getting babies: her line is making Canadian money." And the women ripped Doris apart, limb by limb; and they talked about all her family history and her boyfriend-history. There was a tall thin red woman from

Jamaica who said, "Oh-ho-ho, a worthliss bitch like Doris, stupid enough to let a married man sleep with her, and foolish enough to get herself pregnant! Christ, and this place is so hard, as it is." And it seemed that this was the same thing as taking Doris bodily, and throwing her into a den of hens. Each West Indian woman took a peck at Doris's flesh and Doris's reputation and when they were finished, Doris was like a piece of dried rotten cod fish.

After Doris, they talked about home. Bernice asked another Barbadian, if she knew the Deep Water Harbour had been built; yes, said the woman, it built three years now, child. And then somebody asked about somebody's island, and was told that "things not too bright, soul; not as bright as here"; and the person who asked, relaxed, and seemed to feel happier. It was a sort of madness which gave them strength and moral fortitude to return to their various domestic jobs, and as Dots said, "to fight the fight a next day, and a next night, heh-hehhh!"

Estelle remained aloof but attentive as the conversation turned to the white families for whom these women worked. Bernice was the cheer-leader in this. "My missy tight tight tight as a damn kettle-drum." And the women bawled. "Man, she so damn tight, that once I caught her in *my* kitchen counting the blasted rice grains." The women laughed as if they were hitting all the various missies in Forest Hill, Rosedale, Richmond Hill, all over. It was a field day; and no missy, no matter if she was "Mrs. Queen" from high society, could erase the abrasions of this spiteful flogging.

"But you didn't hear 'bout the one I works for?" asked another woman. "She does not have any decencies, whatsoever. I really do not see how she could be so great, with big maid, cook, and cleaning-woman, when...and this is the gospel-truth, as what Rev Markham just preached about...it would make you puke to see the way she splatters tomato ketchup all over the nice, expensive steaks I cooks for her. God, it is enough to make you bring up your guts!"

"Yes, they ain't no good," Bernice said. "They are not any damn good."

"...one I work for, have money..." somebody was saying.

"Yes, money," Bernice said, having to raise her voice to be heard.

"But they only have money."

"But that is money, honey."

"But listen to me!" Bernice was shouting now: it was *her* revivalist meeting. "Listen to me," she said, shouting less, because she noticed that Estelle was embarrassed by her manner. "Money do not make the man. Money do not make a person into a lady. Money is only dollars and cents. And that can't buy, nor purchase what I call *breeding*."

And a very black, thin, beautiful and proud Jamaican woman said, in distinct and venomous clarity, "All-you tell all of them for me, that all of them could kiss my sweet arse. It is only money, as Bernice said, that give them the right to be called missy. It is only the lack of money that give them the opportunity to call me maid. But as long as there is a will, there is a way. I mean to pull out from this arse country as one big millionaire-woman, hear? Or in the very least, as a woman with a few thousand Canadian dollar-bills in my pocketbook."

When the talking stopped, Estelle was jarred. And when the last laugh and the last giggle had died, and the last trace of the hymn *Abide With Me*, which had closed the service, had faded from Bernice's memory, she and Dots and Estelle and two other women from Grenada walked out into the cold winter afternoon. Some others lingered behind (writing reports for church committees): some of them married, but without husbands with them, because husbands are hindrances; some husbands playing dominoes with the "boys"; or old-talking about girls, with the boys; and some husbands still in the West Indies, waiting for passage money, or a money order, or a birthday card from their wives, or permission from the Canadian immigration department . . . and some letters written back as periodically as a menstruation period . . . and others, middle-aged, and unmarried, like kippers through neglect, like virgins on pensions, but still looking and still lonely, they would crawl back on their frustrated way into the suburbs of wealth and loneliness, and long hard work, along Bathurst Street, and along the various street-car tracks of cold, parallel lines of steel and restrictiveness. And Bernice (before Estelle came up) like the others, would close her apartment door behind her, every night; and make certain that the door was locked, and that she was secure inside. She would make certain to make herself damn safe and sound from men (she always thought of men as Mr. Burrmann); and from the nightmares of men, which haunted and hunted and raped her during the nights of long tension and insomnia. "This is our life, child," she told Estelle, returning this Sunday afternoon from church. "Child, it is a life o' snow and whiteness." By this time, Estelle knew what she meant.

Bernice saw the great threat that was about to change her life, through having her sister with her, and she said, "Life is a funny, funny thing." It was some time before she realized the degree of the threat. She did not know, that despite her age, and her set ways before she came to Canada, she would still be flexible enough to adjust her West Indian puritanism to the new Canadian puritanism.

One day Estelle dropped a hair comb, by mistake. Bernice then realized that she herself had never dropped a comb since she had lived here. And she screamed so hard at Estelle, that Estelle began to shake. But when Bernice caught herself, she was even more fightened than Estelle: (she remembered that once she had dropped a spoon in the kitchen on the tiled floor, and Mrs. Burrmann came screaming into the kitchen, with her hands at her temples, complaining about the din!) It was living alone for so long that made her almost completely independent; and that fashioned her into a tight, selfish orderliness.

Estelle began to smoke. She liked the local cigarettes very much. She began to smoke about fifteen a day. Estelle began to drop specks of ash on the edge of the table. Estelle became less careful, and some ash dropped — by mistake — on the floor. Estelle began to be sloppy with her clothes, and dropped them on the floor. Estelle began to neglect washing her underclothes (she would cram them in the clothes hamper, and Bernice would have to wash them) as frequently as Bernice thought she should. This was the beginning of the trouble.

On Estelle's part, she was a bit peeved by having to wait, sometimes as late as ten o'clock in the morning, for her breakfast. Mrs. Burrmann knew that Estelle was living in Bernice's apartment; but Bernice had not openly asked, nor had she been given permission to have Estelle stay. So the longer Mrs. Burrmann lingered over her breakfast, the longer it took for Bernice to sneak upstairs with the two strips of bacon, a fried egg, a piece of toast (the colour of which was proportional to how close Mrs. Burrmann was to the kitchen) and a teacup of coffee. But when Mrs. Burrmann found out what Bernice was doing, she was mad. "Do you imagine that I am such a cheap-skate, eh, Leach? That you could not bring Estelle down here, to have a proper breakfast with us, instead of sneaking up and down?" Bernice was ashamed. "But Mistress, I didn't mean to give the impression . . . " Estelle preferred to be served in bed, on the chesterfield. She was spending all day and night in the apartment, alone. It was becoming a telling experience: a new country and boredom. She knew all the radio programmes by heart; all the commercials by heart; and many popular songs by heart. In a way, she knew Canada by heart. She would see Brigitte playing with her kids across the street, and Brigitte would wave and say hello; and she had seen the two men with the two dogs; and life had almost become unbearable, when one cold afternoon, she saw this white woman walking towards her (she was at the window), and then she heard her steps coming up to the apartment; and then she heard, "that I was just passing in the car when I happened to remember that you are still here, and I know how dull it can be, in a house by yourself, so I thought we might go downtown, nothing fancy, just to the campus and the library, and have a cup of coffee."

That was the beginning of a great, true friendship between Agatha and Estelle. Together they went to the Museum, the Public Library, the O'Keefe Centre of the Performing Arts to hear Harry Belafonte sing, and the Russian Ballet dance, and to the Park Plaza Hotel to have a drink ("But you-all Cana-dians are funny people. Imagine going to a hotel to have a drink! Back home we have drink in a rum shop. But I won't like to tell you what people back there go to a hotel to do, heh-heh!") and then walked across the street to the Yorkville Village, which was really a shattering experience for Estelle: the freshness about this place, and the young people like rebels and the women who looked as if they were really alive and fresh. Bernice could not understand this excitement. "I don't want to hear nothing 'bout no long-hair beatniks, with lice in their heads, eh!" The only thing Bernice knew about Yorkville Village was what a reporter of *The Globe and Mail* said about it: that a lot of marijuana was smoked there. Like the reporter, Bernice did not try to find out more. Yorkville was to her, irrevocably, a den of iniquity.

Sometimes, in the kitchen, Bernice would think of her life in Canada: how it had changed; the clothes she was now wearing; the broadness of her knowledge about subjects and people she never knew existed. She was very impressed by Brigitte, who told her many interesting things about Germany, about Hitler and the Nazis. To hear Brigitte talk about so powerful a man, made it very real to her, because in the West Indies, during the heyday of Hitler, she was a small girl interested in Frank Sinatra, and Hitler was no more than the swastikas of chalk she used to draw on the church wall. She never imagined Hitler to be a man. She was also very impressed by the wealth of the Burrmanns. Once, Mrs. Burrmann sent her to the bank with a cheque. When she saw the cheque made out to Mr. Burrmann, for three thousand dollars, *exact*, she almost dropped the cheque. And this made her think of Mr. Burrmann as a very powerful man, even more powerful than Hitler was. She did not know him as intimately as she felt she knew Mrs. Burrmann. He never spoke to her affectionately; but he was never rude. It seemed he kept her at the distance a servant ought to be kept: with coldness and civility. He regarded Bernice the way he regarded his secretary: as a machine, to perform certain well-defined jobs. It was also difficult to get to know him, since he spent little time in the home. He was always working. On weekends, he was in the study, studying or preparing briefs — so Bernice imagined, until one day she found him lying on the floor, with his head almost touching the speaker of his record-player system which he had built into the wall; and with the lights out. As she remembered it, he was listening to jazz, a kind of strange noise, with lots of drums and cymbals and screechings. That afternoon, he seemed completely relaxed by the "damn noise"; and when he spoke to her, she noticed that his eyes were red and tired and distant. "That damn man is far from here!" she commented.

"How's it going, Bernice?" He would ask her this many times. Each time, she was made to feel she had just arrived for the job; and he had met her for the first time. Sometimes, she would smile; and sometimes she would smile and say, "Betwixt and between, sir!" And he liked her to say that.

Mr. Burrmann really never felt at home, at home. Not even when, as a boy growing up on Palmerston Boulevard in the guts of old downtown Toronto, in the days when Jews inhabited and ruled that entire section bounded by College, north to Bloor Street, east to Spadina Avenue and as far west as Bathurst Street. He used to spend those days in a "gang." Some of the "gangsters" were young "coloured boys," sons of West Indians who had come to Canada to work as porters on the railroads, and as domestics in white, rich kitchens and homes. Mr. Burrmann was therefore acquainted, from an early age, with domestics. Bernice did not know (not even Mrs. Burrmann from whom he hid it; and to whom he never had the guts to mention it; and who was brought up in a more respectably rich and suburban area of the city) that he had been close to black people throughout his adolescence and university days. Something happened to him when he was fourteen, something which never left him completely, but which came up into his consciousness, periodically, like a badly digested apple. It would sometimes make him physically sick, as it had made him vomit on his clothes that summer afternoon thirty years ago, on the street which is now the main artery in the Jewish Market, Augusta Street. Once, during his university days, when he made a lot of money working in construction one summer, he took the liberty and the expensive fling of seeing a psychiatrist about it: *It was about four o'clock one day, and some guys, me and five others, coloured boys from the neighbourhood who used to go to the public school in the area, well, we were walking through the Market teasing some guys wearing the paius, you know? earlocks, we used to call them pigtails; and wearing their foreign-looking clothes....*

*How did they look?*

*... well, like uniforms, uniforms of mourning. Well, anyway, we were looking for excitement, as guys usually are — looking for trouble. This afternoon in question, the excitement was to be picking apples from the heaps on the sidewalk stands, when the Polish Jews weren't watching....*

*Did you actually steal any, many?*

*Yeah! a lot, and as we turned the corner, Baldwin Street, and just as I was putting my hand on a coupla apples from an old Jewish guy, he caught me and start giving me the chase:* the old Jewish gentleman ran behind them, up Augusta Street crowded with afternoon shoppers, and knocking down stalls and stands and making the live chickens cackle and lay eggs in fright; and the "gang" escaped the old man. But one of them ran right into a large oak of a man who put his arms in the boy's way,

like a crucifix of maple, and when the giant got him into his
arms, he closed them and held the boy until the Jewish gentleman came, and peering over his bi-focals that drooped on his
long nose, he shouted, "That's him!" And although he had
actually seen Sammy Burrmann with an apple in his hand, he
did not see any difference between Sammy and Jeffrey, who
was black. They never saw Jeffrey again. A week later, Jeffrey's
mother went into the Toronto General Hospital with her
fourth baby at the edge of her womb, and she died before the
baby was born, and before she was delivered of her travail.
(The baby was given out for adoption.) That night, Sammy
Burrmann vomited. But he did not have enough guts left, after
vomiting, to confess to Jeffrey's mother, or to the Jewish gentleman who he knew, and who went to the same synagogue on
College Street, that he was the one with the apple in his hand.
The other two black boys in the "gang" stopped stealing apples;
and stopped joining "gangs" that had Jewish members; and
they stopped speaking to Sammy after they found out that the
court had sentenced Jeffrey to two years hard labour for his
first offence. This heavy guilt on Mr. Burrmann's shoulders
followed him throughout his adolescence; a guilt he ended up
by keeping to himself, since he had waited so long to confess
it, or talk about it, in the first place. It was about this time
that he decided to become a lawyer. But even before that, he
had had other experiences of youth, with black people. He
remained on Palmerston Boulevard, near the district that was
predominantly "coloured" at the time, because his family was
too poor to move away, as others had done to escape the "black
scourge." His father did not sell enough scrap iron and parts
of metal bedsteads which the West Indians threw out at their
front gates with other junk, in his horse-drawn chariot, to

enable him to move. And when he died, Sammy and his two sisters and three brothers, and his mother were not left enough money to enable them to move north into what was fast becoming the Ghetto, the area of success. (If you look in the Toronto telephone directory today, you will see two other Burrmanns, men, Sammy's brothers: one is a musician in an orchestra; and the other, is a waiter in a bar downtown. Both sisters died of tuberculosis.) Soon after, Sammy's mother died. When she died, the doctors said she died of arthritis and pneumonia; but Sammy knew she died of a broken heart and a broken love. He never liked his father. When Mr. Burrmann, Senior, died, Sammy laughed; and did not even miss a lecture at Trinity College, to visit the synagogue. He was free now to associate with the black boys he used to know at school and in the bars around Spadina. Sammy also had liaisons with his friends' sisters.

His boyhood days never left him. They never wiped out completely, the taste left in his mouth, by the incident with Jeffrey. These things he thought about when his wife first introduced him to his new domestic, Bernice. His coldness towards Bernice was caused by these memories. The embarrassment that came into his eyes when she turned round once in the kitchen and found him staring at her ("You undressing me with your blasted eyes, you bitch!") was caused by these memories. They made him retreat further into his already introverted nature. One Sunday morning, when Mrs. Burrmann had left to take the children to the municipal skating rink, Bernice found him in a clothes closet which was not used often; and all he was doing was running his hands on an old broomstick, as if measuring it. And once, she found him sitting on the landing that led from the ground floor mid-way between the children's room and hers. She approached him, since she had to pass that way, and all he said was, "How's she going, Bernice?"

"Mr. Burrmann, is you all right, sir?"

"Why?" When he looked up, and saw the concern on her face, he felt he had to say something more. He never knew that Bernice regarded him as a madman; and as a terribly ill-treated man, and husband. "Oh, I was just sitting here, thinking." He said it without losing his dignity; and his superiority as master and man. Bernice just left him sitting there. ("That man, mad as hell, in truth. I hope he don't come trying no damn foolishness with me.") When she reached her apartment, she locked the door.

As the days passed, Estelle found herself smothered by the same triangle of existence that Bernice was restricted to — with the exception that the princess telephone which Bernice used so often, was useless to her, since she knew so few people. Once however, she did call Boysie to find out how she could remain in Canada, permanently (Bernice had refused to talk about it); and he advised her to get a child by a Canadian; or marry a man. "But you have to make sure he is a Canadian *by birth*. That is first!" Boysie sniggered, and Estelle hung up the telephone. But she thought of his suggestion for many days. Boysie came round once, to borrow two dollars from Bernice; and after that day, they never saw him for three weeks; and he never called.

Estelle was becoming worried, and bored. She remembered she knew two Barbadian girls in Canada; one lived in Winnipeg, the other, in Montreal. So she decided to call them on Bernice's princess. Just as she was about to dial, Bernice screamed, "Girl, you crazy as hell? Them is long-distance calls!" Bernice showed her on the map, where Winnipeg and Montreal were.

But Bernice could not escape the image of Estelle's underclothes strewn on the floor. In her mind; in the kitchen; throughout the house; whenever she looked into a cup or a glass, she saw Estelle's panties in the bottom. Whenever she put out the garbage, she saw Estelle lying in the bottom of the pail. There was no escape. She had promised a long time ago, to take Estelle to the WIF Club, but because of the wrong way Estelle rubbed her, she deliberately forgot her promise. She began to spend most of her rest-hour period downstairs in the kitchen; and she would spend them mending, and darning things for the children and Mrs. Burrmann, which she did not have to do. When she was tired mending, she read the newspapers, usually two days old. Once, she came across a magazine, *Harper's Bazaar*, which fascinated her. The magazine was exactly one year three months old, since its publication. She was so impressed by the photographs and the advertisements in it, that she threatened to stop her subscription to *Muhammad Speaks* and *Jet* and to subscribe to *Harper's Bazaar*. She was so frustrated and weakened by Estelle and her attitudes ("Christ, all she has done since setting foot in Canada, is to moan and groan 'bout every blasted thing. She don't even like the food I cooks!") that she found herself drawn closer to the Burrmanns.

One morning, the bubble burst. Bernice discovered that Estelle had used *her* toothbrush. "But I don't see anything serious," Estelle said. Both toothbrushes were the same colour. "It's a toothbrush, Bernice, and anybody could make a mistake like that. Besides, I don't have phthisic...."

"Jesus Christ, look woman!..." But the rest of her anger buried itself. She saw herself strangling Estelle. And when she rushed out of the room, shaking with anger and the frustration of not being able to express this anger (she promised to buy two new toothbrushes next time she went to the drug store) it took her a long time simmering down, in the kitchen. Mrs. Burrmann came in and said pleasantly, "Bernice, when are you going to begin dinner?"

"You don't see me resting, Mrs. Burrmann?" she replied, confusing the object of her hostility, and seeing Mrs. Burrmann as Estelle. But she caught herself, and added, "Soon, ma'am."

"Is something the matter?"

"Estelle!"

"Oh, how's she liking Canada?" Mrs. Burrmann had by now given permission for Estelle to live with Bernice.

"Fine, ma'am." Bernice was ready with the smile and the happy face. Mrs. Burrmann read the face and the smile, and concluded that everything was fine. Drunk or sober, Bernice cautioned herself, mind your business! "Everything is ship-shape."

Today, Mrs. Burrmann looked fresh and happy and young. She lingered in the kitchen (touching dishes and plates on the counter, like a shopper touching fruits to see whether they're ripe) and then said, "Tell me, Bernice, haven't you ever thought of getting married?" The shock was so great, that for some time, Bernice actually couldn't think. But she recovered, and laughed in her expansive manner; and looked Mrs. Burrmann straight in the eyes, and said, "Ma'am, I have put man outta my life, *a long time now.*" Together, they enjoyed the deceit of this declaration; and they laughed, and before Mrs. Burrmann left she rested her hand, her right hand on Bernice's left arm (she was facing Bernice) and said, "Sometimes, you make me feel as if you're my..." But she didn't finish; there was no need.

Spasms of affection like this one, helped to prevent Bernice from thinking too much of the pain in her back. The pain was brought on by tension, and the fact that Estelle hogged up most of the chesterfield, at nights. Bernice had to spend many sleepless nights in the chair by the window. Sometimes, she really preferred to sit there: she could see more of Brigitte's private business. Once, she saw Brigitte in her room. And she saw the policeman, too. What she really saw was a man's form. She could have seen more, but the lights were turned off too quickly. Another night, she looked down to investigate a scratching on the front lawn; and she saw the two men with the two dogs. The men were like two black dots on the white background of winter; and the dogs were like two ants scurrying about. That same night, distracted by Estelle's silence on the entire chesterfield, curdled like milk, the idea hit her. "Now, why I didn't think of that before? I so damn stupid!" She was trembling because she thought Estelle had heard her thoughts. The next day, she mentioned the idea to Dots, on the telephone. "I am going to find a room for Estelle. Expense and location don't matter."

"That's a damn good idea, gal!" Dots went on to say, "She may be your sister, but you will have to pardon me if I say I don't particularly like Estelle. What the hell she mean by calling up Boysie, asking him to help her become a landed immigrant? Estelle fresh!"

"She young."

"Estelle in this country looking for man," Dots said. She laughed and added, "But you don't have to worry, gal. You don't have no man for Estelle to take away...." And so, it became obvious that Estelle and Dots weren't favourites. Dots was envious of her beauty (Estelle was fascinating with a provocative body) and her greater intelligence. "Get her out, before she brings trouble in Mrs. Burrmann's place, eh. Estelle harping 'pon one thing. Canadian citizenship. She want it, by hook or by crook." This was one time when Bernice didn't really want to take Dots's advice. It sounded like a threat. And she was further hurt, because Dots had hung up on her. It was the first time in three years. Bernice began to feel suspicious, and insecure: Dots knew something about Estelle; more than she had said. Bernice felt her friendship with Dots threatened. "But that ain't true!" she said to herself. "Estelle isn' going to leave Barbados and come up here in Canada to turn Dots from me. Sister, or no sister."

And then one day it happened. No one knew that it would: not Dots, not Estelle, not even Bernice. (She had even forgotten she had decided to look for a room.) It happened, perhaps, because it had to happen. Bernice had gone to the store to purchase some vaseline for her hair. Estelle was going to "process" Bernice's hair with a hot comb. Estelle was lying on the chesterfield, watching the snow fall. She liked the snow. She must have been lying there a long time, dreaming and plotting to become a landed immigrant, and seeing her schemes fall like snowflakes, when the knock sounded on the door. She did not move. It must be Bernice come back from the store. The knock was, to her, merely part of her dream. But the knocking continued, and the snow stopped falling. She came out of the dream, and went to the door ("But Bernice don't knock, usually. . . .") and opened the door; and saw, not the white shoes and the brown stockings, but blue denim trousers and mouldy tennis shoes. Raising her eyes, she saw the man in the doorway. He was surprised; more surprised than she. He could see small black circles around the nipples of her breasts which the thickness of the silk nightgown was too thin to hide. He could see right through the apex of her legs; and he thought he could see snow falling outside. All this his eyes took in, in that one glance immediately after the shock of seeing her, cleared from his mind. ("Did my wife actually tell me somebody was up here with Bernice? I seemed to hear her saying something 'bout Bernice's sister. . . . ") Something within Estelle was making the silk rise and fall, just as the wind on a field of snow sometimes makes it rise and fall. In one glance, she saw cold steel in his eyes; and a kind of fright was there, too.

"I'm sorry," he said at last.

"Oh, it's all right," she said, still unsettled. (She knew who he was.) "I thought it was Bernice out here. But Bernice won't knock. She has a key." He remained standing, not knowing what to do next. She felt she had to say something to take his mind off what his mind might have been on. "Well, look at me, eh! Still in bed this time o' day!"

"You must be Bernice's sister."

"Yes, Estelle."

"Well, how's it going?" He turned to go. "I'm sorry."

"I'll tell Bernice you were looking for her."

"Fine."

"Well, you come back when Bernice comes back, eh?"

"Fine." He had not actually moved yet.

"Well, I'd better go and take off these . . . "

"Fine." He was looking at her legs, in the passage of his glance downwards to her ankles. He did not know why he had looked at her ankles, instead of at her breasts. He did not know why he didn't move away as soon as he saw her. Perhaps it was the way she looked; the way she looked at him . . . she looked

at him just as Jeffrey's mother had looked at him when he went
to her home to say he was sorry for what happened to Jeffrey,
and Jeffrey's mother looked at him that way, because she hated
him; and because he was a coward, because he went to her after
Jeffrey had spent two months of his sentence in the Don Jail.
Estelle was looking at him as if he was a small child sent on
an errand too large for his retention; just so did Mrs. Carson,
Jeffrey's mother look at him. And Jeffrey's mother had shouted
at him, and called him "a crooked blasted Jew," loud loud loud,
so loud that the neighbours heard, and that was what caused
him to do the thing that weakened him, and made him always
uncomfortable in front of women. *He had shit his pants, in front
of Mrs. Carson, Jeffrey's mother*... and running without opening
his legs too much, across the dilapidated street of old garbage,
open and fly-infested, and in the eyes of noisy black people,
right across Spadina and up College, until he reached Palmerston Boulevard, with the brown grease slipping down his legs,
and the smell; and there and then, he bathed four times that
night; and since then bathing had become a necessity. When he
was at university, living by himself, he would bathe three times
a day (he never took a shower in his life) and when, later in
life, that was made impossible and inconvenient, he would
spend as much time as possible in the bath tub (to compensate
for the infrequency). Now he stood waiting upon Estelle, as if
he wanted to be scolded again. "I am sorry." But she had
already closed the door, because he had frightened her. She was
not frightened of him; no, it wasn't his appearance, or the
appearance of his motives which she felt she detected; but the
way he stood there, like a fool, like someone without the reality of hinging the past to the present.

Inside the door, she could hear him going back down. She

had latched the door while he was outside; but she unlatched it, later. She went back to the chesterfield, and began to count the snowflakes. She could not think of the snow now: she was thinking of the man; and she was drawing pictures of the man, in the snow, without permitting her mind to linger on the motives of the pictures; yet she was shaking with a nervousness which imprisoned the man in a corner of her mind. The motives were at work; for something had happened; and she knew it. *It is up to me to do something about the something that has happened; because something else is going to happen and it can be up to me to make that something else happen. But I am not sure what.* But before she could decide what to do, Bernice was back, with the vaseline; thinking: *I gotta get a room and get rid of this bitch, I gotta get a room.* Unable to think of this scheme against her sister, and be in the same room with her, Bernice slipped downstairs to find some solace in work. She prepared lunch for Mr. Burrmann and the children. Mrs. Burrmann had gone to do her volunteer work in the Women's Auxiliary, at the Doctors' Hospital, where she sold cigarettes and chewing gum to chronic patients, with a smile.

Bernice was sitting on a straightbacked chair. She had been sitting like this for thirty minutes. Her dress was tucked saucily in the crux of her large wallaba-like legs. One eye was closed (it was on that side of the head which was being *processed*) as Estelle ripped the comb through her tough hair. Suddenly, she laughed out. The comb hesitated. Estelle moved round in front; looked down inquisitively to see what Bernice was laughing at; and said, "This is the first time, in almost six weeks that I see you even smile. Well, God bless my eyesight!" Bernice continued laughing loudly. "Do you know what just enter my mind?"

she asked. "I was laughing 'bout them two fellars who stealed the mangoes, and then couldn't divide them in two, because neither one could count. God! that must have been something. One threaten to kill the other one, if he didn't get his due, although he himself couldn't know what his due was. A simple thing like division by two's. But them two fellars sat down under the street light; one fellar empty all the mangoes on the road, and he started counting: *one for me, and one for you; one for me, and one for you, and . . .*"

"But that was funny."

"You mean the way they solve the counting?"

"No, Bernice. It's funny because the day Agatha took me driving, those are the exact words she used. *There's enough for me and there's enough for you!* Her exact words. And I don't really know if she wanted those words to reach my ears, because the way she was talking, she was talking as if she was saying it to herself. But now that you mentioned the story, I remember what she said: *enough for me and enough for you*, which, as you would agree, is the same thing as saying *one for me and one for you*." She went back to "processing" Bernice's hair. "Bernice?" she said, later, "what exactly could Agatha mean by a statement like that?"

"Agaffa isn't worth worrying about; and she isn't worrying with you. Agaffa accustom to black people, and especially men."

"Yes, she told me about Henry. The parents ripped hell, in truth."

"It serve all them Negro men right, though!" There was bitterness in her voice. Her body stiffened, so that you couldn't help thinking her statement was based on personal involvement. "That girl's father threatened to shoot Henry, you didn't know? Henry won't stop troubling the man's daughter. The man send Agaffa to Europe to forget Henry, and be-Christ, after eighteen months, that Agaffa still come back like a loopy dog, dying o' thirst, and caused the father to ask her to leave home. . . . " Estelle said she had heard about it, from Agatha herself. "And look, I have to confess that that poor child suffered so much for that blasted brute, Henry. And he treats her like dirt. And still she coming back for more?"

"A woman is a woman, Bernice. It doesn't matter what colour she is. And if Henry had fallen in love with . . . " Bernice rushed up out of the chair. The cloth tied round her head and shoulders, dropped off. "How the hell would you know?" she asked Estelle. "You just come? You is one o' the *broadminded* ones, already?" But she sat back down, quieted; and in a changed manner, she admitted, "You know something? I don't know, I do not know, at all. I really do not know, Estelle."

"But do you think you've changed much? Living here?"

"Child, I really do not know."

"To me, you changed; and changed a damn lot, too."

Bernice took a deep breath, it seemed to put her thoughts in order. "Look, child, this idea o' leaving your home and coming into somebody-else country is a damn brave thing, eh. Every day, there's something to remind you that you wasn't born here, that you don't belong here. Christ, sometimes, I shudder in my room, thinking what would happen to me, to Dots, to Boysie, to all the black people in this place, if some o' them blasted African people in Africa decided to kill-off all the white people living in their midst. Child, don't you think that would be a day o' blood and sorrow and sufferation? Just to think of it makes me tremble." Estelle had stopped fixing the hair, to listen; and to ponder the possibility of that happening. "Perhaps, you are more happier, more freer where the hell you come from, I don't know. I have a good few cents stashed away in a bank, somewhere in this place. There's dresses in that clothes closet, as you see for yourself; and be-Christ, I could never hope to get half o' them if I was still in Barbados. Look round this apartment. Telephone, radio-gram, electric iron, and I just had a chat with that man, Mr. Burrmann, and he tell me he puttin' in television in here, next week. Well, what the hell more do I want? Tell me, Estelle. The only thing I don't have, nor don't particular want to have, is a man, goddammit, because man is trouble. And when I balance my life here against my life there, I think I come out on top."

"Still, I think you changed."

"*Change?* Is change, you say? That ain't the word. The word is mashed-up — *destroy!*" She moved her arms round the apartment, taking in all its contents. "All this! all this. And not a ounce o' happiness." She remembered what Dots had said on her return from Barbados recently; and this made her say, "But a man could live anywhere, any place, as long as there is *people* on the earth." The ironing comb was ripping through Bernice's hair; and Estelle herself winced when the comb got stuck, and when Bernice stiffened, anticipating the pain that would crawl up from the roots of her hair. Many mangled pieces of hair were caught in the comb; Estelle would take them out, and drop them; and they would fall like snow-balls into Bernice's lap. Bernice played with them, and balled them into small balls; then joined all the small ones into a large ball. She studied the large ball, looking at it, and wondering, "Estelle, you think snow would ever be black?"

"I suppose it's possible! Anything is possible." But she didn't really think so.

Bernice was happier now; and more comfortable; and

she allowed her mind to wonder and to wander. Estelle too, wandered in her thoughts: *if a man could press a button in a car, as Agatha did, and roll up car windows, I don't see why it's so strange with snow falling outta the skies the colour of black. Man made the car windows and the garage door. But God made the snow; so anything is possible. . . .*

*I would like to bring Mammy up for a month, for a rest, at least. Wonder what Estelle would think o' that.* "Estelle, what about bringing up Mammy?" *I better think 'bout that, yes! 'cause I don't know if young people should live with old people; old people and Canadians always talking 'bout death. Old people are real Canadians! . . . or even bring up Lonnie.*

"Mammy too old to travel."

"It might make her happy, though." *But I wonder why Estelle don't like Mammy? She hasn't said more than two words concerning poor Mammy, since she come up here? I had better leave my money on the bank. Mammy all right. Mammy could walk across the road, and call-out for two three four people by their first names, even before she make another step; Mammy could even enjoy a joke with them; Mammy could walk through Bridgetown, barefooted or in shoes, or with a loaf o' bread in her mouth, eating, but be-Christ, Mammy, you can't do none o' them things in this place. So perhaps, you are better off down there. . . .* "But Estelle, you see any wisdom in a woman like me trying to make her home in this country?"

"I don't know, Bernice, I really don't know. But what really is worrying me, is how you become so important and independent a woman, that you don't have time for one little man round this apartment?"

"Come, finish the hair, child, 'cause I have a hundred and one things to do before nightfall."

"But Bernice, have you ever thought serious 'bout marriage or *anything?*"

"*No.*" And after that, Bernice was silent for a long time, while Estelle worked on the hair. She began to talk to herself, under her breath, mostly; but at times, her thoughts got the better of her, and she would express them, so that Estelle could hear. "You know something? That white woman down there, she could work like a blasted horse, herself, yuh know. Man, Mrs. Burrmann can do as much work, as much house-work as me or you. Sometimes I wonder *why*, with me here, she still killing herself over the house, making a home for Mr. Burrmann, God-love-him, sometimes: looking after them two kids, and still she employing me, and paying me! You think it is because she *must* have somebody beneath her? ... I making sense to you, or I imagining something that ain't there?"

"God, Bernice ... and I talking in your language now! ... this is the kind o' horse-sense I was waiting to hear from you since I arrive."

"Christ, yes, man! and though I don't always have the mind or the inclination to talk what is on my mind, it don't mean that I don't have serious things on my mind ... Listen, Estelle! listen, listen, listen!" She was whispering now. "You hear footsteps coming up here?" Out of the hissing of the hair being fried, came footsteps up the stairs. Quickly, all life stopped. Action halted; and the women waited, staring, to recognize the footsteps. You could see their minds working. "Thank God," Bernice said, "the door lock. Quick! turn off that damn hot-plate!" Estelle couldn't find the switch: she had never before used a hot-plate in her life. "Come, take this!" Bernice gave her the towel which was wrapped round her shoulders to keep the hair from falling into her bosom. Then Bernice pulled out the cord of the hot-plate, and threw it under the chesterfield. The vaseline jar had lost its cover, but she couldn't wait to find it. She threw that, the ironing comb and the rag, used to wipe the comb, into the bathroom. And then they waited for the person to knock. Bernice stopped breathing, it seemed; and Estelle, too.

The footsteps come right up to the door; they wait, and then they turn and go back downstairs.

"But who you think it is, Bernice?"

"Mrs. Burrmann, probably."

"It could be Dots, couldn't it?"

"Dots would call out. Besides, Dots working."

"Yes. And they were heavier footsteps than a woman."

"I wonder..."

"It a good thing you keep this door locked, all the time. You should always keep it so, remembering what I told you Agatha told me about a girl who got raped *in broad daylight*, in her own apartment..."

"You making me nervous."

"...and the girl Dots talked about, the Jamaican, who was working in Willowdale." Estelle thought of something that made her laugh; and then it made her shudder: suppose what she was thinking was really true.

"You *smiling*? Estelle, how the hell could you smile at a time like this?"

"I wonder if..." Estelle began. The she had to laugh out, loudly; and this confused Bernice. "You know something? Those were a man's footsteps out there." And when something like shame settled over Bernice, Estelle taunted her, and said, "A man!"

"But who? Which man could be coming, smelling round me?"

Estelle laughed again. She thought she knew who it was. "Don't get frightened Bernice, man; it is only a man."

For days after, they were talking about it. Dots couldn't explain it; nor could Boysie, who confided in Henry one night at the Paramount. Henry was the only one who pretended to know the explanation. Agatha was told about it by Henry; and she said it disgusted her: she still didn't tell Henry what it was that disgusted her. Some time later, in the Paramount, eating wings and drinking draughts, Henry brightened, and gave Boysie this explanation: "There is *one* tide in the affairs of men — and woman, too — Boysie Cumberbatch." He waited until Boysie manoeuvred a greasy bone out of his front gums. "And that tide, Boysie Cumberbatch, is pussy. Pussy provides the end-all and the be-all of life. It is the tide of life and the tide of death; the tide of love and the tide of pain. The tide of happiness and the tide of sorrowness. *That* is the tide in the affairs of men. And it don't have nothing to do with what that man Shakespeare talked about, neither. . . . " Henry stopped talking, because the bone had now lodged itself at a nasty angle in Boysie's throat; and it was causing him to cough and splutter. Boysie was glad he was choking: he didn't have to reply to the nonsense Henry was talking. He didn't want to smash the student-teacher relationship their friendship had recently grown into. He had carried this "explanation" around for three days. He thought of Bernice, tried to imagine himself the man going up the stairs; and without explanation, he started coughing and spluttering. The prospect choked him.

Recently Bernice had found some solace in reading *Awake*

and *The Watchtower*. (An article in *Muhammad Speaks*, calling upon her, spiritually and morally, to kill the white devil nearest her — Mrs. Burrmann — had shaken her up so much, that she started to fold the newspaper in half, with the front page hidden, and to file it under her chesterfield.) But these two religious papers brought no real solution. Solutions seemed far from her comprehension. Estelle was like the snow, always around in winter, which was always in the room, "always in my footsteps, always in my arse" (these were the private unspoken thoughts, communicated in communion, to God only), like a snake around her neck. She could no longer talk for hours on her princess; she began to feel her movements stiffen with tension; she was irritable: God, it is too much, Estelle have to move out. I can't even listen to my own church services, I can't get a chance to lay-down on my own chesterfield, I can't even hear the word o' God on my own radiogram, I can't even be private, any more! Estelle turned off my church music and put on the blasted rock-'n'-roll. It pains me right down to my guts to see how this snake come in here and is taking over in my place, but be-Christ, I intends to be the conqueror. By Monday forenoon, I putting her in a nice single room, or a furnished flat, even. If it can't happen on Monday, then on my next day off. "It is painful," Bernice was saying to Dots (Estelle was in the bathroom, so she had to whisper into the princess. She didn't even know if Estelle was listening: and this made her chilly and tensed.), "to have to treat *our friend* so harsh. But I been so damn lick-out with work, lately, that I gotta do ... *our friend* coming out ... " And once more she had to hang up. Only once before was she more furious because of an interruption; and that was when she had just dropped her clothes on to the floor, and was about to expire on the chesterfield from all the hard work in the kitchen, and as she said, "Jesus, Jesus!" in relief and anticipation, the two women from *Awake* and *The Watchtower* rapped on her door, because "the lady downstairs told us we could count on you." They had spent her entire rest hour preparing her for God and heaven and a subscription chatting away the sins of this terrible world; drinking all of Bernice's tea. When they left, she told Dots, "You know something, I could have killed them two ashy-faced bitches, just now. What in hell they mean by telling me for one whole blasted hour, that God love me?" Later, she found out, that it was Mrs. Burrmann who staged the meeting, as a decoy to her own conversion.

The tension between Bernice and Estelle, which grew steadily after the toothbrush incident, exploded one Sunday morning. Estelle turned off Bernice's service from the Andes Mountains, and tuned into a rock-'n'-roll piece, *Down Town*, well, be-Jesus God (Bernice was swearing a lot more nowadays), girl! you have gone too far, now. I can't take this. But later, on the way to church that very morning, she consoled herself that Dots and she would find a room for Estelle, on Monday. Estelle had decided to go to church with her: there was nothing else to do on a Sunday morning in Canada.

"I believe in *two* things," Bernice was saying. "In God and in clothes. Clothes clothes my outside, and God clothes my inside. So I protected on both sides. How yuh like me?" Estelle was borrowing a dress to wear to church. She had never got over the amount of clothes Bernice owned. "These clothes, all these clothes you see here, well, they each have a particular function in my life. They may be clothes to you. But to me, they is more than clothes." And that was the truth: for immigration had worked a substantial change in her dressing habits; and other West Indian women would praise her, and say how much she looked like a "*sophisticated coloured Canadian.*" Bernice chose a suit which was given to her last year by Mrs. Burrmann. (When Dots saw it, her mouth ran water, in envy. Bernice told her she had bought it at Eaton's, brand new!) It was a green woollen suit, rich as guinea grass. Estelle had chosen a white dress, whose fabric and style bore no relation to the season of the year. She liked it. But Bernice was not pleased that she had chosen this dress: not because of fashion or style; but because the white dress was her best dress. Estelle told Bernice how young she looked; and Bernice laughed, and said, Thank you, Ess (while thinking Estelle a damn liar); and just then, Boysie blew the car horn, below the window. He blew it a second time, louder; and Estelle held half of her body out, and shouted, "Wait! Bernice putting on her make-up!"

"But Estelle," Bernice said reprovingly, "it don't sound nice to hear a person in this district get on like that, and on a Sunday."

"Perhaps I should have *whispered* to him. You ashamed of something? Or you ashamed of me?"

"I only say that I don't think it look good, decent, to see a person shouting through a window…Look, you had better learn one thing. We is the only coloured people in this district. We have to be on our best peace and behaviour, always. Everything we do, every word we utter, we gotta be always remembering it is a reflection on all the hundreds and thousands o' coloured people in Toronto and in the whole o' Canada." Estelle didn't know whether she ought to laugh; or pity Bernice. "I didn't make it so. I come and find it so, so you don't have to look at me as if I is some, some-some-some, *mad person!*"

Estelle kicked off her shoes in disgust. She threw down her handbag.

"I changed my mind."

"You mean you *not* going to church?"

"No."

"Merely because I had to teach you a little goodness? I, a person, a, the only coloured person in this street...trying to make you understand..."

"No, no, no! Jesus Christ, Bernice, can't you hear I say no? No, no, no!"

Estelle's voice was still screaming in Bernice's ears, even as she went down to the car. Her lipstick was put on badly. It had smeared her lips, and was on her teeth. She was agitated. That bitch, that bitch, was all Bernice could say. She had wrenched the plastic curtains shut, because Estelle was now naked, except for her panties.

"I'm too young," Estelle said, sitting on the chesterfield, "I am too young, man. I not wasting my time in no damn church. You talk to God, and let me talk to man."

"And I hopes to-Christ that you will find one! I kiss this bible in my hand, and I pray and hopes, Estelle Shepherd, that you will find one who will full-up your damn belly with a child, *and a fatherless child, at that!*"

With a problem as serious as Estelle on her mind, Bernice would refuse to seek advice until she had first reached her own decision. Dots frequently gave her opinions, and Bernice would alter them; but by that time, she had already settled her mind on some action she was going to take. She felt that if she was going to find any solace, or reprieve, it had to come from within herself. Sometimes, problems were too large for her.

They would burden her, and then a new problem would come; and she would forget the first one. You know something? Perhaps, Estelle have a point, when she say she isn't interested in God, only in man. Perhaps. (Dots had confided in Bernice that she had spent the first ten months in Canada, in masturbation. "Without a blasted man in my pants, gal! It don't make you feel happier when you, as a woman in bed alone, night after night, hearing the springs in the missy's bed. Ten months I carried the racket o' them creaking springs in my ears and in my pants, gal, twelve months o' loneliness I don't ever want to live over again." And so said; so done: Boysie was brought up from Barbados, shortly afterwards. But Bernice had tried to solve her loneliness in another way. She had seen a future, and permanence, in a young Jamaican man she met on Cecil Street, in those days when you could dance for a whole night for one dollar. It was a place managed by an old West Indian who tried to help "reorientate the islanders to the Canadian way of life." This Jamaican was told by one of his student-friends to "grab the first piece o' pussy, white or black, that come across, old man, 'cause winter does be cold as arse in this country!" And the Jamaican grabbed Bernice. He knew (and she knew too) that it was only temporary; but both insisted that their love affair had to last forever. She invited him to Marina Boulevard on Fridays, when Mrs. Burrmann was usually helping at the Doctors' Hospital; and the student-man would stay the whole weekend; and once he had to jump through the second floor window, when it looked as if Mrs. Burrmann would never leave the house on that Monday afternoon, for her regular cocktails with friends, on the roof of the Park Plaza Hotel. Bernice was thinking of all these things, on the way to church this Sunday. She was in the back seat. Dots

was sitting beside Boysie; and she was grumbling about the
cold weather, and about Mrs. Hunter, and about Boysie
"creeping in this morning at six, but one o' these times, be-
Christ, I am going to track you down!" Bernice tried to close
her mind to all this; and tried to concentrate on the memories
of her student-friend of two-and-a-half years ago, when she
stood at the window, black and invisible, and saw her student-
man walk up and down Marina Boulevard, *five times*, waiting
for her signal that the coast was clear: shhh! snow boots in
hand, shoes in Bernice's hands, stockings walking like ashes
and cats on the hot broadloom; and how on that night when
he ate his first square meal, and he ate her food and her body,
too. And she was very, so very happy. "You don't know this is
the first time in almost a year, that I do *that*," she said, not as
tenderly as she would have liked, because she was out of the
custom of being tender to a man. "I love you, bad. Me and
you..." She had given him money; and occasionally, washed
a shirt for him, while he waited naked in bed, in glee, under
her lily-white sheets. She loved him; oppressively and posses-
sively; and one night, she dressed in her best dress, the dress
Estelle had chosen this morning, for church, to wait for him,
to come, to take her out. Mrs. Burrmann was so happy about
it: she lent Bernice her fur wrap, and a pair of elbow-length kid
gloves. Bernice sat in front of her looking glass, waiting for
him to take her to the annual variety show put on by the West
Indian students at the University. Nine o'clock came. Nine
o'clock went. Ten came. Ten went. Eleven came and went.
Mrs. Burrmann came up to see what's going on, and to say,
"Some men are bastards, Bernice, you got to learn that, early,"
and she went back down, confused and cursing men. Bernice
was so frightened because of the disappointment, that she

started to count her terror in five-minute periods. She was sitting at the window when she saw Brigitte come home in the police cruiser, for the first time, with her policeman. The phone rang. She jumped up. She brushed away the dried tears from the corners of her eyes; and she smiled. Her prince had not forgotten her. She practised her greeting, and then said, "Hello, Michael." But it was Dots on the phone. "I thought you was coming down here at the Education College with that man o' yours." Bernice could hear Sparrow laughing in a calypso, *Not a woman ever complain yet...* "He here, yuh know. That bastard you supporting, he here, licking out your ten-dollar bill 'pon one with long blonde hair!" When morning came, cold and bitter and with a wind, Bernice had not yet taken off the white dress, nor the wrap, nor the kid gloves, which looked as if time had withered them on to her hands — nor had she replaced the telephone receiver. She never wore that white dress again. And that was what it meant to her, seeing Estelle put it on. And never did she set her eyes on her student-prince again. In the kitchen the next morning, tired and sleepy and vexed, she heard Mrs. Burrmann make one comment when she was given back the fur wrap and the gloves: "*Men!*")...But imagine me, dreaming so early this Sunday morning. She then realized, that in all this time, she had said nothing either to Dots or Boysie; but time was now playing tricks upon her; and so was reality. She forgot she was not at her window, waiting for her student-prince, but that she was in a car. She couldn't remember whether it was a moment ago she had seen Brigitte ("Looka that bitch!") taking her policeman through the side entrance; or whether it was that night she waited like Cinderella for her prince to come. She remembered (and still remembers) envying Brigitte, not for the man, *but for possessing a man.* As she closed out that part of her past (which she didn't realize as past), she saw the south-bound traffic on Bathurst thinning out, and Boysie, driving with one hand barely touching the steering wheel. She thought she heard Dots's voice droning, like a voice talking...  "She called me last week, gal. I have ladies calling on me, nowadays. How yuh like that? I belongst to high society these days, gal."

"I always knew there wasn't one damn thing wrong with Agaffa," Boysie cut in. "The two o' you always cussing that woman, but that woman is good as gold."

"And how would you know, Boysie?" Boysie cackled; he enjoyed this kind of a challenge from his wife. But Dots was in her Sunday mood, and she merely added, "Just let me catch you with one o' them! I tell you, *if,* if! I ever catch you with one o' them, well, Jesus Christ himself will have to save you, Boysie Cumberbatch." She let the threat soak in; and she allowed him time to laugh, before she said to Bernice, "Agaffa! Yes, Agaffa called me, gal. At work. And she opened her heart to me. Tell me everything, every-damn-thing: she and Henry was planning to get married, the parents start fussing, and *bram!* She ups and left home."

"*That* is woman!" Boysie exclaimed.

"She left, or she get thrown out?" Bernice asked, not wanting to concede that Henry was worthy of a woman like Agatha. She wanted to smear Agatha too. "I feel she get thrown out. What woman in her right mind would run after a black bastard like him, anyway?"

"Thrown-out, left, or tossed-out, it is the same thing. That is how the white women loves the boys. I know from ex-..." (and when he saw how he almost said "experience," he changed his mind and said), "I know from examples, that the white women gives our boys a damn fair break. So I not surprised that Agaffa left home, stock, lock and barrel to run after Henry. And furthermore. It is love. Love is pain. And pain is love. She love Henry so bad that it caused pain. And by causing pain, it mean it is love."

"But Boysie?"

"Wait, Dots? Where Boysie learn all this 'bout love equal to pain? You sending Boysie to the University?" And they laughed at him, as they always did; it was a vicious, ridiculing, oppressing laugh. It was on Boysie that they took out their bitterness against the white world. But Boysie threw back the laugh on them, and said. "Gorblummuh! one o' these days both you and Bernice will have to address me as Mister Boysie, Esquire, B.A." And they laughed even more at that.

"But Henry damn lucky, though," Dots said, when everybody else had practically forgotten the topic of conversation. "Imagine that! A ordinary ex-porter man, and he has such a rich powerful woman running behind him! Well, some strange things happen in this country."

"That don't matter, Dots. This is one country where it do not matter what kind o' job you have, once you bringing money on a Friday."

"He still blasted lucky! Agaffa is a nice, rich, wealthy girl. And I must say that when she traipsed in your place that time, in fur coat and thing, I hated her like hell. But now, well, it is a different story. She is a lady."

"Henry have a Grand Prize of a woman. And it don't matter a shit to me if Agaffa was white or blue. 'Cause, I says one thing, and it is this. Woman is woman, cunny is cunny, one is one, and two..."

"Watch your mouth, man!" The sharpness in Bernice's

voice cut off further conversation, until sometime later, she said she wanted to talk to Agatha about helping her to find a room for Estelle. Dots said she didn't know her phone number. Boysie said he didn't know it either, but that some funny things could, and do, happen in this country. "Take for an instance," he said, "the time when a man turned up outta the blasted blue and ask me if my name is Boysie Cumberbatch. Now, how in the name o' heaven and hell could a stranger come and ask *me* if my name is really *my* name?"

"That is nothing compared to Clotelle."

"That gal from Grenada?"

"That is the Clotelle I mean. Clotelle who fell prey to one o' them salesman-man, one night..." Bernice re-told the saga of Clotelle, trusting Clotelle, who was waylaid by her own avariciousness for cutlery and by a salesman. The story was known to every West Indian in Toronto, because it was in the newspapers. But the way Bernice told it... ("That salesman-man sweetened-up Clotelle and she signed to buy up everything for the wedding she was planning, because she had just bring up her old boyfriend from Grenada. Clotelle buy-up silvers, knife and fork, spoon, sugar bowl, cream bowl, and the knives and forks even had something called a coat of arms with Clotelle's initials and insignias carved in them. And the salesman-crook told Clotelle they weren't hard to pay for. But when the first instalment payment came, ninety-five dollars and five cents! Clotelle borrowed money from Sacrificial Finance Company and had to turn round and borrow money *needlessly* from Withold Corporation to pay back Sacrificial, and still the interest was mounting up, higher than the skies. And then, one fine day, Clotelle start looking for a new job, where nobody won't find her. But she didn't know that although this

Toronto is a large city, it ain't so damn big that a finance company can't track you down, and find you, and pin you down to
the ground, Jesus Christ, till they squeeze every last drop of
blood and payments outta you, till that debt squared-off.
Three people was looking for Clotelle. They take out search
warrant for her blood. 'Twas Sacrificial — Lord, deliver me
ever, from them clutches! — Withold and the silvers people.
And when they found Clotelle, they found her sticky and
greasy and smelling like a hospital, working off her arse cooking in another kitchen, the Toronto General Hospital kitchen.
Bram! The finance-man and the bailiff-man or whoever the
hell he was, plus the garnishee-man, all two o' them pounced
on Clotelle, and when they get up offa Clotelle, the Hospital
fired Clotelle, and she was *back in the same white woman
kitchen*, working off her fat, cooking for *less* money now,
because she had to beg for the job, and go back on bended
knees, penitent as hell. One stinking eighty dollars a month.
And no rent-free room, neither! She found a dirty room on
Parliament Street, had to take street-car to and from work up
in Forest Hill, and had to pay off one hundred and fifteen dollars a month, instalments. I don't know where Clotelle get the
other thirty five dollars from, and I won't like to guess; but she
had to pay off them loan-sharks. Barracudas, that's what they
is! So, this place *may* look big; but it isn't so big, in truth. Ask
Clotelle, then!") ... Bernice's mind switched from Clotelle to
Estelle, alone in the apartment, and anybody could go up
there; nobody ain't home but Mr. Burrmann, "'cause this is the
time Mrs. Burrmann takes the children skating, and Estelle
probably is still undressed, oh Christ! and I forgot to lock that
door behind me! and she probably still slouching round on
the damn chesterfield, too"... and she took it upon herself

to compose a letter in her mind to Mammy, about Estelle's behaviour:

*Dear Mammy, How are you? I hope the reaches of this letter will find you in a perfect state of good health, as it leaves me feeling fairly well, at present. Estelle here. But things are not working out as I did figure they would work out. But I putting everything in God hands, and all I can do now, is wait. I am making up a parcel with a few odds and ends, to send to you, including a dress and a pair of shoes...* She tore up that letter, in her mind, and considered writing one to Lonnie, who had been resting heavily on her conscience since Estelle arrived; and since she saw the folly of having sent for her. But before she thought more of Lonnie, she began again to think of Estelle, in the apartment alone: "...wonder what she is up to, now? That girl make me so vexed this morning, and I, a Christian-minded person had to tell her such hard things, my own flesh-and-blood, Christ! I haven't left nothing now for anybody to say to her. Bernice, you have treated that girl, your sister, worse than a slut, wishing that a man (her thoughts ran over Mr. Burrmann like a spotlight, travelling from his head to his toes: and she winced the thoughts out of her mind) would breed Estelle, and give her an unwanted child, Lord God!"...

*Dear Lonnie. Sometimes you make me so blasted vexed with all your asking and begging, that I sometimes have to consider myself a woman who must be a damn fool, or mad. Imagine me up here, in this cold climate, working for next to peanuts and supporting a blasted hardback man like you! Lonnie, you think I borned yesterday? You think you is such a Valentino that I am hard-up and crazy over you? Blind you, Lonnie! when I begged you and beseeched you and practically kissed your behind to put a ring on my finger, and make me the lady any decent man would*

*want to make of his woman in childbirth, be-Christ, Lonnie, you
know what you did? You turn and run, and run, Lonnie, 'cause
you was a coward 'gainst responsibilities. And now you have the
gall writing me a letter to ask for a suit to wear to church.
Christmas morning? Well, Lonnie, I think so much of you and
what you stand for, that I advise you to wear the one you was
borned in, if you was ever borned. Go and face the Bishop in that,
heh-heh-ha-hah!* and here her letter ran out, because the power
of her bitterness against Lonnie and against men, was so strong
it burned up her imagination. She addressed herself *directly*
to Lonnie now (she felt she was actually speaking to him, in
the flesh) "*Lonnie, listen to me! if, if I give you a second chance,
if we could fix up things and put our two heads together, you
think you could behave like a man, even half a man?*" (Bernice
herself answered for Lonnie, "Perhaps!" She answered so em-
phatically, she thought Dots had heard.) "*I am going to send a
plane ticket for you, because this country wasn't discovered
for a woman who do not have a man as a companion. But I am
going to watch you with both my eyes. You not playing no games
with me, like this Boysie here, worthless Boysie who is always two-
timing Dots, you hear? Or be-Christ, I kill you, Lonnie! I am
a woman pushing forty years now, and no man hasn't come yet
telling me I beautiful, and that I sweet . . .*"

"But Bernice, how you think the finance people track-down
Clotelle?" Dots was thinking about her over-due payments on
the old Chevrolet, and about the sewing machine she had bought
from a salesman. "Millions and millions o' people in this city!"

"White people, Dots," Bernice said, tidying her mind to
answer. "They have invented every device and contraption for
tracking down people and things. You ain't see they even tracking down the moon these days, child?"

"You know something?" Boysie said. "A German fellar, a immigrant like me, or you, tell me they have a big book with all the names and addresses and jobs of people, living in this city. That book is lock up, always under lock and key in the Parliament Buildings, below there on Queen's Park. This German fellar say, that any man at all, once that man living here — even if he moved in the city for half day! — all you got to do, is consult with that book, and that man is *found*!"

"But Boysie, where do you get these stories from?"

"I is a man who associates with people in the know," he said proudly. "I looks at my position in this country this way. I come into this country, gorblummuh! to *stay*. And I figures that my stay here could only be better if I mix-in with the people in command here, not with West Indians." Not a man with much finesse and modesty, Boysie was always conscious of his inferiority to Dots (he did not think of Bernice in this way) and when he had a chance to make a point, he always overstated it. It was this way with other things too. Like the way he parked the car now: spinning the steering wheel, when he knew it couldn't turn any more; and then allowing the wheel to unwind itself and spin through his hands. He always wanted to impress whoever was present. He was now impressing Bernice and Dots, but particularly Bernice. Bernice and Dots shrugged their winter coats into place; adjusted their hats, and looked prepared. Boysie turned off the engine before applying the brakes, and the car jerked and then stopped. He opened his door, slammed it hard and said, "I think I going wait here, in the car, till you and..."

"You coming with we! Church don't bite."

"But Dots..."

"If you got it in your head to dodge back up there and

crawl behind Brigitte, and you think you leaving me in this hot, stuffy church, listening to that damn fool talk 'bout God, looka Boysie! don't make Satan get in my behind today...." Boysie slammed the door again, and dragged his winter boots through the snow and went into the church. "That bastard!"

"He better be careful that the policeman Brigitte got don't bathe his behind in licks one o' these days!" Bernice said, joking. But deep down she was not joking. Dots made a note of it, too. Bernice saw this; but after all, the damage was already done. They did things to their faces in small pocket compacts; they applied a fresh layer of white powder so that when they were finished, the colour and the texture on their faces were noticeably different from that of their necks. Bernice smacked her lipstick into place.

"Getting out of a car in the winter time is hell, eh, gal?" It was difficult for her to keep her legs closed. A white man, standing opposite and drinking out of a paper bag, was looking at her. "Looka that bitch!" Bernice hadn't noticed. "There! He spying up under me, you can't see that?" Bernice saw him. In a lower voice, Dots said to the man, so that he couldn't hear, "*Spy! Spy, you bitch!* 'cause you never see nothing so pretty, so get a good eyeful!" Bernice almost choked with laughter. The man did not hear; and he did not stop looking and he did not stop drinking. Perhaps he was frozen stiff, frozen dead. Just before entering the church, Bernice told Dots that Estelle wasn't working out at all. Dots commiserated with her.

"I want you to help me look for a room tomorrow. Perhaps you could get Agaffa to see if she know a place, 'cause she would have a better chance getting a better place...."

"Yes, gal."

Mr. Burrmann had been reading *The New Class* by Milovan Djilas, for the past two hours. He would find himself following the argument on page 131, and becoming engrossed in what Djilas was saying; and he would shake his head, and realize he had read the passage already. It had taken him about forty-five minutes to finish page 130. He was worried this morning, a dull Sunday morning; and he was lonely. Mrs. Burrmann had taken Putzi and the children to the neighbourhood skating rink. He had seen Bernice leave for church.

On these mornings, when he was alone, he would read in his study, or listen to very progressive jazz which his wife called "vulgar and certainly not the kind of music a man in your position should waste time listening to, why don't you ever try to improve your mind, you're so damn vulgar for a lawyer!" But jazz and not Beethoven was what Mr. Burrmann grew up with, on Palmerston Boulevard. He used to spend all the time he could, and his money too, listening to black musicians from America, who came to play at the Silver Dollar, and at an inconspicuous establishment, euphemistically named The TNT. With the jazz and black women and whiskey and the crap games, he had had his share of Negro culture. He had thrown dice with the Harlem-like men, and have even consciously imitated their mannerisms, and a few of their diversions, such as smoking marijuana, because he had found his own orthodox life dull and boring. But he had emerged "clean" from all this, because he had his university degree and was ambitious; and he wanted to be a lawyer. One aspect of his Spadina days never left him: it was the complete satisfaction he had known, while in the thighs of a large vulgar-laughing black woman named A-Train, who roared in and out of the El Mocombo Tavern, like an express train, singing rhythm-and-blues. It was

A-Train who had done that *thing* to him, with such vulgarity and completeness, that it never left his mind or body. And he would think of it, as he was thinking about it this morning, and cold shivers would run down his spine like an ecstatic paralysis. When she was finished with him, she held him like a baby in her arms (she was two hundred pounds and had muscles like Mohammad Ali, the heavyweight champion of the world) and put her face close to his, and shouted in his ears, "Sammy baby, you ain't nothing but a child, a little teeny child." And she dropped him out of her arms, and he fell on the broken, many-tongued springs of the rented bed. And he started to cry. "Get to hell out, Sammy. And don't you ever come back till you's a *man!*"

Throughout his married life, the terror of responsibility in bed, plus the fact that he was conscious he was marrying Rachel Gladys Heinne, heiress to a million dollars in slum-house real estate (he had lived in one of those very slum houses owned by Miss Heinne's father, who came to Canada broke, in 1909, from Poland), had instilled a certain resentment for the woman who became his wife; and it accounted (so his psychiatrist told him) for a certain drying up of his energies and his love, whenever he made love to her. He always thought he was going to have a child whenever he made love to his wife; and he was terrified that he would have to marry her: *although at the time, he was already married to her.* His hate for A-Train and the truth she had done to him and had told him; and also Mrs. Burrmann's attitude to sex, did nothing to help untangle the mesh of emotions and deep fears which took him in their arms whenever he wanted a woman. After some time, Mrs. Burrmann herself went to a fashionable psychiatrist in the Bloor Street Colonnade; and she sent Sammy to one in the

Medical Arts Building, several blocks away, on the same street. (He was thinking this morning, that he never did satisfy his own curiosity about this action of his wife's: and he, a man, had allowed her to tell him what to do, and which expert to consult about *his* problems. He resented her more for that: she was being superior again; laughing at him for making the problems and then helping him to solve them.) After the first meeting, his psychiatrist told him, "Sammy, leave, man!" and go home and try "it" in as many attitudes and states of mind until Mrs. Burrmann understood "her natural role." It was all very confusing, and not a little ridiculous. But Mr. Burrmann never tried "it." *It* had already become repulsive to him. And he never did find out what her psychiatrist told her.

The complete destruction of pride brought upon his sensibilities by A-Train, in those loud, whorling-whirlpool Spadina days, would sometimes cause him to search for his lost manhood, among the European coffee shops on Bloor Street West; and later, in Yorkville Village. In his law firm where he was a brilliant corporation lawyer (this was another variation of his earlier ambition to be the best Jewish criminal lawyer in the Upper Canada Law Society's history, which happened midway through the University of Toronto Law School, because he had succeeded in putting Jeffrey and Jeffrey's burden out of his mind; and he had decided he wanted nothing to do with civil rights and people who have those problems: he wanted a fresh, clean un-sordid law practice) he kept to himself, whenever that was possible. But he was always searching: in the evenings he would visit the coffee houses in the Village, where the candle-light was only bright enough for him to read *Playboy* and *Foreign Affairs*; and weak enough for his austere business suit with subtle pinstripe to appear like badly cut, off-the-rack hipster's *threads*. His search would take him into daydreams over the red-and-white checkered tablecloths, between the soot and the flickering hopes of the candles and the "free" women, young and maidened, upright as virgins in common-law packages: and always he would think of bizarre experiences with these women, especially one who was tall and willowy and daring in her walk, and shabby and thin, even for a model, and who wore her hair long and stringy and uncombed like the tail of a horse. There must be a variation; there must be love; there must be women to *try IT in as many attitudes and states of mind until they understood their natural role*: but all the women he had loved, before and after his marriage, always left — they left town; or left life; or left fornication; or left love. But they left; they all left; but before leaving him they told him they had to leave "in order to be fair, because I want you to know before I do anything, since it is the least bit of decency I can do." Many times, in coffee houses, the Penny Farthing, the Act One Scene One, the Half Beat, he tried "it" within the free regions of his mind, *in as many attitudes and states of mind* as time would allow, as it took the horse-hair woman to drink her expresso coffee: but the thought of his wife, in her attitudes, intervened. His wife's attitudes to *it*, when all the things essential to the after-cleanliness of the performance, were brought into the bedroom; and were placed on the marble-topped dressing table. There were clean, fresh, fleshy towels: one for him, inscribed HIS; and one for her, significantly christened, HERS, and "by-God, one of these days, or nights, I'm gonna use the *wrong* towel, HERS! and then I'll see if I contract syphilis, or some damn incurable disease . . ."; and scented by Chanel. The vaseline was there too; not in a cheap jar as bought from Woolworth's or Kresge's; and marked VASELINE, which was really what it was, but in an apothecary's jar which Mrs. Burrmann had bought at an art shop on Cumberland Street. The jar was inscribed OINTMENT, written on skin-colour Band-Aid, in red ink! The most recent passions of sex to come to his mind, were twice within the last three months, when on her insistence, they did "it" twice — on her birthday; and on their tenth wedding anniversary. Mrs. Burrmann was brought up in an orthodox Jewish home with Christian dispositions, and was taught that it was more proper to use phrases instead of the medical terms, which were synonymous with those phrases. She would wear the thin red silk nightgown, bought from Macy's in New York; and silk negligées which did not hide her body, and which were not meant to. And this bothered Mr. Burrmann: this temptation. On those nights of sex, she would come into her bedroom which had a large circular double bed, and which was separated from the other room by a short hallway and a door. Rachel Gladys Heinne-Burrmann (this is how her name appeared on her personal stationery of blue paper; but he called her, when he called her, Glad)... *Glad would lie there, God, on her back, like a cloud fallen to the ground* (he was talking to the woman of his dreams, as she drank her expresso, but she could not hear him, because he did not intend it to be that kind of conversation. He was talking to her spirit, which he knew could hear his words; he was complaining to her, like a child searching faces of adult unconcern for a welcomed ear)... *and she would lie there, still as the dead body of Mary, not Jesus's mother, but Mary who went to call the cattle home and call the cattle home across the Sands of Dee, and whose body was found later, in the moss and sunset beds of floating death, in the River Dee; waiting waiting and preparing as if for a goddamn operation in a hospital, permitting the ether of desire to work itself through her body, and for the Benedictine and Brandy to take the feel of his hands and body, from her body; and with the Vaseline, oh God, no, the* OINT-MENT, *the towels, the wash basin and ewer which she picked up at a bargain in Yorkville Village on Yorkville Street at a shop which sold toilet bowls and other ointmentations.... Christ! that's a good word! must remember that one — ointmentations for bowls and bowels...Sam you're going crazy as hell, loony nutty stark-lark-goddamn crazy!...and Glad'll bring in glasses, two glasses, crystal, the only two of a wedding present; and the tall decanter of B and B. And you, like a goddamn fool, would come in, see her, your wife, and your goddamn head'll start to spin just like the time when A-Train did that awful thing to you, you goddamn little teeny boy* (what A-Train did to Sammy Burrmann, was so tantalizingly ticklishly spine-tingling-gee-gee-gigglish, that he never once clothed the thought of it in words, when he thought of it) *you weren't even a man enough to admit to yourself that you wanted to go to bed with Bernice, your maid.... Goddamn, Sam, you're slipping, baby! going to bed, and you can't even call it by its real name, you goddamn..."Miss? Miss? Would you like to work for me? I'm a lawyer, you know; and I can give you a job in my law firm. Bay Street, right in the financial, fine-arsial centre of Toronto."* He was feeling tired; and he got up, stretched and rubbed his eyes, and continued to read. For the first time, he saw the words on page 131. "What?" he said, almost shouting. He rubbed his eyes and read the passage aloud: *"While announcing that he was freeing man's spiritual personality, he degraded man's civil personality to the blackest slavery."* He could not believe it; he read it, studied it, read it over again. "Blackest slavery? Could Djilas be thinking, even remotely, of Bernice? Or Estelle?" And further down, he read: *"... Stendhal observed how young men and young women carried on conversations only about 'the pastor.'"* . . . So many things were troubling him, in his searches; so many things. He got up from his desk, put on some progressive jazz, and went into the kitchen to pour himself a double bourbon, straight, and without ice cubes. . . .

The snow is falling again. Estelle looks out and sees the skies polka-dotted white on white. She is happy. "Canada is a nice place. I like it here." When Bernice returns she must ask her again about becoming a landed immigrant: *immigrant reçu.* She sits at Bernice's window, and dreams of home: wonder what Mammy is doing now, at this minute? Wonder if the pains in her head are better? Lonnie, poor stupid Lonnie was vexed as hell when I came instead of him. Wonder what time it is in Barbados, right now? God, I bet nobody in Barbados ever saw snow falling so pretty!

Those footsteps that stopped outside the door the afternoon she was "processing" Bernice's hair, were like a thirst that had to be quenched, a tantalizing of the mind that had to be satisfied. But she was frightened: she was faced now with something she had never known in her life, back in Barbados.

Estelle was a woman, upright morally, in the terms of that loose licentiousness of life in a slum area. She was ambitious. Ambitious with men, the way Bernice was ambitious with her bank account at the Royal Bank of Canada. She was sorry she didn't go to church, even after the quarrel. But she decided to remain — *home.* She had actually thought out the word, home. Home to Estelle was any place where she couldn't see Mammy; where she couldn't see the poverty of her village and the villagers; where she didn't have to go behind the house (within the tall rotting paling) to go to the outdoor closet, in

rain, in wind and in the sun. Home was *Away*. Away from that
home. And to make her escape from poverty and the fear of
poverty, finally final, she had put Mammy in the Poor House,
in the care of the parish. This made her nervous and guilty
every time Bernice inquired of Mammy. She had to get rid
of Mammy, which she did, ten months before she left. She
worked it out carefully, in her mind, this terrible fraud she had
to play upon Bernice. It was a fraud; and it was not a fraud.
Mammy was losing her sight and her health; Mammy never
really possessed the sight nor the right of the pen, and she
had to write and read all the letters from Bernice. She spent all
the money sent, on Mammy. This was her great honesty. But
now that Mammy was in the Poor House, Bernice would
probably find out, some day. This fear never permitted Estelle
to relax.

Mammy didn't care to hear about Canada, and the problems Bernice wrote about. Mammy only insisted on signing
her own name at the bottom of each letter, herself. That was
the personal freedom she insisted upon; and she refused to
sign, until Estelle had read to her what she had told Estelle to
write to Bernice, her girl child, "up there in that terrible place,
by herself."

She was thinking of the footsteps again; imagining things,
dreams about the owner of the footsteps: *he is downstairs, having breakfast with his wife and children; and he's just taken a strip
of bacon which Bernice has fried before going to church* (she
dressed herself in Bernice's uniform and body; and herself took
over serving breakfast); she sees dangers in those thoughts, so
she stops thinking them. She thinks of the time Agatha took
her to the Towne Tavern to hear Joe Williams sing and roar
and curse in the blues: *and there's this old black woman in the*

*washroom for women. But what the hell is she doing in there?*
*Does she have to wash their hands? wipe them? kiss their backsides*
*after they use the toilet?*...Through the window, she sees
Brigitte opening her window, holding more than half of her
body through it; and she debates whether to call her, but it
"don't look good, decent to see a person shouting through
a window." Brigitte waves a hand; Estelle looks and a man
appears; and Brigitte closes the window, and the curtains.
Blasted Brigitte, blast her! Estelle says; blast Agatha, blast
Bernice, blast *everybody!* "I should tidy up this damn apartment...I wish, I could wash some panties...I should comb
my hair...I should wash some nightgowns...I would like to
cook a Sunday meal for Bernice...Christ, I can't do nothing,
nothing nothing in this blasted fancy apartment!" There is
nothing in the apartment except a clothes closet, a chesterfield,
a coffee table, two metal chairs, a matching metal table, a
dressing table and a bathroom. Estelle turns on the radio:
church! "Church, church, church, hell!" She turns off the
radio, goes into the bathroom, closes the door, and shouts,
"*Jesus Christ!*" four times. But not even this lamentation can be
heard: her loneliness is soundproof. She opens the bathroom
door, comes to the chesterfield (she is still in her slip) and she
wishes aloud, that she was dead, "I could kill myself now, I
could kill myself"; and she falls on the chesterfield as if she was
really dead, wishing she were dead.

When she opened her eyes, the man was there. Not a word
passed from his lips to her. She did not say anything, either.
When she realized it was he, she raised herself from the
chesterfield, clutching her slip to conceal the black tips of her
breasts and to hide the transparent sweetness of her beautiful

body from his eyes. She was watching him: he was watching
her. She sat back on the chesterfield (there was nothing else her
terror permitted her to do: she didn't wish to scream) and she
held her head down. There were no words; there was no need
for words. He came right inside, finally, through the door
which, for the second time, Bernice had forgotten to lock.
Estelle was frightened. Rape? She had thought of it happening.
She had actually urged it on in her mind; but she had hoped
it would never happen. Now it was about to happen. She lay
back on the chesterfield (things were becoming difficult to
think about, to do) her right hand running down the fresh,
ready-to-cut fields of her right side, beside the mountains and
valleys of her body. Her eyes were on the ceiling: and instead
of God, or a prayer, they saw cobwebs; and she heard herself
thinking, "Bernice isn't such a clean housekeeper as she thinks
she is!"; and her legs, outstretched, dead, not inviting, just
there where he saw them as two plains swept by a wind to
make them look sparse of vegetation. The man came to the
chesterfield, standing over her like a landlord and not a lover;
desire in his body and fear in his eyes; and with a nervous anx-
iety, because of the passion and the lust in his body, which
turned his smile into a criminal's grin. But she had made him
suffer long enough; she would have to save him now — from
his conscience and from the deceit of his white body. Never in
his life, had he seen a naked body which did this paralysis to
his mind...and so, rushed into the luscious valleys and caverns
of her love, he felt himself going down down down into an
inextricably unexplored nothingness. It sucked him up in its
thighs and held him there, suspended; and it made him bawl
in his heart for murder and joy. This was a new pleasure; his
new ecstasy, so complete and so hurtful that it was unbearable

to continue, or to stop. And in the midst of this confusion, he did a very strange thing (though in his life, it could not, through its repetition, be now considered a strange thing) *he actually compared this woman with his wife, and with A-Train:* being careful to note the many attitudes and states of mind. Nothing, nothing before in his life, was like this. It was all driving, all searching, all exploring. Thoughts rushed into his brain: the vomit in A-Train's room above the junk shop on Spadina; the B and B in the drugstore of his wife's bedroom; the coffee-house girl; A-Train's disgust, and his wife's disgust at his incompetence...quarrels between his father and his mother, long ago in the dark, heavy, dog-smelling front room on Palmerston Boulevard; and he saw Dachau and Auschwitz; he saw torment of bodies emaciated, tortured, twisted out of all human form and dimensions; and he saw Jeffrey being beaten by the ugly red-faced white policeman who had recently left the immigrant boat from Ireland; and he saw the pain and the humanity in Jeffrey's mother's face, as she told him, thirty years ago, "You's going to pay for your silence, one o' these good days." He was now like a man in a canefield, ploughing with the threat of rain behind him, and in the skies; a man having to complete his ploughing because of his commitment, because rain and wages are enemies. And a sensation like madness takes command of him: now he is a man in a sea, a rough turbulent foreign sea with the waves coming up to his shoulders and up to his neck and to his mouth and finally into his nostrils. He feels himself called to his grave, to his death, a soaking, wet death. He wants to die; but he struggles to keep off the death which he knows he cannot really keep off; and does not want to withhold. And now a child: the short, fat, well-fed child of Palmerston Boulevard, in the bosom of his mother; naked as the child at night, surrounded by terror and grown people, shapeless as the monsters of shadows on the walls of the curtain-partition behind which he saw once, the movements of his mother, undressing; and everything coming down at once, clothes, thunder and rain, and his father's foreign voice brought back sterner and louder and deeper from the Paramount Tavern; a child, complete even in its willingness to be scourged and loved, and in its willingness to be a child, because a child cannot be anything else.

This was the purity of the action as he writhed in the pain of love; thinking of that country, Poland, far away from his life where his history had begun and ended; thinking there was nothing beyond his semi-illiterate father and his silent mother, nothing further back than twenty years, to his life; of his failures in life and in love, and of his successes in his profession; and of his great insatiable desire for this black woman beneath him.

And she, the woman; the mother, opening herself to take him in, swallowing him, because she wanted to teach him a damn good lesson. For she could see he was a child, dressed in man's thoughts. She was the land. She was the land through which he had to travel like a man exploring, cutting through a jungle of vines that obstructed his path and vision. He was the traveller through this land, searching for the end at the other side, for enlightenment. And she, like the land, possessing *the* power, did not insist on blocking his path; but allowed him the arrogance and the comfort of trampling his feet on the black soil of her body. She was the land. And he, the explorer. She was the land, with her hands cupped before him, like the hands of his rabbi with a crumb of everlasting joy in them, offering this little blessing which he saw as a bounty. She was saying to the machette, Cut, cut, cut, there is willingness here to endure this blessing of the pain and the violence of your search. *Cut!* And he, not wanting to end, though tired, but still wanting to end, was now brushing back the last vines from his path, and from his eyes, using his hands like a madman struggling in a sea with breast strokes of panic. "A-Train! A-Train! Glad! Glad! Coffee-house-girl! look at me now," he was saying. "This is love. Do not let it end!" His pleas shut out the exhaustion from his groans and groins, and he thought he was still listening to a surging voice of a jazz saxophone: the voice of John Coltrane, romping through *Chasing the Trane* alone, unaccompanied in glee and pain. He could see, not hear, the surges of the voice pushing on, straining on, *chasing* on in its turbulence; and a gigantic boulder came down a hill dragging everything in its way with it; the voice in the instrument became a human voice, not the cry of the reed, but the blood and the sweat of the man playing the instrument and of the man listening. They were all three of them searching: the voice, the man, the explorer. But the clearing was in sight. The voice of the man in the instrument was breaking. He could see it, and he could feel it and he could hear it. And she almost completely untouched, merely scratched as a branch in the wind would scratch the land; and conscious that he should not have the pleasure of knowing he had conquered her, she held the land in a death grip and *tightened* the valleys of her thighs until valleys became fjords which stifled him and drained every last drop of song from his body; and she said to him, in a manner he could not hear, *You're going to pay for this, you bastard!* And then she released him from his prison. He saw the horizon coming, and he closed his eyes. He was powerless to see the end. But it had been a journey of love, and a journey of pain and violence. She was laughing because she wanted him to see her laughing; but she was saying inside, *You're going to pay for this rape, white man! Rape!* And the man, unable to face his abuse of beauty and ignorance, scrambled up his shame, and ran out of the room. A-Train was screaming in his ears, from wherever the hell she was, in that noise and jazz of Harlem, *Goo-goo, charlie-pony! goo-goo!*

The man is back in his study. He has bathed. He could not stand the *thought* of the smell. He sits now before the bottle of bourbon (he had emptied half of its contents to give him the courage to climb those stairs to Bernice's apartment) and drinks. The smell of the thought is what he wants to drown. The adventure is over. He is bathed. He smells like a bar of Lifebuoy soap. He has sprinkled a third of his Old Spice After-Shave lotion, and Men's Deodorant, to kill the smell. His thoughts are still upstairs. He feels like a man who has come through two afternoons in one day. He smells her body on his body (even though he lathered thrice and washed it off thrice). He sang in his bath. Had Mrs. Burrmann been home, she would have known. Guilt will not let him feel easy. He feels like a robber. But the smell is on him; and in him. On his shirt (which is a clean, white shirt, laundered by Bernice); and on his hands (he is always putting them to his mouth — not his nostrils); on his mind. And he wonders why.

He opens *The New Class*, and looks at the page; but there is no text on it, only Estelle's body. In the bourbon is the face. He cannot get rid of them. Finally, he decides he does not want to get rid of them. He has a new power and new glory now: his wife drifts into the background of impotence; he feels he is free of the inferiority of being unable to have a son. He knows he can have a son now: from any woman. This man has entered a different zodiac of life. He is in love. With the woman upstairs. And this burden, finally settled and laid down, frees him enough to permit him to take up a book and see the print and read: "*Upon my release from prison, in January 1961...*" He looks at the cover, to find he's taken up the wrong book, *Conversations With Stalin* and not *The New Class*. The mistake is not significant; but things like these, bother him very much. "*Upon my release from prison*"; he turns the words over and over, relishing them. He takes out his pocket diary. He writes down the quotation, on the appropriate date. He wonders whether that morning in January 1961 was also a Sunday morning.

Frequently nowadays, Bernice's meditations and soliloquies took place on the toilet bowl, with the bathroom door locked. Before Estelle came, the door would remain open: and she could spend as much time as she chose in this meditative posture, reading her *Muhammad Speaks*. She could sing her Hymns Ancient and Modern in there; she could laugh at jokes she made up; she could laugh at Mrs. Burrmann and at Dots even — she could do everything, anything in there. Recently, it was becoming more difficult to enjoy this psychological siesta. She couldn't think with Estelle in the room. Once, the weight of her bladder almost crippled her into immobility: Estelle was in the bathroom, running the water; and Bernice was almost overcome, and then she felt her own water starting to drip, drip, her pants were dripping, dripping until she managed to reach the children's bathroom, and there the oppressiveness of both Estelle and her bladder exploded, and she said, "Ahhh!"; and after the comfort of relief, going back upstairs, to find the water in her own bathroom still running and above the noise of the water, Estelle singing "*I Want To Hold Your Hand.*"

"In my own place, I can't even go to the blasted toilet when I have to!" And to think that only the other day she was bragging to Dots about her good judgement in bringing up Estelle, in preference to Lonnie.

"You should have bring up Estelle in the summer, though," Dots felt. "In the summer, the missy and the children and the master all gone their separate ways, and you rule this roost."

"Yes. She gone to Nassau, he to the north, shooting and drinking and the kids at summer camp, Christ! this whole mansion could be mine! Estelle could have slept on my chesterfield, and I downstairs in the kiddies' room."

The apartment was becoming smaller every day; untidier, every hour. Bernice had kept the bathroom clean (even smelling clean) by various toilet washes and detergents. The chesterfield had been covered by a piece of Mexican blanket brought for her by Mrs. Burrmann. But when Estelle arrived, Bernice took it off, and replaced it with plastic cloth. Estelle was raucous. Bernice was shocked to see how her centre table was smeared. This table was her pride. She polished it every Saturday night until she saw her face smiling in it, until sometimes, she thought it was a crystal ball showing her the licentiousness of Dots and Boysie dancing and drinking rum-and-ginger down at the WIF club. She didn't really grudge them their leisure: she had her apartment to clean. It was therefore heart-breaking to see the first smudges like paw-prints walking at random across her table, like the fingers of a cat. On the glass which covered the dressing table top, were the same finger-prints of paws which roamed through lipstick and pink powder. "Powder all over my blasted table top! Clothes dropped behind the bath tub! Estelle's pads staring wide open! Oh Jesus God, when are you going to deliver me from this rat?" (Bernice stopped buying the same brand of sanitary pads when she saw that Estelle's brand was not covered in the green drugstore paper to hide its brand name, and the contents. "I lonely as hell here, and I send for a woman? Christ, am I in love with woman? Am I one o' them?") Estelle's voice grew louder, in the melody of *Down Town*; and Bernice purposely dropped the lid of the toilet bowl; flushed the toilet noisily, and rattled things about. The small bathroom even had a different smell: an Estelle-smell. Bernice held her hands to her head to shut out the noise and the headache. She screamed, "*Estellllllll!*" And Estelle came to the door, opened it quietly and asked, "Bern, dear, are you all right?" All Bernice could do was to take the doorknob out of Estelle's hand, close the door, and ask the turquoise-coloured ceiling, "When?"

Two subsequent events warned Bernice that it would take a long time to get rid of Estelle. The first was that Estelle managed to get her visitor's visa extended (even before the first six months were expired) through the help of Agatha. Agatha had been seeing her fairly often. The second was that Agatha couldn't get the two-room flat which she told Dots was for rent. It had been rented a week earlier. Agatha suggested a rooming house on Huron, or on Sussex, but Bernice said no. "I not sending Estelle so near to that bastard, Henry. Not me. She may be bad, but the bitch is still my sister, and I responsible for her."

"But she ain't a child, gal! And furthermore, you had better watch her, 'cause people talking."

"What you mean, Dots, by people talking?"

"People talking." There was a long pause on the line; and there was something like a laugh. Bernice became tense; she gripped the receiver, and pressed it against her ear, and she thought — no, she was certain — she heard two persons, women, in the background sniggering. "I putting you on your guard. People talking. And I gone now, 'cause I damn busy." Dots cut off the conversation. Bernice did not sleep that night. She worried, she imagined, she put the puzzle of the remark together, and all she saw was a jig-saw of confusion. That night also, she prayed to God, for strength and guidance. But it was long in coming. It didn't come even with the dawn which caught her at the window, thinking: *who could the man be, causing people to talk about my sister?* (Something put it into her head that it was a man; and a married man. She was wise enough to know that people don't talk if there is a single man and a single woman.) *I hope it ain't that man Estelle come up on the plane with, and I hope that bitch Agaffa ain't up to no damn tricks with my sister, 'cause some o' these rich Jewish women horny as hell, and they always on the prowl for excitement....* (She narrowed it down to a man: a married man; a married white man. She thought of and discounted Henry; she had discounted Boysie, the only married man she knew. She knew Dots and every other West Indian woman had been watching out for Boysie. The jig-saw puzzle was falling into place.) *It is a man, I know that, 'cause Estelle don't like women! But which man? It is a man, Lord, but who? Who man?* (She could only fit those two pieces into the puzzle, before she fell asleep.) *A man, but who, Lord? Who man?*

The next day, Bernice saw a FOR RENT sign in the meat store beside the drug store where she was buying some vaseline for

Mrs. Burrmann. In one glance she took in all the information on the sign. She was self-conscious about being caught reading a FOR RENT sign in this exclusive district. When she got back, she made the call from the kitchen phone. And she had to talk softly, because Mrs. Burrmann was in the sitting-room reading.

"You still have the room for rent?" she whispered into the phone. She was self-conscious also about her accent which she feared might be detected, and her chances of renting the room destroyed. So she tried to speak in an English accent. It was the same accent she used when she wanted to impress Mrs. Burrmann, or a salesgirl at Eaton's. "Have you got a room for rent?"

"Oh yes, yes!" It was a secure voice, an old voice. "Are you interested?" But before Bernice could say she was, the voice went on talking as if it had not talked for a very long time, and had to. "Carpets in both rooms, although I'm asking rent for one room only now, and a very lovely window, actually a bay window, and a fireplace..." and before Bernice could say anything, the voice had changed the topic to something else: "and since I'm a Christian person myself, I don't want to force my principles of living on you, so there's a television and a record player in the room also, and don't be shy in using it, because noise doesn't bother me nowadays, since I have a slight difficulty hearing out of one ear...." Bernice didn't think she could afford such a room, judging by its description. But the woman was talking again. "Are you a Christian, too, dear?"

"Well.... Yes, I is a Christian person."

"Oh that's fine! Myself, I'm Baptist."

Bernice didn't know which denomination to give. If she said British Methodist Episcopal Church, the woman might

know she was black; and she didn't know whether Unitari-
anism was a denomination, or not. "Well, I used to belong
to them but to tell the truth, lately I been worshipping at
the United Church, and sometimes, I goes across to the
Christian..."

"Oh my dear, child! Those Unitarian people don't believe
in God. They haven't a religion as such, you know, dear?"

"Yes, but I still regards myself as a staunch Baptist."
Bernice was getting confused. She had the room, and yet having the wrong religion or denomination, it could slip from her.
"I agree with you, ma'am, for I know that them people doesn't
have no religion as such..." (She suddenly realized that she
had been lapsing into her Barbadian dialect. She wondered
whether it had been noticeable.) "... and rightly so, that is one
rational thing that caused me to entertain second considera-
tion concerning worshipping in an institution...."

"Come over, come over," the woman's voice interrupted.
"When you come, and you may come any time, I'll show you
my watercolours, and if you come today, you can sample my
chocolate cake."

That was it. "Estelle, you moving out bright and early
tomorrow morning. Take that!" She had made the appointment while butterflies skiied and mountain-climbed inside
her. She thanked the woman, too many times; and she thanked
God, once; and the woman's God (for who could doubt, that
she and this woman had the same God?). She even smiled with
the music coming from the sitting-room. There was a bit of
a storm gathering in the music, and in her plans. The rest of
the morning went like a piece of snow in the sun, on the first
day of spring. She was so happy, so relieved, that of her own
wish, she took a new glass and a new set of ice cubes into the

sitting-room of music and reading, and dress-making, for Mrs. Burrmann. "But you is a real first-class dress-maker, in truth, ma'am!"

Mrs. Burrmann looked up, and smiled. She too was having a fine day. "Bernice, dear! You look so tired. So why don't you go up and take a rest? Oh! and Bernice? go into my bedroom and you'll see a dress on the bed. Why don't you see if it'll fit Estelle, eh?"

"Yes, ma'am," she said. Turning away, she added, "You handling that needle-and-cotton like a master!" Back in the kitchen, she held back the aquamarine plastic curtains in the aquamarine kitchen and looked out into the back yard. There was a swallow chirping on the fence of icicles. "Spring here, already?" she wondered. She joined the bird in praise of the end of the bitter winter. When the swallow flew away, she knew it had been only one day of reprieve from the blues of winter.

Later that afternoon, the day turned sour. Winter returned. She slipped out from Estelle listening to the Ten Top Tunes, and ran along the sidewalk, unmindful of the slippery ice. Ice to her meant death. Through ice, she had met the most embarrassing moments of her life on Marina Boulevard. It happened one day, returning from Eaton's with a handful of parcels bought with her "charge plate," when she noticed the streets weren't cleaned. It was the first time in the history of Forest Hill that the public works department had made this slip. She saw the ice and she walked cautiously: putting one foot forward and not daring to move the other foot until she could feel her two hundred pounds securely balanced. Crawling like this, as cautious as a hearse in a funeral, she fastened her eyes on the enemy beneath. She was going well. Harry-etta on the ice! And then, Brigitte her friend, looked out and saw her, and called out to her. The left foot did not make contact with anything beneath it; her right foot was already in motion; something like a chill gripped her and took the rhythm out of her body, and she saw nothing but the melting snow man on the Muhlens' lawn. And when she hit, there was a resounding thud. Brigitte opened her window wider than it had ever been opened before, and she shrieked and bawled and laughed and cried, "Darrr-link! darlink!"; and in a twinkling of an eye of shame, all the windows on Marina Boulevard were filled with heads and faces (she saw four faces in one window) that had opened mouths in them. Scrambling up her parcels, all she could think of was the time she laughed in her heart, at the old woman in the long fur coat, with her hands like paws in kid gloves, who fell on her bottom, once. She felt it was more ridiculous to see her, a big black woman, flat on her arse, on the wide white sidewalk. "Darlink, get up. You break you back?" But Bernice was cursing Brigitte, and all the time, rushing and sliding and slipping and cursing (forgetting to brush off her winter coat) through that shameful afternoon, all the way towards hell and Estelle.

But on this afternoon of crisis, she forgot about the snow on the sidewalk. "Ice, man, go to hell, do! I in a damn hurry!" and she rushed over it like Frank Mahovlich in the Maple Leaf Hockey Stadium. When she arrived at the imposing house, accident-free and puffing, and knocked at the front door, the voice within said, "Come in, come in." Bernice cleaned her boots on three mats placed in the passageway, and entered the sitting-room that smelled like heather and retirement. She could smell chocolate cake. She saw the strange watercolours on the brown panelled walls; but she could not see the woman.

When she took off her ear-muffs and her coat and her scarf and her McGregor tartan which was wrapped around her face, she must have only then come within range of the woman's weak eyes. There was a great intake of breath. Perhaps, the woman had difficulty breathing. "Come in, come in," but there was a different feeling in the welcome. "So you are a Christian? I'm so glad you are a Christian person, dear. It is such a decent thing for you." Bernice opened her mouth to ask about the rent, but the woman was still chattering. "I suppose you saw my watercolours on the way in...milk and sugar?...retirement, you know, is a good thing, you know? ...providing you can provide for yourself. Piece of cake? You must try some of this dee-licious cake....Now, take my case...." And she went on to tell Bernice that her husband was a professor in Classics and Philosophy at a university somewhere in Africa (she called the name but Bernice wasn't listening) and that he died last year of some disease (again Bernice heard the sound of the word, but not the word), and her voice went on like a leaking tap.

"But I come to see the room."

The woman settled herself on her cushions, adjusted her pince-nez, and said, "You are coloured, aren't you, dear? Before you leave..."

"But I come to see..."

"I was saying, before you leave, I wish you would take some of these copies of *Awake* and *The Watchtower*. They are wonderful devotional reading. I'm sure you'll find them rewarding. Don't you know, I've subscribed to *Awake* and *The Watchtower* even when the Professor and I were in Africa, for almost twenty years...and I'm so glad for your sake that you have found God, and you're not like those other coloured people who call themselves Black Muslims. . . . It's a shame, don't you think? and imagine! calling some person like me, a *devil*! . . . such a hateful thing, and such a chip on the shoulders. . . ." Her breath was not staying with her; and Bernice hoped it never would. She brought a small lace handkerchief from some part of her body or the cushions (she was all cloth to Bernice: the only flesh visible was her head) and rested it light on her lips. "I am a Christian."

"I am the person . . ."

"You *must* take along those copies, dear. . . ."

"I come for the room."

Something happened then to the woman's eyes; some film of resentment replaced the little life that was in them. "But surely, you didn't . . ." she began, and a smile of graciousness and dignity and old age and very old long-practised deceit and dishonesty took the place of the film. "I was under the impression you came to talk about Christianity . . . you did say you were a Baptist, you know . . . but you must take *The Watchtower.* . . ."

When Bernice stomped herself in her boots, without having said thanks for the tea and the chocolate cake, and the copies of *Awake* and *The Watchtower* (which she found in her hands) all she could think of, was "That bewitched old bitch! She think I got time to sit on my arse . . . but what the hell is *her* problem, though?" She dropped the copies of *Awake* and *The Watchtower* in a garbage can, as she turned the corner. The moment she did it, conscious always of the power of God's words and God's wrath, she realized that it was a bad thing to do. *Looka me, throwing pearls before swines! that blasted insane woman making me cross-up my damn life with bad luck, eh!* . . . and she would have picked them out of the garbage (she had actually bent down) if a car had not been passing at the same time.

Brigitte came out just as she reached home; and Bernice made her walk back with her to the house she had just left. "Read that sign for me, Brigitte. What that sign saying?" Brigitte read the sign in the front window: "Room, for, rent." And still, not knowing what it was all about, she looked at Bernice and asked, "You leaving Mrs. Burrmann?"

Going back home, Bernice was pensive. Brigitte was grumbling about the amount of work Mrs. Gasstein was giving her. She said they had just quarrelled because she had her boyfriend in her quarters. "I tell you, Bernice darlink. Working for these Jews is terrible. I was a Nazi. I am German. I confess to you, Bernice darlink, that as German, I know what Nazis had in their heart about these people."

"Girl, I understand." Brigitte left to go back to her work. Bernice knew that the old woman with the dead husband was Jewish. "Christ, I ain't the only person with a cross to bear. But at times, it seems so."

When she told it to Dots, all the details, all the strange conversation, the tea, the magazines and the cake, Dots was still shaking her head in bewilderment. "I still can't find no loop-holes in that, gal. I can't find nothing to say, 'gainst that old woman. But then again, gal, you and she is two Christians together, heh-heh-heh! She give you religion and a lot o' religion-talk. But be-Christ, when it come to a room for you to live in, she didn't have nothing to say 'bout that. Figure it out for yourself, gal."

The afternoon papers were full of a tragedy. A woman was killed. She had killed herself. But it was a mistake; because she really wanted to kill the child in her womb. The papers said a lot about "the increasing numbers of unwed mothers, both in and out of high school." Bernice read the story on the front page, as Mrs. Burrmann held it; and she wondered why this country had such strange ways of saying things. Now, instead o' saying pregnant women, who went and get themselves pregnant, they calling them *unwed mothers?* Unwed mothers, hell! They is women. Women who find themselves in the family way. But they is still women; and I know of many cases in which them same women usually make better mothers, and even better wives, when their turn come to be wives, much better than them bitches who, through ring, bible and church have their whoring made legal. I know how them unwed mothers must feel, 'cause I went through the same hell and grievances, myself. And it ain't no bed o' roses, darling!

Mrs. Burrmann put down the paper, and the tragedy of those thousands of Canadians, unknown, unfortunate, unwed, and unwanted mothers, faded from Bernice's mind, just as the steam of the kettle disappeared and then died. It is hell, though, she thought. If I had a sister, and she found herself in them circumstances, with no man to father her child, and it was for one o' them worthless bastards in this country, white *or* black, Japanee or Chinee, be-Jesus Christ! and I turn my eyes above to You, I would have to get a half day from You to search for that brute, and when I find him, so-help-me-God, *bram*! (She actually slapped her hand on the kitchen counter. Mrs. Burrmann called her name. "It's only me, ma'am. I here, talking-over a few things with God.") "I think I would *kill* that bastard. The sorrow and the sufferation and the unhappiness to bring into a girl's life!" (Bernice remembered the case of the Jamaican girl, twenty-three years old who was working as a domestic; and she found herself in the family way; and the man didn't stand up, nor own up and say that it was his; and the only help that girl got was the gossip from the West Indian women who spread the story through the whole of Toronto, as if it was the gospel. The gossip reached her employer; and then it reached the people at the Immigration Office; and then the girl was deported.) "A poor single woman in *this* country, with a child that don't have a father? And a two-tone child, at that? Lord, Lord, Lord!" The terror and the tragedy were real, and she was shivering as if she were living through them. "And with all this hospital thing nowadays that you hearing 'bout: blue cross, physicians-and-services, group benefits to pay. This is the first country I ever live in where I hear you have to pay *hard cash* in order to bring a little innocent mortal into this blasted world. They make you pay through your hat, too! You pays to enter them hospital gates. You pays to lay down in that bed. You pays a certain kind o' cash to lay down in a certain bed. You pays to lay down in a certain bed, in a certain ward. You pays again to lay down in a certain bed, in a certain ward, in a certain place o' that hospital. You pays to get a certain kind o' treatment from the nurses. And there is a certain kind o' nurse you have to get before you could even think 'bout paying out ordinary cash. You pays the doctor. If he happens to be your family doctor — *well*! If he happen to be somebody-else family doctor — *then*! You pays the delivering surgeon. You pays the drugs people. You pays the man who knock you out with the smelling salts thing, the anaesthesia-man. You pays for the birth certificate. And be-Christ, when you dead, somebody telling you you still have to pay for deading! Why it is so, like this, in Toronto?" (And there was another case: Bernice was remembering everything now. A

Trinidadian girl...with a nice skin and nice features and nice long hair; and she had a good brain, too. God-love-a-duck! and Satan stepped right in and put the wrong man in that girl's pants. That man took that nice, young girl, and give her a child; kept coming back for more; fooling-up that angel till she was four months and almost showing; and the moment she stepped into maternity clothes that her missy bought for her from Holt Renfrew, that bastard run like a rabbit.) Dots was present when Bernice heard the story over the gossiphone. "Gal, that man run like he was running from a fire that had wings on it."

"And all he had to say is, he is a student."

"Student?" Dots even disliked the word. "Student? He only have time for books and not babies, eh?"

"But still, though, Dots," Bernice conceded. "You can't crucify that boy. As a student, he would have to look after his books. I heard Agaffa say once, that being a student is a funny thing, especially..."

"Student my arse, gal! They all stop being students on a Friday night. You go down at the Little Trinidad, or the WIF Club, the Latin quarter, the Tropics and you see them looking for free woman and cheap domestic pussy, you hear?"

"That is true, too," Bernice said. (And indeed, she could not have said otherwise). Bernice had to stop her thoughts from whirring; and she looked round to see whether Mrs. Burr-mann had finished reading about unwed mothers, or whether she had heard her. When she listened, the only sound in the house, was music: the Third Movement of Beethoven's Sixth Symphony. And then the music ended; and all she could hear was the rustling of the newspaper about unwed mothers, and the tolling of their doom in the glass with the ice cubes and the whiskey. The front door opened just then, and she heard Mr. Burrmann come in. He did not greet his wife, but went straight upstairs to his bedroom. Bernice followed him in her mind, his steps going up ("He walks up them steps in such a qa nmfunny way! This is the first time I really study the way he walks, and it seem like I hear them footsteps before . . . in a dream? Could it be in a dream?") until they were smothered in the broadloom in his room. She returned to her thoughts and the sizzling beef steaks in the pan. "You is the next one, Mr. Burrmann!" She looked into the pan, and saw Mr. Burrmann sizzling. "I am going to cuss you stink as hell one o' these days. You wait till the next time you having in your lawyer-friends, and you come smelling up in my damn face, telling me, Thanks Bernice dear, that was a *fine* repast. Fine repast, my arse! Heh-heh, that sound good, don't it? But I serious now, I going tell you to your face, and in the presence o' your friends, I knows it is a damn fine repast, Mr. Burrmann. But I waiting for almost three years now to see when, and if, you intend to increase my talents from ninety stinking dollars a month, to something a decent human being could live offa. A fine repast deserves a damn fine bonus, you don't know, Mr. Burrmann? . . . heh-heh-heh! I bet the brute will turn red as hell, with shame!"

She finished dinner, and laid it on the table, and waited until they were well into the food before she left the kitchen to take up Estelle's. Estelle had now stopped complaining about the "meagre" meals, and this was a little blessing which Bernice never stopped thanking God for.

"I am going out with Agatha, Bern," she said, eating.

"Yeah?" Bernice didn't like Agatha. She suspected her.

"We are going to the pictures. I'm meeting her at the corner."

"Oh?" Without waiting for more information, Bernice escaped back down to her kitchen.

Mr. Burrmann never ate dinner without his jacket. Even for breakfast, he was dressed. He had got into the habit while at Trinity College; and constant use, after graduation, helped him to retain it, without second thoughts, or self-consciousness. He was a healthy man. He even looked healthy. Five feet eleven inches tall, he was six inches taller than his wife. He did not have what Bernice came to know as "the typical Jewish features"; and she felt that had he so wished, he could pass as an Italian, in summer; a very clear-skin washed-out Negro in winter. But she knew he was a Jew — in more ways than one. Mrs. Burrmann once told her, that as far as she knew, Mr. Burrmann was the first Jew ever to attend Trinity College, in the University of Toronto. He spent four undergraduate years there. He took part in everything: he wrote for the *Trinity Review*, and won a prize once, for poetry; he took part in plays; debated, badly; swam; boxed, and got knocked down more times than he heard the bells of third rounds; and eventually when he graduated, no one was surprised that he had gained First Class Honours in Economics. He was never too modest, nor too self-denigrating in expressing his capabilities. This caused Bernice to ignore him, most of the time. But now, she was watching him eating; watching his movements about the house; noticing his entrances and exits and his long absences. "You know something? Two times in the last two weeks, I notice that Estelle is outta this house at the same identical time as Mr. Burrmann! I wonder what the two o' them up to?...oh hell, you going outta your mind?") She is watching him this Friday afternoon, closely, because it is the first time she has cooked them West Indian peas-and-rice and roast pork;

and she wants to know how much more liberty she can take with the seasoning and the pepper. The glowing candlesticks, like a hand of bananas turned upside down, are throwing just that much light on the food and on their faces and the wine, to make the dining room have a feeling of love and romance. But she can see tension in Mrs. Burrmann's face; and far-away thoughts on his. Mrs. Burrmann eats with a fork only; she cuts up the meat in little bits, and pelicans them into her mouth with the fork. But with Mr. Burrmann, now, it is a fine upbringing she is seeing! She and Dots used to talk a lot, before, about the way their missies ate. Dots said it sickened her to see them eat. "You mean to tell me that a big doctor-man and a big woman with so much necklace round her neck, strangling her, and they can't eat no better than that?"

"You was seeing money at that table," Bernice told her. "Not manners." But Bernice felt superior to Dots, because her "people" had better table manners than the Hunters of Rosedale. It was soon after this that she stole a glance at Mr. Burrmann, at dinner, in the large dining room. She watched him as he brought up the knife to fork, holding the fork *down*; and place that food, with the knife on the fork, man; and with your back straight as a sergeant-major on parade, Lord! bring that fork now up to your lips, man ... open them lips ("Haii!") close them lips over the fork ("Look at that man!") chew now ("God, that is really a man sitting down there, a gentleman!") without all the bones in your face looking as if they going collapse and fall apart. ("You is a man and a half!") She fed the children, and she put them to bed. Mrs. Burrmann went up-stairs soon afterwards. Bernice was still cleaning up the kitchen, when she heard the first signs of a threatening quarrel. It was nothing new. They had always quarrelled; and sometimes they had come to blows. (The first time she witnessed it, she asked Dots to bear testimony: "Well, be-Christ, child," she whispered on the phone in the kitchen, while the fight raged above her head, "I thought only worthless black men uses to beat their wives!" Dots laughed, and said, "Gal, you aren't no true-true Muslim, in truth!") Now, she was wondering what the children were thinking; what they did when they heard their parents fighting.

Mrs. Burrmann was saying, "To me, Sam, you're a man *in absentia.*" Bernice felt cheated: it seemed as if they were deliberately using a language they knew she couldn't understand. Then she heard them coming down the stairs. "Take me into your life, for once. For once." His voice, though not coming down the stairs, was still loud.

"You know what you are? Or would you like me to tell you what you are?"

"You're either going to take me into your life, Sam, or I want you to stop moseying round in mine. Quit sneaking behind me. I'm a woman, and I have needs and I won't sit around here all day all night, if my husband can't fulfil those needs." She was standing now, talking back up the stairs. "I'll have to find a man who..."

"You little, rich, over-educated bitch!"

"I don't bloody-well want you..." She was coming down fast, for he was behind her. "I don't want you bloody-well compartmentalizing me." She brushed past Bernice, who could not move fast enough from the bottom of the stairs where she was eavesdropping. When the front door slammed, Bernice put all the blame on Mr. Burrmann. "You big bastard," she called him. "If I was she, if I was in her place, be-Christ, a saucepan o' hot water would be in your damn face, right now. Imagine you, treating such a nice, decent girl like her, the way you treats her. All you men want is a whore in bed, that's all." But still the words used in the quarrel were bothering her. She couldn't understand many of them. To her, it was a stupid way to quarrel: you either told your man, *Go to hell! Kiss my backside, man!* or *Stop fucking up my life, man, you hear? Or I kill yuh!* "I must say, though," she conceded, "that these white tribes have a damn funny way of doing almost everything." One night Mrs. Burrmann broke three crystal water glasses, in a rage. Mr. Burrmann re-ordered them from Birks the next day (an action which completely confused Bernice; since they were thrown at his head) and Bernice happened to see that each glass cost thirty-five dollars. "Such a blasted waste o' money, womankind and time, I tell you, Dots."

Recently, there seemed to be always fights in the house. On another occasion, just as she passed their room, she hear them talking, warming up for their quarrel. He was using his lawyer's voice, as if talking to a jury. "I must tell you, Rachel, I must tell you, from the bottom of my heart, that it pains me even more than it can ever pain you, that you can't ever seem to carry a child in your womb without goddamn losing it, or doing some damn crazy thing to it. Every man needs a son. I need a son. And that seems to be the simple reason why this is not working out. It is as simple as that." Bernice lingered outside their door, and soon, she too was crying. She didn't know why she was always crying and feeling sorry for Mrs. Burrmann, whenever she heard him talking to her. But in these times, Bernice always forgot the amount of drink which seemed to keep Mrs. Burrmann almost half-dead sometimes; she forgot that one party in particular, when she saw the man kissing Mrs. Burrmann as if he was Mr. Burrmann; she forgot the hard words Mrs. Burrmann had very often used to her. When, however, she had a too busy day in the kitchen, she would remember that night; and more, too: the many times, late at night, when Mrs. Burrmann left in her car, and how, sometimes, she would come back very late and very drunk; and how, many times, Mr. Burrmann had to go out in his pyjamas and housecoat and move the car from straddling Marina Boulevard before the neighbours woke up. And once, Bernice remembered, she saw her parking the car in the metal telephone pole opposite the garage gate. When Bernice thought of these things, she criticized her for being so hurtful to Mr. Burrmann. Then, she really loved Mr. Burrmann. Still, she wondered who was to blame. In her judgement, a marriage going sour like this one, had one blame. One person was responsible for its ruin; one thing; one action.

And Bernice would always remember the night when she herself first made love in Canada, with the student-man; creeping down the stairs with the man's smell in her thighs and his arms round her throbbing waist, to let him out like a woman letting out a dog or a cat, that night when she heard tears in Mrs. Burrmann's voice, saying, "But Sam, I am a woman. I am a . . . the unhappiness you talk so much about, in our marriage, lies . . . " (Bernice was finding it difficult to hear each word) " . . . *right here!*" She thought she heard a muffled sound, like somebody banging a bed. " . . . it is here! here, here, here!" The banging stopped shortly after. On the way back upstairs, Bernice wondered whether the children were having a pillow fight; or whether it was Mrs. Burrmann banging her mattress. "She couldn't be saying that. A young man and a young woman, and *she* saying that?" She thought about it for a long while; but she couldn't make up her mind about it; she hadn't been concentrating because her own body was still throbbing from love.

Beethoven was coming to her where she was working. It was a Wednesday afternoon; and in her mind, she was putting in order the things she had to do the next day. She had to go to the bank. She thought of her low wages again, and wished that something would happen to make somebody say something about a raise soon. But she wasn't going to complain now. Estelle was living in the house. She would wait until Estelle went back to Barbados. "Three years, it is three years I been slaving for that princess in there!" She had waited so long; and still defeat followed upon defeat: Estelle's visa extended three more months; and her utter failure to get a room in which to banish her. "Lord, sometimes I have to wonder who the hell side you are on! You hailing for me, or you hailing for Estelle?" She brushed aside this unsavoury thought, and went back to her raise. "I have to get that raise. If Brigitte herself thinks it is unfair, well it must be unfair, in truth!" She thought next of Mammy. Wonder what Mammy doing right now? She glanced at the electric clock on the wall, over the sink, and it said a quarter to six. "Since seven forty-five I been standing up on these two blasted foots!" "She hurried up drying the dishes; and she put some of the initialled cutlery into the drawer without wiping them. "They could tarnish. I need that raise." Mammy came back into her thoughts, and she looked at the clock again, and wondered what time it was back in Barbados. At this time, a moment before dusk, she knew Mammy would already have brought in her grass-stuffed mattress, from the clothes line and from the sun, and would be shaking it out, and cursing because she never owned a store-bought, spring-and-cotton-stuffed mattress; and soon she would be lying down, in the front bedroom of her small house, fifty yards from the evening waves. Probably dreaming, too. "Poor, sweet, Mammy." Estelle didn't say much about Mammy; she never wrote Mammy once. Bernice had written a letter last month, telling Mammy about the hard times she had with Estelle, and she had sent the letter to Mammy's house in the village. Now, she had write another letter to Mammy, this one, within the regions of her mind; and she hoped it would fly through the air, and get to Mammy right now, and ease some of the painful things she had written in the earlier letter. *Dear Mammy, I love you so much; and we are so far from one another. What I wrote to you four or five weeks gone, concerning Estelle...* ("But Mammy always used to answer back quickly. It is almost four months that I haven't heard a word outta Mammy. Christ, I wonder if it is the money that didn't get posted to Mammy, that have Mammy...") *the things I wrote to you about Estelle, well they are not so bad now. Estelle made a complete somersault in regards to her behaviour to me. I think she likes Canada. And if God work out things the right way, mayhaps, I will even begin to take out papers for Estelle's landed immigrancy...* ("Over my dead body, blind you! All you want is man? Always saying you going out with that Agaffa? But one o' these days, I am going to see who the *real* Agaffa is!") ... *But do you know what I been thinking recently, Mammy? I was thinking that it would do you the world of good to come up here, on a vacation. The little journey in a plane would not kill you, although I know what you think about planes and things that fly. But I am dying to see you. Sometimes I think I will never see you again, in the flesh. However, God understand. In a few minutes, I am going to send down*

*the plane ticket for you. You come up here, and rest your old bones,
Your loving daughter, Bernice.* She felt happier now that she had
communicated with Mammy. And in the same spirit, she
decided to drop a line to Lonnie; just to inquire how he was,
what he was up to these days; and whether he had visited
Terence recently. But before she put the pen to the paper of her
imagination, she pondered the wisdom of bringing an old
woman like Mammy in all this cold weather; whether she
should withdraw the money for the ticket, tomorrow, and
whether she should send the ticket for Lonnie. ("No! I am
going to borrow the money from Mrs. Burrmann. She would
respect me more, and treat me better, because she would want
her money back, heh-heh!") *But Lonnie, are you a man, too?
Every little piece of woman in this place, Canada, have a man
going out every morning in the cold, from eight till five, providing
for her. And it only you West Indian men who sitting down on
your behinds, begging women for money. Lonnie, you don't know
that behaviour is gone out of fashion? And Lonnie, you should be
ashame. But then, how the hell would you know when and when
not to be ashame? But let me tell you this...* She wasn't satisfied
with the way this letter was going, so she destroyed it; and the
paper petals floated and dropped finally to the bottom of her
consciousness, like heavy feathers.

She was almost finished drying, when a chill went through
her entire body. Once before she had had a similar spasm; and
then a fierce thought; something more than a thought, a kind
of vision, in which she saw her father, Pappy, dead. And before
she reached home, she had heard Estelle screaming, and the
whole village gathered at the front door. Pappy had been
washed in, at low tide, drowned. When Bernice told them she
had seen it in a vision, at five o'clock (the same time Pappy was

first seen, like a bundle of old rags on the shore) they called her superstitious, an *obeah woman*. Now, she was having that kind of vision; but she laughed it off, as they had laughed at her, once before. In this vision, she saw Mammy dead. "Looka me, dreaming damn foolishness! It must be the hard work and the cold weather." She slammed the last cupboard door shut; switched off the lights, and got ready to go up to her room. The time was nine o'clock. Before she moved, she looked right and left, and then hastily and stealthily dropped the grease-proof paper parcel into her bosom. And then she smiled. It contained about a pound of Mrs. Burrmann's favourite mild Canadian Cheddar cheese. The cheese had hardly settled itself between her warm, sweaty breasts, when Mrs. Burrmann appeared, smiling.

"Well, well, well!" she said, still smiling.

"Oh God, ma'am, you frighten me." Mrs. Burrmann patted her on her shoulder. "Man, I nearly catch a heart-affection."

"You said that so dramatically, Bern." She handed her her wages, in the customary manilla envelope; and also an air-mail letter. "Tomorrow is Thursday."

"The whole day, ma'am."

"You needn't come down. I won't be here for breakfast, and Mr. Burrmann, well..."

"I understand what you going through, soul..."

"That's all right," Mrs. Burrmann said, interrupting; and cutting off further sympathy from Bernice. "Mr. Burrmann won't be eating here tonight, he's gone back to the office. It must have been a long day for you, today, Bernice." (In her heart Bernice asked, "Woman, you think only today was a long day for me?") Mrs. Burrmann rested her hand on Bernice's shoulder again, very affectionately. It was a gesture of sincere appreciation. "Don't open the brown envelope till you get to your room. There's a surprise in it for you. And have a good night, Bernice."

"Thanks." But Bernice was suspicious: she would always be suspicious with this woman. This time, it was the fear of being dismissed, without notice. Perhaps it was because Estelle had remained too long in the apartment.

"Is Estelle liking it here?" she asked. "I hear she's going out quite a bit, lately, and meeting some of our young men..."

"Well, I going up now, and rest these old bones, ma'am," Bernice said, giving Mrs. Burrmann the sweet smile which she had practised to please her mistress. But hearing about her sister going out with "*some of our young men*" — well, this was nothing for Bernice to smile about. Mrs. Burrmann stood watching her, until she got to the stairs, and then she followed her, and caught up with her. Bernice stopped and looked down from a step higher, looked into the pain and the unhappiness of her eyes. And Mrs. Burrmann knew it; and said in a voice that was deep with sorrow, "Thanks, Bernice, for everything. You've been very good, *really*, to all of us — even though things haven't always been easy for you. Thanks again, and have a good rest." She removed her hand; and went back downstairs. Bernice was shaken: but more important, she did not believe a word of it. It was to her, like a greeting from a stranger, on a crowded subway train. She climbed the rest of the journey to her room; holding on to the bannister where there was a bannister; and where there was none, on to her knee, her left knee which gave her such trouble. When she opened the door, Estelle was writing at the table. Bernice imagined that she was writing on the polish of the table itself. Estelle saw her come in, and she folded the paper, and put it into her handbag. She was already dressed. Bernice went straight for the chair by the window. "Lord!" she said, massaging her knee, pretending it was paining her unbearably. She rolled down her stockings and continued rubbing, saying all the time, "Lord!"

Estelle was ready to go. She said nothing. She napped her handbag shut. She put on her coat (Bernice's coat, really). She went through the door.

When the door was closed, Bernice said, "Lemme see what this one have to say..." and she opened the letter, to see Lonnie's handwriting. Before she got involved in it, she watched for Estelle coming out of the house. Agatha was to pick her up, she remembered Estelle saying. But there was no car parked nearby. Estelle came out. She looked up towards Bernice. Bernice held her head out of sight. And she watched Estelle wagging and stepping high, as if she owned the Boulevard. She was really a beautiful woman. With Estelle gone, there was a great burden taken off her spirit; and Bernice found out that moment, for the first time, that she really was happy that Estelle could find some place to go; and that she had friends — other than Dots and Boysie. Bernice now set her mind to Lonnie's letter, without interruption. *Darling love, Bernice, honey,* (it began) *I missing you bad bad, in a certain fashion. You know what I mean. I am one man who have not start fooling all about the place the moment his woman left the island. I faithful as hell with you, even though you have not write much and say much in the way of how you miss me. But I want you to know this. You may be up in Canada for three years going into four years, but you is still in my heart as you was before you even think about pulling out for the outside world. The child living with me now. I mean Torrence. Your mother treated me*

*worst than if I were a dog. But she is your mother, and I am
not going to say nothing bad concerning her. However, something I have to tell you in regards to Mammy and Estelle, before
she left Barbados. Estelle was spreading it all over the island
that she is not coming back down here. She staying up there. I
hear from a friend of a friend of yours who Estelle write to last
week, that you are taking out papers for Estelle. I am only the
father of your child. Estelle is your flesh and blood. Work scarce
as anything down here. The poor people getting more poorer. I
broke as hell, too. So I beseeching you, Bernice, that if you ever
put your hand on an extra dollar bill, think of Lonnie, and
send down one, because I do not know what I going to do. Roses
are red and skies are blue and the sea is green and I love you.
xxxx. They is kisses for you. Respectively yours, Lonnie, your
No. 1.*

Bernice went straight to the chesterfield and sat down.
The things in the letter: about Mammy; about Estelle; about
home; about her child, Terence, and about Lonnie himself.
It was a good letter; she liked it, and she found herself liking
Lonnie too. At least, he had begun to show some interest
in Terence. She was hearing Lonnie's voice, and the sweet
words he had written at the bottom of her letter: *Roses are red
and skies are blue* . . . and the four kisses! And she felt very
lonely, with a great urge, a great desire for Lonnie, lying on top
of her. She lay back on her back; and spread her legs as if it
was Lonnie who had pulled them apart. And she imagined
Lonnie on her, making love to her; and she began to pant
and breathe heavily, in rhythm to the stirruping which she
remembered so well; and she was feeling good, as if it was real
and she was coming to the end of the race, with the tape in
front of her eyes, and then she jumped up from the bed.

"What sort o' worthlessness is this? Me, Bernice, jerking-off 'pon myself? God, a shame, a shame..." and she went to the bathroom to draw a bath; and wash away the sin of loneliness. She had tried it before (in recent weeks, with Estelle around, not as often) by rubbing herself with her finger to stimulate an orgasm. But each time, the meaning of it frightened her; and she would take a hot bath. Before this bath was ready, she opened the manilla envelope Mrs. Burrmann had given her, and into her lap fell four crisp twenty-dollar bills, an old crumpled ten and a five. Her income had been increased by five dollars a month.

"You make me feel like a man again," the man was telling Estelle. She was looking at the coloured beads, strung on cord, that were the curtains in the Penny Farthing coffee house, on Yorkville. Tension had crept into their friendship, though, because she resented being taken each time they went out, to the small hotel on Avenue Road, where they would rush through an hour of hectic love-making; and where he would rush her on through the lounge, past the desk clerk with the eyes of a spy. Worst of all the compromise in the transaction, was the *look* on the clerk's face, and the *look* in the man's face. And once, when she was struggling with the cigarette machine (although she had two packages in her handbag) while the man paid his cash and got his key, she thought she heard the clerk say, with a laugh in his voice, "She must be a damn good screw, eh, Sam?"

But he could think of no place to take her; and now that it was cold weather, it was very uncomfortable in the back of his car, although it was a large black Buick. They had tried the apartment of a lawyer friend of his, but one night, the lawyer

friend came in too soon (Estelle was standing on her virtues
that night) and caught them putting on their clothes. She felt
humiliated; very compromised. The tension in their affair rose
with the inconvenience of being alone when they wanted to
be. Once, when lust got the better of them, and made them
almost insane with desire and plotting, he took her to the Four
Seasons, a motor hotel in the downtown part of the city. But
the clerk at the desk assumed the moral and ethical responsibility of the entire city, and refused to accept the man's cash.
"Listen Mack," the clerk said to Mr. Sam Burrmann, B.A.,
M.A. LLB (Toronto), "not in here. Take *her* somewhere else.
This is a decent establishment." (But Sam had tried "it" in
that decent establishment twice before, with two different
blondes.) The clerk had said this to Sam, who did not tell it to
Estelle. But she knew anyhow. He went back to his Buick and
they drove around the city, building up mileage and courage;
and thinking of a place. He was conscious of his pride, and of
his position; and in a strange way, was mindful of her pride.
She was his woman: he had not yet begun to think of her as
his whore. But he wanted her badly; and he ate his pride and
burned his oil and gas, and decided on a house on Jarvis Street.
In a window, Estelle saw BED AND BREAKFAST, written on a
dirty piece of cardboard.

"You make me feel like a whore." She was thinking of the
women back home she had seen going into houses like this.
The way she had thought herself so much above them; and
what she herself called them — bitches! — and now?

"You're not, *really*. You're not ..."

"That doesn't mean I don't feel like one."

It took the whole twenty-six ounces of Canadian Club
whiskey to take the evil taste out of both their mouths. Since

that night, the distaste of the house kept them from wanting each other (although they continued to meet) for almost two weeks.

Tonight, however, she was happy. The simple elegance of this coffee house, with its blue-and-white table cloths, and its ordinary painted-over hard bottom chairs, appealed to her. Back in Barbados, only the poorest of the poor would sit on these chairs; and she herself would not sit on them; but in this coffee house, in this country, they were charming to her. The man she was with had just told her he loved her. He did not want her to go back to Barbados. And she was very happy that he said he wanted her: she was also a trifle embarrassed through conscience, because her own motives for giving him her gift of love, were to put him in a position to be exploited. She must not think of these things, though, she warned herself; because she had given him a gift. If he wanted, or felt he had to give her a gift in return (perhaps assuring himself of another taste of her generosity), then she need not feel badly about his motives, at all. And that was what she decided. And having decided, she could then begin to enjoy the atmosphere of the coffee house. The man said he did not like the atmosphere of this coffee house: the music was too commercial, he said. But he came nevertheless, because it was a place where he could hide. He could bring a woman here, and his morals, or his guilt, or whatever it was that made him feel uneasy with a woman, not his wife, all these little inconveniences of conscience could be lost here, because it was taking place in a coffee house, in the Village, "among artist-types and beatniks," as he said, more than once. Before Estelle, when he needed love and relaxation from the professional crowd of Malloney's and the Park Plaza Hotel Roof Bar, he would go alone to the

Twenty-Two (before many advertising men heard about it) or to Seventy-Three Yorkville, where he would sit and sip and dream of getting into bed with the Spanish woman who helped to raise the price, the attendance, and the consumption of expresso coffee, by wearing a pair of panties under a meshed pair of black tights, so suffocatingly tight, that it was uncomfortable for Sam Burrmann to sit quietly. But in the Penny Farthing with Estelle, he was uncomfortable: the customers were mostly young, with beards and long hair, and with a smell of freedom which was really the odour of uncleanliness and laziness.

Her attention was drawn to a big beautiful black man who came in as if he owned the entire street. Estelle was so overpowered by his beauty and his strength which seeped through his expensively tailored suit, that she had to stare. And then a small white man, neat and willowy, prim and feminine, with a beard and a guitar in his hand, said to the black man, "*Hi, baby!*" Estelle had to smile (the man she was with was already becoming jealous of the big black man) and admit that "baby" was a funny way to address this black mountain of a man. But the black man merely said to his friend, "Shit, baby! how you doing?"

"Damn Americans!" her escort said. "Whole place is full of them." Estelle refused to dispute this judgement. "These coffee houses're so depressing nowadays," he went on. "Before, you could come here and relax, meet decent people...but now, well, wherever you go in Yorkville these days, you see a lot o' Europeans, Italians, Germans, Greeks, Americans..."

The small guitar player was giving them a song, in a foreign language. The man with Estelle had to lean over to be heard. "And you know what I heard the other day? All these coffee houses are cells, cells for one thing or the other. If it isn't some kind of nationalism, it is smoking pot. Kids with long hair, kids wearing jeans, kids in bare feet . . . they're spoiling everything."

"You come here often?"

"Well, no . . . sometimes, after work . . . to relax."

"Instead o' going home, Sam?"

"Well, I don't mean it that way, though it is . . . But why are we so serious? Let's enjoy ourselves, eh? Would you like some more coffee?" A short young woman, dressed in black, wearing a white band in her long black hair, came to serve them. Estelle wondered why she had to wear so much black. Agatha had pointed out to her, as they were driving through the West End, that all the women on that street, young and old, dressed in black, were Italian immigrants. And Estelle had looked at them, and had liked them. Black seemed to go hand in hand with Italian immigrants. But this young thing, serving coffee, didn't suit black; and black didn't suit her. Black shoe and black stocking, to boot! Estelle observed.

"That girl's mother is dead, Sam."

"What're you saying?"

"Look at her."

"How did you know?"

"She is dressed in black, from head to foot."

And Sam laughed. "You have a weird sense of humour, believe me." He was still laughing (and he had held out his hand, and rested it on Estelle's knee, under the table) when a black man holding a white woman round her waist, entered. The man was wearing a very small felt hat. Estelle noticed it was much smaller than his head. His clothes were neat; and he was walking with a subtle kind of bravado. When he took off his hat, she thought something was wrong with his head. It was shining. His hair was slicked back, straightened and pasted close to his scalp; (Bernice's hair would have been like that, almost, had she not been interrupted by the footsteps that afternoon. She looked at Sam, and smiled. He was the one who had interrupted them. Only she knew: and Sam!) only the man's shoes were shinier and blacker. The man left his woman sitting, and came up to Sam, as if he had grown up with him. He slapped Sam on his back.

"Sam, baby!" His arms were open, as if to embrace Sam; and all the time he was grinning. "You old motherfucker, you!" Sam didn't know what to do. He had hardly looked at the man long enough to recognize him. It was a peculiarity of his, this inability to look into a black man's eyes.

"I don't think I know you, sir..."

"Shit, baby! Jeffrey! Ain't you remember me, Jeffrey? Me and him and a few other ofay cats who used to gang up on those Jewish rabbits round Spadina in the good old days..." (He was now telling it to Estelle.)

"Oh." He remembered. He remembered Jeffrey being beaten by the policeman; he remembered Jeffrey's mother; he remembered fifteen, twenty, thirty years of things he wished he had forgotten. He had refused to think of it because he still carried the guilt of it with him. Apparently, Jeffrey couldn't (or didn't) remember the cause of his being sent to jail. "Yes, yes!" But Sam was not very enthusiastic.

"The guys tell me you's this big cat now in town, baby! Swinging with the cats of the law. Man, you must be wailing in bread. I see you got you a nice chick, here, baby!" He beckoned to his fiancée; she was coming to join them. A few couples close by were finding the conversation very interesting.

But Sam was nervous. "Hey, Sue! come and meet my old crazy side-kick from the old days, baby. This cat is a lawyer; but me and him used to groove back in them days, stirring up a lot o' shit with the Jews and the Polacks..."

"Look, I'm sorry, sir," Sam said, rising. "We're just leaving. I was having some coffee with this lady, a client of mine, since..."

"Crazy, baby! I sure glad as hell to lay my eyes on you, baby. Gimme your card, man. Me and you gotta get together like in the old days. Perhaps I may throw a case or two your way, eh, buddy?"

"I am sorry, sir, but I don't happen to have a card on me, right at this moment."

"That ain't no problem, baby," Jeffrey said. "Take mine, then." And he slapped Sam playfully on his arm, and said, "Surprise yuh, ain't I? Drop by some time, man." The card was the size of a usual calling card, and all it had on it, printed, was: JEFFREY'S 9223720.

"Okay, okay," Sam said. The waitress was coming with the coffee he had ordered; he was trying to hustle Estelle out. "Look, I gotta go, I gotta go. Give me a call — at the office, sometime."

"Crazy, man!" Even after Sam and Estelle left, Jeffrey was still talking about him to his fiancée. "That cat! That sweet motherfucker been swinging since he was a kid. Only God knows how much coloured babies Sam has in this place. That cat..."

The afternoon the letter came, Bernice wept. It was the same letter she had written home; and now it was returned to her, stamped: ADDRESSEE UNKNOWN. Everyone in the village knew Mammy. Bernice gave only one meaning to this strange message, stamped in black, uneven ink (she made a mental note of the colour of the ink!) and bearing the terrible message. "Mammy unknown in Reid's Village, where Mammy was born and spent most of her sixty-three years?" — except the three years spent in the Canal Zone, in Panama, helping the Americans to build the Canal.

She rushed upstairs to her room, to be alone, to express this tragedy, in tears. She flung open the door, and screamed, "Estelle! oh God, Mammy dead!" And when there was no answer, only the drum beat of the record, stuck in its groove on the player, did she realize that she had seen Estelle leave, earlier. Nobody was home. It was four o'clock. No house was more like a graveyard than this large tomb, this Saturday afternoon, in the middle of spring.

She looked at the envelope again. She saw the handwriting on it; she saw the Canadian postage stamps; she saw the stamp stamped on it, in the Toronto Post Office; the other stamp from the Barbados Post Office when the letter first arrived there; and the series of other stamps made both in Barbados and in Canada, sending the letter on its long last walk back to her. Looking across the street, amongst the colours of spring, she tried to search the curtains at the third floor window, for Brigitte. She could not see her. She did not see her in the yard where the children played. There were no children in the yard. Brigitte had stopped by, late in the morning, to ask her to warn Boysie not to call so often: her policeman friend was becoming suspicious and threatening. And Bernice remembered she had listened, and had promised to tell Dots, but that Brigitte urged her not to. "You not tell Dots. Just Boysie, to warn him." And she had pinched Bernice, knowingly, and like a conspirator; and had left. Bernice sat by the window, trying to gather her thoughts, trying to find some logic to contradict this tragedy. But all she could think of was Mammy: in a small house in a village by the sea, and boarded up in many places with pieces of tin-shingles made of large butter pails from Australia. She thought of the sea which had claimed Pappy's life. She thought of Estelle, and of Marina Boulevard: the waves of leaves, brown leaves, red leaves, brick-painted leaves of spring raged round the front yards of the houses opposite. She could see the leaves taken up by the wind, and sent like sprays all over the yards; and then settling themselves nervously into a heap round the tall scarecrow of the maple tree in front of Brigitte's house. This was too much like the storm which claimed Pappy's life, so she stopped thinking about the leaves, and thought of someone to call. Dots isn't home, there isn't no damn sense in calling that husband o' hers, 'cause he stupid as hell ... Estelle outta the house as usual ... now, what about Agaffa? Agaffa, hell! ... and Henry? ... Henry just as useless as Boysie. There was no one to call. "Mammy dead, far away in Barbados, and there isn't one blasted living soul in the whole o' Toronto Canada, that I could call on for help and assistance?"

She went to the chesterfield for her bible; and she knelt in front of it. Tears made her eyes red as those of a man on a diet of rum; her hands were shaking so much that she found it difficult to turn the pages, and find the portion of scripture she felt Mammy's death deserved. Her fingers moved over the silken pages, rustling them like the wind outside was wrestling with the leaves. She found the section. She read it aloud, her hands pressed together in the attitude of prayer. *"The Lord is my shepherd, I shall not want. He maketh me to lie down in green pastures; he leadeth me beside the still waters. He restoreth my soul...*" She made the sign of the cross, although her present denomination told her not to do this. But she felt she had to do this extreme thing to suit an extreme tragedy. Through her tears, through the filmy vision of her tears, the page looked like a large newspaper page at the bottom of a pool on which the wind was striking. But although she could not see each word, she read the lines because it was a portion of scripture she had memorized from her Sunday school days. "*...thou anointest my head with oil; and my cup runneth over. Surely goodness and mercy shall follow me all the days of my life...*" Her sorrow was running over: there was nothing she could do to contain it. Her former strength of mind now began to crack. She cried and she sang *The Gloria*; and it was this that Mrs. Burrmann heard, that sent her rushing up the stairs to find out "what the hell's going on in this house, Leach?"

She found Bernice, her maid, prostrated and crippled by grief, beside the chesterfield. Without turning, Bernice knew it was her employer, Mrs. Burrmann; and she screamed out, "Jesus Christ, Mrs. Burrmann, Mammy dead! My Mammy dead! God, You is a damn cruel God!" And Mrs. Burrmann, overcome by all this (she herself had experienced death reported to her and to her family, twice, from Europe; and she had witnessed the physical and moral fracture the news had brought with it: how her parents cried and wept and talked about those deaths and other deaths in the family, long into the night) knelt down, and reached out her hand, and rested her hand on Bernice's shoulder. Then her hand slipped, and fell to her side, and soon she found she was holding Bernice's hand in hers. Their bodies were very close. Bernice smelled the *Je Reviens* on Mrs. Burrmann's body; and she smelled it stronger and stronger, almost choking her, until she realized what was happening. Mrs. Burrmann was kissing her on her cheeks. "What are you going to do now? What are you going to do? You'll have to go down..." Mrs. Burrmann was saying, over and over. It made Bernice plunge into new sorrow. "You will have to go home." (Suddenly, in the midst of all this sorrow, Bernice became aware of her job, and her bank account, and of the possibility that Estelle might take away her job.) "Yes, Bernice, you will have to go home." Bernice was about to say she had no money for the plane ticket, when Mrs. Burrmann said, "Don't worry about the ticket, dear, I'll fix that. Try to take it easy, Bernice. Spend a little time, and then come back." She put her arm round Bernice. Her perfume and her lipstick and her lips were touching Bernice's cheeks. Bernice was having short spasms, and Mrs. Burrmann said, "Come, let us pray for strength." Mrs. Burrmann said a few short things in a language Bernice had heard spoken very seldom in the house (once in particular, during a very hectic quarrel, when Mr. Burrmann raised his voice) and when she finished, she smiled and said, "Your mother, so she's dead. Can you bring her back with all this crying? No. But I know you feel bad. So, I think I should bring you some brandy..."

In the heavy silence of the room, Bernice, with tears streaming down her face; and Mrs. Burrmann, with a water-stain on her cheeks, and the leaves in the wind outside: these two women joined together in grief, as they had never been united before, by love.


From the Penny Farthing, where they used to go often; but from which they had been driven, by the resurrection of Sam's friend Jeffrey (Sam later found out that Jeffrey had spent about ten years in jail; nine years for his part in an abortive armed robbery, and less than one year for the theft of apples which he didn't steal, and which in particular made Sam feel very uneasy in his company), they began to seek refuge in the gloomier and more bohemian atmosphere of the Cellar Jazz Club, on Avenue Road. This place was more cosy; and agreeable too, because it had live jazz. He could touch her hand here, he could squeeze her hand here, he could even kiss her here, without being seen, without feeling conspicuous; and most of all, without being seen by black men who disapproved. Some of the musicians were black; and there were some others who sat in silence, fierce and powerful like jaguars, controlled by the beauty of the music, but who seemed to want to explode the moment the music stopped. In this stealth of gloominess, the man reached out and touched her hand. It was very soft and very cool. He held it. Then he gripped it. He tried to send little indecent messages with his fingers scratching the palm of her hand; but he tried to morse-code them in a manner of decency. Estelle thought his hands were rough. "Whatever happens, whatever ... (the music was loud here) ... in spite of everything, I want you to know... (the black drummer was transforming the basement club to the throbbing of Africa) ... I love you..."

"I think I love you, too, man." She did not say it as a lover would have whispered it into his ear. She was listening to the messages being sent to her directly, from the drummer. She was annoyed that Sam talked while the music was talking to her. "You know something? I think I love you."

"Only *think*?"

"When I say 'think,' I mean 'sure.'"

"But you said think, nevertheless."

"I know, I know." For a long time, Sam was quiet; and it

was good for her that the music was loud at this point, so she didn't have to talk. "Look, Sam, I don't know if you started out loving me, as you say, or if you started out wanting to find out something about me, and women like me, or something..." The music was loud again. He was becoming irritable. "And look," she said, when he could hear her, "since me and you been going out all over Toronto, in coffee houses and places where they play jazz and sing folk songs, I have seen a lot o' mixed-up couples. Black man and Chinee woman, Chinee man and white woman, white woman and black man, and at first, it looked pretty to me, because that is the way I think people on earth should live — *together*, you know? But from the last time we were out together, I suddenly got the feeling that people were looking at me, *not* at you. They know you. But the way they look at me..." Sam held his head into his coffee cup, searching it, and searching his conscience and his memory at the same time, for something to tell this woman. He wanted to say something that was different: something like, I am not like the others; I am not like them at all; Don't you see, I am sitting with you? It was a burden which grew heavier from that afternoon when they first made love. He had worked out his excuses and explanations against the discovery of his adultery. Sometimes, he felt he would kill his wife if she so much as found out, and mentioned it; at other times, he felt he would kill himself. But deep down, he knew he would never kill himself; or his wife. He didn't think he was made that way: although he never gave much thought to how he had to be made in order to murder or commit suicide. There were children to consider. There are always children to consider; and he knew the difficulty about this, because he had seen his mother with her children, after his father died, his mother who was too proud and too poor to do very much about her children's neglect.

"Sometimes, I don't think you realize that my sister works in your house, and lives in your house, as your servant. And I live with my sister. Sometimes, I don't think you understand what that means. You don't. To me, and to her."

"I know, I know."

"Heh-heh-heh! but look at the two of us two foolish grown-ups. Sitting down here, hiding. I, from my sister; and you, from your wife. And both of us hiding from what inside here," she said, touching the place where she thought her heart and conscience were located. "I don't have one damn right to do anything to hurt Bernice, hear? Bernice was always like a mother to me. And I suppose you don't have any damn right to hurt your wife, neither. But still...heh-heh! a woman is a real fool..." The waitress was upon them. Her presence was censuring. She cleaned the table with a dirty damp cloth, spending more time to look into Estelle's face and into the man's face, than she spent on the spots of the hard unfinished table. "You don't have to ask me if I love you, man," she said, when the waitress left. "You don't have to, at all. For what we did, what we have done, is something that is either done through love, or wickedness. And I know I ain't wicked. Are you wicked? I don't think you should point your finger at me, and say, and ask if I love you."

"I know, I know."

Just then, she saw Agatha come in. She had just happened to turn, when she saw them (Agatha and Henry) paying Otto, the pipe-smoking cashier at the door, who smoked his pipe with no tobacco in it. Luckily, she was sitting at the rear, in the shadows, beside an unfinished stone pillar. The man wondered

why, suddenly, she had snuggled up to him; and why she had
placed her head on his shoulder. But the feeling was a good
one; and the jazz at that moment, seemed more beautiful than
he had ever heard it at The Cellar.


They were all there. Bernice was packing her suitcase. (Mrs.
Burrmann had called the airport, and there was an early flight
reserved for her, first thing, Sunday morning. Boysie and Dots
had come as soon as possible. They had told Henry, who told
Agatha. And by now, the news of Mammy's death had spread
throughout the West Indian community of domestics, like
typhoid fever in Reid's Village, in 1943: everybody had been
smitten.

They were all there, sitting in Bernice's apartment, as if
they were shadows in the shadows thrown by the one lamp
that burned on the dressing table. Boysie, sipping the expensive brandy which Mrs. Burrmann had left to deaden some of
Bernice's hysteria and screams and grief; and Dots, talking, as
if in her sleep, but talking nevertheless, though she knew no
one was listening; and Bernice, placing her dresses and her
underclothes on the bed, although the suitcase was already
full, and although she knew she was going to attend only one
funeral; not a wedding; and thinking aloud, and crying and
taking a gasp-like breath, each time she remembered something new about Mammy. It was past eleven o'clock: in a few
hours, it would be Sunday.

DOTS: Sitting down here this sad evening, I can't get my mind
to travel back over that salt water and land mass, at all. I can't
get this mind o' mine to take in this sudden, sudden tragedy
which now have this poor girl, packing suitcase and valise,
black dress and hat, to follow her sweet mother, Mammy, to

the grave in. It is as if something blocking the path o' my mind, and my mind can't take up the picture o' grief, from the negative of that grief, because all I can see before my two eyes, is clouds and clouds. Boysie, pass that thing you drinking here, and let me taste a sip, please... The picture of remembering, of remembering back to things and happenings and memories in that damn island, is like a tragedy itself. Mammy gone. That is one fact. Mammy gone and I feel it is my own-own mother who is dead, the difference being that my mother was dead a damn long time ago, even before I born. But sitting down here in Forest Hill, gives this tragedy a damn funny sperspective, as my missy, Mrs. Hunter, would say. This blow of Mammy's death hit me in two ways. It hit me hard hard because I know Bernice here, poor soul, now packing and spending money 'pon plane ticket, when she should be banking that same money 'gainst a rainy day. And second, it hit me hard 'cause I know that death does do some strange things to a man's think-ing, and cause him to wish the wrong thing, and say the wrong thing, and say that death should have hit the next person... Christ! I know three people living today that this death should have hit: my missy, Mrs. Hunter, who ain't worth shit, she is number one; number two is the man who blow-up that church down South with them four tiny beautiful little Negro children and caused them to go to their death; and number three, is anybody like Hitler. A man always wishes death to hit a per-son, anybody, somebody you don't like, but it shouldn't hit a person you like, or you know. That is the three sperspectives through which I see this death. (Just then, the music from downstairs, in Mrs. Burrmann's sitting room, came up to help them think of mournful things. It was the Fourth Movement from Beethoven's Sixth Symphony. Dots listened; and she looked at Bernice, who understood what she heard. Boysie was busy sipping the brandy.) Boysie, you remember? Boysie, stop drinking a minute, and tell me if you remember, or call to mind, how the news o' Lottie's death hit us, as we was relaxing in Dr. Hunter' basement, drinking two beers? You remember when the news o' Lottie's death came, it came in such a strange manner and fashion, that I had to open my mouth wide and say, "Jesus Christ! It isn't, couldn't be true. Lottie not dead." I couldn't believe it was the same Lottie who I had rested my eyes on that very morning, walking 'cross Sherbourne Street going up by Bloor Street, Jesus God, not the same Lottie, flourishing at ten o'clock and cut down at ten-past-ten, the same day. Not the same Lottie? But death came, and *bram*! it take Lottie with it. That is death, Boysie. If you have ears to hear, and if that brandy hasn't start doing something to your hearing and vision, that is what I want you to know concerning death. Death came and take Lottie as she was standing up at the bus stop, waiting for a streetcar. And all Lottie did, according to them two evening papers, the *Telegram* and the *Star*, all Lottie was guilty of, was that Lottie held out her hand, and *pointed*, and then crossed the road going through them crosswalk-things that the city put there to save human beings, pedestrians, from cars. That was Lottie's crime. But death is a blind man who can't see at all, and didn't went to school. And Lottie didn't get half-way 'cross that blasted crosswalk-thing, before this big, big transport truck didn't come and *brugh-guh-dung-dung*! licked Lottie 'gainst a streetcar coming one way and a lorry going the next. Lottie's two hand cut off *cleanclean* as if they was cut off with a carving knife. Lottie's head severed clean as a whistle from Lottie's body, and the blood! Jesus Christ Almighty! the blood in that Bloor Street road, was red and thick and enough to make twenty dogs puke. That was Lottie's death. That is the manner in which death came to Lottie. And be-Christ, that Bloor Street road was full with people, white people, and not one o' them bitches didn't even as much as run to the telephone box opposite the drug store, and call a ambulance, or a hospital or the police, even though Lottie was down there on that cold road and streetcar tracks, panting and splattering-'bout, like a blasted whale. And as I sitting down here, this evening o' sorrow, Boysie, I ask you, Boysie please, *please* be careful with the traffics in this place, 'cause this place is a heartless, cruel place. Please be careful where, and how you driving that damn old trap-heap, you calls a mottor car. Take care, Boysie. Take care. You don't know how, or when, or in what manner death is going to strike. The onliest thing you know, in regards o' death, is that death *bound* and 'bliged to hit one day. And one thing I ask you. As long as you driving that mottor car in this country, please, *please* do not hit a white person with it. *Please*, Boysie! Don't even *touch* their mottor car, then, with the one you driving. 'Cause, I saying something now, in the presence o' you Bernice, and in the hearing o' you, Boysie; something I had buried deep down inside o' me; and it is only Lottie's death that cause me now to call it to mind. More than four years ago, this thing happened, and when it happen, all I could do was to run straight up in Rosedale and lock myself in my quarters, and sit down and shake my head. I think I even dropped a tear or two, too. The unbelief! It is this. I was walking home one night. It was early, man. Ten o'clock didn't even gone, then. A mottor car came screeling round Sherbourne. He ain't watching no traffics, nor no lights. A next mottor car, with a coloured man driving, was coming up Bloor, driving like if he is a gentleman, and as if

the car cost gold. And I had just turned 'way my face to blow
my nose in a Kleenex, when I hear this big report, *blam*! The
man who screeled outta Sherbourne ran right into the car
with the coloured man. Well, both cars stopped now, naturally.
The white man get out. He start crying, begging the coloured
gentleman pardon; he sorry; he say he going to pay to fix the
car. Everybody in the street... by this time, there is twenty to
forty o' we onlookers looking on. Everybody, including the
man in the screeling car, say the coloured man isn't to blame.
Everybody putting the blame where it belongst. And that is on
the white man. Well, the police come. Kreeeeeeeeeennnnnn!
sirens! the police jumped outta the cruiser, and grabbed the
coloured gentleman. Start calling that gentleman nigger-this
and nigger-that; black bastard, where-the-hell-you-come-
from? and then they hold him 'gainst he police car, and started
searching him like how you see they do in the movies, and be-
Christ, they put *all the blame* 'pon that coloured man. *Not one*,
you hear me, not one o' them white people, including the man
in the screeling car, didn't as much as say, Boo! — meaning
that what they saw with their eyes wasn't what the police say
the coloured man do. Not one blasted white person outta
twenty-one to forty-one, could find his tongue. And that is
what I mean when I say, Careful, Boysie, this country ain't
your country. And the police, the white people and the papers
reminds you it is not your place of birth nor belonging, neither. If you, Boysie, was that coloured man that the police
dragged-off so... and I watched the papers weeks after, to see
who will get the blame, 'cause I was smart enough to take
down both mottor car licence... be-Christ! and I still watching to see the justice the police intend to give that coloured
man... if you was that man, Boysie, I would *kill*... (Bernice

had stopped packing, to stand and listen. Her terror for the
police had unhinged all her control; and made her mouth
hang loose. Boysie, struck by this secret burden and concern of
his wife, had stopped drinking)...although you ain't worth
shit, sometimes, Boysie, by-God, I am not such a fool not to
know that you won't be worth *nothing*, if you was dead. That
is what I mean by death, Boysie. Bernice, that is the way I see
this thing, from three or four sperspectives, as Mrs. Hunter
would put it, and in the three or four ways it happen to you.
It happen to you, and I may be next. Me, or Boysie, here.
Death. It sure to come. Death, death...that is death...

BOYSIE: I agree with you. But still I can't agree with all the
three or four sperspectives you mention in regards o' death.
So, I can only say, I agree and I disagree. Though I can't pull
out the words from my brain, in the manner and fashion as
how you just talked...gorblummuh! this brandy going to my
brain! But I agree in these respects. You was right to say death
does come like a thief in the night. I say, however, death is
worser than a fire. You does see a fire, and you does smell a fire.
When you screel, *Fire!* gorblummuh, somebody coming to
help put out that fire. But you can't see, nor smell, death. And
when death *strike*, it ain't one blasted soul, living or dead, to
come trotting. Death is a thief. The biggest ever made and create' in this Chinee world. Death thiefed Lottie. It thiefed
Mammy, too. Mammy, down there in that old house, in
Barbados, didn't know, nor hear, nor smell, death. Lottie, stepping 'cross that crosswalk, didn't know that death was waiting
on the other side. That is the ways of a thief, Dots; and that is
the ways o' death, too.

DOTS: No, no, no, man! You can't say that death is any damn
thief, 'cause for you to say that, you are really saying that death

have eyes to see with, hands to hold with, and feet to walk with. And that death have a brain. Because a thief knows, a thief does *know*, Boysie. A thief, any thief who is worth his salt, always knows beforehand which man stands in possession o' possessions, and which man doesn't. That is the onliest explanation you could give me concerning the thief, whoever he was, that robbed Dr. Hunter. That thief knew who to rob: he knew beforehand, who was doctor and who was maid. That is the difference betwixt death and a thief. A thief isn't blind, Boysie, boy. But death is blind. Death can't, don't, and don't want to see, because death don't have eyes to see or recognize or know who he taketh away, and who he don't and shouldn't, take away.

BOYSIE: Yes ... and no, too! Yes, to that part where you say that death isn't a man, or a thing, or a piece o' anything in possession o' sight and vision. That I could agree with. But everything else is *no*, Dots. Death does thief a man from life. Death does thief a man from his wife. Death does, and could, thief a man from his job, or from his children, like how it thiefed the headmaster o' St. Matthias School, back home, from his eight children in the twinkling of a eye. Be-Jesus Christ, Dots, as I sitting down here, drinking this white woman brandy, that is the only how in which death have the mechanics of being a thief; and it is the manner in which I see this present strategy concerning Mammy's death. Death come to Mammy like a centipee on a dark night, and *steeeennnnng*! Mammy wasn't no more Mammy. Death transform Mammy from one something in a next something else; and even now, even at this very moment o' speech and event, even as we three here mourning over Mammy, the same Mammy might be keeping company with we, in the form of that something else, namely a spirit, or a ghost, or just air...

BERNICE: Boysie, do you see spirits?

BOYSIE: Look round this room, Bernice; look round this room, Dots, and tell me, either one of the two of you, if you don't feel something like a cold draught coming in through...

DOTS: The window, man! It is open. Look man, you old ignorant arse-hole idiot...looka, don't let me lose my temper, do!

BERNICE: You say a cold draught coming in through somewhere?

BOYSIE: A cold draught *is* coming in through somewhere! Look, and listen. Listen! You hear something, like a wind? Bernice, you hear the wind, the cool, cool, cold wind that does blow in your face early, early in the morning when you waiting for a streetcar that does come down the tracks creeping like a snail? I bet you, both o' you, that it is Mammy come back from wherever the hell she is, asking to talk to you, Bernice, because you is her daughter...

BERNICE: It is only the window, open, Boysie. The window open, because I forget to close it. But look, I am going to close it now, man.

DOTS: Look, you ignorant ram-goat!

BOYSIE: You could close that window, be-Christ, till you tired closing that window. But you can't close out the wind that coming in, as Mammy, and as Mammy's ghost. I not talking 'bout a open window, Bernice, because I know when a window is open, and when a window is not open. I talking 'bout a feeling in this room right now. Listen! You telling me there ain't somebody else walking 'bout in this damn room with the three o' we? Now, I is a man, who don't believe in no kiss-me-arse foolishness 'bout dead people coming back and turning into something else, or somebody else. But I stating in a positive way, that...shhhh! listen...

DOTS: It is death. It is death, Boysie, that is in this room with the three of us. A dampening feeling, a feeling like a feeling crawling through this room like water crawling over a floor, and with the floor in darkness, and you can't see the water because the whole damn place is in darkness...

BOYSIE: *Now*, you talking some sense, at last, Dots. I sorry to say so, but you had me thinking that you was stupid as arse, not to agree with me. Something, some-damn-thing is in this room. Maybe it is death; maybe not. But whatever the hell it is, it got me, gorblummuh! real scared.

BERNICE: Mammy dead. But look at that thing, though — Mammy dead. And Estelle nowhere to be found. Dots, Estelle reminds me of the prodigal son: cannot be found at a time like this. I cry till I can't cry no more. It is Estelle's duty to come and assist in this mourning, you don't think so?...

DOTS: Gal, this is a evening of sorrow, and I don't intend to heap more on your head, than you already carrying, nor than you is able to bear. But just the same, since you already down down down with grief and sufferation, a little more can't kill you. So I might as well tell you that everybody else in Toronto know what you don't seem to know. Bernice, you may not like to hear this concerning your sister, Estelle, but...

BOYSIE: Dots, I think you need another sip o' this thing.

BERNICE: Now, let me see... toothpaste, toothbrush, Palm-olive soap, lipstick, under-arm deodorant, perspiration odour, what else?... down there in that island so damn hot! Oh yes! a extra toothbrush, in case this one breaks. Earrings, I got them? Yes, I got them... panties, five pairs, 'cause Barbados sweaty at this time o' year... slips, five dresses, brassieres, mensing pads and powder.... Look, Estelle isn't even present and I packing to leave first thing in the morning, eh!... Death is a funny thing. It could join blood more closer to blood than anything I know. Look, today, death came and death taketh away a mother; but that same death joined me and my missy, Mrs. Burrmann, on bended knee, like if we was siamee twins, join-up to one another by a spinal cord. When I received that letter, marked MAMMY UNKNOWN, sitting right here on this floor, you should have seen the two o' we, child. Black woman and Jew woman together, in grief and sorrow, feeling the same sorrow and feeling the same grief, experiencing the same emotion, as if I were her sister, and she were my sister. And in the midst o' my grief, I had was to raise my head to God, and ask him, Christ, now where the hell could Estelle be?

DOTS: Of a truth I could bear witness to your testimony, tonight, gal, that what you say, is so. You are a woman with grief in your heart. And as I say a moment ago, it isn't my place to add more grief to the toll you already dragging, but as you just mentioned Estelle, and admit to me and to Boysie, that you knew nothing concerning Estelle's whereabouts, although you is her sister, Bernice, I must tell you, although it could mean the end of our long friendship...

BOYSIE: Have another drink, Dots....

DOTS: I talking, man! You don't have no damn manners?... (Mrs. Burrmann's Beethoven was suddenly so loud that Dots could not hear her own voice talking. The music had been loud the whole night; but not so loud. And Dots didn't know that Bernice had heard very little of the night's conversation, and mourning.)

BERNICE: Mark your last words, Dots. Don't let me interrupt whatever you was saying. But I have to add, in fairness to Mrs. Burrmann, down there, poor soul, that when death came this afternoon, it joined us together in one, as no amount of hard work I could do in her kitchen, could have join us. And in the midst o' life, as you say, there is death; well, listen to me now! I adding something new to that. *In the midst o' death, there is life!*

BOYSIE: Amen! I saying amen to that, 'cause it sound like sense to me.

DOTS: Missy and maid? Maid and missy kneeling down in prayer, side by side, because o' death? Oh Jesus God, no!

BOYSIE: It is a good sign, it is a damn good sign, 'cause it show you one thing. Some white people isn't as bad as we does think they...

DOTS: But it mean more than that, though, Boysie! It mean and connote much much more than what you just said. It mean, in this sperspective, as Mrs. Hunter would put it, that white people and black people...

Someone was running up the stairs. They stopped talking to listen. Bernice, as if transfixed, was holding a pair of nylons in her hand.

Estelle bounded into the room.

"God, Bernice, I just heard. Henry told me."

"She dead, all right, gal!"

"Mammy dead," Bernice said. Immediately, she broke down crying, and screaming. (Dots got up and closed the door.) It seemed that her mind broke finally, for she started to roll all over the floor, like a woman in the spirit, at a revivalist meeting.

"How you heard?" Nobody was too keen to answer Estelle. She looked at Dots, and then at Boysie, already visibly drunk from the brandy. Finally, she looked at her sister, who was now merely writhing on the floor, and foaming at the mouth. Still, nobody answered. "Who sent the message, the cable? You got a cable, Bernice?"

"I get *this*!" Bernice reached up for the bible, and took the letter from it.

"But Bernice," Estelle said, "this letter couldn't have come from the Poor House where Mammy..." She checked herself, although it was too late.

"What you say?" Bernice was staring mad. The hand that reached for the bible, and which was resting on the chesterfield, now fell to her side, dead. Silence, like the silence Boysie was trying to explain earlier, came over the room. "*Poor* House? I hear you say Poor House?"

Estelle was weeping now. "I had to put her there, Bernice, because Mammy was losing her control...." Bernice was like a piece of wood, dead wallaba wood. "If you didn't get this letter from *them*, the Poor House people, well Mammy is not dead, Bernice. Bernice, you hear? Mammy is not dead."

"You little bitch," Dots said. "You heard what you just said? You know what you said just now? You said *Mammy not dead! Mammy not dead!* Two times, you say that. You didn't even have the decency to say *Mammy still living*! You couldn't say Mammy still living? Be-Christ, if Mammy isn't dead, she must be living then, eh, gal?"

"Mammy still living," Estelle said.

Bernice began to cry worse than ever. And then she laughed, a short laugh. "Christalmighty! and I would have gone down there by plane, and would have had to pay back every cent of that money for the plane ticket..."

"You are telling we, Estelle," Dots said, ignoring Bernice's words, and speaking slowly, in order to have her words understood, and to have them answered by Estelle, "you saying Mammy is not dead?" Estelle nodded. "Well, how in the name of hell, Bernice, are *you* going to explain all this to Mrs.

Burrmann, tomorrow morning?" And then she remembered her own husband. She looked at him, with a tender feeling, and she said, "And look! Boysie have drunk-up *all* o' Mrs. Burrmann expensive brandy!" And Boysie, hearing his name mentioned, but insensible to what was being said about him, wiped his lips with the back of his hand. He took the glass which was half-full, and rested it beside the twenty-six-ounce bottle of Hennessy Brandy. The bottle was already empty.

# 3

# THE TRIANGLE
# IS SMASHED

Summer came to Toronto like a plague. It was hot. Bernice could not drink sufficient soft drinks, or iced tea, or iced coffee, "cool-aid," or ginger ale — nothing she could do would conjure up a breeze, or reduce the oppressiveness in the room with her. Added to this, Estelle was in the room, too.

All the time, she cursed and said, "Jesus, is it hot!" The green trees round the house turned dumb. Not a breeze came to make them whisper. Each chance she got, she stole a "jumbo"-sized carton of ice-cream from Mrs. Burrmann's refrigerator; and she and Estelle would eat it, although sometimes, (particularly the day following the night that Estelle came home late), she would wish that some of the ice-cream would choke her, and kill her. But still, the sweat continued to pour out of them.

Bernice had not recovered from the shock and the mistake about her mother's death; and she did not cease to hate Estelle for her treatment of Mammy. A new attitude, blanket distrust, a sort of aggressive cynicism came into her life; she wanted to get back at Estelle; at Mrs. Burrmann (although she was not too clear about this vengeance); and at Dots for spreading gossip about Estelle. Shortly after the mistake about Mammy's death, when Bernice first decided that the whole world was against her, she began to get back at the world, via Mrs. Burrmann, who, to her, represented the world. She purposely wasted the groceries. She used too much cooking oil (sometimes, she threw some down the sink) on the lamb chops and the steaks and the pancakes. She wasted the sugar. She methodically over-used the groceries, "because if he or she, don't intend to put more money in my hand, as wages, well she going put more money in the grocer-man' hand, for groceries." It was a successful sabotage: Mrs. Burrmann didn't once ask whether the groceries were running out too fast. "That is the meaning o' money and power, gal!" Dots remarked when she heard the scheme. She didn't think Bernice had it in her; and she said so. "But, have patience, darling. One and one is two; and every five-cent piece does add-up to a dollar bill. Time on your side, gal." But Bernice felt her stealing and her wastage were like stealing from a man who didn't know it, and who didn't miss it; and this caused her, more than once, to abandon her sabotage. But the moment she was annoyed by an action or an attitude, she promptly returned to her corrosive and denuding waste. Now that summer was here, she would have the run of the whole house, to save or denude, as she pleased.

Mrs. Burrmann was thinking of going to Mexico. Mexico, she always said, was far and foreign and exotic; and nobody there knew Mrs. Gladys Rachel Heinne-Burrmann. The children would be going, as usual, to one of the Jewish-sponsored summer camps, in the northern resort area of Ontario, to learn "camp life and leadership qualities," where they were taught how to make wiener-roasts, pottery and to be juvenile-scaled Toby Robbinses and Lorne Greenes. Mr. Burrmann hadn't told anyone yet what his summer plans would be; but he knew they would depend upon Estelle.

Meanwhile, it was no picnic in the third-floor apartment. It was a hot summer. Downstairs, where the family spent most of their time, there was a new air-conditioner. The family and the workmen, had, by a small oversight, missed Bernice's apartment. Every afternoon, Bernice, dressed in her slip and panties only, and Estelle in a housedress (with nothing underneath) would watch Mrs. Burrmann and the children get into the new Impala convertible (her birthday present from her husband) and speed across the Boulevard to the nearby community swimming pool, on Eglinton Avenue West. This was the same pool that Dots had talked about last summer, when Bernice said she wanted to go there, for a bath. Dots said she had never seen a black person in the pool yet. "That is true, too," Bernice agreed. "I now remember that in the three years I been living in this district, I have never see a black person in that damn pool, neither." And this caused Dots to ask, "And how the hell could they still be calling it a *community* pool?" There was no reasonable answer Bernice could give. Soon after, they both forgot about the pool, and the community.

Bernice continued to look at Estelle and blame her for the heat. Too many o' we in this damn little room. It is you, Estelle, causing this heat, she would think. But she never had the courage to speak it openly. She was going out of her mind. The only consolation was the hostility she took out in the form of wasting the groceries. Then, after much thinking about her own condition, and about what Dots said concerning Estelle's long absences from the apartment, Bernice sat down and wrote a long letter to Lonnie. There were things she had to find out; and Lonnie was the only person she could trust. It was not an

honest trust; not an implicit trust, but rather a bargain. Lonnie
wanted to emigrate to Canada, and he wanted money. She
addressed herself to this bargain, and put her cards on the table
of honesty and near-defeat. *My dearest Lonnie,* ("If that don't
make the bastard listen, and feel that I am serious, well, I don't
know what would!") *who I have not treated too good in the past*
(she wrote), *a time comes in a woman's life, when she has to sit
down and make up a tally of things she mean to do, and have succeeded in doing, and of things she mean to do, and did not get the
chance of doing. My dropping you these few lines is one of the
things I had in mind always to do, but which life in this country,
and other things in life, prevent me from putting my attention to.
Estelle up here, as you know. Something gone wrong down there
with Mammy; and I want you to 'vestigate the ins and outs of that
situation in my behalf, and tell me everything. I am not happy up
here. There is a lot of things wrong with this country, I do not have
time to tell you everything that is wrong with this country; but I
will say one thing. Loneliness, Lonnie, is a thing I did not know
to exist against a person, as I have come to know it, in this
Canada. That is one thing. Another thing I could tell you about
my life here, is that money is not all. Money is not all, boy. I was
after money when I put down my name to come up here to work
off my fat in these people kitchen. But I will not make that mistake two times. But yet, according to some of the things that Estelle
been saying, all is not roses down there in Barbados, neither. And
this bring me to something else. You have always written to me
asking for a piece of change. Well, I am going to give it to you. I
can only send you twenty dollars now. But I hope that you will be
able to get some of the things you always wanted to get, with it.
And don't forget to take care of the little boy. Terence is all I have.
He is my future. I only hoping that God will give me the strength*

*to endure this slavery up here, by which time Terence will be a big man to come up and live with me. I have great things in mind for that boy. But sometimes, things is so bad, that I have to sit down and cry and wish that I was back home where I can speak to a friend, or laugh with a friend, or even laugh with myself, if there is no friend to laugh with. You understand what I saying, Lonnie? Canada to me, is only a place to make money in, not a place to live in, or feel relaxed in. These people don't owe me nothing; and I owes them nothing, in return. But I am here, and I have to make the most of a bad situation. I want you to understand, Lonnie, that although I have not sat down and poured out my heart to you as I used to, and as a woman would pour out her heart to the man she loves, it do not mean that you were not always in my mind, and in my heart...* ("Jesus Christ, I am going too far with Lonnie, now! I don't think I should tell that man all this, 'cause he might start imagining things...") *...a young strong woman cannot live in this place by herself. She needs a man...* ("Yes, I gone too far with Lonnie, now!") She waited until a voice within her reasoned with her as to whether she was really saying too much, writing too many personal things, to Lonnie. She hadn't written him in about eighteen months. "The things I am writing that man...suppose he already found himself a woman to live with, Christ! what a shameful position I would be putting myself in! I can see Lonnie showing my love letter to every man, woman and child...." She convinced herself that the inner voice was wisdom. She folded the letter. She folded the envelope, already addressed, round the letter. She tore up the letter with the envelope, and dropped them into the toilet bowel. As she flushed them down, she stood there and composed in her mind, a better letter to Lonnie; a straight-forward one, which he could never mistake as a surrender. She was very concerned about giving in to him; and very proud about her strength and her sexual abstinence, and about withstanding his advances for so long.... *Lonnie, I am sending you this twenty dollars because you ask for it.* ("Can't get nothing for nothing, child!") *Go round by St. Peters Almshouses and visit Mammy for me. Estelle put her there. Tell me everything. The name of the charge nurse, what ward they have Mammy in, everything. Be good to Terence. I am thinking of taking out papers to help you to come up here.* ("Now, I will see what kind o' man that Lonnie is!") This was a much better letter, she decided. More business-like. She revised it twice in her mind, and made a promise that after cleaning up the kitchen tonight, she would write it down, on paper.

They were sitting on the balcony of a coffee house on Avenue Road, Estelle and her man. It was a cool night, one of the first of the summer. They were drinking iced tea. The inside room was crowded, mostly with young people. The men were wearing beards, and the women, mostly, were wearing their hair long. A few were barefoot, Estelle noticed. As they were walking along Yorkville, they met the owner of the coffee house, a European gentleman with long Jesus-like hair and beard, an old bowler hat covering the bald spot of his head, and a cane in his hand. He had a plaster cast on his right foot and leg. "Welcome to Zee Place!" he was telling everyone; and giving out handbills advertising The Place, which was the name of the coffee house. Below and across the street from where they were sitting now, they could see the owner, still hawking his club.

"Beautiful night," the man said, without looking up at the stars.

"Reminds me of the West Indies, of Barbados," Estelle said. "Stars, stars, stars...."

"Like northern Ontario, too. In summer." Earlier, they had been talking about going to Muskoka, or Timmins, for the summer. But she disregarded the suggestion, until, at least, it became a firm invitation.

"Twinkle, twinkle, little star..." She recited the line, and then sang it, softly. "Twinkle little Estelle...."

"...how I wonder what you are!" He touched her hand, ever so softly; and then he squeezed it, and together they laughed. They had forgotten, in their happiness, that others were on the balcony with them. It was summer. It was lovely. For some time, neither of them said a word. At last, Estelle said, "What's going to happen, when she finds out?" He pretended he hadn't heard; but when he saw how childish that was, he pretended he didn't know to whom she was referring. "Your wife." There was nothing he could say to this; there was no pretence he could put up. He had learned early in his relationship with Estelle, that she was a very straightforward woman. Blunt, almost. "You know something?" she said, knowing he wasn't going to answer the previous question. "If I was your wife. And if it was me, in this situation I find myself in now, you know what I would do?" He touched her hand again, expecting kindness, understanding, love even. But Estelle said, bluntly, "I would kill you, Sam."

"Do what?" The tables nearby turned to listen. He had shouted, inadvertently.

"I said I would kill you," she said, much softer, with a whisper of a smile on her beautiful face. The candlelight was shimmering. "Come, let's go. I'm beginning to feel bad." She did not talk to him, until they had come within walking distance of the house on Marina Boulevard. Normally she would get out just before reaching the house, and walk, with him driving behind to guard her. And returning home very late, normally, nobody saw them. (Once Mrs. Burrmann was looking out, from the sitting-room, with the lights out, but she only saw Estelle going in through the side entrance; and although Mr. Burrmann drove up ten minutes later, she suspected nothing.) This time, just as she was about to get out, he said, "Well?" — thereby asking a million questions in that one word: but really trying to find the answer to one question, which had been bothering him for about three weeks, and which he was terrified to ask, in case the answer was what he had suspected. When she didn't answer, he moved closer to her. She stiffened her body against his embrace. He was sensitive to her feelings. He was vexed with her. And he forced his lips over her lips; and although he could feel her teeth against his lips, he still didn't stop. He was beside himself this night, with desire: a brutal, rough, rapist desire. "*I* know, *I* know," he said, trying to make his voice and manner coincide with what he thought was the James Cagney approach to romantic manliness. I could kill you right now, Sam, she was thinking, as he rubbed his tongue on her teeth, forcing her mouth open. (Suppose this bitch was to bite off my goddamn tongue; and he saw blood on his expensive suit, and it splattered all over his car. That made him stop forcing himself upon her. He hugged her; and he kissed her cheek instead.) You make me feel so cheap, she was thinking, as he passed his hand over her smooth skin. I must have been mad to let you do the things you did, all that you have done, and now, you don't have the decency nor the understanding... (He was forcing his hand against her brassiere and her breast: he was making his hand crawl like oil on a piece of glass)...and look what the hell I got myself into! Christ! if Bernice finds out that I let this, this, this-this-bastard treat me like a whore, take me on Jarvis Street...He was very close to her now; and his face was buried in the crook of her neck. He could taste the salt in her perspiration. Estelle remained very quiet. She even rested her hand on his neck. The neck was very smooth. The skin was very smooth. It was oily, too. There must have been too much grease in his hair. She closed her eyes under his hands, and for *one second*, she squeezed hard on his swallow pipe; and she could see the blood pumping through veins in his neck; and then she opened her eyes, and in her imagination, removing his hands, and she reached up and kissed him on the mouth; and she opened his mouth with her mouth, and talked very personal things, very provocative things to him, alone, with a twirling and articulate tongue. She knew she had him within her power. She knew his weaknesses. He was that kind of a man. Be-Christ, Sam, you're going to pay through your arse, man, for the things you done to me, you hear? She could see him laughing with his eyes, weakening in her arms, as she tantalized him with the words of her tongue. "Darling," he said, as if he was panting, and not talking. "Dar-ling."

Estelle traced small circles on his neck, with the compasses of her first finger and her second finger. The circles confused and excited him; and he drew still closer to her. She hated him more deeply, the closer he came. As he embraced, and kissed her, he thought: *goddamn, look what I picked up off the street! look at me, Sam Burrmann, screwing about with this big black nig- Negro woman, goddammit, but baby, you're barking up the wrong tree. I know a lot of men who lay their domestics, screwing and being screwed-up by them; but that's not my scene, baby. I bet you're soon going to tell me you're pregnant. Am I going to feel bad! and weep? Or get the best goddamn abortionist in Toronto, and put you in his goddamn hands? That's a scream!...put you in his goddamn hands, with a little expense, everything'll be fine...so, you're not fooling me, baby. One thing about Jeffrey, that goddamn idiot: he told me a long time how to lay you black broads. You all like a piece of white prick.* And he spoke to her, and said, "I love you, Estelle."

"I love you, too, man."

"Really?"

"Well, how you mean? How you could ask me a foolish thing like that, eh, man?" And she continued to trace circles on the back of his neck; and he continued to hold her close to him. His excitement, and his ecstasy made him reconsider what he had been thinking about her. *Shit, that would be hell for this poor bitch! A man just can't breed a broad and leave her, even if she's a...* But he couldn't call her a Negro, this time; not even in his mind. He thought of his friend the abortionist (unknown to him, his own wife had been treated by this same abortionist; and Brigitte used to work for him, as his cleaning-woman, before she got the job on Marina Boulevard when she was learning to be a Canadian citizen)... *and if Paul plays the ass, there's always the Children's Aid Society! there's always some poor guy looking for a child, so there shouldn't be much trouble to place a Jewisho-Africo-Westindico child! hah-hah! what's one more Negro bastard in this goddamn world? One more mixed-up, mixed kid? But I'm sure Paul'll play ball and help out, or if not...* His excitement was climbing a small wall at the top of which he thought he would reach some kind of manual consummation. But she knew when she had him: and just before that point of arrival — or departure — she withdrew her hand, and ran out of the car, leaving the door open. She knew he couldn't shout after her (he was too near home), that he had to be silent, and self-effacing; silent as he had been with Jeffrey. "You are a white son-of-a-bitch!" she told him. But she didn't know whether he had heard.

Summer was doing something awful to Estelle. It was bringing her closer to Bernice; and it was taking her further from Sam. Apart from her own experiences of arrival, and her taste of summer and fire, she was having her own problems. It was fortunate for her that Bernice escaped downstairs to the kitchen every morning before eight o'clock; the moment she was alone, with the door locked, she would rush to the bathroom, and engage in the violent motions of vomiting. Nothing came up. But she knew that one morning, something was going to come up. This daily dry vomiting had been coming on, more regularly, for about three weeks. Bernice neither witnessed it, nor suspected it. Lately, it was coming at the same time, each morning. In spite of all this, Estelle refused to think too much about it, and refused to interpret it as a symptom of pregnancy; for by so doing, she would be confessing to a defeat of her schemes against the man. But she was frightened. And fear was like a paralysis which kept her in the apartment during the day, allowing her to go out only in the late afternoon. This was one time when being alone did not depress or exasperate her. What exasperation she suffered came through the heat, and the thought of the butterflies in her stomach, and of the man who had put them there. Since winter had turned to spring, she had been going out with Agatha more often; and she had visited many places, and was brought into a wider, more mixed circle of friends in her stay than Bernice had known in three or more years.

The kind of relationship that sprang up between Estelle and Agatha was that of a woman trying to find out everything about her rival, her enemy. On Agatha's part there was more sincerity. She told Estelle many close things, personal things, about Henry: she was angry because he didn't go to night school, and then university, and "raise himself"; he had such "natural ability, it is a shame he does nothing but hate all white people"; and drink himself in a stupor almost every night, either in the Paramount, or in the Pilot. "You know, Ess, sometimes I feel he is so inferior, you know what I mean? There are many things I can't even discuss with him, and when I try to make him feel, feel equal, he starts abusing me and calling me a *white intellectual*... hell! I'm no intellectual! I am a *woman!*" And that was exactly why Estelle was so fond of Agatha. Estelle learned many things about Negro men from Agatha. She knew also, that Henry had caused Agatha to move — she was really evicted because the tenants complained — four times since she had left home, also because of him. That was two months ago. "When I moved into that bachelor apartment, on Prince Arthur Avenue, the building superintendent complained. I was having too many parties, he said. I didn't have *one* party, Estelle. I was only in the place three weeks, and I spent those three weekends in New York, with Henry. And then he changed his tune, and said something like, *Well, you know, Miss... we haven't got anything 'gainst you, but you see, the other tenants, well, they see you all the time with this coloured fella...* and that bastard was a DP! A foreigner! Estelle, I was never so ashamed to be a white person!" (Estelle could not fully understand the dilemma that Agatha had seen herself in.) "It's been like that, three other times, after Prince Arthur. St. George Street... there, the superintendent was all right until he saw

Henry helping me move in. Then he started asking a lot of insulting questions. *Was I married, miss?*...Then Bedford Road, then Lowther, in a so-called old Toronto family home... until now, when I got this flat on Huron and Bloor." But she didn't tell Estelle the worst of all her experiences. It was when she had to move from Prince Arthur to St. George Street. Things were going well, until she needed a reference; and she could only get this from her previous superintendent. It was required because the St. George Street caretaker had seen Henry; neighbours with no love in their heart had caught Henry kissing Agatha goodnight outside her apartment door late one night. The neighbours complained. The superintendent asked her to leave, because, "Miss, this is a decent apartment dwelling." Agatha hired a friend who was a lawyer; and when the lawyer knew he was involved in a racial case, he advised her to drop proceedings, because, "Well, look at it this way, Agatha. It isn't doing you any goddamn good to get mixed up in a thing like this with a Negro chap. You understand what I'm saying? I mean, Negroes are great guys, I subscribe to the NAACP, and I dig jazz and all that, but I'm not advising you now as a lawyer, I'm talking to you as my friend. I'll ask the owners to refund you your three months' advance rent, and I think you should find yourself a place to live. And Agatha, there's a lot of nice guys your kind, around still, yuh know?" This was the seed from which began to grow a smouldering hate for Henry. After this, she loved him less. She had got herself into debt (the moving, packing, lawyer-friend's fees, bottles of sleeping pills and tranquillizer pills and two emergency sessions with her psychiatrist) and she began to weaken under the stress of society and its demands upon her. Once, in a moment of reality — this was her mother's favourite phrase

— Agatha really looked at herself; and toyed with the idea of
going with a man *less* black than Henry: somebody like Harry
Belafonte. Her reputation was being discussed at parties (she
was no longer invited to them) as the poor Jewish kid who got
kicked out of apartments because of her weakness for Negroes.
Somebody suggested making her an honorary president of
the NAACP. When word got back to her, through a mutual,
but tongue-lashing friend, she remained in her Huron Street
room, forcing herself into perpetual sleep, because everywhere
she went, she thought white people and black people were
pointing their fingers at her, and saying *There she is!* It was her
landlord, a painter, and a kind of Bohemian, who got her out
of this depression, by inviting her, *and* Henry to have dinner
with him, and his wife. A new view of the world sprung up out
of the four glasses of Beaujolais wine which her landlord served.

That was Agatha's story, as she told it (in parts, and in part)
to Estelle. But the person whom Estelle sympathized with was
Henry. Secretly, Estelle still felt that Agatha was "stealing one
of our men."

But now, it was summer. Summer brought with it a
remarkable exposure: an exposure of friendliness, of happiness,
of gaiety and of life to the shrouded, over-coated atmosphere
of the city. Summer brought Estelle closer once more to Sam,
who seemed a new man. He took her to Niagara Falls, to
Oshawa where they made cars; he took her across the Canadian
border to Buffalo and to Syracuse where she saw many houses
painted white, like in Barbados. Sam was now driving a white
convertible Cadillac. It was education and excitement. But
Estelle could not speak a word of it to Bernice. As far as
Bernice knew, she was going out with Agatha.

But the excitement was tiring. She was losing her stamina

in the heat. She was losing it because now there was no denying that her physiological condition had changed. The dry vomiting changed to real vomiting. She would come in late at night, and pretend to fall asleep fast, so she wouldn't have to talk to Bernice. She had to do this, because Bernice got tired of sleeping on the two chairs, and she began to make the chesterfield into a bed. She would put Estelle's pillow at *her* feet. She herself wasn't too keen on talking, either. But she had been thinking. Estelle's symptoms were now clear; and she planned how best to tell Sam she was pregnant. It was going to be difficult, since Sam himself suspected; and he had become edged with an over-sensitivity, capable of cutting both ways.

Bernice never stopped questioning herself about Estelle's long absences. Similarly, she never let up on her schemes of sabotaging Mrs. Burrmann's groceries. In these two respects, summer had done nothing to seep her destructive resourcefulness. But she didn't make the same fuss with Estelle, as she had made during winter and spring. One Thursday afternoon, drinking iced Coca-Cola with Dots, Bernice mentioned Estelle; and Dots gave the same explanation for Estelle's absences. "You don't have to take down Estelle's pants and inspect them to know she is taking man, eh, gal?" Dots's straightforwardness wounded Bernice. "You grieving too much over that gal."

"Well, I hope she don't get herself in trouble, though." Sometimes, this was a dishonest wish. "The more I think 'bout it, the more I feel sure that my sister may get herself in the family-way, sometime...."

"You get a room for Estelle, yet?"

"Not yet."

"Same thing happened, eh, gal?"

"Same blasted excuse."

"Only this afternoon I been reading in the *Star*, where it say there is thousands o' white men and white women living together in sin, in apartments, and even in Rosedale!"

"Yuh lie, Dots! Well, I never would guess!"

"And the man who write this story...yuh know something? I think he had a Jew-name, too!...anyhow, he says that once a woman who wasn't married, went up to this real exclusive place in Rosedale, and asked for an apartment. She had the honesty to say she wasn't married to the man she was going to live with. And guess what the superintendent told that lady?"

"I don't read the *Star*, Dots."

"That's true. But he said, It is all right, madam. Most of the people who live here together, as man and woman, isn't married, neither."

"To err is mankind, Dots."

"You just spoke a mouthful! But you have no idea of the amount o' sinning, fornicating and adultering that takes place in this Toronto. But when it happens in the white man's corner o' the world, I think they calls it by another name. Take it from me, gal, whilst you are up here reading *Muhammad Speaks* and a lot o' race books, I am down in Rosedale reading history. I reads *Flash* and *Hush*. Them is two history books which tell me the facts and truths of life." Bernice was very impressed: she promised to get herself these two weeklies. She never expected that everything about this world wasn't contained in *Muhammad Speaks*, after all. "Gal, take it from me. Rosedale is too good for black people." She remembered seeing a West Indian family in Rosedale, recently; to be honest, she added, "Now and then, you find a white man with a heart. Now and then. Take that from me, too."

"Mr. Burrmann, my employer, is one o' them few."

"Why this place so damn hot?" She fanned herself with the tail of her dress and laughed. "Too much black people living in it, these days, gal! It is we who bring this damn heat, you never heard that?" Dots fanned herself some more. "Hey, Bernice! You remember that nurse-gal who was here at the party for Estelle? Priscilla? Well, she engaged to a Canadian man."

"Yuh lie!"

"Gal, you are the only woman we waiting on still," Dots teased; and she laughed her sensuous and suggestive laugh. "Hurry up and get a man. This nurse-gal engaged to married a orderly from the same hospital, the General."

"He is a white man?"

"I said a Canadian man."

"And I ask you if he is a white man."

"He is still a man, gal!"

And swiftly, the heat took possession of them; and they paid more attention to the people passing. Almost everybody was in shorts. Some men in front gardens had already taken refuge in Bermuda shorts. Bernice said she was going to wear her shorts on the streets. "Oh Christ, no, gal! What you think you are doing? Wearing shorts? Not in Toronto! I have never seen a black person in the many years I been here, who was man enough or woman enough, to wear shorts, in public. And I not talking 'bout the shape o' your legs, neither. I am concern with the *colour*!" Bernice said she was talking foolishness, but really she had never seen one either. And she had brought a pair of shorts from Barbados more than three years ago, and never once had she put them on, outside her apartment. "And yuh know something, else? The swimming pools! I don't see black people in them, neither. But I promised one of these good days. I am going to drink a good rum, go up there by the big pool on Eglinton, take *off all my clothes*, every damn stitch, and when them white men see my beautiful body, and I dive-off from that diving board, be-Jesus Christ, you will read about my debut in the three papers. I might even make television on the CBC!" When they stopped laughing, they saw a white woman passing, wearing shorts. Neither of them said anything for a while.

"That is Irene Gasstein, the woman that Brigitte works for," Bernice said, as the woman was going out of sight.

"She look too bad in them shorts! Eh?"

"She look bad all right, but I am not questioning that. I questioning how she could twirl her little stiff backside at me, as if she owns the street, the city and the whole o' Canada."

Dots got up from the window, and began stepping around the apartment, in a parody of Mrs. Gasstein, in shorts. "Looka me! oh Christ, heh-heh-heeee! Mrs. Dotstein!" Then she realized she had exhausted the performance, and she had to face an audience of reality. "This country could never be home, gal. All the black people here, living in this place, called Canada, be we foreign-born black people, or local-born Canadian black people, we are only abiding through the tender mercies o' God and the white man, and . . ."

"Both o' them is white, to boot!"

". . . the landlord," Dots concluded. "The tender mercies o' God, the white man and the landlord. Any time gal, any time, these three gods feel like it, bram! they kick-in our behinds just like they do down in Mississippi. Don't ever forget that."

"But wait! Dots, have you become a Black Muslim, too?" It pleased Bernice to hear Dots talking like this.

"Commonsense, gal!" And she laughed. She got up from the window, and sat on the chesterfield. "You know what I would like right now?"

"A nice long cool drink of mauby from back home?"

"I mean a real wish, something I would *really* like."

"To be back home, right now!"

"That ain't no damn wish, gal."

"A better job, then?"

"A man!" She got up and patted herself between her thighs, slapping it and looking at Bernice, who held down her head in shame. Then she walked over to Bernice, and patted Bernice high up between her thighs, and said, laughing, "Who looking after *that* for you? Take care cobwebs don't get in there, eh?" When the laugh faded and she could see Bernice once more for the film of joyous tears in her eyes, she saw that Bernice was fanning herself with a copy of *Awake.* "I have to give it to Estelle. She really knows how to look after herself...."

"Never mind me, darling," Bernice said, taking the conversation off Estelle. "Never mind me. But I could tell you something interesting, in case you want to hear. Henry been coming after me, darling. Yes, Henry crawling back...."

"Jesus Christ, no!"

"Yes."

"No! that ain't true, gal! What happen to Agaffa?"

Bernice insisted it was so. When Dots realized she was serious, she rushed to her, and held Bernice in her arms, close; and kissed her on her face, and swung her around playfully in a dance. "Here comes the bride, here comes the bride, da da da-daaa, da-da da da dee-da...." And after that, Bernice went downstairs and cooked the two largest porterhouse steaks she could find for herself and Dots; and between them, they drank

a whole bottle of wine that belonged to Mrs. Burrmann. They
were so happy, and so talkative and so drunk, that the moment
they finished eating, they fell asleep. Bernice didn't know
where the Burrmanns were, and she didn't care.


For the past few weeks, Henry had been experiencing greater
insecurity in his affair with Agatha. She did not point her finger of censure at him, and blame him for all her difficulties,
with apartment superintendents. But she made him suffer
in other ways: she would leave her telephone off the hook, and
this would arouse his jealousy, even though she was always
faithful to him from the time they had met; she would refuse
to accompany him to the Paramount and the Pilot, having
suddenly become aware that both places were beneath her
respectability. She did continue seeing him (only on weekends
because of the pressure of essays and seminars in her graduate
course in Zoology) but each meeting contained some tension
carried over from the last one. He wanted to see her more
often; and he imagined that her studies were only a pretence:
that when the phone was off the hook, there was really a man
with her. He could not bear this, because their love had been
a full, rich, turbulent combustion of love, strength and sex.
There was pain too; and sorrow and sympathy: like the two
nights and one day he sat beside her on the bed, holding her
hand to extract the pain that crawled through her body like a
meandering centipede, as the warm poultices he placed on her
infected leg whizzed through her body and brought her, many
times, on the brink of a death-like fainting. And that night,
rushing her to the Emergency Ward of the Toronto General
Hospital; and waiting like a prospective father, smoking and
walking and hoping. When he took her back to her Prince

Arthur Avenue apartment, and had settled her in bed, in the bed he had himself made up with the linen he had washed at the coin laundry on Asquith Avenue, he went round the block to Palmers Drug Store, to fill the prescription. And there he met the first real challenge of his strength in love, and (as he tried not to tell himself) the real repudiation by a white woman, for his love for a white woman.... "Because, this prescription, sir, is a narcotic. Do you understand that?" He did not know that, because he had never been to school very much, and the school he attended never remembered to teach him how to read prescriptions. "This is a narcotic drug you want me to fill. Do you have the name of the doctor? His number? I have to call the doctor to see if he really prescribed this." "Look, woman," Henry said, not really getting the implication in this cross-examination, "this thing belongs to a woman, a friend o' mine, and I only come to get it fixed, because she is in a blasted lot o' pain, and..." And the white-faced, white-laced, white-smocked, white-thinking-right-is-white white woman interrupted him, and said, "I can't just fill out this prescription because you say so. This contains narcotics, and..." Henry has forgotten now what he told that white woman; but he still can remember how he screamed and shouted and asked the entire drug store to bear him witness, and say whether he was on narcotics, because he was black. While the woman-pharmacist herself called the Emergency Ward of the hospital to check, and to get the doctor ("Jesus God, I wonder if my woman is dying...all this time this bitch calling, and my woman might be dying from pain!") a well-dressed white man came to the counter and whispered a purchase of condoms in the pharmacist's ears; and he saw Henry and shouted, "Shit baby! what's happening, Henry?"; and the pharmacist-woman, hearing the white-referee's testimonial, dropped the telephone and filled the prescription. You god-damn motherfucker, was all that Henry could think of saying to her. And what else did he do? — nothing, nothing. God-damn, here am I, a black son-of-a-bitch, trying for once, to be nice to a woman, and this broad is trying to kill the woman, my woman! Goddamn! But he soon forgot the scene in Palmers (he never told it to Agatha, because he didn't think their love was strong enough to endure these malicious interruptions).

Once, when he could stand her withdrawal no longer, he rushed over to her apartment, and banged on the door. There was no one at home. He planned and he plotted what he would say to her: the slaps he would give her; and he rehearsed them over and over, to give him courage. And then she returned, with her hands laden with large books, three hours later. He was shivering in the draughty lounge; and all he had courage to do, was to open the door for her, and say, "Goodbye, I see you're busy as hell."

He never got over the feeling of intellectual inferiority to her; especially when they were in the company of her university friends. She would use words, some of them technical and zoological, which she knew he could not have heard about; and she would ask him, "Have you read this absolutely great novel?", most of which were written by Chinese and Japanese novelists. All he could say, was "Goddamn! how do you know all these things?"; promise to get the novels from the Main Public Library, as she suggested (but the Library was so badly stocked with these "great novels"!); forget about them as soon as he was outside her literary influence; and he would hate her immensely and secretly, for making him out to be a fool. With time and with hatred, he forgot completely about these "great novels," and their authors; and he drank more draught beer at the Paramount; and with the beer, he washed down the servings of his favourite Southern-fried chicken wings. One night, alone and sad (she had kept her promise of never returning to the LADIES AND ESCORTS of the Paramount) he commiserated with a Polish neighbour, sitting at his shiny, circular drinking table. The dust on the floor and the smoke in the noisy, many-tongued room, was irritating him. Perhaps this was why Agatha refused to return here. "Hey, man," he asked the Polish drunkard, "you ever heard of a great Chinese cat who wrote a novel?"

"*Chinese?*" The neighbour knew only one Chinese: the man behind the fish-and-chips and fried-chicken counter. There must be some terrible mistake, his manner suggested.

"There's some great novels written in Chinese, my man. Great works of art those cats produced."

The neighbour looked back at the man behind the counter. The man was frying chips and Southern-fried chicken wings. "You mean that man wrote one of them, sir?"

Henry looked too: at the Chinese man, half-hidden in the smoke screen of cooking smoke and cooking oil. There was also a black man at their table; and he looked too; and he said, "Shit, man! I only got time for hustling a piece o' pussy and a quick buck from the Man, man. I gotta teach these cats how to *love*. I ain't got time for too much education and shit like that, baby. So, I won't know how to dig that Chinese cat, unless he cooks me some swinging Southern-fried. Education? Man, that's the white folks' scene. *I'm loving*, baby."

"There's some good works of art written by the Chinese. Great works. Goddamn!" For the rest of the night, between his dribbling beer-words, Henry would mention the Chinese and their novels to whoever joined the Polish immigrant and himself, at the salted, salt-sprinkled table. When the waiter shouted, "Last call! Drink up!", Henry stumbled home with a blonde woman on his arm; and throughout the turbulence of a night of hatred in bed with her, his literary inadequacy returned to him. Early next morning, when he turned over and saw who she was too close to him, he asked her, "You ever read a great Chinese novel, baby?" The blonde winked and blinked her eyes scarred by rheum and mascara, and said, "Are you crazy?" "Damn!" he said, and hustled her out, right away.

Shortly afterwards, sitting in his room he and Boysie were chatting about what Boysie termed, "life in this kiss-me-arse country." Boysie had brought along a half bottle of rum with a Barbados label on it, but bottled in Canada, by the Liquor Control Board of Ontario. This made him mad, to begin with; but they were drinking it, anyhow.

"How's the woman situation, man?" Boysie asked.

"Goddamn!"

"Man, I didn't think a woman could love me so bad, be-Jesus Christ! I talking 'bout Brigitte."

"You have now begin to see life, Boysie," said Henry, lapsing into his favourite Harlem American slang. "Dig! Those white cats hate our guts for it, baby. But their women *love* us, baby. You dig?"

"That is true." Boysie smacked his lips noisily, and closed his eyes against the punch of the rum. He was drinking his from a tea cup with a chipped rim. Henry was drinking his with ice and water, because he was "no goddamn native like you, Boysie, but a Canadian." He was wearing a tie and a seersucker jacket, while Boysie was dressed casually, in a short-sleeved calypso shirt. "What you just say is true, yuh. I wish I had a woman like Agatha. How she looks after you, man! gor-blummuh, all Dots does do is read *Hush* and *Flash*. But Agaffa, does take you to the O'Keefe and to concerts. Man, I can't understand why the black women in this place refuse to take a leaf outta the white women's book. You understand what I mean?"

"White woman was invented for black man. That is what I know. Goddamn, man, I been through so much white pants in my time in this town, Boysie, baby, that I don't even remember there's a colour problem here. Shit, man, as far as this cat is concerned, there *ain't no colour problem.* Because, dig! when you come down to the level o' undressing a woman, that thing is all the same colour and formation, baby. You dig?"

"Heh-heh-heh!" Nothing tickled Boysie more than woman-talk.

"Let the Man worry 'bout discrimination, baby. You dig? 'Cause I'm getting my due, dig?"

"But you really think a woman like Brigitte could love a man like me?"

"Baby, you better learn there ain't no such thing as love in this. What the hell you talking 'bout love, for? Love? It is hate, baby. You dig? Hate: *h-a-t-e*! Dig! They love you, *not* because they love you, but because they *sympathize* with you, you dig? And I ain't outrightly saying there ain't no love between a black cat and a white chick, dig." Henry was in command: he was enjoying the impact he was having upon Boysie. Nothing was more precious to Boysie than women. And he was always entranced when Henry used his Harlem American slang. The intonations of the voice did something beautiful and powerful to him. "They love *you.* And you hate *them.*"

"Is that true, though?"

"Well, dig again, baby. Dig this. I'll tell you something 'bout me and my chick, Agatha. Man, one night it was hell in this bed. I'm thinking of all those black people lynched and killed, all those black cats, murdered and slain, all those black chicks raped and dehumanized, demortalized, *de*-whatever-the-hell-you-want-to-call-it, and dig! man, I'm *driving* and *driving*, baby. It was driving, driving, driving. Hell broke loose, baby. I'm thinking of going down to the Civil Service Commission on St. Clair, and the Man there telling me, No jobs, buddy; so you dig? Down at the Unemployment Insurance Commission and the Man there telling me there ain't no jobs. Down at Eatons during one Christmas rush period, and the Man there telling me, there ain't no jobs. I'm thinking of the Man, you dig? The Man. The Man. The Man. No jobs. No jobs. No jobs. That's what the hell I'm thinking of, baby. And I'm driving like I'm *crazy*. And the broad, she's *bawling*. You dig? Wailing! Man, she's yelling her little head off, Love me, baby, she says, *love me*! But me, baby? I'm thinking how I got this goddamn Man by his balls, man you dig me, you dig what I'm doing to this Man? I'm punching him in his arse with all my goddamn hate, baby. I'm driving. Man, I am so cool and hip to that chick, that I know I ain't going stop driving till I kill her. And shit, baby, you think she was thinking about my driving, or feeling my driving? You think that chick was hip to what I was thinking of the Man? Goddamn, baby, *she* was thinking I *was loving her*. But, man, I was *re-paying*! I was re-paying *her* for what her brothers do to *my* sister, you dig? There ain't no such thing as love, baby. It a re-payment. A final goddamn re-payment." Boysie was overcome. "Dig," Henry commanded him; and went to the telephone. "I'm going to show you now, how stupid these broads is. Look man, I'm going to call up Agatha and you will hear how crazy this chick is behind me...so, dig!" Boysie did not recover from this devastating comment on his love for Brigitte. It was insulting. It was humiliating. But it was instructive. He was not convinced, however, that Henry himself believed all he had said. Boysie just loved. He hoped that Brigitte just loved too. There was nothing else in it, that he could think of. But he had to confess that Henry was among white women much longer than he was. Henry was on the telephone now. And Boysie, forever mesmerized by his friend's personality, rested his chipped tea cup of rum on the floor, and listened attentively. He even repeated under his breath, some of the phrases Henry was using to Agatha. Gotta see how these going go over 'pon Brigitte, man, he promised. "Hi, baby!" Henry said, louder than necessary. The slang and the alcohol in his acquired vocabulary, were making him poetic. "Ain't you never going to come over and give you daddy some loving, honey?... I'm here all by my lonesome, puffing and pining for you, baby. Just pining my old self, waiting for you...." He put his hand over the mouth-piece. "Come here, you arse-hole, and learn a lesson from a pro." Boysie came and stood beside Henry. Henry removed his hand, and said, "Baby, I want you to tell me how much you love me. Tell your daddy-o.... What you say? I know already how much you love me?..." He shrugged his shoulders at Boysie; Boysie took the wink and the hint, and went back to his rum which was waiting for him, in the tea cup. "Well, baby, I'll be seeing you, later tonight." Henry then put down the phone. He had dialled his own number.

"Gorr-blummuh!" Boysie exclaimed, very impressed by his friend's technique. "That woman love you real bad, man."

"That ain't love, Boysie Cumberbatch, good God, man!

how much times I have to tell you there ain't no such thing as love. That is a *re-payment*. You dig that, now!"

Bernice never liked to be by herself when travelling on the subway, or in a streetcar. She was always nervous and self-conscious, particularly when it was crowded. She would imagine that they wanted to push her under the wheels; that she was unclean; that she was some kind of interloper; that she was without rights to sit on *their* subway. All these persistent thoughts came to her, because it seemed that whenever she was by herself on a subway, or in a streetcar, the newspapers were always filled with photographs of white people beating up black people: and she could not see any physical difference between the passengers in her streetcar and those from the States, shown in the photographs. She always tried to find out what they were thinking: no one had the courage to *say* what he was thinking (her egotism would not allow the possibility that they were really thinking about their first and second mortgages). No one ever said a word to her. But she knew they *looked* it. She became self-conscious, first, one day when a pregnant white woman entered the streetcar, and not finding a seat, except the half-seat beside Bernice, decided not to sit down, although the car was rocking, and was jammed.

But riding south today, on the Eglinton–Union Station subway, with Estelle beside her, it was different. Still, she was not settled in mind: two days ago, Brigitte had told her, again, some distressing news about Boysie. She had threatened to tell Dots, but Brigitte asked her not to; assuring her that she herself could handle the problem. Ignoring her companion, Estelle, Bernice recalled (even complete with Brigitte's accent) the shameful story of Boysie's fornication — that was the word Bernice used to describe his behaviour. "He is a damn fornicator. Coming now to muddy-up my waters, Dots' waters, Estelle's waters, every blasted black person's waters, that stupid-foolish..." She had condemned Boysie immediately. She had given neither Boysie nor Brigitte time to check the truth of the story: *"my friend, he sees me talking to a man, and he start to threaten me. Oh my God, Bernice, never have I seen a man so cruel and so jealous. So cruel! You know my friend, the policeman? Well, he get into the car and drive down this street after the man. And when he don't see the man, he come back and give me this."* (Brigitte pulled down her left eyelid, although the blow had landed between the eyes. It was black-and-blue.) *"He tell me he is going to watch out, every night for this man. He say, Let me catch this coloured bastard playing round you, again, just once more, and I kill him."* It was then that Bernice told her, "Between me and you, Brigitte. Me and you is friends for a long time now. Jesus God, what the hell you see in Boysie? You can't find nothing better than *that*?" It was at this point that confusion started. Brigitte said, *"I don't say it is Boysie, Bernice darlink,"* (now, Bernice was cursing Brigitte, in her heart) *"but my boyfriend, he say the man looks like Boysie. He insist it is Boysie, because he see me talking to Boysie one day when he came to see you. It isn't Boysie. It is Henry."* (and this almost killed Bernice: she couldn't even think about it) *"And my friend, the policeman, he said somebody jumped him... what is jumped... jumped him? and he is sure it is Boysie. So I tell you, do warn the Boysie, for I like not the violence...."*

It was this story which was now occupying her mind, as she travelled downtown with her sister. And although it had happened two days before, still she couldn't stop worrying about it. She wished and she hoped the policeman would catch Boysie, and put a few stiff lashes in his behind — although Brigitte had pointed out that it was really Henry. Still, Bernice imagined that it was Boysie; it should be Boysie. She wanted to will it so. This was the kind of confusion she had been going through since the night she sat with Dots and Boysie, keeping a wake for what she thought was Mammy's death. After that night, her mind seemed to be eating itself away: reality and hope and wishing were becoming mixed into one; and it might have been mainly this mental condition which caused her to brag to Dots one afternoon, that she was now a landlady, the owner of the house which Mammy left in her will to her. She had willed Mammy dead. Secretly, from the time of the returned letter, she wanted Mammy dead: her disappointment that Mammy was still alive, was greater than her disappointment that Estelle had put Mammy into the Poor House. Sometimes, Estelle would find her mumbling to herself, talking about when Mammy was alive: *now, I am a big landlady, and be-Jees, I am only renting to black people, 'cause I learn my lesson, and I am going to be the biggest discriminator in the whole o' Canada* — although the house was in Barbados. Dots noticed this transformation; and it worried her. "Boysie, you think that somebody who *knows* a person is still alive, and always talking as if that person is dead, is a person in her right mind?" Boysie didn't know; but when she told him it was Bernice she referred to, he said, "Bernice want a stiff man. That is all Bernice want. *Man.*"

There was one incident in her life which bothered her very much; and which up until now, she had been unable to face; an incident contributing to her great fear of being alone on a crowded subway. It was when a child, a small child, raised its eyes from its mother's and saw Bernice opposite, and said, slightly too loud for it to be a secret, "Mummy! *Look!*" Nobody but that child knew he was awed and impressed by Bernice's beauty. But Bernice, because she was Bernice, hated everybody in the subway coach, and everybody was white. The child in the subway was curious. His mother was embarrassed. The passengers nearby, were embarrassed, because they saw that Bernice was embarrassed. Each time the child said, "Look!" his Mummy called him darling, and said, "That is not *nice*," and would laugh as if she was contradicting herself. "That is not nice, darling." When the train eventually reached the station at College Street, Bernice rushed out, pushing her way through the embarking and disembarking innocent crowd; and she hogged her way up the cement steps to the exit. *(Looka you-all move outta my blasted way, before I lick-down every damn one o' you. You-all think you own the earth! Move, move move move, move! I am in a damn hurry!)* and entered Eaton's College Street store. She asked four times for the ladies' washroom; rambled four times; eventually found it; entered it; bolted the door behind her; shut out all the white noises, all the white people in the world; sat on the clean, detergent-smelling toilet bowl (which was white) with the cover still pulled down, and covered and woolly; and she cried for fifteen minutes.

On this subway trip, Estelle is thinking of Sam. She feels she wants to tell somebody she is pregnant. She feels, one minute, she must keep the child (after all, look who his father is? A big lawyer!) the next minute, she wants to get rid of the child. ("Me? Bring a fatherless child in this world?") And she thinks that if anybody finds out, if Bernice, if Dots, if Boysie, if Henry — not Agatha whom she thinks is more understanding. "I think she told me once that she had a little trouble herself, too, and that she had to . . . " — this may cause Sam's family to

be destroyed; his career may be, too. It does not really matter
to Estelle that she is pregnant by a married man. It does not
matter that her sister is this man's domestic. It does not matter
that she has to return to Barbados, with this burden in her lug-
gage.... *You see the nice, smooth-skin thing that Estelle gave
birth to? Darling, that child is the prettiest, sweetest baby I ever
seen! It too pretty! and it got a nice complexion too; and it isn't no
worthliss Bajan like the rest o' we. It is a big Canadian, and almost
white, at that!"*...Estelle does not see it as a burden, because
the people back home do not see it as a burden. What matters
is that Sam does not love her. Sam has used her. She has used
Sam too, but she thinks that is different. She is not sure he
loves her; ever loved her. She decides to keep her secret, within
her throbbing womb. But she is terrified.... *Suppose his wife
was to come upstairs one morning, and decide to get on ignorant,
and shout and screel and bring the police and Bernice! Oh Christ,
what would I do?*...because she thinks Mrs. Burrmann smells
a rat, because one night, creeping in late after leaving him in
the car, a few doors down the street, just as she put on the
night latch and turned, there was Mrs. Burrmann, face to
face.... "Oh, Estelle," she said. "I'd like to speak with you for
a minute." Estelle was stiff with fear. And this caused Mrs.
Burrmann to say, "*If* you don't mind." It didn't make Estelle
feel any better; only more resentful. But in a sense, she was
glad that the confrontation had come, at last, for she had been
uneasy a long time. She followed her into the sitting-room,
rehearsing in her mind, all the defences she was going to put
to Mrs. Burrmann. She was going to tell her: *your husband
came to the apartment, I didn't call him; your husband started
it first, I didn't call him; your husband forced me, I didn't call
him; your husband loves me, I didn't hate him.*...But all Mrs.

Burrmann said, was "Sit down, please, Estelle." She turned up the record player, and it was the *Shepherd's Hymn* from Beethoven's Sixth. Estelle knew, from the tone of the music, that the tone of the meeting would not be quarrelsome. "Tell me, Estelle, oh . . . you would like a drink, wouldn't you?"

"Yes, please."

"I see you've been having a rather *interesting* time, here." Estelle didn't like the use of "interesting." The knock-out blow was sure to follow quickly.

"Yes, please."

"You know, sometimes at night, I see you coming in." Estelle was preparing her defence again. "But don't you think you are out rather late, for a woman . . . alone?"

"No, please."

"I'm probably too sensitive to these sort of things," she said, giving her the drink of whiskey and water. "I spend so much of my time alone. That is why I saw you tonight, and have seen you many other nights. I was going to call you before, when I see you coming in, late, and invite you in for a drink and a chat about your country, but I thought . . . "

"That's all right, ma'am."

Mrs. Burrmann was watching her closely, peering at her through the crystal glass. "You see, my husband works very hard, many times late at night. . . . "

"Yes, ma'am."

" . . . and that is why I spend so much time by myself, alone." She paused. Estelle could see she was staring at her, through her glass. It was this pause that got Estelle completely mixed-up.

"Well, Mrs. Burrmann, I am a bit tired now, you know, so I think . . . "

"Yes, yes," Mrs. Burrmann said, getting up; still holding her drink. She touched Estelle on her elbow, and walked with her to the stairs leading up to Bernice's apartment. She was very pleasant, very graceful, very aristocratic. Estelle was confused by this formidable opposition. "You see, Estelle, I am still stronger than you, although you are so young... and beautiful, I might add. Me, well, I've been knocking around for a long time. Built up quite a resistance, too." When Estelle reached the foot of the stairs, and said goodnight, Mrs. Burrmann remained to see her go up. "I hope we'll have a drink and a chat, another time, soon." (Exactly five seconds later, Mr. Burrmann entered through the front door.)

On this afternoon trip with Bernice, in the middle of summer, she was still thinking of Mrs. Burrmann's words: *I am still stronger than you*; and she decided that Mrs. Burrmann knew all about her affair with her husband; and probably about her pregnancy, too.

"Estelle, you can't imagine," Bernice was saying, "you have no idea how lonely I feels sometimes when I am in a crowded subway train! It is something I can't explain to you, really, or to none o' these people sitting down here with me. I think a man would have to be in my shoes for him to understand the feeling and the sensation I talking about."

"I think I am beginning to get that same feeling, myself, Bernice." But she was thinking of Mrs. Burrmann's words; and of Sam, who hadn't contacted her for about four days.

Henry had been waiting for five hours for Boysie to come. He was in a morose mood. It was now one in the afternoon; Boysie had promised to arrive at eight, to help Henry move his belongings in the old Chevrolet. For five hours now, the landlady had been clunking up and down the shaking stairs. She would clunk down, open Henry's door, look in, say "Oh!" in a short aggressive tone, as if he had startled her, sexually; and then she would clunk back up the stairs, muttering all the time, in her shaking retreat, "I have that room to clean, Mr. White. I have to clean that room, Mr. White.

Cardboard boxes, previously used to ship Tide, for washing whiter than white; a Modess box which had no motto on it, and which neglected to advertise its contents; a Kleenex box; an Uncle Ben's Rice box, and a flat six-container box marked O'Keefe Ale, were in the room with Henry. These five boxes contained his possessions — except his ten suits. They were arranged like the turrets of a fort, all round him. The landlady had earlier ripped off the sheets and the pillowcases from the bed. He was sitting on the stained, lipsticklicked bed, soiled by day-dreams and night-dreams, dry-dreams and wet-dreams; and beside him, were five bank books from five commercial banks in metropolitan Toronto: the Bank of Montreal, the Bank of Nova Scotia, the Canadian Imperial Bank of Commerce, the Royal Bank of Canada and the Toronto-Dominion Bank. There was also a book from the National Trust Company. (He had opened an account there, to impress Agatha; and to reap the benefits of four and one-half per cent interest, as against three from the commercial banks. He had deposited twenty dollars when he opened this account; but "circumstances beyond my control" forced him to withdraw nineteen dollars, a day later — unknown to Agatha — and that had left one hundred cents, trusting and entrusted to keep his trust account open!) He picked up one bank book, and studied it. It was his favourite: the dark, wine-coloured book with the motto — "*My* Bank, to 5,000,000 Canadians!" — (he felt like a red-blooded Canadian himself) from the Bank of Montreal. Agitation gripped him. He snatched up the book from the Trust Company. He looked at his one hundred cents balance. He looked at the date it was posted. He had only six months to keep this account open with one hundred cents. He felt so sick, the time had expired, that he spat on the floor, on Miss Diamond's ringed and smudged congoleum floor. The greenish gloyish paste made a soft slapping noise, and for a moment, it seemed to stare at him. Henry glared back at it; and shut it from his mind, by wiping his foot on it. In the process, quite accidentally, he made a cross. "Goddamn!" The cross frightened him; but he had been frightened already by the colour and thickness of the sputum (both made alarming meaning about his strength and his health); so he eradicated the cross, by wiping his foot at the four points. "Gottdamn!" — he had made a *swastika*. "Control yourself, baby! You're going shit crazy!" He pulled a cardboard box over it, and hid it. Studying the wine-coloured book again, he smiled. Fourteen thousand dollars and twenty-three cents was the balance. He smiled again, took out his Papermate ball point pen, and as smoothly as butter, wrote in *another* naught, making the total one hundred and forty thousand dollars. And twenty-three cents. "Damn! one little nought, and I multiply this balance *ten times*! Crazy!" He thought for a while, whether he should also increase it from twenty-three cents, to two hundred and thirty cents. But that didn't make sense. "Goddamn! that ain't sense, in dollars and cents, *or* in sense!"

His last legitimate deposit in this bank account, had been posted months before, in August. It was fifteen dollars. Since then, there were no more; and there was no work. He was living on unemployment cheques. As a man of slightly over fifty, it was extremely difficult to find a job: employers were thinking that before they would get one week's decent honest back-breaking work out of Henry, they would have to put him on their pension plan. He felt the civil service commission had discriminated against him; as it had against Boysie. One summer morning, a few years ago ("Shit, man! that was in 1961, man!") Henry took a streetcar to the head office, and he filled out an application form. He was interviewed by a very old white-haired, dentured and dainty woman, who smiled a lot with him, and said (after the interview), "Thank you, sir. We'll call you." Henry was still waiting for the call; sometimes, he and Boysie would joke about it.

When he had first shown this bank book to Boysie, long ago, Boysie's eyes popped out. "Gorblummuh! man, I didn't know a black man could have so much money!"

He took up the other bank books, and totalled his fortune. It came to five dollars and fourteen cents. The banks were scattered all over the city; the nearest one requiring at least, twenty cents for a one-way streetcar journey. He searched in his pockets, under and inside the cushions in the old, stained chesterfield, under the bed and in the corners, near the milk bottles which sometimes, in stress, saved him the creaking climb to the bathroom. He looked again, and at the bottom of one bottle, he saw a nickle. "Was I peeing nickles, baby?" But he took it out nevertheless. "Money, money, I gotta have money!" His woman, Agatha, was coming to see him; and he needed money, in case she wanted to go out. She might want to go to the Plaza Room or The Roof, or the Twenty-Two, but that *cost goddamn bread, baby.* It had always been very embarrassing for him to enter a crowded bank, with lunch-time pay-cheque people, and he, standing there before the bland blonde teller;

and the line of jogging Friday-spending Friday-withdrawing people with mists and vapour in their mouths, in a hurry to get back outside in the biting snow and winter; and he, having to wait long until the teller tells the accountant who tells the teller something again; and then the accountant searching for the account, probably lost now, because his favourite bank had just instituted its new IBM Banking System; and then the card, found at last! Henry, gritting his teeth and his modesty, as the teller tells him, in a tone as if she is telling the world, "Are you withdrawing the whole forty-four cents, Mr. White?" And he, answering in a pin voice, "How much would keep the account open?" This happened once — and the last time! — in his favourite bank, the Bank of Montreal, at the corner of St. George Street and Bloor, in the heart of money and the university. "Well, sir," the fortune-teller tells him, "it usually takes a dollar. . . . " Behind me on that cold damn day (he tells himself for the benefit of his memory, and because he can laugh at himself now) I see this big cat, tanned and looking groovy, although it is still the middle o' winter; and he's impatient as hell, and he pushes this cheque through the hole, and Christ! when my eyes rest on it, goddamn! EIGHT HUNDRED DOL-LARS, EXACT, I see stamped in that cheque. And I didn't and still don't, think that was fair, because this is the way I look at it: why should one cat have so much fucking bread? And from that day, I decided to make my own deposits at home, and have some bread too, 'cause I can't get a job and work for it honest!

But Boysie, who had heard the story before, had his own impressions of Henry: he, Henry White, a well-dressed-always-in-black, black man, as usual in a three-piece suit, although un-employ', pin-striked and striped, trouser-cuffed, waistcoat and watch-chain, enough to hang a cow, with a gold watch-chain that don't have no watch attach to it, because there ain't no blasted watch ("McTamney's the pawnbroker people keeping the watch for me, for a while, man.") and walking 'bout the place like if he owns the whole o' Toronto.

On the afternoon, when the teller came back to the counter, to talk to Henry, Henry was already running out of the bank, without the money. The teller, ignoring the man with the large cheque, tiptoed and shouted, "Oh, Mr. White. *Mr. White!*" But Henry wasn't looking back. Just as he reached the cluttered door, a small African gentleman, a student, dressed in a long heavy over-sized overcoat, grey peaked cap and red earmuffs, with the colours of his college to complete the impression the affliction of winter was having upon him, entered. Everybody in the bank was now looking towards the door. The teller was shouting, "Oh, *Mr. White!*" And the gentleman from Africa, thinking there was some mistake, made two short glances, one to his right and one to his left, and still unable to see why the teller was calling *him* Mr. White, gripped his heavy, learned, book bag, and ran out. "Goddamn," Henry said now, remembering all this, as if it had happened yesterday. "One hundred and fourteen thousand dollars, and I don't own one fucking cent of it!"

It was now three o'clock. Boysie hadn't come, Agatha hadn't come. So, he unpacked the five cardboard boxes, rearranged their contents in the room, and said, "Blind you, Miss Diamond, try and get me out!"


As the summer established its decision to remain summer, Bernice realized she had never enjoyed herself like this, in all her time in Canada. She and Estelle had spent most of this particular afternoon, walking through most of the department

stores, through Eaton's and Simpson's, and through some of
the small exclusive shops; and had tried on very expensive
clothes (even corsets) which they had no intention (nor money)
to buy. Now, they were pausing from their window-shopping,
window-hopping spree, to sit on two stools in the rock-'n'-roll
bar. Before going in, Bernice looked left and right, and then
laughed and said, "Lemme check if my pastor, or a member of
my congregation can see me going into this den of iniquity,
darling!" But she went in merrily: she was at home, characteristic as the lemon rind on the mouths of the hastily washed
glasses. Five young men with hair as long and as curled as a
woman's, were singing *I Love You, Yeah Yeah Yeah!* as if they
meant it personally, for both Bernice and Estelle. And Bernice,
thinking that they meant it, and wanting them to mean it,
threw a kiss for one of them — no one in particular: just the
first one to see it — and all five saw it, and returned it. "This
is living, child! Something to drink now, Ess, darling." After
the set of songs, the five female-looking young men came over
to them, and bought two rounds of drinks for them, and
talked and laughed about a "real crazy-old time we had where
you chicks are from." They hadn't asked where Bernice and
Estelle were from. But they had had their crazy old time in
Nassau last summer. Bernice was never so happy before. "Christ,
look! Estelle, you know something? I am moving down here,
man! The life is downtown, man, down here. Forest Hill and
the Jews up in there, stifling my arse, man, heh-heh-heh!" And
Estelle, more surprised than in agreement, agreed. "Look, let
we pass round by Henry now, and find out 'bout renting
rooms down here. Let we drop in at the WIF Club where I
promise to take you ever so long ago, and eat some *good*
West Indian curried chicken, gal. *Let we live it up* the whole

day, 'cause today is Thursday, my day, Berniceday! Today is Berniceday, not Thursday, no more!"

Walking along Yonge Street, going north to College, they came next to a large display window with very large photographs of celebrities. Bernice thought she recognized the face of a black woman. "Christ! I didn't know she is one o' them, too!" But Estelle could not appreciate it; so they continued walking. "Look, take this," Bernice said, folding her hand over a crisp ten-dollar bill, and then folding her hand into Estelle's, and with her other hand, closing Estelle's hand. "This is a ten dollar. You are big woman. Lick it out, child. Lick it out! and buy whatever the hell you want to lick it out on, 'cause this is summer, and we having a *ball*!" Estelle was speechless. "The WIF Club next! WIF Club, look out, 'cause here we come!" They got on the streetcar for the WIF Club; then Bernice held over, so the woman behind wouldn't hear, and said, in Estelle's ears (making Estelle slightly annoyed because Bernice's breath was hot against her ear) "Look, Estelle, I vex vex as hell that I have allowed myself, a young woman like me, not even forty years yet, to stick myself up there in Forest Hill with all them rich Jewish people, and pine-away my soul, work my fingers to the bone, till I come like some, some-some-some...Christ! it is no wonder that I was thinking like a Black Muslim, whilst I was up there, all that time!"

"But Bernice! Are you going outta your mind, or something?"

"Yes, I mad as the devil in hell, gal! I am a mad-woman, today. I *living*!"

"Sure! The people in this streetcar must be thinking so, too."

"Well, let them think so." She turned round, and opened

her mouth to talk, when Estelle, fearing greater embarrassment, nudged her in the ribs. Bernice held closer and said, "Heh-heh!" a smothered cackle coming from the back of her throat. "But I learn something today, uh-huhm! I learn something good good today. I learn that if a black person don't come out from that place called Forest Hill, once in a while, God in heaven knows that she would turn into a real first-class Black Muslim. I telling you what I know. But child, *today is my day*!"

It was summer. It was lovely. The men were bright in shirts that had almost all the colours of the rainbow in them; and in tans, too; and some of them looked coloured, if you were not careful to look a second time. Bernice was playing a game with herself, trying to spot which man and which woman had black blood in their veins. The women, frilled and light in clouds of petticoats that seem to blow kisses; and in dresses of kites in the wind, in the eyes of the men and the stares of the men; their dresses of sky-blue, white, pink (which was fashionable this summer) cream, Jacob-coloured, exposing that upper burnished tint where the sun and a man's lips touched the breasts when they were bathing in the sun . . . summer!

"God, sometimes, I really like this place!"

"Is the summer, Estelle, dear. Summer, girl. You don't understand this is summer? Girl, I would be a fool, Bernice Leach would be a thorough fool to say she is thinking 'bout going back to Barbados when it is summer in Toronto. And you ain't see nothing yet. Wait till it is something they call *Indian* summer. Well, that summer is even ten times more better than the white people summer! Indian summer."

"The buildings, though! The buildings is the thing I can't stop admiring, in this place. And that place, what the name is now?... yes, the City Hall. Those two big powerful things going up in the skies as if they want to knock down the whole skies... and down in Eaton's, when I didn't think I was ever going to stop going up in that elevator. Lord, I had a funny feeling, like the feeling you get when you are flying in an airplane... and it pleased my heart to see some of our girls working there! Those coloured girls really looked nice, working there."

"And didn't you see *that* one? A real nice jet-black girl? Not one o' them wishy-washy ones who are passing, or wishing they could pass for something white; but a real pure-pure black girl, working in the Bank of Nova Scotia, downtown? Well, I tell you something, I intend to change my account from the Bank o' Canada, if they don't smarten up and employ a black person in their bank. Because this is the modern times. And if a black person isn't good enough to work in their bank, be-Christ, *my* black money isn't good enough to bank in their bank, neither. How yuh like me, child?" The streetcar rumbled on and rambled on, with Bernice pondering the wisdom of changing her account to another, integrated bank; and Estelle, admiring the people and the buildings.

"You know something?" she said, when the streetcar was less noisy. "I think I now understand what Sam was saying, when..."

"Which Sam?" Bernice snapped, apparently not completely engrossed in the plan to change her bank. "You couldn't be meaning the Sam Burrmann, that cheap bastard, I works for, up in Forest Hill, who won't raise my pay...." And she laughed, because she felt it was preposterous for Estelle to be referring to that Sam Burrmann.

"But did I say Sam?"

"Sam, hell! Forget Sam, girl — whichever Sam you mean."

She held Estelle by the arm, as they got off the streetcar. When they reached the bar in the WIF Club, Bernice greeted one of the owners, "Geary, honey? How, man?"

"So-so," he said, shrugging. "Betwixt and between."

"Me, too," she said, resting her hand on his shoulder. Then to Estelle, she said, "You want to try another one o' them drinks we had at that place on Yonge Street? . . . one o' them . . . what the hell the bartender-fellar call' it?"

"D'Aquiris."

"D'Aqua-what? D'Aquarri? . . . oh-hell!"

When the telephone call came, at five o'clock, it was Boysie. "Goddamn, man!" Henry was vexed. "Are you a man or a boy, Boysie Cumberbatch?" He was using his best Harlem American idiom. He was shouting so loudly, that he hardly heard Boysie's voice complaining . . . "and they take the damn car, man. They take the car. This morning. . . ." Again, Henry said, "Goddamn!" the way he thought a born Harlemite would say it, stressing the last syllable.

"Man, I didn't know they could come into your place, and take up your car, in this country, man," Boysie was lamenting. "That vehicle is mine. I paying for it." He lapsed into a long paragraph of his choicest abuses, in which he did not repeat one phrase. When Boysie was feeling good, he could curse for five minutes without using the same word twice: this afternoon, he was in top form. "Be-Jesus Christ!" he said, with the usual faint trace of a smile in his voice, "first thing this morning, before I even rubbed the blasted booby outta my kiss-me-arse eyes, the bailiff-man knocking down the door. Dots run out in her nightgown, just a housecoat on, wearing no panties, 'cause she had just got outta bed, and I thinking it is a detective or a police looking for me concerning what I told you 'bout Brigitte...."

"Goddamn, you's paying your dues now, baby."

"...and Dots, trying hard not to expose all her fronts in front o' the man, and as the man push this summons in Dots' face, be-Christ, Dots start one big worthless bawling. A summons, Henry! They send me a summons, man. *Mr. Boysie Cumberbatch versus Nells Used Car Lot, Without Prejudice.* God blind them in hell!... it say here, I is the defendant, gorblummuh, and old Nells is the plaintives.... But you know what this *versus* mean, though?"

"It means you's against the Man, baby!" There wasn't any sympathy in Henry's voice: there was only derision. "You're learning now how to meet that Man, baby!" He was becoming more proficient in the dialect of his adoption. "And when you get that son-of-a-bitch, I want you to kick in his balls for me."

"Henry? Henry? Man, I can't make head nor tail outta what you telling me, man. But listen! I broke. I was taking money offa Dots' bank account to spend 'pon Brigitte, and Dots was taking off money too, at the same time. Now, all the damn cheques bouncing 'bout this place, and Dots mad as hell, man!" He went on to tell Henry the money was spent at the Cellar Jazz Club and the Riverboat where Brigitte liked to go, because good folk singers performed there; and at the Pilot Tavern, where she was very impressed by the many artists and artist-types who drank beer there. In the midst of all this, Henry started laughing. Boysie started to laugh too, to ease the tension. "But this ain't no damn laughing matter," he went on to say, still laughing. "Not at all, because three days ago, Dots went down in Simpson's and write out a big cheque for a new dress, and that cheque bounced too. And when she figured out that she had enough money in the bank the day before, to cover the cheque, then the blasted war was declared. Number one, is the cheque. Number two, is that I get in at six this morning, from..."

"Seeing Bridgey?"

"You damn right, baby!" Boysie said, and sniggered.

"Goddamn!" Henry screamed, applauding Boysie. And then he said, "But that's your cross, old man."

"The bailiff-man, the policeman that Brigitte have, the cheque, be-Christ, and now, the mottor car, too?"

"Goddamn," Henry said. For a while, no one spoke. "But Boysie Cumberbatch," Henry said later, "you know what you're looking for?"

"What I looking for? Man, that is a blasted queer question to ask a man who has lost mottor car, outside-woman, and gorblummuh! who stand close to losing a wife, too! all in one morning."

"Who are you, Boysie? What you looking for, Boysie?"

"Well, now that you ask me that, let me put it to you this way, then, Henry." After considering for some time. "I is a man who don't have no big lot o' formalized learning nor education and them sort o' things, like Agaffa. I is one man who came to this country through the back door, as I tell you. Now, you know, you could bear me out in this, that I been seeing hell to lay my hands 'pon a job, 'cause I isn't a idle man. Gorblummuh! sweat have poured offa my back like rainwater, pulling hand-cart and working in the canefield in Barbados, so work don't scare me. But I been seeing them civil service people, the Imperial Oil people, Shell Oil, paint factory after paint factory, mottor car factory, be-Jesus Christ, Henry, the whole bunch o' them bitches. And you think they would give me a job? I can't say, really and truly, *ergo* and *quod erat demonstrandum*, that I get any lot o' money outta this country, Canada. So I would have to conclude, in answer to your question, Henry, that I is a man who, therefore, only want a piece o' woman regular, a piece o' change in my pockets, and gorblummuh! a woman who could support me, and a piece o' automobile to take me and transport me going and coming from that piece o' woman and that piece o' change."

"Goddamn."

"You understand now, what I wants outta this life?"

"Goddamn!" he repeated, and then hung up, with the promise to listen for Boysie, later. Henry went back to his day-dreaming. He had reached a stage in life, at which it was easier to lie in bed all day, and dream; a stage at which he was becoming so weak from the exhaustion of thinking, that he could not see much difference between the day and the night: both were nightmares. He was experiencing something like a suspension of time; and he would spend the days, and the nights too (when he wasn't out with Agatha) waiting; waiting as if he was waiting for somebody or some event, like an enemy, or a detective (he had not forgotten the night on Marina Boulevard when he struck that policeman) or a bailiff — who came often, and wasn't let in. In these moods, he would think of Agatha. Agatha, in some way, put him into these moods. Sometimes, before she arrived, he would pull himself out of these apathies, and prepare himself for the long walk through the university grounds, through Queen's Park, Victoria College grounds, Charles Street and then to the Pilot, to spend the night drinking; or it would be the Paramount (with, or without — recently without — Agatha). He was thinking of his life now; and he asked himself the same questions he had just asked Boysie: "Henry, who are you? What are you?" He looked round the untidy room, at the three large photographs of Agatha, each inscribed, *Forever*; and he told himself, aloud, so that he could hear his own answer, "You ain't no goddamn celebrity, baby! You ain't no Sammy, Davis, and you sure ain't no goddamn Harry Belafonte, neither; and you ain't no goddamn heavyweight. . . . " The phone rang. It was Boysie.

"If Dots call," he said, "tell her I gone down by Jees-and-Ages, playing some dominoes, hear? But I really going up by Brigitte — just in case."

For a while Henry just listened. He despised him for doing this; but it was a strange ambivalent hostility. "Look, Boysie," he said. "What you think of Bernice? What you think about me and Bernice getting together?"

"Bernice?"

"I am having second thoughts 'bout Bernice, man. She is my people."

"And what about Agaffa?" Boysie asked.

"Never mind." But the doubts had already set in, to eat away at his decision to spend his life (if it came to that, voluntarily, or by force of circumstance) with Agatha. Recently, comparing Bernice with Agatha, he was unable to decide on one of them; he was unable to break off one relationship and embark on the other. *Why can't there be some nice goddamn black chicks in this town? Goddamn! Man, I know I don't, and can't love Bernice; and I know I can't ever love Agatha, because I don't have that pain in my heart for either Agatha or Bernice. It is only sympathy, baby, sympathy. Not the kind o' pain that love is, baby. Because, pain is love. And love is pain. And I don't have to be no goddamn postgraduate at no goddamn university, to know pain from love, and love from pain, and when love is pain and pain is love, goddamn!* "And that motherfucker, Agatha, always telling me, 'I love you, Henry, God, how I love you....'" Somebody was pounding at his room door. The aggressiveness in the knocking pushed away the suspension of time. He cursed the landlady, who he thought it was ("Goddamn rent again, baby!") — and who it was. She handed him a letter, sent SPECIAL DELIVERY. When he took it, he remembered the summons Boysie had received earlier today. It was time for Agatha to come. But he was still going to read her letter, which called him, *My dear Henry, I am sorry indeed...* He skipped that page, and began again at the fifth page, the final page, mid-way in which she was saying that *although I am guilty of having fooled you into believing this could work out; and having fooled myself into feeling so, too, through rationalizing my guilt feelings, I must tell you the truth now. A friend of mine in social work at the university with me, has helped me to work out my problem. I shall not see you again. It is bad for me. But I shall always love you. And I hope that you will not hate me, but love me, even though I have done this cruel thing to you. But you were always the stronger vessel, and I, the weaker. Forever, Agatha. Goodbye, Henry.*

For some time lying there, facing the ceiling, his hands under his head, and knitted together, he pretended he didn't give a damn: after all Agatha was just another rich broad looking for kicks; just another Forest Hill kid, rich and young and bored; or a Rosedale kid, just like those goddamn weird kids up in the village. "Shit, baby, you ain't never going to make this cat weep, and break up, oh no, baby!" But he had to look at her four photographs, and at the face which was really a beautiful face; and at the boast she had written on the face of each photograph, each one taken in a different season of year and love: *Forever.* He looked at the clock ticking like a bomb, and it showed him the time of day, and the time of happier days when Agatha would be sitting on the dirty bed in that very room, right here, look man! right here where I'm sitting now! and would be drinking tea or coffee or wine from his chipped tea-cups; or sitting combing the evidence (of having lied to him in his bed) out of her long brown hair; and suddenly, he wished and willed her present, but all he got was her perfume, the perfume of her perfume, the perfume of her body, the perfume of her body after sex . . . and the things that came to his mind (as her body came to his senses) were little things, the happy things, the joyful things, such as the night when they walked through Queen's Park when the snow hid the ground for seven inches; and they held hands, he an old man, sedate and a bit embarrassed to be seen so gay and happy, holding hands and playing in the snow; and she, young, flighty and flirty, gay and giggling, deep as the snow, in love with him. Then she said, picking a line from somewhere, "Bet people'll think they've been hippos! What would you do if you saw two hippos?" Before he could say anything sensible (if indeed he had anything sensible in mind to say: not having been exposed to hippos before — only hippies) she threw a snowball right into his face, and turned him into a checkerboard. And the two of them stood like gigantic icicles in the middle of the park bound by snow, kissing. He tried to put this out of his mind, by going to his drawer to search for the leaflet which he had received a long time ago, from the Canadian Anti-Apartheid Association. He had thrown it into a drawer, or somewhere, because he was happy then, and he had his woman beside him. But now, he was searching for it. He remembered vaguely, that it asked him to march. March with us on . . . a certain date! He couldn't remember the date: perhaps the day of Mars and March had passed. But when he pulled out the first envelope, it contained the remnants of a red rose she had stolen from a garden in residential Lowther Avenue, last summer. ("With this rose, I thee dub, my lover, forever," she had said.) He was remembering that now. He reached into the back of the drawer and searched; and eventually, out came the leaflet to march. "Goddammit! I shouldda been marching a long time!" But he had a few days in which to decide. He thought of the march, and he thought of Agatha. He tore up the leaflet; and he held the rose in his hand, and he cried. "Goddammit, that's a great woman, my woman, and I love her, 'cause I'm feeling that goddamn pain...." Losing her was too much for him.

When Estelle heard what the man said, she asked him to repeat it. He repeated it; and still she refused to believe she was hearing properly. "Is that what I mean to you?" She had already sensed it. "Is that *all* I mean to you, Sam?" Dishonesty and a sense of the dramatic were becoming characteristic now that she knew she was carrying his child. Sam disowned the child. "Are you kidding?" he shouted, when she told him. He was refusing to be honest. He had found out he wasn't really impotent. She had found out that she was just a woman, another cheap woman. Yet, had she been back home and this had happened, she would have chosen to keep his child as the forceful weapon to remind him of his past. "Is that all I mean to you, Sam?" There were tears now. But she could have told him a long time ago, all that she meant to him. Her own grandfather had told her grandmother what *she* meant to him. Why should it be any different for her? He had just told her she should have the child ("... if you're telling me the truth, if, if you're telling me the child is mine, well all right. But a man is never sure a child a woman say is his, is his." Estelle got so mad, she screamed, "Christ, man! a woman knows! A woman knows!" And when he found that he was blundering, and didn't have the courage to say he was unfair to her, he said, "How the hell do I know it isn't Boysie or, or what that other one's name is, Henry, or somebody like them. It could be one of your own people!"), but perhaps, she should give it up for adoption. It was easy, he said. Many women do it; they sign the paper and the child is adopted, and it goes into a rich, loving home, perhaps the child even gets a university education. "A child like yours, a child with a strike against it to begin with, a coloured child, *must* have a home, must have at least one chance in life...." He said it all depended on *her*, since it was *her* child. "You would have to decide, Estelle."

They had talked in Bernice's apartment, while she was at church, and Mrs. Burrmann had taken the children out. Sam had worried about her being pregnant for a long time, but he had decided that when she told him, he would not be kind to her; he would be cruel, and make her hate him, and make her kill the child. He did not feel he really cared for her: never did. But he was still worried. She sat watching him, hating him; and he sat watching her, hating her, hating himself for having got mixed up with her. Time however, had become a complete circle: it had begun here in this same room; and here it ended. It had begun on a Sunday morning; and now, on this Sunday morning, it ended. "You have to get rid of the child. There's no question about that," he said. Estelle was expressionless. She was not crying, she was not angry, she was not sulking. She just looked at him. "I don't want people to be talking about..." and he decided it was unwise to finish what he was going to say.

He had begun by talking about his summer plans so as to evade the real problem on his mind. Mrs. Burrmann, he said, had decided on Mexico; the children were going on the Monday, to Camp Kipawawa, and he was thinking of going to some northern Ontario resort area to fish. But he hadn't included her in his plans (though, to be honest, she didn't expect it); and it was then that the real discussion started.

"I never thought I would come to this, to be here, sitting in front of the man who put me in all this trouble, all this damn trouble.... Look, you forget that I came up here on a vacation?...and do you want to know something else? If I thought it would do something *bad*, something bad bad bad, to you, I would kill this blasted child in my womb. But that isn't bad enough for you!"

"Okay, okay," was all he said, and all he could say. And to change the conversation, he told her he had arranged with a friend at the Bedford Road immigration office to help her take out landed immigrant's papers. "That's what you want, isn't it?" That was the last word he said to her. That was the last time he saw her. That was the moment when the house suddenly became as quiet, and as silent as a sea without a wave.

Time was no longer time. Bernice did not now belong to time. Time had no dominion over her; for she was time. A good, summer afternoon time. Time had changed her in such a short time, that her own sister could not understand what was happening. It was a new Bernice. It was a summer Bernice. And time was long and heavy with Estelle.

"I have a plan for you, Estelle," Bernice said. They were walking along College Street, near the Toronto General Hospital. She was thinking of a job in the hospital for Estelle. She thought of Priscilla who had attended Estelle's welcoming party. "I made up my mind to help you. You are staying with me, 'cause I need company. But before you go and do the wrong thing, listen to me. I am going to figure out a way to make you a immigrant, if it means changing your name from Shepherd to Estelle Leach. As a matter of fact, from this afternoon, I am calling you Leach. Don't forget that. 'Cause today, I claim you as a sister." Estelle remained very quiet. She had already laid her plans to remain. Sam was going to work on his friend in the immigration office; now, Bernice was coming out with a similar idea.

"You know something?" Estelle said. "I wouldn't mind being a nurse, at all."

"You are *going to be a nurse!*"

"I always wanted to be a nurse."

"Gal — as Dots would say — you is almost *that* right now!"

And they passed the ugly, silent hospital. It was proud and self-centred, hiding within its dirty brown brick, all the mysteries of diseases, and the curses and the cures of those diseases, which in a short time, Estelle would be learning about. Just as they reached the corner, a long double line of people was marching towards them. Some were carrying placards; some just walking; a few black persons (mostly women) were walking and holding down their heads as if they thought they should not be seen; and all of them were mumbling a song which had a very bad and lugubrious melodic line. Estelle could see the placards saying: CANADA IS NOT ALABAMA and END RACE PREJUDICE NOW and BLACK EQUALS WHITE and NEGROES ARE PEOPLE. Estelle hurried on to see better. The leaders came into full view: a Jewish man, wearing a pair of glasses that had one eye-lens darkened, holding hands with a black woman. And there was a tall black man, proud as a prince, and he too was wearing glasses, dark glasses. The line passed and passed, until they were opposite about five black men; and when the men saw Estelle and Bernice (who was visibly upset and annoyed) they stopped singing, shut their mouths, and hastily looked the other way. Bernice walked off, as the lights changed; and she pulled Estelle behind her, saying, "Come woman, we don't have the whole day, standing up watching a bunch o' black people walking 'bout the place, making themselves look more foolish."

"It is just like in the South," Estelle said, a little sad she had to leave the marching. "I remember now that I saw coloured people marching like this, on television...."

"Child, they been marching down South, up South, up North, all over the States. Whenever you open a newspaper, whenever the summer come, whenever you turn on the damn television, all you seeing these days is a lot o' stupid black people marching 'bout the place." She made a wicked rasping noise with her lips, to show her disgust. "Black people praying, kneeling down all over the street, won't let traffics pass, making trouble. Praying and kneeling down, and when they tired doing them two things, they getting beat up all over the damn place. Christ! it sickens me to my stomach to see what this blasted world o' black people is coming to." She shook her head, from side to side, to show how despondent she was with this aspect of life. "And these niggers in Canada! Well, they don't know how lucky they are!"

"I think you are wrong, Bernice. I think you are wrong, wrong, wrong." Bernice gave her a cruel glance. "Now, if I was a person living in Canada, and if I knew about this marching-thing, I would be in it. God! and I would be in front, too, leading! Just like that lovely black woman at the head, hooking up with that Jew man, as if she is the Queen o' Tonga, be-Jees, and singing loud loud, too!"

"You, too?"

"Christ, yes! I am a Muslim, you didn't know that?"

"But this is Canada, dear, *not* America. You and me, we is West Indians, not American Negroes. We are not in that mess. Leave that damn foolishness to *them*, you hear? 'cause we grow up in a place, the West Indies, where nobody don't worry over things like colour, and where you aren't condemn because you are blacker than the next person, and..."

"Woman, what the arse are you saying, at all?" When she realized how she had spoken to Bernice, she was trembling. But she was now fed up with Bernice's dishonesty. "Look, be-Christ! Bernice you is, are, my sister. But I am saying you are *wrong*." And she decided to end the conversation there. Bernice said nothing else.

They walked on, both of them pretending to be friends, while each one knew the other was cursing her. "Sickening," Bernice said, at last sitting down in the WIF Club, grateful for the relief from seeing the marchers, and from walking. On the way, they heard the bells ringing in the tower of the university. They stopped to listen: Bernice shaking her head, sadly; and Estelle amazed. But they left the bells and the melody behind them. Men and women were laughing in the WIF Club; patting one another on the back, and saying, "What happ'ning, man? Oh hell, I can't see you these days, man!" and a friend would say, with a smile, "Christ, man! things rough man, things *rough*!" And while they were there, a tall Jamaican entered, and shouted, "Rass, Small Island!" greeting a small, toughly put-together Barbadian man, who seemed to have forgotten how to smile. Turning to the other four men sitting at the bar, drinking, he added, "Baje, here, is a hell of a skins-man, eh! I see him hustling a blonde skins last night, man!"

Bernice took her mind off the merriment of the men, to comment about the marchers, "Blasted stupid black people walking 'bout the white man road, with signs! They don't know how to look for work? Every one o' we seeing hell in this place, but we ain't making trouble.... Mr. Geary, how, boy?" Mr. Geary came over, smiled, patted her on her shoulder, and wished her the best. "Can't complain, boy," she told him. "And how things?" He said, "Betwixt and between," and then moved back into the curry and the steam and the ackee and cod fish that spurted and sputtered beautifully out of the kitchen.

"Well, I declare," Estelle said, picking up the discussion after Mr. Geary left. "Something really has happened to you, Bernice. First it was the Muslim newspaper that was your bible, and now, it seems like it is *The Watchtower* and *Awake*."

"That is the way life is," Bernice said. "And anyhow, this is summer, child. So let we fill our guts with some o' Mr. Geary's nice curry-chicken, and get merry and drunk this peaceable Thursday afternoon...." And they did that.

The sun was arrogant enough to suggest, through its glorious golden brightness, that it was going to catch the whole evening on fire. Bernice and Estelle, many hours after they had eaten and had drunk and were merry, were sitting, waiting, watching to see if the sun was going to keep its word. They were silent; almost respectful. The carilloneur's music was helping to make the evening into a theatre. They were listening; almost dreaming.

"Bells *playing* hymns? Well, what the hell this white man can't do, eh? heh-heh-heh!"

"Hymns *and* songs, darling. This is something you would never see in the West Indies," Bernice said; and then ridiculed the West Indies, in the way she laughed.

"This is a funny country, in truth." Estelle then looked up at the clock, which said five-twenty-five; and at the tower. But she couldn't find the man nor the hands nor the bells.

"And this is why I tell you, Estelle, that I gets blasted vex when I see a pack o' black people marching 'bout the road, looking like arses."

The bells were ringing hymns now; and their voices were fresh on Estelle's heart. They were washing out the problem that lay at the bottom of her womb; and she wished they could wash her clean of all personal problems. "I still can't believe it is me, Estelle Shepherd, who..."

"*Leach!* Not Shepherd, child, you are a Leach by name, now, heh-heh!"

"Still, I can't imagine that I could be here, and a man could be there, up there, playing hymns on bells."

"Listening to them bells make me think o' Mammy and death. One day when I was alone in that apartment, I start thinking as if Mammy was really dead, you don't know that. Christ! and I even thought I had inherit the house in my mind..."

"Listening to that man up there, making me think of life and wanting to live. Life..." You could see how the bells were working on her face. The put a kind of fear on it; a fear for the wonderful power which was in the hands of the carilloneur. They were doing something beautiful to her. Bernice's face, in her concentration, looked haughty and proud and beautiful, too.

"Ess, what hymn he say he playing now? You recognize it?"

"*The Day Thou Gavest...*"

"*Lord is Ending! Amen.*" Bernice said. "That is the hymn they took Pappy to his grave with, you remember, Ess? You don't remember when they take Pappy outta the sea, drowned, how I cry and cry and cry, and people from all over the neighbourhood came and look in at the hole in the coffin? What a beautiful funeral Pappy had! Old women bowing down their heads low low and saying, Thank God, Pappy going up to his Maker!"

"That is one day I don't want to remember."

"Christ, Estelle, the weeping! the weeping and the crying and the singing. And you remember too, that I was the only person who insisted that they buried Pappy while he was still living, and really wasn't dead yet?"

"He was dead, Bernice. Pappy was dead as hell, too!"

"Yes. But only after I make certain he was really dead, though; not before... and you remember, Estelle, you remember how all the people who couldn't follow Pappy in mottor cars, stood outside their houses, and the walkers, then the riders on bicycles, then the cars, forty-nine cars Pappy had following him, and everybody was so sorry that Pappy didn't make the fifty, a round number, 'cause then, that would have been a funeral to end all funerals... Well, listening to the magic and the goodness in that damn bell now, bringing it back to me, as if I was in a theatre watching a movie, two times, from beginning to end." Bernice started to hum with the bells. Her voice, not a good singing voice, was struggling; and Estelle held her hand, and gave her strength, and joined her, singing. Just then, Henry came across the walk, from the little bridge nearby.

"Goddamn!" he said, surprised to see them sitting there. Estelle immediately dropped Bernice's hand. He sat beside them, unfolded a large blown-up photograph of three policemen with three night sticks beating up one black woman. "Goddamn! Look at this." Estelle looked and shuddered. Bernice snatched it from him, folded it in its original creases, tore it into bits and tore the bits into confetti, and then spread them to the wind, as if she was planting seed. "Goddamn, woman, are you crazy?"

"Don't come here and spoil the peace for me, eh, Henry?"

"I just come from marching."

"Well, go 'long back and march."

"I saw you," Estelle said. Henry sat between them now, listening to Estelle, and very impressed by her interest. He took out a cigarette and lighted it.

"And why you didn't jump in the line, and shake yuh body-line, heh-heh!"

"It don't have nothing, not a damn thing to do with Estelle. Estelle is a West Indian, you forget? It ain't her business, Mister Henry."

"Goddamn, that is your fight, too, baby! West Indian, Canadian, American, Bahamian — we is all niggers to Mister Charlie!"

"You may be one o' them," Bernice said, disdainfully, "but not me. I was sitting down here, listening to the niceness in these bells."

"Fuck the bells! Excuse me, Estelle."

"Man, what you say?"

"I say, fuck the bells!" He got up and sat beside Estelle. "You sitting down on the white man grass, in the white man university, listening to the white man playing bells, goddamn, and telling me what? Next thing you are going to tell me, is that you ain't no more West Indian, you is a goddamn Canadian, and a white one, too!"

Bernice sat up straight, and with great arrogance and scorn, said, "The only way I am going to beat him is to listen to him. And that is why I sitting down here." Henry ignored her. Never before in his life, had he come to despise a woman so completely as he despised Bernice. Big, black, stupid arsehole woman, he said to himself. But as soon as he realized he had said that about a black woman, his own people, he was sorry; and he altered his sentiment to: this big stupid woman.

"You see Boysie recently, Estelle?"

"Where Estelle would see Boysie?" Bernice snapped. "That bastard ain't dead yet. If he ain't careful, Dots will soon bury him, though!" She was thinking of Brigitte and the policeman's threat. "Boysie had better watch his pees-and-queus!"

"Shit, woman! you *must* be having your period! Goddamn!"

"Why you don't come and find out, if you is a man?"

"Listening to these bells," Estelle cut in, a little embarrassed, "reminds me of back home..."

"Baby, I won't tell you what they remind me of..." Before he could finish, he noticed something was happening to Estelle: she seemed to be having trouble breathing. He saw her jerk her neck, the second time (Bernice merely gave her a reproving glance), but he didn't know that at that moment, vomit had spurted up into her mouth. She held her mouth shut. She looked anxiously at Bernice, and then she wallowed it round in her mouth, debating what to do with it. The taste of slime nauseated her, and she wallowed it into a large ball of spaghetti-worms, and swallowed it back down. She closed her eyes, bent her head slightly forward, and gave it easy passage back down. She clapped her chest twice.

Bernice was mumbling about deaths and funerals again. "I remember the dress I wore to Pappy's funeral, it was a shark-skin piece o' material. I had got it at a sale." The worms were in Estelle's stomach; and they were beginning to climb again. "You remember the undertaker-man? Well, I will never forget that bastard! Dressed-down in black from head to toenail, he comes and put dirt on top o' Pappy, and that bitch, when nobody wasn't looking, unscrew every last piece of the silver handles from offa the coffin. *Every piece* of that silver, he take off and bram! Into his pocket they went."

"That is the brand o' West Indian motherfucker we will have to kill off!" Bernice was insulted by Henry's language, and she said so. Estelle was too busy with her health problems to care. "We got to treat them just how the Mau-Maus killed them, 'cause that is the only way the West Indies will be free, and could ever lift up this blasted emastipated black race, goddamn!"

"Now, that's the most sensible thing I ever heard come outta your mouth, Henry!" And to show him she approved, she rested her hand on his leg, with the feeling of a warm handshake. Meantime, Estelle was feeling things in her stomach. She tried to jerk them back down. But they came up nevertheless. She got up and went behind a small building that had plenty of ivy strangling it. In that short nightmare trip (in the twelve steps it took her to get there, during which she had covered every detail of her stay in Canada) the vomit had gone back down; and she was thinking she should turn back, and walk back to Henry and Bernice and sit down. But when she stopped, considering (she was thinking of what Sam had said to her the last time they met), something in the vomit changed it mind, and she could barely reach the building, when the slime and the disgust and the hate for Sam within her, rebelled like a storm and she yawked and yaawked and puked through her nostrils and her mouth at the same time; and only God knew why it didn't come through her eyes. She looked at the vomit, and she thought she saw Sam in it. The bells were ringing still; but she did not recognize the tune. When it was over, she wiped her mouth and blew her nose with the pink tissues which she had taken from the Ladies' Room at the WIF Club; put powder and lipstick on her mouth, and a whiff of perfume to kill the perfume in the vomit, and went back to them. Bernice was still groaning something about how Pappy looked in the grave. Estelle wished it was *her* unborn child in that grave. What would Bernice say when she found out that she had taken something, which might put the child in Pappy's predicament? "Exactly round this time o' day, I remember, I was standing up beside Pappy's grave, screeling my bloody head off!" Henry had long ceased to listen: he had developed the art of seeming to be listening, while in fact, he was sleeping. He could sleep with his eyes open.

The bells were not ringing now. Without the bells, they became bored with each other; and with time resting heavily upon them. Estelle was wondering when she would have to vomit again; and thinking of Sam, and the *thing* inside her. Henry was thinking of his woman, Agatha, because the peace and the stillness of the evening reminded him of his exhaustion and drowsiness after sex with her. Bernice was thinking of a home; of a big stone house on a hill, with a lot of chickens and ducks and pigs running about the yard. Now, at this exact hour, she would be calling her flock, "Chick-chick!

chickeer! chick, here!" The man in the tower was thinking of what to play next. The clock said it was six-thirty. Time was here. Time, time, time. And all three of them needed more time: time in which to correct the hour-hands of their mistakes.

You can hear Henry and Bernice breathing heavily. Estelle chews on a blade of grass, to prevent herself from thinking. Two days ago (before Sam mentioned abortion) she had decided to take something; mainly because she could not see Sam's love changing from winter to spring. Time. Estelle what are you going to do with your time? Time that you need for the baby to be born; to grow in; in which to kill the baby; in which to recover from the murder of birth? And Bernice, what is your time? Time in which to change Estelle's name to Leach; time in which to look for a husband; time in which to see if there is any point wasting time on the man beside you, yes, on Henry. And Henry, what can time bring you, you old goddamn two-time loser? Can time change time? The carilloneur's voice had just begun to speak, probably in answer to all of their questions, when Estelle's mouth was wrenched open and the vomit was all over her silk dress with the red dots (which belonged to Bernice). Bernice felt a few warm sprays on her cheek; and so too, did Henry. Bernice was going to hit her, for being "so damn common," but Henry intervened.

"This chick is goddamn sick, Bernice, you can't see that?" Estelle remained sitting, apparently too stunned to move. She sat looking foolishly down at the vomit.

"But look at this bitch, though! Just look!" Bernice said.

The nearest refuge was Henry's room. Henry was holding Estelle's left elbow, just touching it, ashamed and embarrassed to be seen walking beside a sick woman. People were looking at them. Time had left them, as the sun had. It went behind a cloud, and as far as Bernice was concerned, it might as well have been one long endless night. As they got near Henry's room, they passed a man, lying on his back on the front steps of a boarding house, with a transistor radio lying on his stomach, playing Beethoven. Bernice recognized the tune of the Storm movement, and she looked at the man, and in her mind, she kicked the man and the radio into the gutter. "That blasted music!" And once, during their retreat from the bells, Estelle had a violent spasm, and Henry barely got his handkerchief out in time, and held it to her mouth, and the vomit spluttered on the handkerchief, and on his hands and on Estelle's dress, and some of it dripped into the gutter. It was then that a West Indian man and a white woman were passing; and the man pulled the woman faster on. It was then too, that Henry felt like running away, leaving his handkerchief (white and linen and initialled and perfumed by Agatha), but he didn't have any strength left. He shrugged his resignation away, and said, "Goddamn!", and put his arm round Estelle's waist.

"Blood!"

It was Bernice who saw it first. Henry turned his back on the blood. But Bernice stared at it, as it appeared on Estelle's dress, like an underground spring; and a million visions of its origins and cause, went through her mind. This is a wicked woman, there ain't no doubt about it, she thought; this woman done something damn bad and foul. Bernice could see herself losing her job, she could see policemen (whom she hated to the bottom of her guts) she could see her bank account disappearing like snow in the sun, she could see Dots and Boysie and Miss Carmeeta Anne Bushell and Priscilla the nurse, all laughing at her, because of what had happened to Estelle. Most of all, she would lose her job, and she was determined to hold on to that, regardless. Lose her job, and have to attend to Estelle till a baby come? *Jesus Christ! whose side you on?* The blood was coming still. Estelle was on her back (Miss Diamond had made up Henry's bed) muttering things, which if they were loud enough, would still not have made sense, either to Bernice or Henry.

"Come, come, Henry," Bernice said, a new urgency, and a new strength now springing from her, "Come, man, this is one o' we, and we have to join together now and close-up ranks. We can't sit down here the whole night whilst this girl bleed 'way herself to death. We got to put our two heads together and do something." Estelle was losing blood steadily; and probably losing consciousness. Bernice knew what she had done: since she herself had done it once before, in Barbados. It was this feminine sympathy that brought her close to Estelle. Bernice knew what to do: Brigitte had told her. "I tell you, Bernice, darlink, we live in a society with wealths. But I tell you, it is too, a society with crime and a society with unmorality." They had been drinking imported German beer which Brigitte had brought over for Bernice.

"You see this Marina Boulevard, well, I tell you, darlink, it would shock you to know the married women, the single women, and the divorced women on this street, who go to abortions. They have the money. And they have their own doctor. I see them, because before this job, I work for doctor who do that, and he make millions." She held Bernice, and leaned over and whispered a name in her ear. Bernice almost dropped her beer glass. "Yuh lie!" she said, her eyes rolling. "Yes,"

Brigitte said; and put her glass to her head. "Jesus God!" Bernice exclaimed. "And not for him neither," Brigitte told her. "Now that is what breaks up marriage, darlink." Brigitte herself knew the things to do; and she taught them to Bernice.

"I stepping out here a sec," she told Henry, after making a preliminary examination of Estelle's condition. Henry was about to resent it, to question her. "Don't *move*." But he was frightened: suppose Agatha come now, goddamn! Or suppose my landlady come now!

"But where you going?"

"Where the hell you think? To bring back the RCMP?" She looked at him, and saw him so pitiful, and so stupid, that she became arrogant with him. "She is my sister, yuh know." Still he wasn't settled in mind. "I have a phone-call to make."

"Use my phone, then."

Before she answered, she smiled, and patted him on his back, as she would have patted a child. "Thanks, Henry. You is a kind man. But this is woman-to-woman business."

"Oh."

"You understand?" She put her arm round him, and for a very brief time let it remain there. "Now, show me the nearest drugstore. I need a few things, for this girl." And Henry directed her. The moment she left, he became frightened. *Goddamn, a woman bleeding in my bed! and suppose my woman come now* (he remembered he hadn't any woman now; so he put that thought away) *suppose Boysie was to drop in now, goddamn! or, or...* (He couldn't think of anybody else; he felt so sad he had no friends, nobody who could make him feel dramatic in this moment) *...somebody, anybody could knock now.* Since there was no one who could come, possibly, he had to think of other tensions; and he sat as far as possible, from the bed: *this*

*goddamn woman, on vacation in this goddamn country and to
find herself in a goddamn mess like this, this could kill Bernice;
but when I think about it, some o' these West Indian women think
they is princesses and queens and virgins in old age, so it ain't
no wonder a lot o' white cats screwing left and right, and it
ain't no fucking wonder, tambien, that this bitch here get herself
in rough waters. You think she would give me a little piece? You
think I could get me a nice black chick, goddamn, in Toronto?
You're crazy, baby? I see every half-pretty black chick shacking
up with some goddamn white man, shit!...I wonder if Boysie
get piece? Boysie is such a smart Bajan bastard...*someone was
knocking on his door. He jumped up. He listened. He looked
to see whether Estelle was sleeping — or dead — and waited
to see if it was Bernice. The knocking continued. ("That goddamn landlady, again?") but he didn't recognize the knocking
(and something about the perfume that came under the door,
told him it wasn't Bernice), and he looked again to see if the
knocking had awakened Estelle (and it had), and then he
heard the voice, "Henry? It's me, Agatha." He stood a foot or
so, away from her, on the other side of the door; and could
not, and did not want to talk to her. He wished she would go
away. ("This goddamn broad.") He knew she knew he was
home: Estelle had just started to cough.

"Henry, Henry? I know you're in there." Henry couldn't
move. (Goddamn! ain't this a bitch? Man, I never yet stand up
in one spot, like this, and couldn't move, just because of a goddamn woman!) He wanted to open the door and drag her in
and throw her on the bed, and give her some good love-blows,
for all the worry she had caused him; he even wanted to touch
her hand; and kiss her; and sit down and watch her knees
which he had spent many hours doing. He began to curse

Estelle in his mind; and Bernice too; and Boysie — for causing all this. Agatha gave the door one final, violent kick, "You
bastard! I know you're in there." And he followed her disappointed footsteps from his door, to the outer door, to the
front door, seven steps...one, two, three, four, five, six, seven
...then down the path cluttered with empty beer bottles and
cigarette butts and packages, and he waited with her, in his
imagination, until she fumbled (as she has been fumbling for
the three years she's visited him) with the latch on the front
gate which Miss Diamond promised to repair. In his mind
still, is Agatha; and he can see her as she walks to the corner of
Baldwin Street, gives one last dirty look at the house and disappears in the late shopping crowds rambling from the Jewish
Market and from the bars and stores. Henry opens the door,
and looks out. He knows she is not out there. But he has to do
it, has to look, for that was his woman, the woman he loved
more than he knew.

He closed the door, and returned to the chair, where he
had been keeping guard.

"Why didn't you let Agatha come in?"

"Oh man! That broad's a real drag, man." He knows he
lies: she knows he lies. "She's sick, too. Always bugging me,
always..."

"Thanks, Henry," Estelle said. "Boy, look how I causing
everybody trouble, eh."

Bernice returned with the necessary information and
instructions from Brigitte, whom she had called; and with the
supplies from the drugstore. She even brought two baby-beef
sandwiches on kaizer rolls, two butter tarts (one day she ate
ten in Eaton's restaurant) and a package of chewing gum for
Estelle. Henry wondered why chewing gum. Bernice shrugged

her shoulders, smiled, and with a little embarrassment, said, "To chew, nuh, man!" He took the sandwiches, smiled and said approvingly to himself, This goddamn woman!

They worked long to relieve Estelle of her pain; and to moderate the bleeding. Henry found a bottle with some whiskey, and they shared this. Bernice was in such a nervous state (although she did not show it) that she knew she needed something more than the word of God to help her through tonight. In any case, Henry never owned a Bible. Occasionally, he would look at her, shake his head, and confide to himself, Goddamn, this is a great woman! He had already placed Agatha in that category of women to be called up, when there were no better ones around, when Bernice said, quite simply, "Just passed Agaffa going along Spadina."

"Who? Who?" He was taken completely off guard.

"That bitch looked at me, and look off, be-Christ, as if she think she is the Queen!" It made Henry sad; and Estelle uneasy. "Wonder who the hell she think she is! She could come in my place and eat-up all my curry-chicken, though..."

"Some women are funny in truth," Henry said. "You didn't know that, did you, Bernice love?" He watched her to see how she reacted to "love." She did not react. "Man, I used to pass this chick every morning. I met her at a party, some place. The day after the party, she passed me on the street. Every morning I passing this nice chick and she ain't saying one goddamn word to me. And then one evening, a knocking on my door! And as Boysie would say, Gorblummuh! when I open the door, I nearly drop down dead. The *same* woman!"

"Jezebel!"

"Wait, you ain't going to ask me who she is?"

"Agaffa! She is the jezebel!"

"Jesus Christ, Bernice! You is a genius!" But he had made up the entire story — every detail. He said, "Goddamn, you is a real woman." He went to her, and put his arms round her, congratulating her. She felt good to him. Bernice gave him a look that was preserved for years, on ice.

"Left me out! Left me out, man! What happen to Agaffa? She wearing her chastity belt these days?" It stunned him. And it stung. Goddamn! he thought; but this time it was not complimentary. Estelle was still in pain. She had been suffering greatly, from the beginning, although she said nothing about it.

"You own a hot-water bottle?" Bernice asked him, tears in her eyes, when she could almost feel the tight-fisted grip of pain in her sister's abdomen. "Lend me your hot-water bottle, man."

"Hot-what? Goddamn, Bernice I ain't no woman, baby." But Bernice wasn't impressed by his Harlem accent, and she didn't take her eyes off him. He said, "I don't even have a woman."

"Looka, man, everybody in Toronto knows you sleeps with Agaffa, you hear?" And she laughed like Dots, and said, "Well, heat-up some hot-towels for me, then, man. The night ain't waiting on we. Come, get up offa your backside."

Bernice turned out to be an excellent nurse. She worked like an army of moths: silently, efficiently, and without feeling like a Florence Nightingale. Even Henry was no longer upset by the emergency and by the blood. He made a partition of thick cloth (one of Miss Diamond's woollen sheets) which held Estelle in her own private ward. Bernice would hand him a neatly wrapped newspaper parcel, and tell him, in the manner of a head nurse talking to an orderly, "Put that somewhere, safe, man!" This was the part he didn't like. But he would unlock the door; slip out; throw the parcel into a garbage can at the corner of the street; slip back inside; lock the door behind him, and take a good shot of whiskey to steady his nerves. At the end of each return journey he would say, "God-damn!" He felt badly doing it. On the third trip, he had to watch a policeman, very carefully, for fifteen minutes, before he disposed of the parcel. The policeman had seen him throw away the second parcel. "Goddamn cop!" But he had fled back to his room, and had taken a large shot of whiskey. He hoped the third trip would be the last. Trouble happened on the fourth trip. As he turned the corner to approach the garbage can, the whiskey now having taken away most of his care and caution, two drunks decided to argue and push each other around, on the sidewalk. Henry was too near the garbage can to turn back. The policeman was approaching. Just as he got near, one drunk fell and overturned the can, and the three newspaper parcels which were on top, tumbled out and ran about the sidewalk. A woman, talking to another woman, saw the contents and screamed and ran. Some men, still enjoying the fight, saw the parcels and they swore and moved on. Henry couldn't move. The policeman was still coming closer. He was almost upon him, when just then, realizing the predicament he could be in, Henry gripped the parcel and fled. "Goddamn!" he said, but only after he had locked the door behind him. He decided to keep the fourth and the fifth parcels in his room, until morning. Morning was seven hours away.

Estelle has stopped bleeding. She is resting now. Bernice is tired and a bit worried ("Bright and early, six o'clock, tomor-row morning, I got to be in that blasted kitchen, *again*. God!"). Henry offers her a drink. She takes the bottle from him, and drinks from it. She takes a second larger drink. And Henry smiles in his heart. The whiskey is working love and pain inside him. Bernice is on the couch. He gets up from the floor, and sits on the arm of the couch, near her. She merely glances at him. She is tired. The night is old, very old. Time is again on her hands, and on Henry's.

"Goddamn," he comments.

"How are you and Agaffa getting on, boy?"

He refuses to fall into this trap; and he refuses to answer. Instead, he offers her more whiskey. Bernice takes the bottle, and takes a large mouthful, from the bottle. Henry draws closer to her (still sitting on the arm of the couch) and is almost touching her now. He actually touches her, but something tells him, it is still too soon to be familiar.

"You and that gal not setting horses too good these days, I hear."

"Goddamn white woman!" He is doubtful: she's asking a damn lot about Agatha! With the whiskey on his brain, he decides to make his move; and he fashions his words of courtship and seduction, in the poetry of his choicest Harlem American. "You's a goddamn cool woman, you don't know that, baby? I shouldda been grooving with you a long time ago, but I make a real big goof." Bernice smiles. She likes to hear him talk like an American, now; and he does it well.

"Christ, man, you left out a good woman like me, for *that*? For Agaffa? Heh-heh!"

"Goddamn, baby, I copped out of a swinging chick, for a weirdee, baby." Bernice smiles. Henry sees for the first time, that she is really a very beautiful black woman. He becomes more confident. "You want to know something, baby? I feel like kissing you right now. On them nice purple lips o' yours."

Bernice's lips quiver. She has never been in this situation of electrifying seductiveness before. But he thinks the time is not ripe for the kiss. He wants to make her wet her pants first. Peace, and slumber and a rich feeling of seduction are in the room now. "I always was wishing I could groove with a woman like you. Big! Nice! A woman who could whip me up a good goddamn home-cooked type o' meal. Wash my threads, and other laundries, be-Christ, even better than the New Method Laundry! A real..."

"What the hell is wrong with Agaffa, niggerman? She is too precious?" She removes his hand from her shoulder. He lets it fall, as if it is a dead hand. His spirits fall too. Bernice gets up and checks on Estelle. "Sleeping," she tells him. She looks round, and sees the photograph of Henry shaking hands with the Prime Minister of Canada. It was taken a long time ago when he was chosen Porter of the Year. At the bottom, he has written, in pencil, *Mister Henry White, Porter of the Year, shaking with the prime minister.* "That is you?" she asks, although she recognizes him. "When you come to think of it, you ain't a bad-looking man, neither."

"I's the man for you, baby."

"Watch your mouth!" But she blushes. He cannot mistake the blush, which comes like a violet on to her face; and he puts his hand, his left hand, on her shoulder. She does not remove it. He allows it to fall gently, imperceptibly; and stops it from falling just as it enters the plains above her breast.

"Isn't it, Bernice? Bernice, say something, baby. Isn't it?" He is closer to her breasts. She notices his hand, and says nothing. Something between his legs quivers. Progress and time and pain are his. He is touching her now. "Isn't it, baby?" She feels soft. Why, goddamn, didn't I find this out before now?

This broad is goddamn soft, more softer than Agatha, man! He puts Agatha swiftly out of his mind, and says, "Isn't it, Bea?" Bernice holds her head down, in shame, in embarrassment. Henry's courage mounts, and so does his passion. His hand leaves the plains and enters the gorge between her breasts. He cannot swallow for fear. Tension comes to his mind.

"Why you don't stop feeling-me-up, Henry?" she says, like a virgin. His hand freezes in the warm steepness of her bosom. Be goddamn careful, Henry, he scolds himself.

"Look, woman, don't be foolish," he says. "Sweetheart, we're made for one another." He tightens his hand round her waist, and brings her close to him. And she comes willingly. "So, what you say, Bernice?"

"Why is you feeling me up, man?"

"What yuh say?"

"You feeling me up."

"Ain't it? Ain't it, eh, Bernice?" And he comes even closer; his lips quivering to touch her lips. Something like a feeling of wire is working itself through his body. "Eh, lovey-dovey?" His voice is now hoarse with tenderness. He decides not to speak again. She frees her right arm; and he thinks she is freeing it to embrace him, and seal this long-overdue pact. The arm comes loose. He relaxes, because he must be cool to enjoy this woman. To himself he says, Goddamn, I know she was only playing hard to get, but be-Christ I is a born Cassanova, baby! Bernice's arm is loose, and just as Henry moves to kiss her, it strikes him, *plax!* right in the soft part of his jaw. Whiskey and success fled immediately from his brain. For a very long time, he is speechless. Bernice is a big, strong woman.

"What the hell you take me for?"

Off and on, for the next few days, Estelle was bleeding. And Bernice kept quiet about it. She would leave Estelle alone on the chesterfield in nightgown and housecoat (which Bernice had come to accept) while she did her work downstairs; but at night, she would sit beside her, and talk to her, and try to comfort her. Never once, in all the time that passed since they sat that summer afternoon listening to the bells, did Bernice mention a word about her sister's condition; or attempted abortion. Bernice bore it silently, like a priest with a secret taken in confession. There was a new bond, stronger than the hostility that was once there, which now bound these women, sisters, together. Bernice had consulted with Brigitte again. There was no cause for further alarm, Brigitte diagnosed; she would do her best for Estelle, because Estelle was her friend's sister. And it seemed too, that this misfortune brought Brigitte into a tight, oathbound triangle of sincerity and sympathy. Bernice had to think about it, one night sitting, watching, nursing Estelle: "Jesus God! and to think of the bad things I have said about that German girl, Brigitte! Christ, you never know who is your real friends, till the time comes! And now, I got Brigitte at the head o' the class in my friendship book." Subconsciously, she had placed her old friend, Dots, at the bottom; because she knew she could never tell Dots about Estelle; that Dots would spread it all over the WIF Club, and further.

Life for Bernice, these days, was centred once more in the kitchen. She could not, and did not use the telephone very often; and the radio was usually turned off, to allow Estelle some rest and quiet. It became the kitchen; and after this, the window in her room, where she kept a steady vigil on Estelle's condition; and on Brigitte's activities with the policeman. Dots

telephoned on three occasions to say she had heard something
about Estelle; but Bernice carefully guided the conversation
away from that topic. Dots was actually looking for gossip.
One day, while looking out, Bernice caught a glimpse of Dots
coming across Marina Boulevard. She moved from the window, and waited. It was about ten days that Bernice hadn't
talked to her; and apparently she was coming to find out why.
She came in; Bernice could hear her coming up the stairs; she
knocked and she waited, certain that the door was going to be
opened for her. When she realized that it wasn't, she lingered
there, muttering, "But I swear I just see Bernice at the window... don't tell me that I seeing spirits!" She knocked again;
and called out, "Bernice, gal, you in?... Estelle?" And when
she saw she wasn't going to be let in, she gave the door one last
heavy pounding, and went back downstairs muttering *all these
years she say she is my friend, I running up here the moment she
have a toothache; and now, because she could laugh with Brigitte,
and the two o' them could sit down, and talk everybody's business,
she saying I not good enough for her! But I learn my lesson, today
I learn my lesson*... and Bernice looked at Estelle, and smiled,
as they both heard what Dots thought of them. The telephone
rang. Bernice refused to answer it. It rang a second time, longer
than the first. Bernice merely smiled at Estelle. Later that afternoon, she happened to be sitting at the window, when as she
was about to go downstairs, she saw Dots coming out of the
house where Brigitte worked. But look at that whore, though,
eh! Bernice noted.

Because the Burrmanns were leaving within a few days for
their summer holidays (Mrs. Burrmann to Mexico, as she said;
and Mr. Burrmann, "somewhere in the north"), they had asked

Bernice to work on this day, Thursday, normally her day off. She didn't mind working, for she had to be close to Estelle, anyhow. She did not know whether they knew about Estelle's condition; so she was always on the alert. She even called Brigitte, to find out (without making Brigitte suspect she was being questioned) whether she had disclosed anything to Dots. Brigitte reassured her, "Hell, no, darlink! This is something a woman does not talk about." Still tense, still apprehensive, she called Henry to check on his trust. Henry was swift to see that she was indebted to him, in spite of the night he tried to seduce her. So he made a date with her, to take her to the Little Trinidad to hear the Trinidad calypso singer, Mighty Sparrow, who was in town. Bernice accepted. "Goddamn!" Henry said, remembering the frustration of that night, and the distaste and the self-hatred: that he had tried to seduce a woman, while her sister was lying on his bed, sick. "Goddamn, Henry, baby! You're weird, baby!" He never forgave himself for this behaviour. And he was glad that Bernice agreed to go out with him; 'cause never mind she is stupid as hell, sometimes, she is a good woman. He was so happy, and excited about taking Bernice on a date, that he didn't mind when Boysie came to ask advice about dealing with Brigitte. Henry was thinking, Goddamn, man, I just lost my woman, and this man coming to *me*, for advice!

"I never knew, Henry man, that a man could be so blasted happy with one o' them women!" He could not contain his elation and his success. It seemed to have gone to his head, more than the rum he was drinking. "The first time I see Brigitte naked, oh Jesus Christ...."

"That's a lot o' woman, eh, boy?"

"But how you did feel the first time, Henry?"

"What first time?"

"When you and Agaffa first had rudeness together...."

"Like a king!"

"Man, I didn't know what the arse to do!" Boysie took a large mouthful of rum, washed it round in his mouth, and then swallowed it. "The first time, after all these days I rushing the woman, and gorblummuh! When I tell you that she likes dicky, I mean dicky man! Henry, when I see them legs, Jesus Christ, you don't know I nearly went mad...."

"Goddamn, Boysie, you's a goddamn sex maniac!"

"But you could remember the way you did feel, the first..."

"Like a goddamn king, Boysie. Like a goddamn king!" But Henry was saddened by the way his first conquest was affecting Boysie. He could see Boysie leaving Dots, because of Brigitte; and Brigitte turning Boysie's head behind his back; and Brigitte eventually destroying Boysie, because he was in love with a symbol.

"Cover up for me, man," Boysie asked him. "Dots going call you; and you would know what to say." He left, as happy as a lamb in love. He was seeing Brigitte the following day, Friday.

Standing in the kitchen sometimes, during these past days of tension and worry, Bernice realized, with some degree of surprise, that she never really did get to know Mr. Burrmann. Even after three years. She knew he ate properly, like a gentleman. When he is at home, there is a great absence of noise. This is all she knew about him. She knew a little more, perhaps: she knew the shape of his hands; and the shape of his fingers. She remembered once, when a fingernail was broken (she noticed it while she served the main course), he had trimmed it before she served dessert. And since she saw the back of his head more than the front, she knew also, when he needed a haircut. "I wish I could get inside that man's head," she wished one day, watching the back of his head. But she knew she never would: not even Mrs. Burrmann seemed able to.

Bernice didn't spend much time these days worrying about Mrs. Burrmann, who was busy preparing for her Mexican holiday. She had been drinking less; but Beethoven was still being played, as loudly as ever. Bernice wondered whether this record would ever wear itself out: the record seemed everlasting; the record and her problems were so similar.

On the Friday, sometime before lunch, Estelle took a turn for the worse. She had a temperature of 101 degrees. Bernice was going frantic. This was the relapse which Brigitte had warned her about. While Bernice prepared lunch for Mrs. Burrmann, who was leaving on the afternoon plane, she worried about Estelle: should she tell Mrs. Burrmann, or should she wait until she left. "On this one day, this damn woman gotta have lunch at home!" Mr. Burrmann arrived home and he too, was having lunch. "Oh Christ! look at my crosses today!" Beethoven was playing, although nobody was listening. It was the Fifth Movement, *in allegretto*, the Shepherd's Hymn and Thanksgiving. She recognized them; but today, there was nothing to be thankful for.

"Well, Bernice, I hope you enjoy the summer," Mrs. Burrmann said, waiting to be served the soup. "I'll be away for about two weeks or so."

"Yes, ma'am. Have a good time."

"Thanks. The kids won't be back from camp before I return, so you'll be free. I hope Estelle will get a chance to see some of our lovely country before she goes back."

"Yes, ma'am." And as she was about to serve Mrs. Burrmann, the bowl slipped and the hot soup fell into her lap. Mrs. Burrmann lost her colour, and her temper.

"You clumsy..." But she caught herself in time. "Oh, I'm sorry, Bernice ... guess everybody is a bit shaky with the excitement of leaving..."

"Darling..." Mr. Burrmann said. (It was the first time in three years that Bernice had heard him use this term to his wife.) "It's nothing.... We're all excited today, somewhat...."

"I'm sorry, Bernice. Forgive me, Sam, darling," she said. (Bernice could not understand what was taking place in this house!) "Imagine that this is the first time in how-many-years?... three, that Bernice has ever spilt anything.... We should give her a reward...."

"I'm sorry, ma'am," Bernice said, not feeling sorry at all. But that was the end of it. Nothing more was said, either by Mrs. Burrmann or her husband. Shortly afterwards, Mrs. Burrmann came downstairs in another, more beautiful, summer frock. She was carrying the soiled dress; and she came to Bernice, put one arm round her neck, kissed her on her neck, and gave her a ten-dollar bill and asked her to give the soiled dress to Estelle. "Take care of Sam, for me, please!" ("What the hell is this I hearing?" Bernice thought.) "That's for your good record ... one spill in three years; and take care of yourself, Bernice." Before she left the house, she turned the record player off. The house seemed so odd without Beethoven in it.

"I'll run you up to the airport, dear," Mr. Burrmann shouted from where he was, somewhere. Bernice noticed this act of kindness, of love. Some damn thing happening or have happened in this household, she thought. And I don't know what it is! And apparently, because she could not understand what was taking place, what transformation had set in, she threw the soiled dress into the garbage pail. But she kept the ten-dollar bill. "Some damn thing taking place between them two. He loving her up, and she loving him up, just as if they going on a second honeymoon. . . . "The house was hers. But it was like holding dominion over a battlefield. Her summer was spoilt. Spoilt beyond repair. But she was glad that soon, she would be completely alone in the house, to take care of Estelle, more efficiently. "Estelle, child," she said, "I coming up soon, and spend some time with you." She was back in her old habit of talking, and arguing aloud, with herself. Before going up, she decided to call Henry. She was thinking a lot of Henry these days: sometimes, she told herself she was a fool to have offended his show of love that night; sometimes she reassured herself that she was better off to be alone, without a man. She was nervous now, because she had nothing to talk about. Her dullness was one of the reasons Henry thought might cause him to stop seeing her. "I am getting scared 'bout Estelle, Henry," she began, talking to Henry on the telephone. "Estelle running a fever, and I don't know what to do."

"Well, you can only wait," he said. And as far as he was concerned, the conversation was over. Bernice didn't know what else to say. What she wanted to say, and what she wanted to know, was too personal; and she did not want to be embarrassed. "Look, Bernice, talk! I busy as hell, and I expecting a important phone call."

"You-all men always busy when somebody decent want to talk business with you! I call you like a human being, to ask you a simple question concerning Estelle, and all you could tell me is, you busy, you busy. But be-Christ, you never too busy running after white woman!"

"Goddamn, Bernice."

"It is all right, though. It is all right. Monkey say wait...
and I is only Bernice. I ain't a lady, like Agaffa...."

"Goddamn, Bernice! That is different. Anyhow, listen to
me! I am a man. I know what I'm doing. If I, a black man, is
going with a white woman, well, goddammit, that's my fucking business, and furthermore, it is different from a white man
screwing a black woman like Estelle, or..." But it was too late.
When she heard her sister's name, she threw down the telephone. She had spoilt it. She knew it. At the other end, Henry
felt he had spoilt it, too; for he was just beginning to have a
genuine interest in Bernice. He did not love her — not the
way he had (and still did) love Agatha; but he felt he could learn
to love her. "Goddamn," he said. His whole day was spoilt.

Bernice was worried too. She had visions of white men
raping her sister; and in each case, the men had no faces. She
saw one man who resembled Mr. Burrmann in physique; and
when she went round to look, the face was the face of Henry.
She was going mad, insane; tied up in her hate and bitterness.
She went up to look for Estelle, and she sat beside her, and
rubbed her back with alcohol, and ran her hand over Estelle's
hair, and pulled the covers up; but she was still confused by
the visions of men without faces. She went back down to get
some orange juice for Estelle, and on the way up, she met Mr.
Burrmann. Something strange went through her body; she
suddenly disliked him intensely; and wanted to kill him.

"How is Estelle?" he asked, in an off-hand manner. "Is she
all right now?"

"Yes, Mr. Burrmann."

"I thought she was not feeling well...."

"Well, no, sir," Bernice said, "really and truly, she ain't

feeling so good. But she is past the worst now." He handed her two envelopes. One was from Barbados, from Lonnie; and the other contained her wages.

"I'll be leaving first thing tomorrow morning," he said. "So, take care of the house. I'll whip up something for myself, so you needn't bother to prepare dinner now, and, oh... tell Estelle... here's the gentleman's name on my card... tell her not to forget her appointment on Monday morning. Ten." Bernice took the card, greatly puzzled, but not wanting to seem inquisitive. He reassured her, "It's all right. Estelle'll understand." Bernice waited until he closed the door of his study, before she opened the manilla envelope with her wages. "Christ!" she exclaimed, when she saw the amount. They had given her an increase in wages. She made a mental note right then, to put an end to her sabotage of their groceries and drinks. Two hundred and fifty dollars a month was her wage now. But she did not understand why this sudden increase. "They are up to some blasted trickery with me, I bet yuh," she told the money, putting it into her apron pocket. And there was, suddenly, and with reason, a new brightness, a new cheerfulness to her summer. She hoped Estelle would get better soon, so they could enjoy the summer and the money. But her exhilaration died as quickly as it came. She had to read the letter from Lonnie. And she sat down, anxious to get back to Estelle with the orange juice, and read: "*Darling, Bernice, love, This is Lonnie. I am pining after you real bad these days. I was going to write you long long time before now, but since I had to look after the business you ask me to look after, I could not write before this time. I visited Mammy. She is in the Poor House, all right. But I think it is a good thing that Estelle put her there, because after I had a talk with Nurse Forde who is the charge*

*nurse in charge of Mammy, Nurse Forde told me that Estelle was*
*right to put Mammy there. Mammy put on weight and she fat.*
*Nurse Forde say not to worry. Mammy is in good hands in the*
*Poor House. Nurse Forde say she remember you. The island look-*
*ing like New York these days. People building new buildings,*
*almost everybody — but me — have a new car that they buy*
*on the time-payment plan, and a lot of American ships in the*
*harbour and the whole town full with those blasted noisy Yankee*
*sailors. But with me, things bad as usual. Rough, rough as hell,*
*if you ask me. But I am not going to ask you again to send for*
*me, because that is a decision that only God could make you*
*decide...*

She could take no more of the letter; she folded it; and was
about to rip it up, when she changed her mind, and put it in
her pocket. She must remember to keep it in her handbag, and
read it sometime later. She climbed the stairs, slowly, thinking
of Lonnie and of Henry, and of her increase in wages... and
thinking of Estelle. "Poor Lonnie," she said, "poor little stupid
Lonnie!"


Violence had always been close to Bernice. Frequently in her
dealings with Mrs. Burrmann, and with the children, this violence seethed beneath the surface of her smiles. She had contained all this for three years, in a situation which was no bed
of roses. Even at times, when violence seemed to her the only
honest, dignified solution to a problem (one such problem was
Estelle's earlier behaviour; and another Mr. Burrmann himself), she had still kept it off. Sometimes, she told herself
that the blood Estelle had lost, and was still losing, was not
caused through violence; but through love. Sometimes, she
wanted to kill Estelle. Mainly, she thought of her sister as

someone abused by love. But Bernice learned to live with it; and Estelle herself, had apparently accepted it as a small portion, a taste of her new life, her life in a new world. Reading the Muslim newspaper, *Muhammad Speaks*, as diligently as she used to, Bernice somehow never accepted returning violence and hate for the white world, as the paper seemed to suggest. And it was this violence, and this hate, which caused her to change eventually to reading *Life* magazine, because too, it contained many colour photographs. She was thinking about all this part of her life, this Friday night, while sitting at the window in her apartment. Estelle was resting; though she still carried a temperature.

"What you think is going to happen, Bernice?" For a while, Bernice had to ask herself if someone had spoken, so accustomed was she to the silence in the room. "Bernice, are you there?" The room was in darkness. Bernice had turned off the dressing table light, as soon as the car parked in front of Brigitte's house. She had turned off the light because she thought she recognized the car. She had seen it parked there many times before. It was Boysie's car. (He had redeemed it. from the people who had towed it away, because of overdue payments.) Estelle called her again, and before she could return from giving her the orange juice, the man got out of the car. She couldn't recognize the man, but she swore it was Boysie. It could only be that whoring Boysie, she said. Bernice looked up at Brigitte's room, and swore at the curtains because they were too thick for her to see through them. She could see only movement in Brigitte's room. She never once saw reality. "Blasted curtains!" she swore, and Estelle heard her.

"Bernice?"

"Yes, Estelle."

"I'm really sorry, Bernice...about everything."

"I understand, child."

"I wrote Mammy a letter today, while you were downstairs." Bernice remembered her own letter from Lonnie. She made a note to finish reading it.

"That's good, Estelle."

"I want you to post it for me, tomorrow."

"That's all right, Estelle."

"And Bernice?"

"Yes, Estelle."

"What you think will happen? I don't think I'm getting better...you think I'll have to go to the hospital?"

Bernice moved from the window to the chesterfield, and sat beside her. She began rubbing her back with her bare hands. She got some more rubbing alcohol and used that. Estelle said it made her feel better. Bernice went back to the window. There was another car parked behind the first one. "That's damn funny!"

"You say something, Bernice?"

"No, child. I just here, talking to myself." She looks harder now, feeling something is about to happen. She thinks she recognizes something like an aerial sticking up from the roof of the second car. She looks harder still, and sees two forms, two men, sitting in the front seat. Something is going wrong, she says to herself. She looks up at Brigitte's room, the room is in darkness, and she smiles. But immediately afterwards, she is ashamed of herself for smiling. Christ! she whispers. Two policemen in uniform get out of their car, and inspect the other car. Bernice can see they are talking about it, but she can't hear. One spots his flashlight all over the car, and inside too, and finally on the licence plate. The other one writes down something in his book. And then they get back inside their own car. They light cigarettes and wait. The light in Brigitte's room is still off. Bernice waits, too. Estelle is sleeping now. The room has become frighteningly quiet. She hears a noise. It is Estelle breathing. The policemen smoke and wait. Oh my God! she keeps on saying.

Violence comes to Bernice's mind. Violence, violence is in the air, like the humidity in the summer night. She can taste it, she can smell it in the heavy breeze coming up to her. A light goes on in Brigitte's room. The red tips of light go out in the waiting car. And now, Bernice thinks she hears the leather seats creak. They wait. The light in Brigitte's room goes out again. And when no shadow comes from between the houses; and when the red tips return inside the waiting car, Bernice goes to the princess telephone to call Henry. There is no answer. She is frightened now, she feels alone, she needs company. His phone rings and rings, and still no answer. She dials Brigitte's number next; and someone lifts the receiver, and before she can speak, a voice says, "Wrong number," and the phone is slammed in her ears. Bernice lights a match to check the right number; and she finds she has dialled the right number. She dials again. She can hear it ringing (so she thinks) from her bedroom window; but nobody answers. Holding the telephone in one hand, she checks her address book. Lord have mercy, she prays. She moves with the phone to the window: the policemen are waiting. She has an impulse to scream for help, to scream for murder, to just scream, scream for anybody. Control yourself, Bernice, she tells herself, while she dials Brigitte's number. At last, Brigitte answers. "Yah?" Bernice, feeling the violence before it happens (how did she know there was going to be violence?) almost loses her voice, and has to whisper, as if she is really whispering across the street, so the policemen won't hear. "Brigitte? Me! Me, man! Bernice!"

"Yah!"

"He out there! Somebody out there! Two o' them. In front, in a car. . . . " Bernice hears when Brigitte rests the phone down on a table, and walks to the window. She looks out to see the curtains being parted slightly. Yes, she says to herself, there the bitch is.

"Thanks," Brigitte says nervously.

"Brigitte?"

"Yah?"

"*He*, there?"

"Yah?" There is a quiver of nervousness in her answer. Bernice is becoming infected by her terror.

"Brigitte? Look, for Chrissakes, don't let Boysie come out now, for God sake, Brigitte."

"Yah." And the telephone is put down.

Bernice goes back to the window. A policeman gets out; spots his flashlight up to Brigitte's window; sees nothing; flashes it on the windows of the adjoining houses; sees nothing also; then on Bernice's window, and gets back into the car. The car lights go on, and the car drives away noisily. Bernice sees lights in Brigitte's room go on, and then off; and she waits. She leans out and sees only one car. *Run, Boysie, run! Come out, Boysie, boy, come come before they beat you up, and kill you! Come, come, Boysie. Run cross the road now, and even come up here in my place till them two bastards leave. Run out now, Boysie, Boysie, oh Boysie, poor Boysie*...and she leaves the window to call Dots, to warn her about the violence which will be done to Boysie. It is late, past midnight, but she has to call, even if Mrs. Hunter is vexed. The phone rings a long time ("In a way, it is

a good thing, that you are sick in bed," she says, looking at
Estelle, "'cause I know where you are, tonight, praise God!"),
and while she waits, she adjusts the covers, and smiles. Nobody
comes to the phone, and Bernice puts it down just as a tapping
on the sidewalk grows louder. She follows the tapping with her
nervousness, and when the tapping turns into two men, she is
disappointed. The two men are holding hands. They are the
men with the two dogs, but this time, without the dogs. They
look up at her, at her window, (as they do, out of habit, each
time they pass), and she holds her head out of sight (as she
does each time they pass). When they are out of sight, the
street returns to its violence and silence. "I wonder where those
two brutes now coming from?" Estelle hears her talking to herself, and she moves in her bed. Bernice follows the tapping,
until it disappears at the south end of the window. Her eyes
now accustomed to the darkness, she looks back north, and
thinks she sees something move. Something, some-damn-
thing, or somebody is moving 'bout out there? The night does
not answer her; there is only the dramatic violent waiting; and
Bernice, waiting too. Then, from between the houses, comes
a shadow, a man, Boysie? The man comes out in front of the
house, sauntering ("Brigitte must have given him something
damn sweet, heh-heh!"), and just as he turns to look up, to
wave goodnight, or probably thanks, or to give Brigitte the
all-clear signal (although Bernice sees no one at Brigitte's
windows), two other shadows appear from the shadows, and
pounce upon him. "Goddamn!" Bernice hears the man ex-
claim, but it is muffled by a blow in the mouth. That is his last
word. Bernice sees him make a start; sees the two shadows
knock him to the ground; and hit him all over his body, in
heavy, vicious blows which land in the right, silent, places.

They beat him thoroughly, and they beat him professionally, and they beat him without a murmur. They do it quickly, so quickly, she can't believe her eyes. One of the shadows runs up the street, and soon afterwards, returns driving the car with the aerial. He parks behind the other car. The shadows lift the man off the ground, and drop him in the front seat of his own car; and then they drive off. And the street returns to its respectable quiet. No light comes from Brigitte's room.

Bernice saw it happen, all of it, and she didn't have the courage to lift a finger, to move, to scream, to call for help. She didn't whisper any advice, as she had done earlier. It was too real; and too much of a dream at the same time. The brutality and the violence. She was still at the window (how long, she could not tell) when the car with the aerial returned. It stopped behind the parked car; a policeman got out; looked up at Brigitte's window, and then walked between the houses. The light went on in Brigitte's room; Bernice could see the police-man's body outlined against the movie-screen curtains; and in a short while, the policeman came out again. "I scared the liv-ing shit outta that broad!" Bernice heard him tell his compan-ion. They both laughed. "*She* won't talk."

"Well, anyways, we got this bastard, at last."

They got into their car and drove off, quietly. The other car was still parked. Bernice saw it all. The violence and the brutality. She was about to undress for bed (although she knew it would be hard to sleep tonight) when she glanced at her sister, and saw *her* suffering; and decided that no matter how late it was, she had to call Dots . . . *suppose that is Boysie out there, dying from those blows, suppose they left Boysie out there, bleeding to death.* . . . The phone didn't ring long, before someone answered.

"Dots, Dots? Where Boysie?"

"Christ, gal! You wake me up in the middle of the night to ask me damn foolishness?"

"Something bad happen to Boysie, Dots! Something..."

"Bernice! Boysie is here! He here laying-down side o' me, snoring like a drunken man. How you mean something happen to Boysie? Bernice, are you going mad as hell?" And in her rage, she dropped the telephone. A chill went through Bernice's body. *I am losing my mind? Could I be really losing my mind?* She closed the window, and the noise disturbed Estelle.

"Bernice, what time is it?"

"Two just gone."

"I've been thinking, Bernice...."

"Yes, Estelle."

"I don't really want to live in this country, Bernice. This place isn't made for me...or for you...neither. I think I want to go home."

"Yes, Estelle."

"You think you could post the letter to Mammy, in the morning?"

"Let us wait and see if there is going to be a morning, first, girl."

"In the morning, then."

Bernice was about to undress in the darkness; but there was no need for the darkness now. And yet she didn't want to turn on the light, because there was still a man out there, beaten up, and she had done nothing about it, and she felt the light would be too bright a finger pointing at her conscience. Estelle was talking again, and moaning; and in pain.

"Bernice, I am feeling worse....I have to get something for this pain, man. I have to get something for this pain...."

She turned the light on, and when she saw the blood in the

bed, she almost lost complete control of herself, and of her senses.

"Jesus Christ, Estelle! . . . why you didn't say something?"

Estelle was jabbering all the way down the speeding streets, and the lights were flashing backwards as the cars stopped to let the ambulance through. The siren was crying and Bernice was crying. In all her life in this country, she had seen and heard ambulances whizzing by, crying for the road, and she had seen people stand and wonder, "Who's in there, this time?" And never once did she imagine the time would come when she would be travelling in one of them.

Estelle had got worse. Bernice had spent half an hour trying to get a taxi. But it was Friday and a bank holiday, and taxis were scarce. She had tried to get Brigitte, and there was no answer. She had tried to get Henry, and there was no answer. She didn't call Dots. Everything was like a photograph, out of focus, and blurred by speed. The ambulance had come screaming across the Boulevard; and in that death of night and silence, had caused all the lights in the street to be turned on. Never had an ambulance ventured screaming on this Boulevard before! On the way out, Bernice saw a light burning in Mr. Burrmann's study.

The driver had come to the front door, by mistake; and in spite of Bernice's instructions to come to the side door. And after that, there was a quick succession of people, faces, comments and gossip; and finally, the siren and the traffic stopping, and the lights speeding into one line of colour; and Estelle muttering.

"I have to go to the immigration people in the morning, Bernice. Sam would be vexed if I didn't go. . . . I have to go . . . he said so, Bernice . . . did he tell you so?"

"Shh! Don't talk, Estelle. Don't talk."

"I want to have my baby, Bernice, I want to have my baby...when I have my baby, Bernice...do you know...do you think they're going to take it away...I want to have it, and I have to go to see a gentleman...."

"Don't talk, Estelle, we soon get there, so don't talk."

They reached the hospital. The Toronto General Hospital, where Bernice wanted Estelle to be a nurse. The attendants rushed her through the Emergency Admitting entrance, and on to another stretcher on wheels. Events and people now ceased to mean anything to Bernice. There was no recognition of reality; just the long corridors of cement shining, and the shining walls and the fluorescent lights, and almost everybody in white. And then the ward, and the doctor, smiling and white and dressed in white; and the questions: Have you any other children, miss? Have you had a miscarriage before? (A miscarriage?) How much blood has she lost? When did the bleeding first become noticeable? How long has she been bleeding? You are her sister, aren't you? Was there any tissue?

And the head nurse, Priscilla (one of the two young women who attended her welcoming party), now vicious, ferocious, an aggressive nurse, black, tightly built and commenting, "Another black whore! Oh Lord!" to the white nurse who didn't want to comment on a racial subject, or patient. "They don't even have any shame!" Priscilla said, making it clear to the white nurse that there are two kinds of black women. And Bernice, standing stupidly and frightened, by the door of the ward, seeing the porters lift Estelle onto another stretcher, and wheel her out of the room to the Operating Room; and Bernice left alone now, with Priscilla, who had forgotten that she had seen Bernice before ("I wonder if I know this face!") in Bernice's own apartment; and who had eaten Bernice's peas and rice and chicken. The waiting, the waiting, the long fluorescent wait; nurses walking harmlessly, uselessly by, while her sister is lying on a stretcher, dying; and the black one, every now and then, passing near to Bernice, and grumbling purgatory and damnation on her own black race, because it has let her down in front of the white nurses and doctors.

"What you waiting here for?" she snapped, as if Bernice is a dog. "You don't see they just take her down to the OR?"

"My sister, ma'am," Bernice said, "I waiting for..."

"Look, we don't want nobody waiting 'bout here, hear?" she said, cutting off Bernice. "Go down by the Emergency Waiting Room, if you want to wait. That is where you wait, down there. Not here."

And a white porter came to Bernice, and rescued her; and took her down, by elevator. He showed her the waiting-room near the Operating Room. There was a man waiting there, too. Bernice waited (the man was standing with his back to her) and then a doctor came out, and she stood up, wondering whether this was Estelle's doctor; but the doctor talked to the man who was waiting. "Why the hell you couldn't get her here sooner, Sam?" The doctor knew the man. "I'm sorry. But we're doing all we can.... I'll call you later, at home.... Will you be home?" Nothing of what was said really registered with Bernice; nothing could register now.

She cried and cried; and walked out of the hospital crying, until she realized she was in a taxi riding back to Marina Boulevard, back to the house, in Forest Hill.

As she pays the taxi driver she pulls the letter from Lonnie out of her pocket, by mistake; and this she carries in her hand upstairs, into her apartment. She reads, but she does not know what Lonnie is really saying to her, although she reads: *But for old times sake, I begging you to send down a few dollars because St Matthias Church having the annual outing, and I am naked as a bird's arse. I need a new suit. So see what you could do. Your loving man, Lonnie. PS Roses are red/Roses are blue/My love is true/Until I dead. Lonnie.*

... hours later, she was holding the letter from Lonnie in her hand, thinking of Lonnie, thinking of her need of Lonnie; or of Henry. (The parked car was no longer there, she noticed. So the man, whoever he was, couldn't be dead.) "Oh Lonnie, poor Lonnie," she said. She heard Mr. Burrmann come in. And she became very frightened to be left in the house with him, alone. She gripped Lonnie's letter firmly in her hand, for protection from Mr. Burrmann. She was thinking of Estelle, and of the man who had been in the waiting-room with her. Then the telephone rang. The hospital must be calling her, she thought. When she took up the receiver, she heard Dots's voice, although she couldn't follow all she was saying: "... and I never knew that this place was so blasted cruel, Bernice, gal. Jesus God! when I see Henry's face this morning ... six o'clock this morning, Henry returned Boysie's car that he borrowed last night ... this morning when I rested my eyes on that poor man's face, Jesus God, Bernice ... and nobody, not even the police, can't tell me nothing. Boysie, and Mrs. Hunter ripped hell when they saw Henry ... but not one blasted person in the whole of Toronto can't or won't say how Henry come to get his face smashed in, his eyes swell up big big till they almost dropping out of his head.... Jesus God! this is a savage world...." Dots went on talking and talking.